Praise for Sheri WhiteFeather

"WhiteFeather's heartbreaking yet beautiful tale showcases her complicated, complex couple's fortitude and strength."

—*RT Book Reviews* on *The Texan's Future Bride*, 4.5 stars

"Genuine and full of heart, heat and depth...intense, sensual and exhilarating."

—*RT Book Reviews* on *Lost and Found Husband*, 4.5 stars

"A passionate, heart-stopping adventure of love and forgiveness."

—*RT Book Reviews* on *Cherokee Dad*

"WhiteFeather tells a passionate and touching story that fans of the Connelly Dynasty will definitely not want to miss in *Cherokee Marriage Dare*."

—*RT Book Reviews*, Top Pick!, 4.5 stars

Praise for *USA TODAY* bestselling author Judy Duarte

"Duarte's fateful second-chance romance is amazing, starring a couple whose teenage love produced an adorable lad who is a testament to resilience. A tragic twist gives them all an opportunity to become a forever family."

—*RT Book Reviews* on *The Daddy Secret*

"Duarte's romance is part mystery and all drama when secrets, betrayals and feuds fill the pages, and the love story is refreshingly pure yet sensually stimulating."

—*RT Book Reviews* on *Tammy and the Doctor*

"Judy Duarte's superb *Their Unexpected Family* pulls the reader deeply and satisfyingly into the hearts and minds of the characters."

—*RT Book Reviews*, 4.5 stars

HOME ON THE RANCH:

TEXAS VOWS

SHERI WHITEFEATHER

USA TODAY **Bestselling Author**

JUDY DUARTE

Recycling programs for this product may not exist in your area.

ISBN-13: 978-1-335-02042-0

Home on the Ranch: Texas Vows

This edition published by arrangement with Harlequin Books S.A.

For questions and comments about the quality of this book, please contact us at CustomerService@Harlequin.com.

Printed in U.S.A.

CONTENTS

Sheri WhiteFeather is an award-winning, bestselling author. She writes a variety of romance novels for Harlequin and is known for incorporating Native American elements into her stories. She has two grown children who are tribally enrolled members of the Muscogee Creek Nation. She lives in California and enjoys shopping in vintage stores and visiting art galleries and museums. Sheri loves to hear from her readers at sheriwhitefeather.com.

Books by Sheri WhiteFeather

Harlequin Desire

Marriage of Revenge
The Morning-After Proposal

Billionaire Brothers Club

Waking Up with the Boss
Single Mom, Billionaire Boss
Paper Wedding, Best-Friend Bride

Harlequin Special Edition

Family Renewal

The Bachelor's Baby Dilemma
Lost and Found Husband
Lost and Found Father

Visit her Author Profile page at Harlequin.com, or sheriwhitefeather.com, for more titles.

THE TEXAN'S FUTURE BRIDE

SHERI WHITEFEATHER

To Judy Duarte and Crystal Green for supporting my dreams and always believing that they will come true.

Chapter 1

What the—?

As Jenna Byrd steered her truck toward the Flying B, she noticed a man walking along the private road that led to the ranch. Or stumbling was more like it. He didn't look familiar, but he didn't seem out of place, either. His dusty jeans, plain T-shirt and battered boots were typical small-town Texas attire. He was missing a hat, though. Had he lost it somewhere? His short dark hair was decidedly messy.

Jenna frowned. Clearly, he was snockered in the middle of the day. Cowboys could be a hell-raisin' breed. Of course she didn't dally with that kind. Although she was hoping to find a cowboy to call her own, she was attracted to well-behaved men, not rabble-rousers who could barely put one foot in front of the other. He was ambling toward her pickup instead of away from it.

Good grief. She couldn't just leave him out here. The Flying B was about five miles down the road, and in his condition, he would never make it. And why he was heading toward the ranch was beyond her.

She stopped her truck and sighed. She knew he wasn't a Flying B employee. She'd made a point of meeting everyone on the payroll. Jenna owned a portion of the ranch. She and her sister and their cousin had inherited equal shares of the Flying B, and they were going to turn it into a B and B.

She rolled down her window and said, "What are you doing out here?"

He looked at her as if he wasn't really seeing her. His deep brown eyes were glazed. He didn't respond.

She repeated the question.

He blinked at her. He was probably around her age, thirty or so, with tanned skin and striking features—handsome, even in his wasted state.

Curious, she tried to figure him out. Maybe he was a whiskey-toting hitchhiker. Or maybe he was affiliated with another ranch in the area and after he'd tied one on, he'd mistakenly taken the wrong road. There had to an explanation for his disorderly presence.

Hoping to solve the dilemma, she asked, "Who are you?"

"Who are you?" he parroted.

This was going nowhere. "You've had too much to drink."

He squinted. "I have?"

"Yes."

"I don't think so."

Easy for him to say. He was too drunk to know the

difference. While she debated how to handle the situation, he staggered a little more.

"I feel funny," he said.

No kidding, she thought.

"I've got a headache." He rubbed the back of his head. When he brought his fingers forward, the tips were red.

Her pulse jumped. He was bleeding.

She parked and leaped out of her truck. Had he gotten into a brawl? Overly intoxicated men were prone to that sort of behavior. But whatever he'd done, it didn't matter. All that mattered was getting his wound treated.

"My cousin's fiancé is a doctor. He lives at the ranch where I live, and I think he's home today. If he isn't, I'll take you to his office."

"No. That's okay." He wiped his hands on his pants. "I'm better now."

Obviously, he wasn't. She slipped her arm around him and realized that he didn't smell of alcohol. Most likely, he hadn't been drinking, which made his condition a bigger cause for concern. He was probably dazed because of the injury.

"Come on. Let's get you into the truck."

Shouldering his weight wasn't easy. He was about six feet, packed with lean muscle mass. At five-five, with a slight build, she was no match for him.

He lagged against her, and she held him tighter. Nonetheless, he kept insisting that he was fine, which clearly wasn't the case. He was definitely confused.

Once he was seated, she eased away from him and closed the door. She got behind the wheel and reached for her cell phone. She called Mike Sanchez or "Doc" as he'd become known in these parts. He was at the ranch.

She asked him to meet her at the main house and told him that she was bringing an injured man with her.

"The back of his head is bleeding." She glanced at her passenger. He was staring out the window with those glazed eyes. She lowered her voice. "I don't know much about these things, but I think he has some sort of concussion. I found him wandering along Flying B Road."

"Don't worry, Jenna," Doc replied. "Just stay calm and get him here."

"I'm on my way." She ended the call, then started the engine and headed for her destination.

The cowboy turned to look at her. "Are we on a date?"

Yikes. Talk about befuddled. His condition was worse than she thought. "I'm taking you to see a doctor, remember?"

"Your hair is pretty." He reached out as if he meant to grasp a loose tendril of her wavy gold locks.

Jenna's heartbeat skittered. He didn't make contact, but she could almost imagine how his tortured touch would feel.

Almost. She focused on the road.

"Very pretty," he said.

She gripped the wheel, and to keep him from reaching for her hair again, she redirected his thoughts.

"What's your name?" she asked, rephrasing her original "Who are you?" question.

He furrowed his brows. It wasn't a trick question, but he didn't appear capable of a response. He didn't know his own name.

"It's okay," she said. "That's why I'm taking you to see a doctor." Besides, all they had to do was look at his ID to see who he was. Everyone carried identification with them. Still, not knowing something as simple as his name wasn't a good sign.

He leaned against the window, then closed his eyes. She hoped that he wasn't going to pass out. That wouldn't be a good sign, either.

She increased her speed, bumping along the road, her truck flanked by green pastures and grazing cattle.

Finally, as the main house came into view, she breathed a sigh of "thank You, God" relief.

The dashing young doctor was waiting for her on the wraparound porch. Tammy, her equally fetching cousin, was there, too. Jenna had only met Tammy recently, when all of the inheritance whoopla had begun. None of the heirs had grown up on the Flying B or visited when they were kids because their families had been estranged from each other. So, when they'd gotten called to their ailing grandpa's bedside, and when he'd died, they'd wept for a man they'd just begun to know.

She glanced at the cowboy beside her. Now wasn't the time to think about men she barely knew. Or death. Or anything bad.

Jenna stopped the truck, and Doc opened the passenger side and escorted the patient into the house.

Once Jenna exited the vehicle, Tammy approached her, and they went inside, too.

Doc didn't waste time. He was already examining the stranger, who sat on the edge of a sturdy leather sofa, looking as confused as ever.

Jenna stood back and frowned. "Do you recognize him?" she asked Tammy. "Do you know if he's from around here?"

"No."

"Me, either." But dang if he didn't make her tongue

stick to the roof of her mouth. She couldn't get his tortured attempt to touch her out of her mind.

Just a few feet away, Doc was telling the patient that he was going to need a couple of stitches. In fact, Doc was preparing to patch him up. But the cut itself was incidental. What obviously concerned Doc were his other symptoms.

Apparently Jenna was right. Indeed, he had a concussion.

Thing was, his identity was still unknown. He wasn't carrying any form of identification; Doc checked his person.

"What do you think is going to happen?" Jenna whispered to Tammy.

"I don't know."

Neither did Jenna. But it was clear from the examination that he had no recollection about himself or how he'd gotten hurt.

After his cut was sanitized and stitched, Doc made arrangements for him to be treated at the local hospital. He spoke gently to the patient, then explained the situation to Jenna.

"I'm going to order a CT scan," he said. "At this point, it's impossible to know the severity of his trauma."

"What's the worst-case scenario?" she asked, making sure the stranger was out of earshot.

"Bleeding in the brain."

She shivered.

Doc concluded, "But let's not get ahead of ourselves. Let's get a thorough diagnosis first."

"I want to go to the hospital with him." She was unable to bear the thought of abandoning him.

"That's fine. A police report will have to be filed, too,

since we don't know who he is or what triggered the injury. He'll be admitted as a John Doe."

Jenna didn't like the impersonal sound of that. But she didn't like any of this. She preferred to have her ducks in a tidy yellow row, with carefully laid plans, no matter what aspect of her life it concerned. She'd even created a list of the type of qualities she wanted her future husband to have, a man who would be nothing like her father. She used to be disappointed in her dad, but these days she was downright ashamed of him. A humiliating skeleton in his closet had surfaced.

She glanced at the stranger. Did he have skeletons in his closet, too? Even if he did, it was none of her concern. She was going to see him through this injury and forget about him.

Doc and Tammy took him to the hospital, and Jenna followed them in her truck.

She sat in the waiting room while he underwent the CT scan. Was she going to be able to forget about him? Already she was feeling oddly attached, as if she was responsible for him somehow.

She glanced over at Tammy, who occupied the seat next to her. "Thanks for keeping me company."

"It shouldn't take long. Rather than wait for a written report, Mike is going to look at the scans himself, along with the radiologist, of course."

"It's nice having a doctor in the family."

Tammy quirked a smile. "Very nice." She stood up. "Do you want some coffee?"

"Sure."

"How do you take it?"

"Cream and sugar."

"Coming right up."

Jenna watched her cousin head for the vending machine. She was a petite brunette, thriving on newfound love. She and Jenna formed a bond when Jenna had helped her with a makeover that had caught the doctor's eye. Tammy was a tomboy turned hot tamale. She could still ride and rope with the best of 'em, but she also looked darn fine in feminine attire. The girl could cook up a storm, too. Soon the Flying B cook would be retiring and Tammy would be taking over as the down-home B and B chef.

Tammy returned with two cups and handed Jenna one. She took a sip. It tasted better than expected.

Jenna said about the stranger, "I can't help but wonder who he is. What his name is, what his family is like."

"Hopefully he'll remember soon."

"I just hope the scan comes out all right." She drank a bit more of her coffee. "He said some weird things when we were in the truck. He told me that he liked my hair, then he asked me if we were on a date."

"That must have been awkward."

"It was." She frowned. "What sort of treatment do they do if someone is bleeding in the brain?"

"I have no idea, but you shouldn't be dwelling on that."

"I know. But I'm the one who found him."

"Finders keepers, losers weepers?" Tammy put her cup beside a dog-eared magazine. "Did you ever say that when you were a kid?"

"All the time. But I hope that doesn't apply to this situation."

"Like someone is left behind weeping for him?"

Jenna nodded, and they both fell silent. But it seemed better not to talk. Other people had just entered the waiting room with somber looks on their faces, as if they were afraid that they might be left weeping for whoever they were there to see.

Time ticked by.

Then Tammy looked up and said, "There's Mike," as her fiancé strode toward them.

Jenna got to her feet, with Tammy on her heels.

Doc said to them, "The results were normal, but we're going to keep him overnight for observation."

"Then what?" Jenna asked.

"Then we'll reevaluate his condition in the morning."

"Do you think his memory will return by then?"

"It's possible. Oftentimes these sorts of lapses only last a day or two. But it could continue for a while. It's hard to say."

"Can I see him?"

"Once we check him into a room, you can visit him."

By the time that happened, the stranger was asleep. Doc and Tammy went home, and Jenna sat in a stiff plastic chair beside his bed and watched him. She used the opportunity to study his features: dark eyebrows, a strong, sharp nose, cheekbones a male model would envy, medium-size lips with a bit of a downward slant. That made her curious about his smile. Was it bright? Crooked? Brooding? She noticed that he was harboring a five-o'clock shadow. The sexy scruff made him look even more like the cowboy she assumed he was. The hospital gown, however, didn't; it robbed him of his edge.

He stirred in his sleep, and she frowned. Although he had a semiprivate room and the curtain was drawn, the TV of the older man next to him sounded in her ears. A game show was playing, a program that had been on the air since she was a kid. She'd never actually seen it, not all the way through. But she'd gotten used to hearing the noisy show in the background when her dad used to watch it, much like she was hearing it now.

Tuning out the sound, she studied the stranger again. Because she was tempted to skim his cheek and feel the warmth of his skin, she kept her hands on her lap. She even curled her fingers to keep them still. Being this close to him while he slept wasn't a good idea. She should go home, but she stayed for as long as the hospital would allow, already anxious to return the following day.

In the morning, Jenna had breakfast with her sister in the main house, surrounded by retro-style gingham accents in the kitchen. Unfortunately it was too early to head over to the hospital. With the exception of spouses and significant others, visiting hours were limited.

She'd barely slept last night, wondering if the stranger would recoup his memory today.

She glanced across the table at Donna, but her sister didn't look up. She was busy texting, in between sips of fresh-brewed coffee and bites of a Spanish omelet, courtesy of the soon-to-retire cook.

Jenna continued to study Donna. They'd always been different from each other. Jenna, a certified horseback riding instructor, loved everything country, and Donna, a magazine writer turned marketer, loved everything city. As soon as the B and B was off the ground, Donna would be returning to New York, where she lived and worked. Jenna, on the other hand, planned to stay at the ranch and help run the B and B with Tammy.

Donna finally glanced up. "What?" she said.

"Nothing."

"Then why were you staring at me?"

"I was just thinking about how opposite we are."

"We're siblings, not clones."

"Yes, but you'd think that we would have more in common. Or look more alike or whatever." Although both were blonde, Donna was a year older, three inches taller and wildly curvy. She had the figure of a 1940s pinup, while Jenna was small and lean.

Donna shrugged and went back to texting, and Jenna considered how distant their relationship was. Her sister had trouble connecting with people on an emotional level, but Jenna could hardly blame her. They'd been raised in a go-your-own-way environment.

Tammy entered the room, and Jenna immediately said, "Hi."

"Hello, yourself." Their cousin sat down and greeted Donna, as well. Then she turned back to Jenna and said, "Mike left a couple of hours ago to check on our patient."

Her stomach fluttered. "He did? Any word?"

"From Mike? No. But I'm sure he'll call when he can."

Donna quit texting. "What patient? Who's sick?"

Jenna answered, "I found a man yesterday. He was wandering around on the road with a concussion." She went on to explain the details. "Hopefully he'll be better today."

"Wow," Donna said. "Can you imagine losing your memory?"

No, but Jenna wouldn't mind forgetting about the mess their dad had made of things. But he'd been notorious for disappointing her, even when she was a child. He'd never been there when she needed him. He'd been too busy with his corporate job. He rarely attended parent-teacher conferences or planned birthday parties or took his daughters to the movies or engaged in the types of activities that would have made them seem more like a family.

She glanced at Donna. Funny thing about her sister. Before the skeleton in Dad's closet had surfaced, Donna used to idolize him. He'd been her hero, the person she often emulated, particularly with her workaholic, career-is-king habits. Not that Donna would ever admit how deeply he influenced her. But Jenna was keenly aware of it.

Clearing the Dad-clutter from her mind, Jenna said to Tammy, "I was planning on going to the hospital later, but maybe I should wait for Mike to call."

"It might take him a while to check in," her cousin replied. "He has a lot of rounds to make. Why don't you head over to the hospital now and look in on the man? I can tell you're still worried about him."

"I can't see him until noon."

"Says who?"

"The hospital visiting hours."

Tammy waved away the rules. "They probably won't notice if you slip in a little early."

"I think it would be better if I went at noon." She wasn't comfortable taking liberties. She preferred to play by the book.

Tammy didn't push her out of her comfort zone and neither did Donna. They allowed her to be her regimented self.

When the time rolled around for her to get ready, she donned classic Western wear: a broomstick skirt, a feminine blouse and a nice pair of boots. She freshened up her face and fluffed her hair, too. Not that it should matter what the stranger thought of her appearance. If he was better today, this would probably be the last time she saw him.

She arrived at the hospital at twelve o'clock sharp and went to the nurses' station, where she inquired about the patient's condition. They informed her that he was awake and coherent, and once everything was in order, Dr. Sanchez would be releasing him.

So, he *was* better.

She thanked them for the information and continued down the hall. A moment later, she stalled. She was nervous about conversing with him.

Pushing past the trepidation, she proceeded. She entered his room and passed the TV-watching patient. Today he was engaged in a sitcom from the seventies. He didn't glance her way, and she left him alone, too.

She moved forward and came face-to-face with the stranger. He was sitting up in bed. His gaze zeroed in on hers, and her heart went bumpy.

"Good morning," she said, keeping a calm voice.

"You're the girl from yesterday."

"Yes."

"The blonde I thought I was dating. I'm sorry about that."

Dang. Did he have to go and mention it? "It's okay. You were out of it."

He nodded, and she took the seat next to his bed, the same spot where she'd watched him sleep. "You look healthier." Still a bit worn-out, she thought, but an improvement nonetheless. "I heard that Doc will be releasing you."

"Yes, but I'm supposed to take it easy."

"You can't go kicking up your heels just yet?"

"No. Not yet." He smiled a little.

It was sinfully crooked. The *bump-bump* in her chest returned. "I'm Jenna, by the way. Jenna Byrd."

"Thank you for what you did. Jenna," he added softly.

The bumping intensified. "I'm glad I was there to help." She scooted to the edge of her chair. "So, what's your name?"

He furrowed his dark brows. "I don't know. I still can't remember anything, aside from you bringing me to your ranch and coming here."

She gaped at him. "Your memory hasn't recovered? Then why is Doc releasing you?"

"Because I'm not dizzy or confused, and my vital signs are good. I have what's called retrograde amnesia, but they can't keep me in the hospital for that. Besides, my memories are supposed to return. It's just a matter of when."

She didn't know what to say. He was still as much of a stranger as he was before.

He said, "The sheriff was here earlier. He took a report. He took my fingerprints, too." He held up his hands and gazed at them. "If I'm in the system, they'll be able to identify me that way."

He might have a criminal record? That wasn't a comforting thought. "Do you think you're in the system?"

"I don't know." He lowered his hands. "But the sheriff doesn't want Dr. Sanchez to release me until the results are in. So we're waiting to hear. I guess the police want to be sure that there isn't a warrant out for my arrest before they put me back on the streets."

"Do you mind if I wait until you hear something?"

"Why would you want to do that?"

Because she still felt responsible for him. Or was it because she was so doggone attracted to him? That wasn't a comforting thought, either. Confused and covering her tracks she said, "I'm interested in knowing who you are." And hoping that he was an upstanding guy.

"At the moment, I'm no one."

"That's not true. Everyone is someone."

He glanced away. Obviously her comment hadn't made a dent in his amnesiac armor. She wanted to reassure him, but how could she, especially since he might be wanted by the police?

Just then, double sets of footsteps sounded, and Jenna turned around in her chair. The stranger shifted in the direction of the approaching people, too.

It was Doc, making a crisp-white presentation in his lab coat, and next to him was a tall, stocky lawman.

As the air grew thick with anticipation, the stranger shot Jenna a quick glance.

Trapping her in the moment they'd been waiting for.

Chapter 2

Amid the silence, Doc caught Jenna's attention. She expected him to ask her to leave, but he merely nodded an acknowledgment. Maybe it was going to be okay. Maybe there was nothing to be concerned about.

The lawman said to the patient, "I'm Deputy Tobbs. The sheriff assigned your case to me."

"Do I have a record?" the stranger asked bluntly.

The deputy shifted his weight. "No, you don't. Your fingerprints aren't on file, but I'm going to investigate further. I'll do my best to uncover your identity and discover what happened to you. I'll be questioning everyone in the area, in case you work around here or were visiting someone."

"Someone who hasn't noticed that I'm gone?"

"It could have been a surprise visit and you never made it to your destination. It could have been a number of things. I'm inclined to think that you were assaulted and robbed, possibly carjacked, which would account for you wandering around on foot. But we'll have to wait and see what turns up."

The stranger tugged a hand through his hair, stopping short of his injury. "It could be worse, I guess." He addressed Doc. "Are you going to sign my release papers now?"

"Yes, but first we need to figure out where you're going to go."

The stranger replied, "Is there a homeless shelter in the area?"

The deputy answered the question. "There's one in the next county, about thirty miles from here."

"Then that will have to do, if they'll take me."

"I can give them a call," the deputy said.

No way, Jenna thought. She wasn't going to let him go off like that. She would worry about him. Still, did she have a right to intervene? Regardless, she couldn't seem to hold back.

She said to the stranger, "You can stay at the Flying B until you regain your memory or until Deputy Tobbs finds out who you are. We're turning the ranch into a B and B, and we have guest rooms and cabins on the property."

"I can't stay there."

Jenna persisted, especially now that she'd made up her mind about saving him, or whatever it was she was trying to do. "Why not?"

"I just can't. I shouldn't."

"Sure you can," Doc said, supporting her idea. "It would be a good place for you to recover."

"I don't know."

Jenna frowned. "What's not to know? Just say yes."

He frowned, too. "Are you always this insistent?"

Was she? "Sometimes." Considering from the time that she and Donna were kids, the one lesson their father had always taught was to go after what they wanted. "But Doc agrees with me, so you're outnumbered."

"Consider it part of your treatment," Doc said. "I could keep a better eye on you, and being surrounded by fresh air would be a heck of a lot nicer than being holed in a homeless shelter."

The deputy interjected. "Sounds like you've got it worked out."

"We do," Jenna assured him.

"Then I'm going to take my leave." He placed his card on the rolling stand beside the bed. "Call me if you have any questions," he told the man with amnesia. "And if I need to reach you, I'll stop by the Flying B." The deputy turned to Jenna. "You should introduce him to everyone at the ranch. It's possible that someone there will recognize him."

"I will, just as soon as he's feeling up to it."

He turned back to the patient. "You take care."

"Thank you," came the polite reply.

Deputy Tobbs said goodbye to everyone and left the room, a hush forming in his absence. Jenna wondered if Doc was going to depart, too. But he stayed quietly put.

She said to the stranger, "You're going to need another name, other than John Doe."

His dark gaze caught hers. "Some people have that name for real."

"I know. But it's doubtful that you do."

"Then you can pick one."

"You want me to name you?"

"Somebody has to."

Jenna glanced at Doc. He stood off to the side, clutching a clipboard that probably contained "John Doe's" charts. Anxious, she crossed her arms over her chest. Doc's silent observation created a fishbowl-type effect. But he had a right to analyze his patient's reactions.

Was he analyzing her, too?

She'd been bothered by the John Doe reference from the beginning, but now that she'd been given the responsibility of changing it, she felt an enormous amount of pressure.

Could Doc tell how nervous she was?

She asked the stranger, "Are you sure you don't want to come up with something yourself?"

"I'm positive."

He sounded as if it didn't matter, that with or without a makeshift name, he still considered himself no one.

Reminding her of how lost he truly was.

As he waited for the outcome, he thought about how surreal all of this was. He felt like a ketchup jar someone had banged upside the counter, with memories locked inside that wouldn't come out.

Emptiness. Nothingness.

His only lifeline was the pretty blonde beside his bed and the doctor watching the scene unfold.

"What do you think of J.D.?" she asked.

"The initials for John Doe?"

She nodded. "I always thought that using initials in place of a name was sexy."

He started. Was she serious? "Sexy?"

She blushed, her cheeks turning a soft shade of pink. "I didn't mean it like that."

Intrigued, he tilted his head. She'd gone from being aggressive to downright shy. "How did you mean it?"

"That it's mysterious."

"Then I guess it fits." Everything was a mystery, right down to his confusion about dating her. Was she the type he would've dated in the past? Or did he even have a type?

"So we can start calling you J.D. now?" she asked, obviously double-checking.

He nodded.

"And you're going to stay at the Flying B?"

He nodded again, still feeling reluctant about being her houseguest or cabin guest or whatever. As far as he was concerned, a homeless shelter would have sufficed.

She said, "When I first saw you, I assumed that you were a cowboy, maybe an employee of a neighboring ranch. I hadn't considered a carjacking, but I wondered if you might be a hitchhiker. I'm glad the deputy is going to talk to everyone in the area about you. Then we'll know for sure." She glanced at his clothes, which were hanging nearby. "You were certainly dressed like a local cowboy, except that you didn't have a hat. But I figured that you'd lost it somewhere."

He followed her line of sight. The T-shirt, jeans and worn-out boots he'd been wearing were as unfamiliar as the day he'd been born. "I don't have a recollection of doing ranch work."

"You don't have a recollection of anything," she reminded him.

"I know, but wouldn't I have a feeling of being connected to ranching? Wouldn't it be ingrained in me if that's what I did for a living?" He turned to the expert. "What do you think, Dr. Sanchez?"

"I think it's too soon to be concerned about that. You just need to rest and let your feelings fall into place when they're meant to." He smiled. "I also think you should start calling me Doc."

"Okay, Doc." He preferred less formality, too, and already he'd gotten used to hearing Jenna say it. A moment later, he shifted his gaze back to his unfamiliar clothes.

Jenna said, "You put some miles on those boots."

"I must have thought they were comfortable." He noticed that the toes were starting to turn up. "I guess I'm going to find out if I still like wearing them."

"Yes, J.D., you are," Doc said, using his new name. "In fact, you can get dressed now, if you want. I can send a nurse in if you need help."

"No, I can handle it."

"All right. Then I'll go get your papers ready, and Jenna can step out of the room and come back when you're done."

J.D. got a highly inappropriate urge, wishing that he could ask her to stay and help him get dressed. He even imagined her hand on his zipper.

Hell and damnation.

He should have insisted on going to a shelter. Clearly, being around Jenna wasn't a good idea.

She and the doctor left, closing the curtain behind them. J.D. got out of bed and walked over to the closet, still thinking about Jenna.

He cursed quietly under his breath, stripped off the hospital gown and put on his Western wear. He grappled with his belt. He fought the boots, too. They felt odd at first, but he got used to them soon enough.

Curious to look at himself in the mirror, he went into

the bathroom. He didn't recognize his reflection, with him wearing the clothes. He was still a nowhere man.

Luckily, the hospital had provided a few necessities, like a comb, toothpaste and a toothbrush. Still standing in front of the mirror, he combed his hair straight back, but it fell forward naturally, so he let it be. They hadn't provided a razor, so he had no choice but to leave the beard stubble. It was starting to itch and he wanted it gone. Or maybe it was the image it created that he didn't like. It made him look as haunted as he felt, like an Old West outlaw.

J.D. the Kid? No. He wasn't a kid. He figured himself for early thirties. Or that was how he appeared. But he could be mistaken.

Blowing out a breath, he returned to his room and opened the curtain, letting Jenna know that she could come back.

She did, about five minutes later, bringing two cups of coffee with her.

"It's from the vending machine," she said. "But it's pretty good. I had some last night when I was waiting for your test results." She handed him a cup. "It has cream and sugar. I hope that's okay."

"It's fine. Thanks. I don't have a preference, not that I'm aware of, anyway." He sat on the edge of the bed, offering her the chair. "You've been putting in a lot of time at this place, hanging out for a man you barely know."

"I'm starting to get to know you." She smiled. "You obviously like coffee."

"So it seems." He drank it right down. "I had orange juice with breakfast, but this hits the spot."

"We have gourmet coffeemakers in the guest cabins. You can brew yourself a fancy cup of Joe tomorrow morning."

"That sounds good, but maybe I shouldn't stay there. You don't need the burden of having a guy like me around."

"You can't back out. You already agreed. Doctor's orders, remember?"

Yes, but his recovery didn't include the stirrings she incited. Even now, he wanted to see her blush again. He liked the shy side of her.

"When this is over, I'll repay you for your hospitality," he said.

"Just get better, okay? That will be payment enough."

"You're a nice girl, Jenna."

"And you seem like a nice man."

"You thought I was drunk off my butt when you saw me stumbling around. I remember you telling me that I had too much to drink."

"I retracted that when I saw that your head was bleeding. How is your head, by the way?"

"Still hurts a little."

"How about your feet?"

He squinted. "My feet aren't injured."

"I was talking about your boots. How do they feel?"

Oh, yeah. The boots. He glanced down at the scuffed leather. "Fine." He motioned to hers. "You've got yourself a fancy pair."

"These are my dressy ones. Sometimes I go dancing in them, too."

"I have no idea if I know how to dance."

"You can try the two-step and see."

"Right now?" He teased her. "Up and down the hospital corridor?"

She laughed. "Later, smarty, when you're up to par."

Were they flirting? It sure as heck seemed as if they were. But it didn't last long because he didn't let it.

He knew better than to start something that he was in no position to finish. She seemed to know it, too. She turned off the charm at the same instant he did.

Tempering what was happening between them.

As a bright and bouncy nurse wheeled J.D. out to Jenna's truck, he said, "I'd rather walk."

"It's hospital policy," the chipper lady said. "Everyone leaves in a wheelchair."

He made a face, and Jenna smiled to herself. Machismo. He certainly behaved like a cowboy.

She stopped smiling. She was actually taking this man home with her, and she knew darn well that he was as attracted to her as she was to him.

But they weren't going to act on it. They were both cautious enough not to let it take over. So it would be fine, she assured herself. He would be a recuperating guest, a patient of Doc's, and nothing more.

She turned on the radio, and they listened to music instead of talking.

Finally, when they were on the private road leading to the ranch, he glanced over at her and said, "Déjà vu," making a joke about repeating his car-ride experience from yesterday.

She tried to make light of it, too. "Your first encounter with it."

"That I'm able to remember. I probably had déjà vu in my old life."

His old life. That made it sound as if he'd become someone new. She supposed that, at least for now, he was a different person. But since she didn't know who he was before, she couldn't compare the old with the new.

"I wonder if I should put you in the dream cabin."

"The cabins have names? Is that part of the B and B thing?"

"No. The dream cabin is what everyone on the ranch has been calling it, for years, amongst themselves. So we call it that, too. It has an old feather bed that used to belong to our great-grandmother. She had the gift of second sight, and her visions came in the form of dreams while she was sleeping in it."

"Interesting family history."

"The bed is magical."

He openly disagreed. "Your great-granny having visions in the bed doesn't make it magical."

"Other people have had vision-type dreams while sleeping in it, too. Tammy had dreams about Doc. Then later, he had a life-altering dream about her, and he wasn't even at the cabin when it happened to him. But we figured that her dreams triggered his, so the feather bed was still part of it."

"Maybe you shouldn't put me in that cabin."

"Why? Don't you want to have a dream that might come true?"

"It just seems like something that should stay within your family."

"Doc wasn't in our family until he and Tammy got engaged."

"I'm not going to get engaged to anyone."

Their discussion was barreling down an uncomfortable path. She struggled to rein it back in. "I wasn't insinuating that you were."

"I don't understand the point of me sleeping in the bed."

"You might have a dream that will help you regain your memory."

"I can't imagine that."

She parked in front of the main house. "Anything is possible. Wait here and I'll get the key to the cabin." She went inside, wondering why he wasn't more interested in the bed. Didn't he want to regain his memory?

She returned with the key, and he sat in the passenger seat, looking tired and confused.

He said, "I don't mean to offend you, Jenna, but I don't know if I believe in magic."

Ah, so that was it. He was a skeptic. "You just need to recover, J.D. and let the rest of it happen naturally."

"Magic isn't natural."

"I didn't used to think so, either. But I've become open-minded about it since Tammy and Doc had their dreams."

He didn't respond, but it was just as well. She didn't want to discuss the details of Doc and Tammy's romance with him.

She took him to the cabin. They went inside, and she showed him around.

"This place was locked up for a long time," she said. "But we aired it out and put some modern appliances in it."

"Like the gourmet coffeemaker?"

She nodded. "Eventually we're going to use it as one of the rental cabins. We think people will be fascinated by the magic associated with the bed. Of course we can't guarantee that they'll dream while they're here."

"You can't make that guarantee for me, either."

"No, but I think it's worth a shot."

They entered the bedroom, and since the bed had already been presented as a focal point, it stood out like a sore thumb, even though it had been designed to look soft and inviting. The quilt was a soft chocolate-brown, with a sheepskin throw draped across it.

He ran his hand across the sheepskin. "Have you ever slept here?"

A sinful chill raced up her spine. Suddenly she was imagining sleeping there with him. "No."

"If you believe in the bed's magic, why haven't you tried it yourself?"

"There's nothing I need to dream about. Besides, there's another story about someone who stayed here that's been bothering me."

He frowned. "Who?

Jenna winced. She should have kept her mouth shut. "Someone named Savannah Jeffries. She was my uncle's girlfriend when they were younger." She was also the woman who'd had a scandalous tryst with Jenna's father, but she wasn't about to mention that part.

"Did she dream while she was here?"

"I don't know. Tammy accidentally discovered a secret Savannah was keeping, though, and now my family has been talking about hiring a P.I. to search for her."

"Why? Did she go missing?" He wrinkled his forehead. "Was there foul play involved?"

"No. She left town on her own. When Tammy first discovered her secret, all of us girls—Tammy, my sister Donna and I—tried to find out things about her on the internet, but nothing turned up."

"Sounds like you want to find her."

"I'm curious about her, but I'd just as soon let sleeping

dogs lie." She purposely changed the subject. She wasn't prepared to discuss Savannah's secret or the possible ramifications of it. "Doc will have my hide if I don't let you rest, so I'm going to get going. But I'll come back and bring you something to eat. I'll bring some extra groceries and stock the fridge for future meals, too. Oh, and I'll see if I can drum up some clothes that will fit you." She motioned to his rugged ensemble. "You're going to need more than one shirt and one pair of jeans."

"You don't have to fuss over me."

"I don't mind."

"You're going above and beyond."

"I want you to get well." She left her cell-phone number on the desk. "Call if you need anything."

"How long are you going to be gone?"

"Probably a couple of hours. You should try to nap while I'm gone." She walked to the door and glanced over her shoulder at him.

He stood beside the feather bed, looking like a man in need of magic.

Chapter 3

After Jenna left, J.D. didn't know what to do with himself. He didn't want to take a nap, even if he was supposed to be resting. He glanced around the room, then eyed the landline phone.

Already he felt like calling Jenna and telling her that he needed something. But what?

Companionship, he thought. He was lonely as hell.

He sat on the bed, then went ahead and reclined on it. Damn. The feather mattress was heavenly.

J.D. considered his whereabouts. He was hellishly lonely on a heavenly bed? Talk about an odd combination.

The amnesia was odd, too. He couldn't remember anything about himself, but he knew what year it was, who was president, what the world at large was like.

He closed his eyes, and unable to resist the bed, he dozed off.

He awakened hours later, the red-digit clock glaring at him. He hadn't dreamed. His subconscious hadn't created any thoughts or images.

He got up and waited for Jenna to return.

She arrived with a light knock at the door. He answered her summons eagerly.

Her hands were filled with grocery bags.

"I'll take those." He lifted the bags and carried them to the kitchen.

She went out to her truck and came back with containers of fried chicken and mashed potatoes.

"I'm not much of a cook," she said. "This came from the diner in town. I picked it up when I got the groceries."

"I hope you're going to join me. It looks like there's plenty for both of us."

"Sure. I'll eat with you." She walked into the dining room to set the table.

After the plates and silverware were in place, she returned to her truck for the rest of the stuff she'd promised. He could see her from his vantage point in the kitchen.

Upon reentering the house, she called out to him. "The clothes belong to a ranch hand who, I think, is about your size. I'll put them on the sofa for you. There's a nice little satchel with toiletries, too. Donna had them made up for the guest rooms and cabins. She's handling the marketing end of the B and B. She's been redecorating, too."

Interested in talking to her, he crammed the grocery bags in the fridge and met her in the dining room.

"What do you do, Jenna?"

"I'm a horseback riding instructor. It was my profession before I came to the Flying B. I've always been a country girl, even when I lived in the city. I grew up in Houston."

"I assumed you grew up here."

"No. Tammy, Donna and I inherited the ranch from our grandfather, and Tammy's brothers inherited some undeveloped land on the west side of the property. All of us were rewarded money, too, with stipulations of how it's to be used. The girls are supposed to keep the ranch going, which we decided includes the inception of the B and B. And the boys are supposed to take advantage of the mineral rights that go with the land, so they'll be commissioning a survey. Our grandfather left us a portion of his legacy, but we barely got to know him before he passed away. Our families were estranged from him and each other."

They sat down to eat. Curious, he asked, "Who was estranged, exactly?"

"Our dads. They're twin brothers. They hadn't spoken to each other or to Grandpa since..."

She didn't finish her statement, and he wondered if the rift had something to do with Savannah Jeffries and why she'd left town.

He said, "Who knows who my family is or if I even have one."

"Everyone comes from somewhere."

"Yes, but I forgot who they were. I mean, how important can they be?"

"You have a head injury. That's not your fault."

He popped open a soda can. "It still feels personal."

"Your life will be back on track before you know it."

Would it? At this point, he couldn't see past his amnesia. He couldn't imagine who he was. "I fell asleep while you were gone."

Her eyes grew wide. "Did you dream?"

"No."

She seemed disappointed. "Maybe you will tonight."

He didn't reply.

A short time later, they finished their meals and went into the living room. They sat on the sofa, and he checked out the clothes, which consisted of a handful of shirts and a couple of pairs of Wrangler jeans. He noticed a package of unopened boxer shorts, too. "Where did these come from?"

"I bought those at the emporium in town. I took a chance that you wore that type. I took a chance on the size, too." She paused, a sweetly shy expression on her face. "I hope it wasn't too forward of me." She quickly added, "I got you socks, too. Did you see those?"

"Yes, thank you." But buying him socks wasn't nearly as intimate as buying him boxers. "I appreciate everything you've been doing for me."

"I borrowed the clothes before I went into town, and then, while I was shopping for groceries, it hit me that you might need those other things, so I made a quick trip to the emporium."

"I feel badly that you've been spending money on me."

"It wasn't that much."

He begged to differ. He knew how expensive it was to live these days. He returned his attention to the clothes, glad they hadn't cost her anything. "These should fit. What's the ranch hand's name who loaned them to me?"

"Caleb Granger. He isn't aware of the loan, though. He's out of town on a personal matter, but he left some of his things behind."

"You borrowed them without his consent?"

"I didn't. The foreman did. When I mentioned that I needed clothes for someone who was about the same size as Caleb, he went into Caleb's cabin and got them for me. I never would've done that. I don't know Caleb very well."

"You noticed how he was built."

"He's tall and muscular, like you. Women notice those sorts of things."

Curious about this Caleb character and the comparison she'd just made, he asked, "Are you interested in getting to know him better?"

"Oh, my goodness, no. The last I checked, he had eyes for my sister. But I don't think she's aware of his interest in her, and now that he's out of town, it doesn't matter anyway."

"It might when he gets back."

"For him, maybe. But for her? I doubt it. I can't see Donna dating a ranch hand. She's Ms. New York. Not that I have a right to criticize her."

"Why? Are you a fussy dater, too? Are you as picky about your men as your sister is about hers?"

She glanced away and started fidgeting. He'd obviously struck a chord. He should have left it alone, but he was too damned curious to drop it.

"Come on, Jenna. Fess up."

"There's nothing to fess."

He frowned, suddenly imagining her in a bad relationship. "Did someone hurt you? Did you get your heart broken?"

"Oh, no. It's nothing like that."

He felt immediately better. She'd been so kind to him, he didn't want to envision someone being unkind to her. "Then what is it?"

"I guess it won't matter if I tell you. But you're probably going to think it's dumb." She blew out a breath and continued, "I made a list of the qualities I want in a man, and I'm following it to the letter."

Well, then. That certainly wasn't what he expected. "I hope you find what you want."

"Me, too."

In the next curious instant, he wondered what sorts of qualities she was after. "Maybe you can show me the list sometime."

"I don't think that's a good idea."

"Why? Do you have sexual things on it?"

She straightened her spine, looking like a sweet little prude. "I can't believe you asked me that."

"Hey, you're the one who gave me a sexy name, remember?"

"I already explained that I didn't mean that literally."

"I know." He shot her a smile. "I was just teasing you."

"You have a wicked sense of humor."

He wondered if a sense of humor was on her list, but decided not to push the issue or tease her anymore about it.

Still, he couldn't get the list out of his mind. Sooner or later, he would probably ask her about it again.

He set Caleb's clothes aside and picked up the toiletry satchel. "Is there a shaving kit in here?"

"Truthfully, I've never taken inventory of what Donna puts in those, but she's a really thorough person, so I'm betting there is. I grabbed that from the supply room. I didn't even tell her that I was taking it."

"Let's see how thorough she is, shall we?"

"Sure. Let's see."

He opened the bag and started removing the items,

placing them on the coffee table and reciting them, one by one. "Soap. Shampoo. Conditioner. Lotion. Toothpaste and mouthwash. Ah here we go. Shaving cream and disposable razors."

"Donna came through."

"Yes, she did." He reached into the satchel again. "There's a small box of some kind. It's wedged at the bottom." He dug it out of the bag and as soon as he held it up, he wanted to shove it back inside.

Condoms.

He looked at Jenna and she stared back at him. He couldn't think of a thing to say.

And apparently neither could she.

Jenna wanted to strangle herself for not checking out the items ahead of time. She wanted to strangle Donna, too, for being far more thorough than necessary.

Before the silence swallowed them alive, she managed a lame comment. "I guess my sister really did think of everything."

"She sure did." He seemed relieved that Jenna had broken the ice. He even smiled.

She was relieved that the moment had passed, too, but she struggled to summon a smile. Her heart was still beating with a quick cadence.

He put the condoms next to the razors. "Are you close?"

"What?"

"You and your sister?"

Funny he should ask. "No. I was just mentioning that to her this morning. How unalike we are. How we don't communicate all that well to each other."

"Did you discuss why?"

"No, but it's because of our family dynamics when we were growing up. Our parents got divorced when we were little, and we lived with our mom. Then she died when I was eight and Donna was nine."

"I'm sorry."

"It was ovarian cancer. I still miss her—Mom and I were close. Donna never bonded with her, or anyone, for that matter. But I think Donna wished she'd been closer to Mom. Sometimes, after Mom died, I used to catch her gazing at Mom's pictures in the most horribly sad way, but then Donna would look away, as if she didn't want me to know how badly she was hurting."

"What happened to you and Donna after your mom passed away?"

"We went to live with our dad. But he worked a lot, and we learned to fend for ourselves. I always wondered about my grandfather and his ranch. Secretly I wanted to meet him. But I knew Dad was estranged from his family, so I didn't talk to him about it. Dad isn't easy to talk to."

"You are."

She felt her cheeks go warm. "Really?"

"I'd tell you about myself if I knew who I was."

"The way I'm blabbing? Somehow, I doubt that."

"You're not blabbing. I asked you about your family and you're answering my questions."

In way too much detail, she thought. But it felt good to get some of it off her chest. "The American dream was lost on my family."

"How common is that, really? How many people get to live that kind of life?"

"I don't know. But someday I want to create a family of my own, one that will be bonded and true to each other."

"Husband, kids, picket fence?"

She nodded. "I want a man who shares my love of the country. I feel blessed that I inherited part of this ranch. It's everything to me now, and I want it to be everything to my future husband."

"That stands to reason." He paused. "So, what was your grandfather like?"

"He went by the name of Tex. He was an ornery old guy, but charming, too. I regret not having the opportunity to know him better, but I'm grateful that he welcomed me into his life when he did." She thought about everything that had transpired recently. "Doc was his private physician. That's how he and Tammy met."

"And then they had dreams about each other that came true?" He glanced toward the bedroom. "If you don't mind me asking, what were those dreams?"

She'd avoided mentioning them earlier, but she supposed it didn't really matter since Doc and Tammy spoke openly about their experiences. "Tammy dreamed that she and Doc had a romantic evening in this cabin before it actually happened."

Clearly, J.D. wasn't impressed. "That's not very groundbreaking."

"Tammy worked hard to catch Doc's eye. In fact, I helped her with a makeover. She was a tomboy for most of her life and didn't know how to doll herself up."

"Doc doesn't seem like he's from around here."

"He isn't. He's originally from Philadelphia, and he came here to pay a debt to the man who put him through medical school, and that debt involved caring for our grandfather." She shifted on the sofa. "Doc was planning on leaving afterward and going back to his life in the city, then he fell in love with Tammy. He dreamed that they were happily married with three kids."

He frowned. "That's not a magic dream. They're not even married yet, and there aren't any kids."

"They're going to be married, and the kids will come later. Besides, they both dreamed about the same little dark-haired girl."

"Really?" He was obviously surprised.

"Yes, and someday that little girl is going to be born to them." Jenna was certain of it.

J.D. didn't respond, but she was glad that they'd had this discussion. Offering him a break, she said, "You should probably rest again."

"I won't be able to take another nap."

"You can watch TV."

"I don't like TV."

"So you do know something about yourself."

"I'm only saying that because when I turned on the TV in the hospital, it bored me."

"Then it probably bored you before you got amnesia, too."

"I don't know, but the man next to me sure liked to watch it."

"Yes, he did. I didn't care for his taste in shows." Especially the game show that reeked of her childhood. Jenna had always been sensitive about her youth, but even more so now that she was dealing with the Savannah Jeffries issue and her dad's part in it.

"What do you watch?" J.D. asked.

She pulled herself back into the conversation. "The news mostly. I like Animal Planet, too. Sometimes I watch romantic comedies."

"Is that what's called chick flicks?"

She nodded.

He got up and stood beside the living-room window. "So, how long have you had that list of yours?"

Dang. He was back to that. "Awhile."

"How long is awhile?"

"Since I was twenty-five, and I'm thirty now."

"Five years? That is awhile. Have you been refining it?"

"I added a few things about the ranch since I came here."

"About your future husband loving this place?"

"Yes." Restless, she reached for the clothes she'd loaned him. "But the list is mostly the same as it was five years ago. I knew what qualities I wanted in a man then, and I still want him to have those same qualities now."

"I couldn't begin to make a list. I don't know what I expect out of myself, let alone someone else."

"You'll know all about yourself once your memory comes back."

"I still can't imagine making a list."

"Then you're probably not a type-A personality like I am."

"I suppose not." He motioned to the clothes. "Is that part of your type-A nature?"

She glanced down. Apparently she'd been folding and refolding the same pair of jeans. "I'm just..."

"What?"

Nervous, she thought. But she said, "I'm just trying to help you get organized." She quickly folded each article of clothing, then went after the toiletries, dropping them back into the bag. She made sure the condoms went first, keeping them out of sight and out of mind. "I'll put all of this away for you."

"Sure. Okay. Thanks." He smiled a little. "I was going to leave everything there until I needed it."

So much for blocking the condoms from her mind. He wouldn't need those while he was staying at the Flying B, would he? Not unless he found a local girl to mess around with once he started feeling better.

Jenna frowned and headed for the bedroom.

He tagged along. "What's wrong?"

"Nothing."

"You seem flustered. If I'm too much work for you, just leave that stuff, Jenna. I'll take care of it."

"I'm not flustered." She just didn't like envisioning him with another woman.

As opposed to him being with her? She reprimanded herself. She shouldn't be entertaining those sorts of thoughts. J.D. could have sex with whoever met his fancy.

Trouble was, he met the physical requirements on her list. Of course she knew that being sexually attracted to someone wasn't enough to sustain a relationship. Every piece of the puzzle had to fit.

While she put his borrowed clothes in the dresser, he sat on the edge of the bed.

"You should stay in this cabin after I'm gone," he said.

"Why?"

"So you can sleep here." He patted the bed.

Her pulse went haywire. "I already told you there's nothing I need to dream about."

"I was talking about the comfort factor."

"I have a comfortable bed in my room."

"Do you have an old feather mattress?"

"No."

"Then I'll bet it doesn't compare. I sank right into this bed. It's pretty darn amazing."

She glanced away. "I'm glad you like it."

"It's interesting that you don't think you have anything to dream about."

She turned to look at him again. "What do you mean?"

"Seems to me that you'd want to dream about the man you're hoping to marry."

"I don't need to see him in a dream. I'll know who he is when I meet him in person."

"You'll recognize him from the list? That must be some list."

"It is to me. But most people probably wouldn't think much of it."

"Where do you keep it?"

"I have a file on my computer. But I keep a copy in my purse, too."

"You carry it around?" He flashed his lopsided grin. "That's over the top."

His cavalier attitude annoyed her. "Keeping it close at hand helps me to stay focused."

"So you can checkmark it when you're on a date?" His grin got even more crooked. "I feel sorry for the poor saps who take you out, having to live up to whatever your expectations are."

"Your sense of humor is wearing thin, J.D."

"Sorry. It's just that I've never met anyone like you before."

"How would you know if you've ever met anyone like me?"

"I wouldn't, I guess. But logic tells me that you're one of a kind."

"You think I'm weird." She tromped into the bathroom to put his toiletries away.

Soon she felt his presence behind her. She sensed that he was looming in the doorway, watching her. She ignored him. The condoms were the last items she put away. She placed them in the cabinet under the sink, stood up and turned in his direction.

He said, "I don't think you're weird. I think you're sweet and beautiful and unique."

He was looking at her with tenderness in his eyes, and now she longed to reach out and hold him. "Thank you. That was a nice thing to say."

"I meant every word."

The bathroom was small already, and now the walls were closing in.

"I should get going," she said.

"You don't have to leave yet."

She glanced at her watch. "It's getting late."

"But I want you to stay." He didn't move away from the doorway, trapping her where she was.

J.D. scrambled for an excuse to keep her there. "I need you to help me put the groceries away."

"You already put them away."

"I just put the bags in the fridge. I didn't unload them."

"Oh, my goodness. Really? There was frozen food in those. And canned goods and…" She shook her head. "You should have unpacked them."

"So help me do it now."

She made a *tsk-tsk* sound. "Who doesn't look in a grocery bag to see what's in it?"

He smiled. "A guy recovering from a concussion?"

She returned his smile, and he realized he'd just

charmed her. It made him feel good inside, but a bit anxious, too. He shouldn't be asking her to spend more time with him.

"Come on," she said. "Let's put the food away properly."

He cleared the doorway, allowing her to pass by him. As her body breezed by his, he got a zipper-tugging sensation. He took a rough breath and followed her to the kitchen. While he was walking behind her, he checked her out. She was lean and gently toned. Had he always been partial to small-framed girls?

She made a beeline for the fridge and removed the bags. Together, they unloaded them. She'd gotten him a variety of stuff to choose from: frozen pizza, fresh fruit, ready-made salads, boxed macaroni and cheese, sandwich fixings, canned chili, soup and crackers, pudding cups, cereal and milk.

Meals designed for a bachelor, he thought. "Thank you again for everything you've been doing for me. I really do intend to repay you."

"All I want is for you to get better," she said, repeating what she'd told him earlier. "That will be payment enough."

"I'm glad you didn't get anything that requires cooking skills. I don't think I'd be very good in that regard."

"We have that in common."

He nodded. She'd already mentioned that she wasn't much of a cook.

After they completed their task, he said, "Will you sit outside with me before you go?" He was still looking for excuses to keep her there, and since the cabin was equipped with a quaint little porch, it provided a cozy atmosphere. "We can have some pudding."

She accepted the invitation, and they settled into mismatched chairs. The air was rife with something sweet. Honeysuckle, maybe. Foliage grew along the sides of the building.

As he spooned into his dessert, he looked at Jenna, impressed with how beautifully she fit into the environment. Her hair caught the setting sun, making it look even blonder. He couldn't explain why her hair was a source of fascination. Was it because his was so dark? His skin was a lot darker than hers, too.

"I wish I could cook," she said, her mind obviously back in the kitchen.

"You could learn, couldn't you?"

"I don't know. Every time I try to make something, it tastes awful. Maybe I'll ask Tammy if she can give me some pointers."

"The way you gave her pointers about dolling herself up?"

Jenna smiled. "It might be a good trade."

"Sounds like it to me." He studied her again. She certainly knew how to make herself look pretty. Whatever she was wearing on her lips created a warm, kissable effect. "You can use me as a guinea pig if you want."

"For my cooking?"

Or kissing, he thought. "Yes, cooking."

"You're already suffering from a head injury. I don't want to poison you, too."

"I'm sure I'd survive it."

"I'd rather not take the chance."

"I probably won't be here long enough anyway." No poison food. No soft, sweet, poison kisses, either. He needed to stop thinking about how alluring she was.

"Do you like the pudding?" she asked.

He glanced at his cup. He'd only taken a few bites. He'd been too busy admiring her. "Yes, it's good."

"Butterscotch is my favorite."

He noticed that she'd barely made a dent in hers, either. "You're not gobbling it up very quickly."

"I'm savoring it."

"So am I," he lied, when in fact, he'd been savoring her.

"This is nice, sitting out here with you."

"Thanks. I think so, too." He couldn't envision anything nicer. Well, actually he could, but he'd warned himself not to obsess about kissing her. "We're becoming friends."

Friends and only friends, he reiterated.

While a soft Texas breeze blew, he asked, "What's the name of this town?"

"Buckshot Hills. I'm surprised no one told you before now."

"It must have slipped their minds."

"It slipped mine. I wonder how long it will take for Deputy Tobbs to start questioning the locals about you."

"Soon, I hope."

"Once you're feeling better, I can take you on a tour of the Flying B and introduce you to the people who work here, like Deputy Tobbs suggested."

"Wouldn't it be ironic if I was on my way to visit someone at the Flying B when I got hurt?"

"It would certainly solve the mystery, and quickly, too."

There was a mixed-up part of him that wished he'd been on his way to visit her, that she'd been his agenda. No matter how hard he tried, he couldn't seem to control his attraction to her. He even worried that he might have an intimate dream about her tonight, with or without a so-called magic bed.

After they finished their pudding, she said, "I really should go now."

He didn't try to stop her. It was better to have some distance between them.

She left, and he watched her go.

About an hour later, someone rapped at the door, and he jumped up to answer it, wondering if she'd returned.

But it was Doc, with his medical bag.

The other man said, "Jenna told me that she put you up in this cabin. How do you like it?"

"It's fine. But I don't believe that the bed is magical. I know you do, though."

"I'm a man of science, but I've learned that sometimes logic doesn't apply."

J.D. didn't respond, and the subject was dropped. Regardless, the feeling remained. He was still concerned that he might have a sensual dream.

Doc examined him and recommended more bed rest. J.D. followed orders and went to sleep early that night. He didn't dream about Jenna.

Much to his shock, he dreamed about himself, with an emotion-packed glimpse of who he was as a child.

Chapter 4

Jenna looked across the table at Donna. They were having breakfast together again, and today Donna was paging through wallpaper samples that were stacked beside her.

"We really should stop meeting like this," Jenna said.

Her sister glanced up and rolled her eyes. But she smiled, too, lightening the moment.

After their mom died, they rarely shared a meal. They would just grab their food and go. Actually, they hadn't dined together all that much when Mom had been around, either. She'd been depressed over the divorce, then she'd gotten sick.

"Our childhoods sucked," Jenna said, thinking out loud.

Donna crinkled her face. "This isn't a discussion we should be having."

"Why not?"

"Because sitting around wallowing in the past isn't going to change anything."

"I wasn't wallowing." She was trying to have a meaningful conversation. "It wouldn't hurt to talk things through once in a while."

"I don't see the point in crying over spilt milk. We need to focus on the B and B and making it a success."

"That's what we've been doing."

"Then let's not lose sight of it."

Jenna considered her sister's determination. A failed business venture had put a dent in Donna's bankbook, damaging her self-esteem and putting her glamorous life at risk. The B and B was her chance to make up for it.

Donna lifted a paisley-printed swatch. "What do you think of this for the bedroom that overlooks the garden?"

"What garden?"

"The one I'm designing with the landscaper. I told you about it before."

"No, you didn't."

"Oh, I'm sorry. I thought I did. It's going to have a redwood gazebo and a boatload of flowering perennials. Daisies in the summer, Texas bluebonnets in the spring. It'll be a perfect spot for weddings and special events."

"It sounds beautiful, and I think the wallpaper is pretty, too."

"I don't know." Donna gave the swatch a critical eye. "Maybe I should use a Western pattern. My goal is to create an idyllic atmosphere but without infringing on the natural environment."

"You're doing a great job so far."

"Thank you."

"I've always admired your sense of style." Jenna

hadn't been born with a gift of flair, not like her sister. "I learned how to put myself together from watching you."

"Really?" Donna seemed surprised, maybe even a little embarrassed by the praise. "Well, you know what? You did a spectacular job of helping Tammy with her makeover. She looks like a million now."

"It was fun, and she nabbed the prize, too."

"The Prince Charming doctor? You'd never catch me playing the role of Cinderella."

For a moment, Jenna was tempted to tell Donna about Caleb's interest in her, but she figured it was pointless since it wouldn't go anywhere, anyway. She said instead, "I gave J.D. one of the toiletry satchels you created for our guests."

"Who's J.D.?"

"The man with amnesia. That's what we're calling him until we know his real name. It's the initials for John Doe. I offered to let him stay at the ranch until his memory returns or until the police uncover his identity."

"I wonder which will come first."

"I don't know. I put him in the dream cabin."

"Did he like the toiletries? I labored over what brand of shampoo and conditioner to order."

"I'm sure the shampoo and conditioner will be just fine, when he's able to use them. For now, he isn't supposed to get his stitches wet." But that was the least of Jenna's concern. "Why did you include condoms in those bags?"

"Because other top-notch establishments provide prophylactics to their guests. Actually, I was thinking that I should use little baskets to display everything instead of the satchels. What do you think?"

"Baskets would definitely be better. No surprises.

I nearly died when J.D. pulled the condoms out of that bag."

Donna furrowed her delicately arched brows. "Don't tell me you have a crush on him."

"What?"

"Why else would you want to die over a box of condoms?"

"Because I barely know him."

"Are you sure that's all it is?"

"Yes."

"Good. Because Flying B romances are chock-full of trouble."

"That isn't a very nice thing to say about Tammy and Doc."

"I wasn't talking about them. It's nice that Tammy is walking around all shiny and new."

"So, you were talking about Savannah Jeffries? Maybe it's time for us to have a discussion about her."

"I'd rather not." Although the detachment in Donna's voice was evident, so was the vulnerability. "Savannah Jeffries has nothing to do with our future."

Jenna wasn't so sure about that. Already Savannah was affecting them. "We can't ignore it forever. We're going to have to vote on the P.I. issue."

"Not at the moment, we don't."

True. The rest of the family had to decide, as well—the rest of them being Tammy and her brothers, Aidan and Nathan.

The fathers were being excluded from the vote, mostly because Jenna and Donna didn't want their dad to have a say in the mess he'd made. As for Uncle William, Tammy said that he preferred to be left out of it anyway, as he just wanted the whole thing to disappear. *The way Savannah had disappeared,* Jenna thought.

Suddenly her cell phone rang. She glanced at the screen and saw the landline number from the dream cabin. She walked away from the table and answered it.

"J.D.?" she said.

"I hope I'm not disturbing you."

"No, not at all. How are you feeling?"

"Truthfully? I'm overwhelmed. The bed worked, Jenna. I dreamed about myself last night. A memory dream. Do you want to come by and I'll tell you about it?"

Her heart struck her chest. "Yes, of course. I'm on my way."

The call ended, and she approached table. "I have to go," she told Donna.

Her sister turned in her chair. "Is everything all right?"

"Yes." At least she hoped it was. J.D. didn't say if his dream was good or bad. *Overwhelmed* could apply to either.

She left the house and climbed in her truck. The cabin was within walking distance, but only on a leisure day. She wanted to hurry up and get there.

She arrived within a matter of minutes, and he was waiting for her on the porch.

She ascended the steps and they stood face-to-face. He was clean shaven, and without the stubble, his strong-boned features were even more pronounced.

He was wearing one of Caleb's shirts, but he'd left it unbuttoned. The jeans were Caleb's, too, and they fit him a little snugger than his own. She assumed that he had a pair of the new boxers on underneath.

"Do you want to talk out here or go inside?" he asked.

"It's up to you." Where they conversed didn't matter. She was distracted by him: his abs, his navel, the frayed waistband of his borrowed jeans. Even his bare feet seemed sexy.

He said, "Let's stay out here."

Normally the outdoors soothed her. But being around J.D. was turning her into a jumble of hormones. She'd lied to Donna about not having a crush on him.

Instead of taking a chair, he sat on the porch steps. She had no choice but to sit beside him, far closer than a chair would've allowed.

"Was it a good dream?" she asked quickly.

"Yes, but it was troubling, too. I saw myself as a boy. I was about ten. I was in a barn, grooming a sorrel mare. I grew up around horses, Jenna. I could feel it during the dream."

"Why is that troubling?" She thought it was wonderful. She'd pegged him as a cowboy from the beginning.

"I was the only person in the dream. I didn't get a feeling about my family. For all I know, I could have been a foster kid who was too old to get adopted."

That struck her as an odd thing for him to say. Was it a memory struggling to surface? "Were you sad in the dream?"

"No. But I was with the mare, and I felt a connection to her. She made me happy."

Horses always made Jenna happy, too, but they gave a lot of people joy. His bond with the mare didn't prove or disprove what type of childhood he'd had. His foster care/adoption comment was too specific to ignore, though. "Maybe the dream will continue on another night."

"Maybe."

She studied his chiseled profile. "What did you look like as a ten-year-old?"

"Why does that matter?"

"I just want to know." To see him through his own eyes.

"I was on the small side, a skinny kid, and my hair was sort of longish. A little messy, I suppose." He shrugged, but he smiled, too. "I was wearing a straw cowboy hat, and I had sugar cubes in my shirt pocket for the mare."

She smiled, as well. She liked envisioning him as a youth and she liked the boyishness that had come over him now. He seemed wistful. If he hadn't made the foster-child remark, she would've assumed that he'd had a solid upbringing. But he had made the remark, and it weighed heavily on her mind.

"Tell me more about the dream," she said. "Were you in Texas? Is that where you grew up?"

"I don't know. I didn't get a sense of the location."

"What was the barn like?"

"I couldn't tell how big it was, but it was well maintained."

"Did you get a sense of how long you'd lived there?"

"No."

"But you sensed that you'd been raised in an equine environment?"

"Yes."

"So if you were a foster child, then all of the homes you'd been placed in had horses? How likely do you think that is?"

"I have no idea." He changed the subject. "So, why don't you tell me about the horses on the Flying B?"

"We have plenty of great trail horses that Tex used to

favor and that anyone on the ranch can use at their leisure, but I'm still acquiring school horses."

"For your riding instruction?"

She nodded. "They have to be able to accommodate any level of rider. I'll need a string of them for group lessons, but I'm being extremely cautious, hand-selecting each one. I have two wonderful geldings, so far."

"Will you take me to see them?"

"Today?"

"Yes, now. Today. I want to know how being around horses makes me feel in person. You can introduce me to the employees on the ranch, too, and see if any of them recognize me."

"I think I better check with Doc before I take you on a tour. You've only been out of the hospital for a day."

"I feel fine."

"I still think I should talk to him." She removed her phone from her purse and called Doc, but she got his answering service. "He's supposed to call me back."

"When?"

"As soon as he's able."

J.D. stood up. "I'm going to get ready."

He went into the cabin and came back, carrying his socks and boots. Jenna couldn't blame him for being anxious, but what if he was jumping the gun?

"Doc might not think you're ready for an outing," she said.

"He will if you tell him about my dream. Besides, I'll go stir-crazy just sitting around here."

After his boots were in place, he buttoned his shirt and tucked it into his pants.

"I forgot my belt." Off he went to retrieve it.

She took a moment to breathe, as deeply as she could.

Watching him get dressed was making her warm and tingly.

He returned with the belt halfway threaded through his belt loops. She should've turned away, but like the smitten female she was fast becoming, she trained her gaze on his every move.

This was crazy. Now she felt as if she had a concussion, and she hadn't even taken a hit to the head. Not literally, anyway. Figuratively, she'd been struck and struck hard.

Determined to keep her wits, she thought about her list. Aside from his physical attributes and his newly discovered connection to horses, he didn't meet her requirements. First and foremost, the man she chose had to be as marriage-minded as she was, and J.D. didn't seem like the husband type. Nor was she foolish enough to believe that he was going to dream himself into that role.

He sat beside her, pulling her out of analytical mode and back into a heap of emotion. His nearness caused a chemical reaction.

Fire in her veins. Pheromones shooting from her pores.

Before the silence grew unbearable, she said, "If you were raised around horses, then I'll bet you're a skilled rider."

He shot her a half-cocked grin. "Give me a bucking bronc to ride and we'll see."

She laughed, albeit nervously. She hadn't recovered from his nearness. "All I need is for you to get tossed on your head. Doc would accuse me of trying to kill his patient."

Finally the doctor in question called, and Jenna spoke with him.

Afterward, she told J.D., "He said it was fine, as long as you don't stay too long or wear yourself out."

"I knew he would agree." He reached over to give her a hand up.

Being touched by him didn't help her condition. She was still fighting fire, pheromones and everything else that had gone wrong with her.

"Are we going to walk?" he asked.

"I think it would be better to take the truck."

He glanced out in the distance. "How far is it?"

"Not that far. But too far for a man with a head injury," she amended. "Doc said not to tax your energy."

"Did he specifically say that I shouldn't walk?"

"No, but I'm saying it." For the second time that day, she avoided a leisurely stroll.

After they got in the truck, he turned toward her. "Thanks, Jenna."

"For what?"

"Putting up with me. I know I'm taking up a lot of your time."

"It's okay. I want to help you through this." And once he was completely well, she could try to resume some order in her life. "Look at the progress you've made already."

"Because of you and your family. You really should stay in the cabin after I'm gone, even if it's just for one night."

"The bed in my room is fine."

"The bed in your room doesn't induce dreams."

She repeated what she'd told him before. "I don't need to rely on magic. Things will happen for me when they're meant to."

"But you seem tense."

She started the engine and headed toward the stables. "There's a lot going on in my world."

"Like the Savannah Jeffries issue?"

"Yes."

"If you need a sounding board, I'll lend you my ear."

"I tried to talk to my sister about it this morning."

"But she didn't want to discuss it?"

"No."

"I'm here, if you need me," he reiterated.

There was a part of her that wanted to tell him the whole sordid story, to lean on his shoulder and let him wrap her in comfort. But relying on him wasn't the answer, especially with her troubled attraction to him.

She parked in front of the stables and introduced him to the ranch hands who were nearby. None of them recognized him. Neither did Hugh, the loyal old foreman who'd snagged Caleb's clothes. But she didn't expect Hugh to recognize him, especially since she'd already described J.D. to him.

"You can meet everyone else on another day," she told J.D.

He agreed, and she took him to the barn that housed the school horses.

"This is Pedro's Pride," she said as a tobiano paint poked his head out to greet them. She opened the gate and they went into his stall. "But I just call him Pedro."

J.D. approached the horse, and it was love at first sight. Man and beast connected instantly. Jenna stood back and marveled at the exchange.

"He's big and flashy," J.D. said, "But he has manners, too."

As he roamed his hands along the gelding's sturdy frame, the horse stood patiently. Jenna wasn't quite so calm. Seeing J.D. this way heightened her feelings for him.

He said, "If Pedro carries a rider the way you say he does, then you found a gem."

"You look as if you found a gem, too. In yourself," she clarified. "I can tell that you're in your element."

"I am. It feels right." He tapped a hand to his chest. "Here, where it counts."

In his heart, she thought. "That's how I feel every time I come out here."

"You're lucky that this is your life's work."

"It's probably yours, too. You just can't remember the who, what and where."

He remained next to the gelding. "How long will Caleb be out of town?"

"I think he's scheduled to come back next month. Why?"

"If you need someone to fill in for him until he gets back, maybe you can hire me. Then I can repay your kindness by working it off."

Yesterday, he'd been unable to acknowledge that he might be a cowboy, and today he was offering to be a ranch hand. But given the circumstances, his offer made sense. "I'll have to talk to Hugh about it, and to Doc, too, of course. You can't start working until he gives you a clean bill of health." She added, "And you'll get the same wages as everyone else. Repaying my kindness doesn't mean that you'll be working for free."

"I won't let you, Hugh or Doc down. I'll do a good job."

"I'm sure you will." But it was only temporary, she reminded herself.

J.D. wasn't going to be part of the Flying B forever.

* * *

J.D. glanced at Pedro, then at Jenna. He felt perfectly at ease around the horse. But around the woman? Not so much. The zip-zing between them jarred his senses.

He wanted to do right by her, to work at the ranch and make himself useful. But somewhere in the pit of his stomach, he wanted to run to the nearest bus stop and leave Buckshot Hills, Texas, far, far behind.

He'd seen the way she'd looked at him when he'd gotten halfway dressed in front of her. True, he'd been antsy about meeting her horses, but he shouldn't have buttoned his shirt or zipped his jeans in her presence, especially since it had been a fantasy leftover from the hospital.

"How are you feeling?" she asked.

He blinked. "What?"

"I want to be sure you're feeling well enough to continue."

"I'm doing fine." Except for his bad-to-the-bone hunger for her.

"Then let's go to the next stall."

They proceeded, and she introduced him to Duke, her other school horse, whose original owner, a lover of old Westerns, had given him the same nickname as John Wayne. He was a friendly sorrel with a blaze and three white socks. J.D. approached the gelding, anxious to get close to him.

"He resembles the mare in my dream. His markings are similar." And it made J.D. feel like the boy he once was. "If I had a sugar cube, I'd give him one."

"You can spoil him next time. And Pedro, too."

"I wish I could ride him."

"Next time," she said again.

"How old were you when you started riding?" he asked.

"Ten."

"The same age I was in my dream."

She nodded. "I was one of those kids that collected horsey stuff—pictures, books, toys, stuffed animals—but other than a few pony rides, I wasn't around them. Then, two years after Mom died, I asked Dad if I could take riding lessons. He agreed, but he didn't take an active part in it. He didn't drive me back and forth or watch me during my lessons. He hired a babysitter for that, and once I got old enough to go on my own, I hung out there all the time, before and after school, on weekends, in the summer. It was a magnificent equestrian center. My home away from home."

"So, what did you look like when you were ten?" he asked, interested to know the same thing about her that she'd wanted to know about him.

She smiled. "I was a skinny kid with longish hair."

He smiled, too. She'd stolen his line. "Did you favor straw hats?"

"Are you kidding? I still do."

"I haven't seen you in a hat yet."

"You will. Speaking of which, you're going to need one once you start working here. I can give you one that belonged to my grandfather."

"You don't have to do that."

"Tex wouldn't have minded. He probably would have given you one himself. I think your dream would have fascinated him."

He thought about his unknown family. "Do you think I was a foster kid?"

"I don't know. But your comment about possibly being too old to be adopted gave me pause."

It gave him pause, too. "Most people want babies or toddlers, not older kids." He frowned. "Don't they?"

"I don't know anything about adoption, J.D."

He searched her gaze. "Would you ever consider raising someone else's child as your own?"

"Truthfully, I've never really thought about it before. But I love children, so if it was something my husband wanted to do, I would certainly consider it. What about you?"

"Me?" He took a cautionary step back. "I don't think I'd make a very good dad, adoptive or otherwise. I'd have enough trouble dealing with myself, let alone being a parent."

"My future husband is going to be father material. That's one of the most important qualities on my list. I want him to bring our children presents, even when it isn't their birthdays. I want him to help me read to them at night. I even want him to dress up as Santa Claus and sneak past the tree on Christmas Eve."

Surprised that she referred to the list she'd been protecting, he said, "I wouldn't be able to do any of that." Even now, he felt as if he were on the brink of a panic attack. "Marriage, babies, birthdays, Christmas."

"I wasn't implying that you should."

"Neither was I." He fought the panic, forcing his lungs to expand. "I was just making conversation."

"About how different we are? I already figured that out."

Of course she did, he thought. She analyzed the men she was attracted to. She weighed them against her list.

She said, "After your identity is restored, you can return to whatever type of lifestyle suits you."

He nodded, knowing that was exactly what he would do. Nonetheless, it didn't give him comfort. The fact that Jenna found him lacking made him ache inside.

An ache he couldn't begin to understand.

Chapter 5

A week passed without J.D. having any more dreams and without the police uncovering any information about him. But at least Doc said that he was well enough to work. And ride, which he'd done, but only minimally. He hadn't had the opportunity to spend a lot of time in the saddle yet. Mostly his work entailed maintenance in and around the barn.

As for Jenna, his hunger for her was getting worse. In spite of the fact that they were completely wrong for each other, he felt like a thunderstruck kid.

Today he was mucking out stalls, and she was reorganizing the tack room. Every so often, as he moved about the barn, he would catch sight of her in the tack room doorway, and his heart would dive straight to his stomach.

"J.D.?" a male voice said, drawing his attention.

He turned to see Manny, another ranch hand, coming toward him. By now, J.D. had met all of the other employees on the Flying B., including the household staff. Manny, he'd learned, had a thing for one of the maids, a girl he talked incessantly about. J.D., however, hadn't said a word about his forbidden interest in Jenna.

Manny flashed a youthful grin. He was all of twenty-two, with curly brown hair and a happy-go-lucky personality. J.D. wished he knew how to feel that way, but the more time that passed, the more he sensed that his emotions had been screwed up long before Jenna had found him and brought him here.

Manny said, "A group of us are getting together at Lucy's tonight. You ought to join us, J.D. It might do you some good to get out."

"Who's Lucy?"

"It's a place, not a person. Lone Star Lucy's. The local honky-tonk. So, do you want to go?"

"Sure, okay. Thanks." He didn't have anything else to do.

Manny grinned again. "Some of the household staff is going, too."

J.D. cracked a smile. The other man's infectious energy seemed to demand it. "I take it that means the gal you're hot for will be there?"

"Heck, yeah. And I'm going to stick to her like glue. You just watch me."

"I don't doubt that you will." J.D. couldn't seem to stop from asking, "Are any of the Byrds going?" He wanted Jenna to be there. He wanted to see her as badly as Manny wanted to see the maid.

"No."

"Why not?"

"Nobody thought to invite them, I guess. We haven't mingled with them outside the ranch."

"Then maybe it's time."

"You can ask them to come, if you want. I wouldn't count on the prissy one showing up, though. She wouldn't fit in." Manny chuckled. "What's her name? Dana?"

"Donna. I met her briefly, a few days ago." A quick introduction when Jenna had taken him inside to meet the household staff. "She doesn't seem easy to get to know." Which had given him a clearer understanding of the lack of closeness between the sisters.

"I've seen her walking around, dodging manure and sniffling from the hay. I'm surprised she's lasted as long as she has."

"I'll invite all of the Byrds to keep from being rude." And to keep it from seeming as if he only had Jenna in mind. "It would be nice to see Doc and Tammy out on the town."

"Yeah, Tammy is country folk, and Doc is getting there, too. Make sure you don't forget about Jenna, not after everything she's done for you. I think you should buy her a drink."

"I agree. I'll do that, if she accepts the invite." He tried to seem casual. "She told me that she likes to dance so maybe I'll two-step with her, too, if I can keep up." He still wasn't sure what kind of dancer he was, but he was willing to find out if it meant having Jenna as his partner.

"Great. Sounds like a party to me. I can give you a ride. Let's say, about eight? I'll swing by your cabin."

"All right. See you then."

Manny returned to work, and J.D. put down his rake and walked over to where Jenna was. He entered the tack room, and she looked up from the bridles she was hanging on wooden pegs.

He got right to the point. "Manny asked me to join him and some of the others at Lucy's tonight. It would be nice if you, Tammy, Doc and Donna wanted to meet us there."

"Donna would never go to Lucy's."

"Yeah, that's what Manny figured. How about you? Do you want to go?"

"I don't know if it's the right place for me, either. From what I've heard, it caters to a wild crowd."

Hoping to thwart her concern, he said, "I'll protect you from the crazies."

"You will, huh?" She laughed a little. "And who's going to protect me from you?"

"If Doc and Tammy go, Doc can keep me in line. He can tranquilize me if I get too rowdy."

She laughed again. "Then I'll make sure they come along."

Damn, but he liked her. "I thought maybe you and I could dance. Or I'd like to give it a try anyway."

"That sounds nice."

"We're leaving around eight. You can head over about the same time if you want."

"I'll do my best."

Before he overstepped his bounds, he said, "I should get back to work now."

"Me, too." She made a show of jangling the bridles in her hand.

"Bye, Jenna."

"Bye."

He walked away, dreading the day he had to say goodbye to her for real. But at least for now, he had the chance to hold her while they danced.

Jenna walked into Lone Star Lucy's, where scores of people gathered. Doc and Tammy couldn't make it, so she'd ventured out on her own—clearly a stupid thing to do, especially at a bar like this.

She didn't have a clue where J.D. or the Flying B employees were. Everyone looked alike in the dimly lit, sawdust-on-the-floor, tables-crammed-too-close-together environment. Most of the men were bold and flirtatious, with their hats dipped low and their beer bottles held high, and most of the women wore their makeup too heavy, their hair too big and their jeans too tight.

As she made her way farther into the room, she noticed the dance floor. A digital jukebox provided the music. Way in the back, she caught a glimpse of pool tables.

J.D. had said that he would protect her from the crazies, but already she was getting hit on.

A cowboy with slurred speech leaned over his chair and grabbed her shirtsleeve. "Where are you going in such a hurry?"

She tugged her arm away. "I'm looking for someone."

"I can be your someone," he replied.

It is time to leave, she thought. She turned around and ran smack-dab into J.D. He stood there, like a wall of muscle.

"Is that guy bothering you?" he asked.

Her pulse went pitter-pat. "He was, but he isn't anymore."

Slurred Speech had gone back to his beer.

"Where's Doc and Tammy?" J.D. asked.

"They had other plans."

"You should have let me know you were alone. You could have ridden with us."

"You and Manny?"

"And some of the other guys."

"A truckload of testosterone? I don't know about that."

"We would have made room for you, and you could have sat up front with me."

She envisioned herself squeezed in the middle, practically sharing the same seat with J.D. "Taking my own truck was fine."

"I'm just happy you're here. You look damn fine, Jenna."

"Thank you." Her boot-cut jeans were as tight as every other cowgirl's in the place. She'd gone easy on the makeup, though, aside from the crimson lipstick that matched her fancy silk blouse. She hadn't overdone her hair, either. She wore it loose and soft.

He kept looking at her with appreciation in his eyes, and his dark gaze whipped her into a girlish flutter. She'd wanted to impress him, and she had.

"Come on," he said. "I'll take you to our table."

He put his hand lightly on the small of her back, and as they weaved their way around other patrons, he never broke contact. His gentle touch heightened her girlish reaction to him.

He motioned with his free hand. "Over there."

She saw the Flying B group, with Manny smiling big and bright amongst his peers.

There were nine people in all, including her and J.D. He'd saved a seat for her. He'd saved seats for Doc and Tammy, too. But as soon as it became apparent that they weren't being used, they were quickly snatched up by people at another table.

Jenna was greeted by the Flying B employees. The other women in attendance were part-timers from the housekeeping staff. Their names were Celia, Joy and Maria, and they looked a lot different here than they did at work. Celia's boobs were busting out of her top, Joy had eyeliner out to there and Maria's dress hugged her curvaceous hips. They smelled of the same flowery perfume, too, a telltale sign that they'd gotten ready together, sharing a bottle of whatever it was. Overall they seemed like nice girls who'd gone into Lucy's mode for the night.

J.D. turned to Jenna. "Would you like a drink? I'm buying."

"You shouldn't spend your money on me." She knew he'd gotten an advance on his pay, but it wasn't much.

"Are you kidding? I owe you more than a drink."

She offered a smile. "You owe me a dance, too."

His smile matched hers. "First a drink."

She considered white wine, but changed her mind. "I'll take a longneck." She motioned to his bottle. "The same kind you're having."

"I'll get it from the bar. It'll take the waitress forever to work her way over here." Before he left, he finished his beer, which apparently had been almost gone. One last swallow.

He stood up, and she watched him walk away. He had an awfully cute butt. But before someone caught her admiring his backside, she turned her attention to the people she was with and noticed that Manny had eyes for Maria. She seemed flattered by the attention, leaning toward him when he talked and laughing at silly things he said. Now she understood why Manny had orchestrated this get-together. He wanted to make something happen with Maria.

J.D. returned with Jenna's beer. She thanked him and noticed that he'd gotten himself another one, too.

She hoped that he didn't overindulge. It was bad enough that she'd assumed he was drunk when she'd first seen him, lest it come true this evening. She still knew very little about J.D and his habits. Of course he knew little about himself, too. Each day was a new exploration.

Earlier, he'd joked about having Doc tranquilize him, and she'd laughed at the time. But it wouldn't be funny if he got carried away.

Luckily, he didn't. He sipped his second drink slowly.

"We should share a toast," he said.

"To what?"

"Us spending the night together."

She blinked at him. She also felt her skin flush. Suddenly, she was racked with heat. Her nipples shot out like bullets against her bra, too. "We're not spending the night together."

"That isn't what I said."

"Yes, it is."

"No, it isn't," he countered. "I said that we were spending the night *out* together."

"You left off the *out* part."

"I did? Are you sure?"

She nodded. She knew the difference.

"It's noisy in here. Maybe you misheard me."

"You goofed up, J.D." He'd made a Freudian slip or whatever mistakes like that were called.

"I'm sorry. I didn't realize..." He fidgeted with his beer.

Now she wished that she would have kept quiet. "I'm sorry, too. I shouldn't have pointed it out."

The subject was dropped, but that didn't ease the moment.

Just when she thought it couldn't get any worse, Manny glanced across the table and said, "When are you guys going to dance?"

"In a while," J.D. responded.

"You don't look like you're having a very good time." Manny cocked his head. "Either of you."

Jenna piped up. "We're just being quiet while we finish our drinks."

"Liquid courage," J.D. said. "I'll probably suck out there."

Manny replied, "You should have done a test run at the ranch and danced around the cabin."

J.D. made a face. "Now how stupid would I have looked?"

"Pretty dang dumb." The other man grinned. "But at least you would've known if you were any good."

"I don't think it would have been the same without a partner. I won't know until I try it for real."

"We're going to dance later, too," Manny said, and moved closer to Maria. "We're waiting for the songs we picked to play."

He turned back to the rest of the group, leaving J.D. and Jenna to their silent agony. Heaven help her, but she wanted to spend the night with him, to make love, to sleep beside him in the dream cabin. But she knew that being with him would create emotional havoc. Dallying with a man who was destined to disappear from her life wasn't part of her get-married-and-have-babies plan.

"Should we pick some songs, too?" he asked. "It might help us relax."

She appreciated his attempt to make things better. "Sure. Let's give it a try."

He stood up, and like a knight in shining armor, he pulled back her chair. "Chivalry" was one of the husband-requirements on her list. She frowned to herself. As always, her list was tucked away in her purse.

They proceeded to the digital jukebox and waited for the people in front of them to make their selections.

When their turn arrived, he said, "I like the old-style jukes better."

"Me, too. But we live in a digital world now."

"Some things should remain the same."

Like chivalrous men, she thought, fighting another frown. Tonight, of all nights, she shouldn't be referring to her list, especially since J.D wasn't in the running.

He scanned the songs. "The jukebox might be new, but at least the music is classic country."

She stood beside him. "Oh, I love this song." She gestured to "Breathe" by Faith Hill.

"That's a romantic one."

"I wasn't suggesting that we dance to it. I was just saying that it's a favorite of mine."

"Do you like this one, too?" He pointed to Faith's duet with Tim McGraw called "Let's Make Love."

"Now you're being smart." And making a naughty joke about his Freudian slip. "You and that wicked sense of humor of yours."

He flashed a dastardly smile. "Are you brave enough to dance to it with me?"

Was she?

"Are you?" he asked again.

Why not? she thought. At this point, it seemed better

to acknowledge their chemistry than try to avoid it. "Go ahead and push the button. But we'll probably smolder on the dance floor and make everyone jealous."

"If I don't step all over your feet."

"That would certainly ruin the ambience."

"I can't guarantee it won't happen." He chose the song. "Any more?"

"I think one is enough, considering. Don't you?"

"Yeah. We probably shouldn't bite off more than we can chew." They stepped away from the jukebox and he said, "Did you know that Manny has a thing for Maria?"

She looked across the room and toward their table. "Yes, I noticed that he's into her. She seems to like him, too. They'll probably start dating after tonight."

"That will make Manny happy. Who knows how long it will last, though?"

"They're young. They have lots of time to find who they're meant to be with."

"Do you think everyone is meant to be with someone?"

"No. But only because some people seem happier when they're single."

"I can't imagine being married. Just thinking about it makes me panic."

Absolute proof that they were wrong for each other. "It has the opposite effect on me. The thought of being married makes me feel calm."

"Do you have the ceremony planned out in your mind? The style of dress you'll wear and whatever else women daydream about?"

"Actually, I don't. I purposely haven't done that. Otherwise the wedding becomes more important than the marriage."

"That's a grounded way of thinking."

She appreciated his praise and even preened a little. "Thank you."

"Look at you. All pretty and smug. I still think your list is goofy."

"You're just miffed because I won't let you see it."

"Has anyone seen it?"

"I showed it to Tammy after she and Doc got together." She'd needed to confide in someone, and Tammy had been the logical choice. Sharing it with Donna would have been way too awkward.

"Can you blame me for wanting to see it? How am I supposed to leave the Flying B without knowing what type of man Jenna Byrd wants to marry?"

"You can come back someday and meet my husband."

"And tell him that we danced to 'Let's Make Love'?" You should pick that for your wedding song."

"Ha, ha. Very funny. And for the record, we haven't danced to it yet."

"We will. But if I'm a lousy dancer, it's going to ruin the song for you."

Maybe having it ruined would be better than feeling its sensual effect, she thought.

Just then, "Save a Horse (Ride a Cowboy)" came on, adding a bit of fuel to the fire. What timing. The crowd exploded with hoots and hollers and country wildness.

J.D. gestured to the table. "Hey. Manny and Maria are getting up."

She followed his line of sight. Sure enough, the younger couple was headed toward the dance floor.

"They must have picked this song," J.D. said.

"So it seems."

"Can't say as I blame them. They'll probably have a great time with it."

Jenna nodded. No doubt they would.

He kept watching. "Yep. There they go."

She watched, too. They were definitely having a great time. Whenever Maria would bump her hips, Manny would flash a big happy grin and mimic her movements. Jenna couldn't fathom scooting around to the song, while she was in the presence of the cowboy she'd vowed *not* to ride.

"Should we go back to the table?" he asked.

She nodded, and they resumed their seats. Then J.D. leaned over and quietly asked, "Do you think it's becoming obvious that we're attracted to each other?"

"Obvious to whom?"

"Whoever is around us."

She glanced at the Flying B employees who were left at the table. "I'm sure it will be when we dance. We're going to smolder, remember?"

"If I don't blow it."

"You won't."

"They'll probably talk about us."

"It doesn't matter." Instead of fretting about the curiosity that would ensue, she justified being gossiped about. "It's just an innocent flirtation. It's not as if we're going to go home together tonight."

He turned quiet, and the anxiety of waiting for the song they'd picked was almost too much to bear.

Then, about fifteen minutes later, it happened. The first melodic chords of "Let's Make Love" began to play.

Their gazes locked. Hard and deep.

It was time for them to dance.

Chapter 6

J.D. reached for Jenna's hand. "Ready?" he asked, even if he wasn't sure if he was ready himself.

"Yes." She accepted his hand and they walked onto the dance floor.

He took her in his arms and drew a blank. Here he was, holding a beautiful woman, and he still didn't know if he could dance. He couldn't seem to move, so he simply stood there, locked in position.

"Are you all right?" she asked.

"I'm more nervous than I thought I'd be."

"Do you want to forget it? You're under no obligation to—"

"No. I want to try." He listened to the melody, the lyrics, the singer's voice, letting those elements guide him. Slowly, he began to relax and dance with her.

A gentle, heart-stirring two-step.

Mercy, they were good together. Beyond good. Beyond imagination. They gazed at each other the entire time.

"You absolutely know how to do this," she said.

So did she, but her skills were never in question.

As they rocked and swayed, the other dancers barely existed and neither did the bar. Everything was out of focus, melding into misty colors and scattered light. All he saw was Jenna, her fair skin and golden hair.

He brought her closer. "I'm glad I met you. I'm even glad I lost my memory."

"I'm glad we met, too. But you shouldn't say that about having amnesia."

"It's giving me a chance to start over."

"This isn't starting over, J.D. It's a break from your other life."

"I don't care about my other life."

"You shouldn't say that, either. It's important to care about who you are."

How could he care about something he couldn't remember?

They didn't talk anymore, and he was grateful for the silence. He didn't want to disturb the bond. He wanted the luxury of knowing her in this way.

He was in the moment. He was part of it. *John Doe and Jenna Byrd,* he thought. He danced with her as if his amnesia depended on it, the heat between them surging through his veins.

This was a memory he would never forget.

When the song ended, his vision cleared and the bar came back into focus. But it didn't put him on solid ground. He longed to kiss Jenna, to taste her ruby-red lips.

"I need some air," he said. "How about you?"

"Definitely." She looked as dazed as he felt.

He escorted her outside, and they stood in front of the club, with a view of the parking lot. Other people were out there, too, standing off to the side and smoking, the tips of their cigarettes creating sparks.

Speaking of sparks…

J.D. was still feeling the fire. Apparently so was Jenna. Her voice vibrated. "I warned you that we were going to smolder. I've never danced with anyone like that before."

"I doubt I have, either." He struggled to put it in perspective. "How long do you think that song was?"

"Three, maybe four minutes."

"That's nothing in the scheme of things."

"I know. But it was beautiful." Her eyes drifted closed.

"Maybe you really should use it as your wedding song."

She opened her eyes. "I could never do that, especially not after dancing with you to it. That wouldn't be fair to my husband."

"Would it be fair to him if I became your short-term lover?" He couldn't help it. He wanted to have a dazzling affair with her. "I'd be good to you, the best lover I could be."

"I'm sure it would be amazing." She crossed her arms over her chest, and the protective gesture made her look achingly vulnerable. "But if we slept together, it would complicate my feelings for you, and I would miss you even more after you're gone."

Her reaction made him feel guilty for suggesting the affair. But he still wanted to be with her. Regardless, he said, "You're right. It wouldn't work. It wouldn't solve anything. We need to focus on being friends, like we agreed on from the beginning."

She nodded, but she didn't uncross her arms. She still looked far too vulnerable. He wanted to reach out and hold her, but he refrained from making physical contact. He'd done enough damage for one night.

He glanced at the smokers. They kept puffing away. As he shifted his attention back to Jenna, the headlights from a departing car shined in his eyes. He blinked from the invasion.

"I've never actually had an affair," she said.

He blinked again. He hadn't expected her to offer that kind of information.

She continued, "I've only been with two men and they were my boyfriends. Neither of them was right for me, though."

"They weren't husband material?"

"I thought they were at the time, but I misjudged them. That's part of why I created the list. I needed something definitive to use as a guide. I've always had specific ideas about family, considering how messed up mine was, and writing everything down was the best way I knew to stay focused on my priorities."

He considered the time line. She'd told him that she'd started the list when she was twenty-five and she was thirty now. "You haven't dated since then?"

"Yes, but just casually."

"So, you've been celibate for five years?"

"I'd rather wait for the right man. Besides, I haven't been overly attracted to anyone, not until..."

Dare he say it? "I came along?"

"Yes."

He blew out a gust of air from his lungs. She did,

too, only in a softer manner. Still, they were mirroring each other.

Then, awkward silence.

The smokers stamped out their cigarettes and returned to the club, making it quieter.

More awkward silence.

"Maybe we should go back inside, too," he said.

A strand of hair blew across her cheek, and she batted it away. "I think I should go home, J.D."

And get away from him and their madly wrong-for-each-other attraction, he thought. "I'll walk you to your truck."

"Thanks." She led the way.

They didn't speak. The only sound was their booted footsteps.

Once her pickup came into view, she stated the obvious. "We're here." She hit the alarm button on her key fob.

If they were dating, this would have been the time to kiss her.

He made a point of keeping his distance. "Be safe."

"I will." She got in her truck and started the engine.

As she drove away, he gazed into the dark, feeling much too alone.

Jenna paced her room and finally ended up in the kitchen, heating milk in a pan on the stove. When she was little, her mother used to give her warm milk and now she thought of it as comfort food.

She poured it into a coffee mug and wandered the halls in her pajamas. It was after midnight, and she didn't expect to run into anyone else at this hour.

She was wrong. She noticed that one of the empty

guest-room doors was open and a light was on. Jenna poked her head in and saw her sister.

She crossed the threshold and said, "What are you doing?"

Donna spun around, her hand flapping against her heart. "You scared the daylights out of me."

"Sorry, but it's not daylight." A dumb thing to say, she supposed, since that was a technicality of which they were both aware.

A beat of silence passed before Donna replied to her original question. "I have too much work on my mind to sleep."

"Is this the room that's going to overlook the garden?"

"Yes, and in my sleep-deprived state, I'm still debating on what wallpaper to use."

Jenna replied, "I couldn't sleep, either. Or relax or sit still. But I guess you already figured that out."

"What are you drinking? I hope it's not coffee. You'll be wired all night if it is."

"It's warm milk."

Donna didn't react. But to do so would have opened the door to a discussion about Mom, and Donna was apparently more cautious than that.

"I went out earlier," Jenna said.

"Where to?"

"Lone Star Lucy's."

Donna crinkled her nose. "That yee-haw bar? Whatever for?"

"Some of the ranch hands and maids were meeting there, and J.D. invited me, too. He invited all of us, you, me, Tammy and Doc, but I was the only one who could go."

"No one told me that I was invited."

"Would you have gone?"

"Not a chance."

"Then what would have been the point in telling you?"

"Protocol. I would have declined the invitation myself." Donna took a chair near the window. "Did that place live up to its reputation?"

Jenna sat on the edge of the bed. "Nothing crazy happened while I was there." Nothing except the way J.D. made her feel. "I left early, though."

"You weren't having a good time, I take it."

"Actually, I was enjoying myself." *Far too much,* she thought.

"Why is that a reason to leave early?"

"Because I danced with J.D. and then he suggested that we have an affair."

"You said that you didn't have a crush on him. I should have known you were lying."

Donna's reaction actually made her seem like a big sister. Or heaven forbid, a mother.

Jenna replied, "I'm not going to sleep with him."

"Right."

"I turned him down. I swear I did." She'd never confided in Donna about things like this before. Girl talk between them was a foreign concept. But she continued, hoping it was going to get easier. "I told him that it wasn't a good idea, and he agreed that we shouldn't."

"I'll bet he only agreed because you turned him down. If you would have said yes, you'd be doing it right now instead of roaming around in your pajamas. Be honest, Jenna, you're having trouble sleeping because you want to climb into bed with him."

"Of course I want to. But I'm smart enough to know when to keep my pajamas on."

"They're pretty, by the way. A bit of silk, a bit of lace."

Jenna clutched her cup. She suspected that Donna had more to say about her sleepwear.

She did indeed. The older sibling added, "They're actually pretty enough to wear on a stroll down to his cabin and crack open those condoms I inadvertently provided."

"You're supposed to be talking me out of being with him, not tempting me to do it."

"I already tried to talk you out of it. I warned you that having a Flying B romance would be trouble, but you didn't listen. You danced with him anyway, a dance that prompted him to suggest an affair."

"He took it back."

"Uh-huh. Well, go traipse down to his cabin and see how quickly he jumps your bones."

Jenna scowled. Girl talk with her know-it-all New York sister sucked. "I'm going back to bed."

"Alone?"

"Yes, alone." Jenna stood up, preparing to stomp off.

Donna rolled her eyes. "You're acting like you did when we were kids."

"I am not."

"Yes, you are. You were always melodramatic."

"You mean like this?" For the heck of it, Jenna stuck out her tongue.

Donna shook her head, and they both laughed. Jenna got a surge of warm and fuzzy, of the closeness that had been missing between them all these years.

But before she could bask in it, the moment ended and Donna withdrew again. She said a quiet good-night, and when she turned away, she stared out the darkened window. Was work the real reason she couldn't sleep? Or did she have something else on her mind?

Jenna went back to her room. Figuring out Donna was impossible when she could barely figure out herself.

She walked over to the mirror and gazed at her reflection. No way was she going to go to J.D.'s cabin dressed like this. Besides, he was probably still at the bar. Not that his whereabouts mattered.

She ditched her milk and got into bed, pulling the covers up around her ears. She was staying away from him for the rest of the night.

The following morning, Jenna finished up some work in the barn, but she didn't come across J.D. She didn't see him anywhere. Curious, she checked the schedule and discovered that it was his day off. She glanced at her watch. She planned on taking Pedro out for a trail ride, and if she brought J.D. along, he could ride Duke. Both horses needed to get away from the barn, and it would be good to take them out together.

Was that an excuse to see J.D., to spend time with him?

Maybe, but it was also important for her lesson horses to get accustomed to the trails. So why not kill two birds with one stone? It would be nice to pack a picnic, too, and enjoy a long leisurely ride.

She suspected that J.D. was anxious to put time in the saddle, and this would be a great opportunity for him to do that, if he didn't have other plans for the day. The only way to know would be to ask him.

As she walked to his cabin, her heart started to pound, mimicking the erratic motion it had made when she'd danced with him. If only she could keep her attraction to him in check. But at least she'd had the good sense to refuse his offer of having an affair.

She arrived at his place, but instead of approaching the cabin, she sat on the bottom step, hoping to quiet her mind. But it didn't work. In that lone moment, she thought about Savannah Jeffries and her connection to the cabin. How could Savannah have had affairs with two men, brothers no less, when Jenna could barely contain her feelings for one man?

"Jenna?"

She stood up and spun around. J.D. stood in the doorway, gazing at her.

"Hi," she said, feeling foolish for getting caught off guard.

"What are you doing?" he asked.

Aside from wondering about Savannah? "I was just sitting here for a minute, before I came to see you. What are you doing?"

"I was planning on going for a walk."

She didn't ascend the steps. She stayed where she was. "Would you like to go for a ride instead? On horseback," she clarified so he didn't think she was inviting him to go somewhere in her truck. "I can ride Pedro, and you can ride Duke. We can take them out by the creek."

"Are you kidding? I'd love to. When?"

"We could go now, but I was thinking that we could have lunch on the trail. I can head over to the main house and throw something together before we leave."

"Mind if I tag along?"

"Not at all. It would be nice to have the company."

He closed the cabin door and joined her.

While they walked beside each other, she asked, "How long did you stay at the bar last night?"

"Until it closed. I would have left earlier, but that's

how long everyone else stayed and I didn't have a ride back."

She forged ahead into her next question. "Did anyone say anything?"

"About us? Everyone at the table did, especially Manny. He asked me if we were going to hook up, but I told him no, that it was just a dance. It was an easy explanation."

"Do you think he bought it?"

"Why wouldn't he? It was the truth."

It wouldn't have been the truth if she'd agreed to sleep with him, but she kept that to herself. "I'm glad it's over."

"The explanation or the dance?"

Her heart thumped. "The explanation. The dance, too, but not because I didn't like it."

"I know you liked it, Jenna. We both did. But we probably shouldn't talk about it anymore."

Or think about it, she reminded herself.

Once they were in the kitchen, she opened the fridge. "Is ham and cheese okay, with lettuce, tomatoes and peperoncinis? That's about as fancy as I get."

"Sounds good to me. But my culinary skills aren't any better than yours." He watched her set everything on the counter. "Are you going to ask Tammy to teach you to cook?"

"Actually, I think I am. I'd feel better about being a wife and mother if I could offer my family some home-cooked meals now and then. Plus there's that old saying, 'The way to a man's heart is through his stomach.'"

"I'm still willing to be your guinea pig. I can give you an honest opinion and tell you if your lessons are working." He flashed his lopsided grin. "And if they aren't, Doc can pump my stomach."

"All in the name of helping me nab a husband? Oh, gee. That's mighty gentlemanly of you."

"It's the least I can do since I messed up your wedding song."

"That was never intended to be my wedding song." She jabbed his shoulder in a playful reprimand. "And we're not supposed to be talking about the dance, remember?"

His grin resurfaced. "Sorry. My bad."

"Very bad." But she understood his need to flirt. She was doing it, too, even if she knew better.

He offered to help, and they built the sandwiches together, working well as a team, unskilled as they were.

She snagged a pepper and ate it. "I love these."

He snagged one, too. "Spicy and sweet, like a girl I know."

More flirting. "You wish you knew her."

"A guy can dream."

"In the dream cabin? Those aren't the kinds of dreams that are supposed to happen there."

"Then I'm safe because I haven't done that yet."

Yet? She decided it was time to change the subject. "We should get going or we're going to be starving by the time we make it to the creek."

He tossed a couple of apples into their lunch sacks. "I'm ready."

So was she. They went to the barn, saddled the horses and packed their saddlebags with food and water.

They rode for hours. The weather was perfect and the ever-changing terrain was riddled with towering trees, fallen branches, stony surfaces, grass, weeds and wildflowers.

J.D. was a magnificent horseman. He looked strong

and regal on his mount. Jenna had to keep stopping herself from admiring him too deeply.

Upon reaching the creek, they set up their picnic, using a blanket they'd brought.

"This is beautiful," he said as a butterfly winged by.

"It's my favorite spot on the trail." She sat across from him. "Heaven on earth, as they say."

He unwrapped his sandwich. "I appreciate you sharing your favorite spot with me."

"That's what friends are for." She just wished that the platonic stuff was easier. "It's nice having a male friend to talk to."

"About finding a husband?"

"And other things." She removed the wrapping from her sandwich, too. "I was thinking about Savannah Jeffries earlier. That's what I was doing when you came out of the cabin and saw me. I think about her a lot."

"You actually haven't told me much about her, other than she was your uncle's girlfriend and Tammy discovered that she was keeping a secret."

"I can tell you the whole story now." Suddenly this seemed like the right time, the right place. "It's sordid, though." She steadied her emotions and started at the beginning. "Tammy first learned of Savannah when she overheard some of the household staff talking about her. Employees who've been around the Flying B a long time. Not like the young maids we socialized with at Lucy's."

He nodded in understanding.

She continued, "According to what Tammy overheard, Savannah didn't just sleep with Tammy's dad. She slept with mine, too."

"Damn," J.D. said.

Jenna's thoughts exactly. "Savannah was Uncle William's girlfriend when he was at Texas A&M, and that's why she was staying at the ranch. He was on summer break from university. He'd been in a car accident, and she came here to help him mend. My dad was home that summer, too."

"Giving Savannah the opportunity to mess around with him, too? That's some heavy stuff."

"It gets worse."

"I'm listening."

"Tammy uncovered an old grocery list in the cabin. It was from the time when Savannah was staying there."

"Why is that relevant?"

"It had an E.P.T. pregnancy test on it."

J.D. started. "That was her secret when she left town? She was pregnant?"

Jenna put her sandwich aside. "She might have been. But there's no way to know for sure. That's why we need to decide if we should hire a P.I. to search for her."

"The family vote?"

She nodded. "If Savannah was pregnant and she gave birth, then the child could belong to either man. Of course he or she wouldn't be a child anymore. They would be the oldest of all of us."

"I think you should hire the P.I."

"Really? Because I was going to vote no. As much as I want to uncover the truth, I'm afraid it will open a can of worms we're not prepared to deal with."

"I understand your concern, but I think it's important to know if there is another member of your family out there. Just think, Jenna, you could have another brother or sister. Or another cousin. That's epic."

Too epic, she thought.

He asked, "Are your dad and uncle going to vote on it, too?"

"No. Just the kids. Donna and I don't want our dad having a stake in it, so that means leaving Uncle William out of it, too. But he made his position clear. He would just as soon never see Savannah again. He's not trying to influence our vote, though. He'll accept whatever all of us decide."

"Does your dad want to see Savannah again?"

"I have no idea, and I don't intend to ask him. Donna and I are no longer on speaking terms with him."

He frowned. "So what's the holdup? Why haven't you voted yet?"

"We're waiting for Tammy's brothers to come back to the ranch. They went home after Tex's funeral and are scheduled to return next week. They have their own business. They're general contractors, and they've been busy with work. When they have time, they're going to help do some renovations around here."

"For the B and B?"

"Yes." She glanced at the body of water and the way it shimmered. "Are you absolutely convinced that I should vote yes?"

"I would if I were you."

"Because family is important? You keep saying that yours doesn't matter because you can't remember them."

"That's because I don't think I have anyone."

She felt lonely for him, but confused for herself, too. Was he right? Should she vote yes?

"Tex hired a P.I. to keep an eye on all of us," she said. "He felt badly about not knowing his grandchildren, so he used someone to find out about us and report back to him."

"That's nice that he cared so much about you. I wonder if he would've condoned the use of a P.I. to find Savannah now that there's a possible child involved."

"I don't know." She pushed the P.I. out of her mind and moved on to a new topic. "Do you want to take a road trip with me this weekend? There's an equestrian center north of Houston that has some school horses for sale."

"Sure, that sounds great. Is it affiliated with the center where you used to work?"

"No. But it's a nice place, and they have some horses that are worth seeing. There's only one motel near there, so I'll book us a couple of rooms ahead of time."

"I can sleep in the truck."

Spoken like a true cowboy. "Humor me, J.D., and accept a room." She smiled. "Way far away from where mine will be."

He laughed. "On the other side of the motel, huh? It's a deal, if you let me buy you dinner while we're there."

"As long as there's no dancing involved."

"There won't be, I promise."

"Then it's a deal for me, too." She was determined to keep their upcoming trip friendly and light.

With absolutely no distractions.

Chapter 7

The trip was long, but interesting. J.D. enjoyed Jenna's company. She was a hell of a woman: smart, pretty, funny, sweet. She knew how to handle a rig, too. She was driving a Dodge dually and gooseneck horse trailer that had belonged to her grandfather, with the Flying B brand prominently displayed.

They arrived in the evening, too late to go to the equestrian center. But they knew ahead of time that they would be cutting it close, so they'd already made arrangements to see the horses in the morning.

"Let's check into the motel, then get some dinner," she said. "In fact, there's a diner there where we can eat. Then we don't have to go back out again."

"Sure. That will work." He didn't blame her for wanting to stay put for the night. She'd been behind the wheel for hours.

The motel was a typical roadway-style place, located in a rural area. The restaurant next to it was a rustic building with a yellow rose painted in the window, and across the street was a gas station with a little convenience store.

She parked the truck and trailer. "The equestrian center is just up the road. It'll be easy to head over there in the morning."

"I'm sorry I wasn't able to help with the driving. You must be beat."

"I'm a little tired, but it's nothing a hot meal can't cure." She glanced over at him. "Besides, you'll be able to drive once your identity is restored and you have access to your driver's license. I wonder how long it will be before the police uncover anything."

"I don't know, but Deputy Tobbs is probably right about me having been carjacked and robbed. That scenario seems to make the most sense."

"Do you remember how to drive?"

"I have a sense of it. I'm sure that when I get behind the wheel it will feel natural."

They exited the truck and went into the rental office. The middle-aged woman behind the counter greeted them, and J.D. realized that they probably looked like a couple, as if they would be staying together. That was quickly dispelled. Jenna asked for two rooms.

Afterward, she handed him his key card. "Your room is next to mine."

For lack of a better response, he made a joke. "What happened to putting me in a room far, far away from yours?"

She smiled. "What can I say? It would have been weird. The clerk would have thought you were a leper."

"I'm just an amnesiac. That's not nearly as bad." He smiled, too. "You can't catch my forgotten memory."

Her expression turned somber. "Sometimes I wish I could."

He assumed that she was referring to the Savannah Jeffries scandal. "I'm sorry you're at odds with what's going on with your family."

"It helped talking to you about it."

"I'm glad you trusted me with your feelings."

"You're turning into a really good friend, J.D."

"So are you, Jenna."

A beat of intimacy passed between them, but she filled it quickly. "Are you ready to eat? We can bring our luggage into our rooms after dinner."

He nodded. His luggage was a duffel bag he'd borrowed from Manny, and hers was an airline-style carry-on with a push-button handle and wheels.

They entered the diner. It had the same rustic appeal inside as it did on the outside, with battered wood booths and antler light fixtures.

A hostess took them to a small corner booth, and they scooted in beside each other. J.D. studied the menu, but Jenna only glanced at hers.

"I already know what I want," she said. "I've got a hankering for a burger and fries. A chocolate milk shake, too."

"That sounds good. I'll get the same thing." He set his menu down. "But with a root-beer float."

The waitress arrived, and they placed their orders.

While they waited for the meals, he asked, "Where in Houston did you grow up?"

"It's about sixty miles from here. Mom stayed in our

old house after the divorce, and Dad got himself a new place, but it was in the same neighborhood."

"A suburban area?"

She nodded. "Near shopping malls and schools and everything else a family might want, I guess. I prefer the country. Always have, always will."

He glanced out the window. "I like this area. It has a great view."

"That's the Sam Houston National Forest in the distance."

"It's impressive."

"Yes, it is." She frowned. "My dad was named after Sam Houston. Sam Houston Byrd. My uncle's full name is William Travis Byrd. But less people know who William Travis is than Sam Houston. Dad got the biggie."

She always scowled when she mentioned her father, but he understood why, considering the Savannah situation. Still, he wished it wasn't troubling her so badly. "You should discuss the details with your dad."

"The details?"

"About what happened all those years ago."

"I don't want to hear about his dirty little fling with his brother's girlfriend."

"I'm talking about the impact it had on his life and the family rift it caused, not the physical stuff between him and Savannah."

She set her jaw. "I know what you meant."

Dang, she was stubborn. "I'm just saying that maybe you should try to make things right with your dad."

"I'm not going to right his wrong."

"There are two sides to every story."

"His side isn't a story I care to hear."

He decided to drop it for now, with the intention of

broaching the subject another time. The way this was gnawing at her wasn't healthy.

During the lapse in conversation, their food and drinks arrived. She dived in, as eager as a bear coming out of hibernation.

"I'm sorry for getting testy," she said.

"You'll feel better now that you're getting some chow in you."

"It's yummy. The milk shake, especially." She sipped from a red-and-white-striped straw.

"My root-beer float is good, too."

She smiled. "Sugar highs."

He could get high on her smile, if he let himself. Let himself? Hell, he already was.

As a distraction, J.D. looked out the window again, where the view erupted into hills, valleys and scores of trees.

She followed his line of sight. "I hope you didn't get the impression that I'm at odds with the real Sam Houston. It's not his fault that my dad ended up with his name."

"I didn't think you disliked *Colonneh.*"

"What? Who?"

He blinked, as confused as she was. He didn't know why he'd said *Colonneh.* Not until his thoughts jumbled into a feeling, a memory, and struck him like a warrior's arrow. "Oh, God, Jenna, I'm related to him."

"I don't know who you're talking about."

He turned to look at her. "Sam Houston."

He gaped at him. "*The* Sam Houston?"

"Well, not him, exactly. But to the band of Cherokee that adopted him."

Another gape. "You're Cherokee?"

"Part. A quarter," he added, amazed by how quickly this information was tumbling into his mind. "That's how I'm registered with the tribe."

"And you're certain that you're affiliated with the band that adopted Sam?"

"Yes. This stuff just hit me, memories that zoomed into my head." And it made him damned proud, too. "Pretty cool, huh?"

"I'll say." She studied him with awe. "Was *Colonneh* Sam's Cherokee name?"

He nodded. "It means The Raven."

"Oh, that's right. His other name was Raven. All Texans should know that. But to actually know someone whose ancestry is connected to his..." She paused. "Do you recall anything else about yourself? Like who told you about your heritage?"

"No. But I'm from Texas. I'm not sure what part I hail from, but it's my homeland." He smiled, feeling a bond with the Lone Star State, with Sam, with the Cherokee blood running through his veins.

"I'm happy for you, J.D."

As she leaned toward him, his heart knocked against his chest. She was almost close enough to kiss. All he had to do was make his move to close the deal. He studied her mouth, then lifted his gaze. She was staring at him, too.

"We aren't supposed to be doing this," she said.

"We aren't doing anything but looking at each other."

"But we want to do more."

"We've wanted that since the beginning."

"We can't."

"We could," he corrected. "But we agreed that we wouldn't."

Regardless, they were damn close to breaking their agreement. She even wet her lips. Unable to help himself, so did he. But then Jenna moved away from him and grabbed her milk shake, sucking viciously on the straw. Unfortunately, her diversion didn't help. It only managed to give him a wildly sexual feeling, worsening his urges.

After their meal ended, they got their luggage from the truck and proceeded to their rooms. But they didn't unlock their doors. They just stood there, trapped in their attraction.

"We better go," she said.

He motioned with his chin. "You first."

She fumbled for her key card, digging around in her purse. She found it and gripped the plastic a little too tightly. "I'll see you in the morning."

"Okay." He didn't trust himself to say anything else. He was still thinking about her mouth on the straw or, more accurately, about kissing her senseless.

She went inside, and he waited until she closed the door before he blew out his breath.

And wished that he was spending the night with her.

Jenna stood in the middle of her room, wondering how long it would take J.D. to enter his. *This is crazy,* she thought, *absolute insanity.* She wanted to forgo their friendship pact and become lovers.

Then why not do it? Honestly, what did she have to lose?

Her heart, for one thing. If she fell in love with him, she would be setting herself up for a world of pain. It wasn't as if J.D. was going to stick around and marry her.

But he wasn't even husband material, so what was the likelihood of falling in love with him, anyway?

There was nothing wrong with uncommitted sex. True, it wasn't Jenna's style, but maybe she needed to rethink her immediate priorities. Later, she could find a man who had the qualities on her list. Later, she could walk down the aisle with Mr. Right. But at the moment, *Mr. Right Now* was *right* next door.

Still, she stalled.

Needing more time to contemplate the issue, she stripped off her clothes and drew a hot bath. Determined to relax, she pinned up her hair and soaked in the tub. She even closed her eyes. Then she lost all sense of reason and conjured an image of J.D. pulling her into his arms. So much for contemplating the issue. She knew darned well that she was going to cave into temptation.

Should she invite him to her room or go to his? Jenna didn't have any experience at this sort of thing.

She sat upright and scrubbed clean, careful not to get amorous with the soap. Touching herself wouldn't help her cause.

After drying off, she moisturized her skin. She brushed her teeth, refreshed her face and let down her hair, too.

Maybe it would be better to invite him over. That way she didn't have to get dressed. She could wrap herself in her robe and stay naked underneath.

What if he rebuffed her advances?

Oh, sure. As if that was going to happen. She knew that J.D. wanted this as badly as she did.

She slipped on her robe, a silky garment that caressed her flesh. Better though, would be the sensation of J.D.'s hands.

Without further hesitation, she dialed his room.

He answered on the second ring. "Hello?"

"It's me," she said, instead of reciting her name. Who else would be calling him at the motel? "I was wondering if you wanted to come over and hang out."

A slight pause. "For how long?"

Here goes, she thought. "All night. I want to be with you, J.D."

His voice turned graveled. "Are you sure?"

Her nerves jangled. "Yes."

"I just got out of the shower." His voice remained rough, anxious, sexy. "I need to get dressed."

Was he fully naked? Or did he have a towel tucked around his waist? She didn't have the courage to ask. Instead, she said, "I just got out of the bath. And I'm in my robe." Fair warning, she decided. No surprises.

"Damn. I'll hurry. But first I have to run across the street to the convenience store."

Obviously he intended to buy condoms. The motel didn't provide them, not like Donna had done for the guest accommodations at the ranch.

"I can't believe this is going to happen," he said. "Are you sure you're not going to change your mind?"

"I'm positive." She didn't have the strength to back out. She needed him, more than anything. "I'll see you soon."

They ended the call with eager goodbyes, and she returned to the bathroom to check her appearance. She even opened her robe and looked at her naked self in the mirror.

Her nerves went nuts. What if he found her lacking? What if he thought her hips were too bony or her breasts were too small? Dang it, why hadn't she been blessed with a figure like her sister's?

Jenna closed her robe and tied the belt. She couldn't do anything about her body. She was what she was.

She headed for the bed and sat on the edge of it. He'd said that he would hurry, but it felt like forever.

Finally, a knock sounded on the door.

She leaped up and answered it. There stood J.D. with a small paper bag in one hand and a plastic yellow rose in the other. Their gazes locked, and he extended the rose.

He said, "It's not the prettiest flower, but it's all they had."

She accepted his gift, assuming that the convenience store was selling them as souvenirs. "I think it's wonderful that you thought of me." And she would cherish the rose, simply because he gave it to her. "Come in, J.D."

He crossed the threshold and closed the door. Silence sizzled between them. He glanced down at her robe, particularly at the area where it gapped in front, revealing the hint of flesh between her breasts.

She didn't make an effort to close the material. Nor did she feel self-conscious about her lack of cleavage. He obviously liked what he saw.

He said, "Promise me that you won't have regrets later."

"I promise."

"What about the comment you made before?"

She considered his question. "You mean on the night we danced?"

He nodded, repeating her words and making them clear. "You said that if you slept with me, you would get attached and it would only make my leaving more difficult for you."

She replied as honestly as she could. "That crossed my mind tonight. I even considered how terrible it would be if I fell in love with you. But it's become more difficult wanting you than not having you, so I'm not going to worry about the future. All that matters is the here and now."

He reached out to touch her cheek. "Someday you'll find the man you're meant to marry."

"I'm counting on it."

But that didn't mean that she didn't appreciate him, exactly as he was, at this very moment. His hair was damp from the shower and although he'd combed it back, stray pieces fell on to his forehead. His hasty attire consisted of jeans, an untucked shirt, no belt and his usual battered boots.

He removed the condoms from the bag and opened the box. "I'm going to put these beside the bed for when we need them."

She handed him the flower. "Will you put the rose there, too?"

He set everything on the nightstand and returned to her. Then he took her into his arms and kissed her. The kiss she'd been waiting for. The kiss he'd been hungry to give her. Their lips met softly at first, but he deepened the contact quickly, using his tongue to intensify the feeling.

She flung her arms around his neck, and he held her body close to his. She could smell a citrus aroma—the customary soap from the motel—on his skin. She'd bathed with the same type of soap, and somehow that made their union seem even more sensual.

J.D. released the tie on her robe and the garment drifted open. He stepped back to look at her, and her heart thudded in her ears.

"Take it all the way off," he said.

Suddenly she went shy, her self-consciousness kicking in. But she did his bidding and removed the robe so he could fully see her.

"I should have put the lights on low," she said.

"No. It's perfect like this. You're perfect. Turn around."

She made what she hoped was a ladylike pirouette. When she faced him once again, he was smiling. She smiled, too. His crooked grin was infectious.

He anxiously led her to bed.

She watched while he discarded his clothes. They reclined on the mattress and started kissing again. Only now, caressing was involved. He roamed his hands along the lines of her body, making her skin tingle. She stroked him, too, gliding over flesh and bone and strong male muscle.

"I can't remember being with anyone else," he said. "But I'm glad I can't. I want this to be my first intimate memory."

His words affected her as deeply as his touch. "You certainly haven't forgotten how to entice a woman."

"You make me want to entice you."

He climbed on top, pinning her hands above her head and making her his willing prisoner. She studied his features. Now that she knew about his Cherokee roots, his heritage seemed magnificently obvious.

"Being with you is everything I imagined," she said.

"For me, too." He released her, but only because he was moving down her body and making a moist path with his tongue.

She arched and closed her eyes. He did things a man had no right to do, things that ignited a fire, things that made her melt all over him. By the time she opened her eyes, she could barely see straight.

He reached for the protection, ripped into a packet and sheathed himself. He was impatient, but so was she. She didn't want to wait another second.

He entered her, and their lovemaking took flight, with Jenna matching his glorious rhythm. As she moved her hips in time with his, prisms of colors spun in her mind, binding them together, almost as if they were one.

But they weren't, she told herself. This was a pleasure-only affair. No heartstrings, no commitment, no ties. J.D. wasn't hers to keep.

And he never would be.

Chapter 8

J.D. couldn't keep his eyes off Jenna. He wanted to devour her in every way imaginable. The experience was so new, so exciting.

He said, "Have you ever heard someone say that sex is overrated? Well, that's not true. Not when it makes you feel this way."

In lieu of a response, she wrapped her legs around him, and the experience got better and better.

He glanced down at her, intrigued by the sinuous manner in which she moved. Her skin was creamy and smooth, soft and fair and so unlike his. The wonderment was almost too much to bear, but she seemed as fascinated by him as he was by her.

She said, "I'm so glad you remembered something about yourself tonight."

"At least I know that I'm from Texas."

"Not only are you from here, you have a connection to Sam Houston. That makes the yellow rose you gave me even more special."

"Next time it will be a real flower. I'd give you hundreds of roses if I could."

"I always imagined rose petals on my honeymoon. All over the bed."

"Don't put fantasies like that in my head."

"You're not interested in marriage, J.D."

"No, but I like the flower-petals idea. It sounds sexy."

"And romantic."

"That, too." He covered her mouth with his. He also slipped his hand between them and heightened her pleasure.

Heat. Beautiful urgency.

He ached to give her a release, to shower her with everything she needed, everything she desired. They weren't a couple, nor were they on their way to becoming one, but for now they belonged to each other, and that was an aphrodisiac neither of them could deny.

Enthralled, he watched her, and with carnality bursting at the seams, she shuddered and climaxed. Unable to hold back, he lost himself in the passion, too.

Spent, he fell into her arms and stayed there for a while, allowing her to bask in the afterglow. She nuzzled his chest, her hair tickling his skin. In a deliberate show of affection, he skimmed a hand down her spine.

After they broke apart, he went into the bathroom to dispose of the condom.

He returned to find her sitting up in bed, with the quilt tucked around her. She looked sweetly tousled. Well-loved.

No! Not loved. He frowned at the mind slip. Making love wasn't love. In this case, it was miles apart.

Before she noticed his unease, he softened his expression and approached her. "Do you want a cup of tea? They have the herbal stuff."

"That sounds good."

He used the coffeepot to heat the water. He didn't brew himself any. He didn't drink hot tea. In fact, he wasn't sure why he'd offered some to her. Was it to keep his mind in check? Or was there someone from his past who favored tea? He honestly didn't know. In spite of his Sam Houston breakthrough, the bulk of his memories remained blocked.

"Cream and sugar?" he asked.

"Sugar. One packet."

He fixed the drink and brought it to her. "It's chamomile. It's supposed to be soothing."

She took the cup and tasted the fragrant brew. "It's just right. Thank you."

He sat beside her, his thoughts drifting back to the flower conversation, as well as to something she'd previously said. "You told me that you haven't planned any of your wedding details. But you have."

"The rose petals on the bed? I saw that in a movie, and it appealed to me. But we shouldn't do it. It wouldn't be right for our affair."

Because it would make their affair seem like a honeymoon? "I agree that we shouldn't."

She made a perplexed expression. "Funny, how we're always talking about what we shouldn't do."

"That's because we're being noncommittal."

She nodded, then clutched the tea with both hands, as if she needed an extra dose of warmth. Was she thinking about the man she was destined to marry and wishing he was here instead? Or was J.D. the only man on her mind?

Either way, he said, "If you want to snuggle, I can hold you tonight while you sleep."

"That would be wonderful." She leaned against his shoulder. "I like to spoon."

"Me, too. I think." He tossed out a smile. "I can't remember. But I'm sure I'll like it with you."

Soon they settled in for sleep, extinguishing the lamp and taking the aforementioned spooning position, with the front of his body pressed against the back of hers. He slipped an arm around her waist, creating a cozier connection.

She sighed, the feathery sound proof of her contentment. Grateful that she was satisfied, J.D. whispered a gentle, "Good night."

"You, too," she responded, using an equally soft voice. She tugged at the covers, getting more comfortable.

Although he closed his eyes, he wasn't able to sleep, at least not right away. He could tell when Jenna drifted off, though, mostly by the change in her breathing. Her limbs seemed looser, too.

Finally he joined her, and in the morning, he awakened before she did. With dawn peeking through a space in the drapes, he sat up and gazed at his lover.

Such delicate repose, he thought, tempted to touch her. But he kept his hands at his sides. He didn't want to rouse her. He wanted to see her while she was unable to see him. He realized that it was his way of shielding his confused self from her, of continuing to hide behind his amnesia.

And taking an odd sort of comfort in it.

* * *

As Jenna awoke, she sensed that she was being watched. She squinted, struggling to get her bearings. Then she saw J.D. sitting next to her, the sheet draped around his waist, his dark gazed fixed on hers.

"Morning," he said, skimming his thumb along her cheek, as if he'd been waiting all morning to do that.

"Hi," she replied quickly, reminding herself not to get attached. Thing was, she wanted to grab him and never let go. But what woman wouldn't feel that way, considering how affectionate he was?

He took his hand away. "You still look sleepy."

She sat up and clutched her portion of the sheet, shielding her nakedness, more out of caution than shyness. "I suppose I am. What time is it?" She couldn't see the clock from her side of the bed.

"A little after six."

"Dang. I hadn't planned on getting up this early. We're keeping rancher's hours, even on a road trip. But I guess it stands to reason, considering we live on a ranch."

"I don't live at the Flying B, Jenna."

"You live there for now." Everything was temporary: his job, his living arrangements, their affair.

"You're right. I do." He leaned closer. "Can I kiss you? Or is it too early for that?"

Her pulse spiked. "It's never too early for a kiss."

He reached for her, and she released the sheet, allowing it to fall to her waist. Their mouths met and mated, and she slipped deeper into the moment.

There was no denying it; she was getting attached. But she would do her darnedest to cope with his departure when the time came.

Sweet and tender, the kiss continued. J.D. had a way of making her feel special, even if it wasn't meant to last.

He pushed the sheet completely away, making it easier to roll over the bed and take her with him. She landed on top, and he smiled. He obviously wanted to make love in this position.

But so did Jenna. She desired him in all sorts of ways. Her heart pounded from the want, the need, the anticipation.

He secured a condom, and the shiny packet glittered. He opened it and concentrated on his task. She suspected that they were going to go through the protection quickly.

"I'm glad we have more of those back at the ranch," she said.

He glanced up and smiled again, a bit more devilish this time. "That's for sure. Now let's get you seated, nice and tight."

He circled her waist, giving her a boost while she straddled him. She impaled herself, and the sensation nearly knocked her for a loop.

With a powerful grip, he lifted her up and down, setting a rocking horse rhythm. "You look like a cowgirl."

She latched on to his shoulders, mesmerized by his broad strength. "I feel like one, too."

"We're good together." He kept her within his grasp. "And it's good that there aren't any future worries between us."

"You mean no plans to stay in touch after you leave?" *No phone calls, emails, texts,* she thought.

He nodded, morning shadows playing against his skin. "You're still okay with that, right?"

"Yes." She was determined to accept it, the best she could. After he was gone, she would accept the blessing of having known him and move on with her life. "All I want right now is to make this happen."

He kissed her hard and rough. "Then do it. Make it happen."

Quickening the pace, she rode him with every ounce of hunger she had, bucking wildly, and leaving them both breathless when it was over.

J.D. took a minute to collect his thoughts, then he said to Jenna, "You blow me away."

"Likewise. Sex with you packs a punch." She climbed off his lap and sagged like a rag doll.

"Relax and I'll be right back." He got rid of the condom and returned to her. "Do you want me go to the diner and get some breakfast?"

"Sure. I'll shower while you're gone."

"I need to shower, too, and shave. But I left my bag in the other room."

"You can do that before you get breakfast. It will probably take me longer to get ready than you, anyway."

"Women and their hair and makeup." He twined his fingers around her golden locks. "I like you the way you are."

"Messy from going cowgirl?"

"Definitely." He noticed that her mouth was swollen from his kisses. Talk about hot. And sinful. And beautiful.

After a beat of soul-stirring silence, she pushed at his chest. "You better go. Before we end up ravishing each other again."

"Good thinking. Or else we'll never leave this bed."

"They'd find us, dead from exhaustion."

He laughed. "With a plastic rose and a box of condoms beside us. How embarrassing would that be?"

She laughed, too. "Proof that we need to control ourselves."

"And eat and be normal?" He climbed into his rumbled clothes. "What should I bring back for you?"

"Ham and eggs, with any kind of toast. It doesn't matter."

"How do you like your eggs?"

"Scrambled is fine."

He gave her a quick kiss, but it didn't satisfy the urges stirring inside him. He wanted to linger, to get his second wind, even after the jokes they'd made.

He headed for the door instead. He was too damned eager to have her again. But what did he expect? He couldn't remember being with anyone but Jenna.

He glanced back and saw that she was watching him. She even chewed her swollen lips, pulling the bottom one between her teeth. Neither of them had the affair down pat. She seemed overwhelmed, too, and possibly on the verge of telling him to forget breakfast and come back to her.

But she didn't give in. And neither did J.D.

He went to his room, and after he showered, shaved and donned clean jeans and a fresh shirt, he walked to the diner and ordered their meals.

Food in hand, he returned to Jenna and noticed that the door was ajar. She'd obviously left it that way for him. He entered the room. She was fully dressed, crisp and pretty in a Western blouse and jeans, with her hair in a ponytail.

"That's a good look on you," he said.

"Thank you."

The certified riding instructor, he thought. She definitely fit the part. The whole purpose of this trip was to shop for lesson horses, not have lust-burning sex.

He put the food on the dining table, which was positioned by the window and equipped with two padded chairs. “Okay if I open the drapes and let more light in?”

“Oh, of course. I meant to do that.” She glanced at the takeout containers. “Which one is mine?”

“They’re both the same. Ham and eggs was the special, with home-fried potatoes. I got wheat toast and lots of jelly to go with it. Ketchup and salt and pepper, too.”

“I made coffee while you were gone. Do you want a cup?”

“Sure.” He could use some caffeine. “Did you drink yours already?”

“No. I was waiting for you to come back.” She poured two cups and set them on the table, along with the little basket that contained powdered creamer, sugar and the accompanying stir sticks.

They sat across from each other and fixed their coffee. Next, they opened the plastic utensils he’d gotten from the diner and doctored their meals. He squeezed ketchup on his eggs, and she used it on her potatoes. Both were generous with the pepper and light on the salt. She favored the grape jelly, and he went to town on the strawberry.

Would this be considered post-sex compatibility? *No,* he thought. *Not quite.*

She took deliberately small bites. She wasn’t as ravenous as she’d been at dinner last night. Either that or she was trying to behave properly. He was, too, still mindful of his hunger for her.

She lifted her coffee and studied him from beneath

the rim of her cup. "I wonder if you know any other Cherokee words besides Sam Houston's Raven name."

"It's possible, I suppose. Who knows what's locked inside my brain? But I should probably count my blessings that I remember how to speak English, let alone my ancestor's language."

"My ancestors are from Sweden. On my mom's side. The Byrds are Texans, through and through, but they originated from England, with a little gypsy tossed in. I didn't know about the gypsy part until Tex told us about our great-grandmother and the feather bed."

"It was foolish of me not believe in your great-grandmother's magic when you first mentioned it to me. The Cherokee believe in magic, in dreams, in visions. It's part of my culture, too. A medicine man is a called *di da nv wi s gi,* and it means 'curer of them.'"

"So you *do* know more Cherokee words."

"Well, damn. Listen to me." He grinned, stunned and pleased that it came so easily. "I guess I do."

She reached across the table to touch his hand. "It's nice to see you looking so happy."

"It's nice for me, too." And so was her caring touch.

"You know what, J.D.? I don't think you were a foster child. I think someone in your family taught you about your culture, and I think you were surrounded by it."

"You could be right. If I was a foster kid, I would probably be missing the Cherokee side of myself instead of recalling it in such a positive way."

As their hands drifted apart, she said, "It's still odd, though, that you seem to have knowledge of the foster-care system and how the older kids rarely get adopted."

"Maybe I knew someone else who grew up in that world."

"Someone who must have been important to you."

The tea drinker, perhaps? If there was such a person. "I don't know. It's all a bit weird. If I had a family, parents who nurtured me, maybe even brothers and sisters, then why do I get the sense of not having anyone in my life?"

"Maybe you just haven't remembered them yet."

"Or maybe something went wrong with my relationship with them. Maybe they turned away from me or I turned away from them. The positive connection I feel to my heritage doesn't mean that other aspects of my life aren't screwed up. Maybe I'm holding on to my heritage so tightly because it's all I have."

"I agree that there's something going on with your family. Otherwise you probably wouldn't be advising me to vote in favor of finding Savannah and the child she might have had. And you wouldn't be trying to encourage me to give my father a chance."

"Are you having a change of heart? Are you going to take my advice?"

"I'm considering the vote."

"But not squaring things with your dad? Sleeping with his brother's girlfriend was a lousy thing to do. But judging him without hearing his side of the story isn't fair, either."

"There's nothing he could say that would make me feel okay about what he did."

"Then forgive him to lessen the burden on yourself."

"I wish I could, but I can't." She moved a forkful of eggs around, mixing them with her potatoes. "If only my mom was still alive. I would talk to her about this if I could." She paused, apparently considering how the conversation would go. "If she were here, I think she would tell me to stay away from Dad and just let him be."

"Why do you think she would say that?"

"Because she never pushed Donna to open up. She accepted that my sister was distant, like Dad in that regard."

Curious, he asked, "Does Donna favor him in her appearance, too? Because I envision that you look more like your mom. And since you and Donna don't really resemble each other, I figure each of you took after a different parent."

"You got that right. I'm my mother's daughter."

He hadn't meant to imply that she didn't have anything in common with her father. "What does your dad think about you and Donna turning the ranch into a B and B?"

"He hasn't given us his opinion. But we don't want him butting into our business or trying to talk to us."

"When's the last time you saw him?"

"At Tex's funeral."

"If I were him, I would be proud of you and your sister. You make a hell of a team. And Tammy. The three of you are going to make the B and B a tremendous success."

Her eyes lit up. "Thanks. That means a lot to me. And thanks for caring about my feelings. Even if I don't follow your advice, I appreciate your motives." She motioned between them. "You and I make a good team, too. I'm glad I brought you on this trip and that you're going to check out the horses with me."

"So am I." He was eager to go to the equestrian center and help her in any way he could, and he couldn't agree more—they were a damned fine team.

In and out of bed.

Chapter 9

Jenna hit the jackpot. She'd purchased two wonderful geldings and now she and J.D. were almost home, traveling down the Flying B Road and heading toward the ranch.

She glanced at the man she'd spent the night with. They'd behaved in a professional manner at the equestrian center. No hand-holding, no public display of affection, nothing that indicated that they were lovers.

"What's going to happen now that we're back?" she asked. "How are we going to handle this?"

"What do you mean?"

"Our affair. Are we going to sneak around and keep it a secret? Or let everyone know that we're together?"

"I'll do whatever you're comfortable with."

"What would you prefer?" Before she went out on a limb and expressed her feelings, she desperately wanted to know how he felt.

"Truthfully? I'd like to be open about it. We're both consenting adults and have a right to be together. We don't have anything to hide, not as far as I'm concerned. But if you would rather go the secret route, I'll respect your wishes."

He'd said exactly what she'd hoped he would say. "I completely agree. Sneaking around seems cheap, and it would make me feel cheap. I don't want to call dirty attention to ourselves, and if we have a secret affair and get caught, it will seem too much like what my dad did with Savannah. Even if the circumstances aren't the same, it would affect me that way."

"I'd never want to do anything that would make you feel badly about yourself." He leaned over and kissed her cheek. "This is a nice thing we've got going."

She smiled. "Very nice."

They arrived at the ranch, and she drove to the barn. Although it was still daylight, dusk would be closing in soon. As they prepared to unload the first gelding, Manny and Hugh, who'd been working nearby, moseyed on over to greet them, obviously curious about the horses she'd purchased.

Jenna got a little nervous. She knew that she shouldn't, not after she and J.D. agreed that they had every right to disclose their affair, but now that they were actually in the company of Flying B employees, she wasn't sure how to act.

J.D. behaved in a perfectly natural way. He unloaded the horse and talked to Hugh and Manny about both geldings and what great finds they were. By the time the second horse was unloaded and placed in his stall, Jenna was able to relax, too. She realized that J.D. was going to handle it.

He said to the other men, "Normally I wouldn't bring something like this up, but I'm concerned about ranch gossip. Jenna and I are dating now. So if you notice us hanging around together or Jenna coming and going from my cabin more often than she did before, please treat the situation with respect."

Hugh replied, "I understand. People talk, and you can't stop their tongues from wagging. But you don't want them talking out of turn." He addressed Jenna. "I'll admit that I've done my share of talking over the years. But never in a hurtful way. And I won't do that to you, either."

"Thank you." She couldn't be more pleased with his reaction. Hugh was as honest as they come, and he'd been around since the Savannah days, witnessing the devastation firsthand.

Young Manny was another story. The Savannah situation had occurred long before he'd been born. No doubt he'd heard about it, though, especially since the past had been unearthed. But Manny only seemed concerned with the here and now.

A cheeky grin broke out on his face, and he said to Jenna, "I knew you two were going to hook up. Maria and I are seeing each other now, too. We should go on a double date somctime."

"Sure." She smiled at him. "Maria seems like a nice girl."

"She's the best. I'm right crazy for her."

Jenna hoped J.D. was feeling the same sense of boyish craziness for her, regardless of how short-lived their affair proved to be. She glanced over at him, and he winked, making her heart spin.

Hugh nudged Manny. "Let's go. It's about quitting time."

Manny was still grinning. To the new lovers, he said, "See you guys."

After the old foreman and the young ranch hand were gone, Jenna spoke to J.D. "Thanks for taking care of that."

"You're welcome. I figured that we needed to get it out there, better sooner than later." He reached for her hand. "Do you want to stay with me tonight? Or are you planning on sleeping in your own bed?"

"I'd like to stay with you, as long as you don't think it's too soon."

"Too soon for what? We already went public with it. In fact, maybe you should just move in with me."

Stunned, she stared at him. "Move in?"

"To the cabin. It would be nice to have you there every night, and now that my memory is starting to improve..."

"You only remembered a few things. Granted, they were really important things, but it was just bits and pieces."

"Yes, but look how quickly it happened. It's probably just a matter of time before everything comes rushing back. And then I'll be leaving."

"So we should cram in as many days together as we can?"

"It works for me."

It worked for her, too. She wanted as much of him as she could get and for as long as she could get it. Still, it wasn't something she'd expected. "I'll move in with you, but I need time to prepare. I want to talk to Donna and Tammy first."

"About us?"

She nodded. “I can’t go skipping off to stay with you without explaining it to them.”

He laughed. “Skipping?”

She play-punched his arm. “You know what I mean.”

“Yes, I believe I do.” He kissed her, long and slow, and she wrapped her arms around him.

After the kiss ended, she said, “Will you take my luggage to the cabin? There’s no point in me hauling it back to the house. I should probably pack a few more bags if I’m moving in with you.” She paused to ponder the situation. “God, that sounds weird. Us living together.”

“I know, but I figure it’s going to be more like a vacation since it’s probably going to be so short.”

“That’s a good way of looking at it.”

“It will be fun. A romantic adventure.”

“I think so, too.” One more kiss, and they parted ways.

As she exited the barn, the horses she’d just purchased whinnied, calling out to each other and adjusting to their new home. Jenna was making an adjustment, too.

She walked to the house with an emotionally cluttered mind. She came to the porch and ascended the steps, grateful that she owned a piece of the ranch. If J.D. was the type who wanted to settle down, she could easily imagine sharing her home with him.

But he wasn’t, and it was pointless to entertain those types of imaginings. Someday she would meet the man from her list. J.D. wasn’t him, and all of the wishing in the world wouldn’t change the nature of their relationship. She had no choice but to accept it.

She opened the front door and saw Donna, sitting on the sofa, tapping away on her iPad. Although she was dressed casually, she managed to look elegant, as always.

Tammy was in the living room, too, paging through a

magazine. She looked lovely, as well, and appeared to be dressed to go out. On the floor beside her was her purse.

Jenna approached both women. She was glad that she'd come across them together, rather than having to summon a meeting or speak to them separately.

Tammy glanced up first. "Hey," she said. "You're home from your trip. How did it go?"

Obviously Jenna had plenty to say about the subject, but she started off simple. "I bought some new lesson horses."

"That's great. Maybe I can see them tomorrow? I don't have time tonight. I'm waiting for Mike to call—we're meeting in town for dinner."

"Tomorrow would be fine. I'd like for you to see them." She didn't make the same offer to Donna. Her sister's allergies acted up whenever she went near the stables.

But that didn't stop Donna from sensing there was more to the conversation than met the eye. She asked, "What else is going on? Besides the horsey stuff?"

"A lot." Jenna sat beside her, with Tammy directly across from them. "I took J.D. on the trip with me, and we're lovers now. But it's just an affair."

Tammy frowned. "There's no commitment involved?"

"He isn't the right man for that."

Donna put the iPad down. "I figured that you'd end up sleeping together. It was obvious how much you wanted him."

"As long as you don't get hurt," Tammy put in.

"I won't. After he leaves, I'll go on with my life and he'll go on with his." She dropped the rest of her bomb. "But we're going to live together for the duration of his stay. I'm moving into the dream cabin with him, and we're going to treat it as a vacation, of sorts."

"That sounds too easy," Donna said.

Before a feeling of sadness crept in, Jenna shoved it away. "Actually, J.D is getting closer to recouping his memory." She relayed the Sam Houston/Cherokee information. "He thinks it's only a matter of time before the rest of it comes tumbling back."

Tammy scooted to the edge of her chair. "That's fascinating. Okay if I tell Mike? He should know."

"I'm sure that would be fine. I think J.D. would appreciate you passing it on to Doc. Come to think of it, J.D. should probably inform Deputy Tobbs, too. The more information the sheriff's department has, the better their chances are of uncovering his identity. In case he doesn't remember everything on his own."

After a stream of silence, Tammy said, "This is off topic, but I already told Donna while you were on your trip, and it concerns the three of us. I heard from my brothers this morning. They'll be here on Wednesday, so if that fits into your schedule, we should plan on having the vote that day."

Jenna's stomach went tight. The P.I. Savannah. The possible child. "J.D. thinks I should vote yes. He thinks it's important to know the truth and embrace it."

Tammy replied, "That's what I'm going to do," making her upcoming vote apparent.

Donna scrunched up her face, indicating an opposing opinion.

Jenna said, "I haven't made a decision, but I'm leaning toward yes. I'm curious about Savannah, but I'm even more curious if there's another Byrd out there. What if it's someone who needs a family? Who would like to have us be part of his or her life?"

"What if it's someone who doesn't?" her sister countered. "If another other Byrd exists, he or she could want nothing to do with us. These types of things don't always turn out hunky-dory."

"I know, but after being around J.D and seeing how lost he is from not being able to remember his family, it's hard for me not to consider how important family is."

"Does that mean you're okay with what Dad did, too?"

Jenna scowled. "Hell, no. That's a whole other matter." Even if J.D. thought otherwise. "Dad created this mess."

Donna blew out her breath. "I'm glad you haven't gone completely over to the dark side."

Jenna found herself saying, "You know it's possible that Savannah isn't the hussy I've been assuming that she was. Dad could have seduced her into being with him. He could have taken advantage of her. You know how brazen he can be when he wants something."

Donna didn't disagree. But she didn't say that she was cutting Savannah any slack, either.

Jenna asked Tammy, "How do you think your brothers will vote?"

"I don't know. We'll just have to wait and see." Tammy's cell phone rang from her purse and she reached in and grabbed it. Obviously it was Doc. She all but glowed when she answered the summons. She got up and walked away to talk to him, waving goodbye to Donna and Jenna, and leaving them alone.

Neither said a word. The impending vote was only two days away, but the results, whatever they turned out to be, would last a lifetime.

* * *

Jenna arrived on J.D.'s doorstep with a slew of luggage and a worried expression, and he got worried, too.

"What's wrong?" he asked.

"I'm getting freaked out about the vote. Tammy's brothers will be here on Wednesday."

He took her luggage and brought it inside. "You already knew they were coming sometime this week."

She followed him inside. "I know. But now it seems so final."

"Are you sure you're not freaked out about *this?*" He motioned to the air between them. "About staying with me?"

"Why? Are you freaked out about it?"

"No." But he feared that he might have pushed the boundaries of their relationship, drawing her into something she couldn't handle.

"I want to stay with you. In fact, I think it's going to be a relief getting away from the main house for a while."

"So it's really the vote that's bothering you?"

She nodded. "If we search for Savannah, we'll know for sure if we have a brother or sister or cousin. And if we don't, I'll always be left wondering."

"So what are you going to do?"

"Vote yes."

He knew she'd been considering it, but she looked as if she'd just made up her mind for certain. "You'll be doing the right thing."

"Tammy is voting yes, too. But I think Donna is going to vote no."

"What about Tammy's brothers?"

"Tammy doesn't know."

They sat on the sofa together. "Does it have to be

unanimous? Because if it does, it sounds like you're going to be deadlocked, regardless of how Tammy's brothers vote."

"We already agreed that the majority will rule."

"Then it still has a shot of going through."

"I hope so. Because I want to talk to Savannah and hear her side of what happened all those years ago."

"You're willing to hear her side, but not your dad's? He's the man who raised you. Who fed you and clothed you. Savannah is a stranger."

"Yes, he's the man who did all of that. But he's also the guy who turned Donna and me into the basket cases that we are."

He couldn't believe what he was hearing. "I barely know your sister, other than what you've told me about her, but from what I can tell, she isn't a basket case, and by God, neither are you. You're beautiful, hardworking, independent women. And if your dad helped shape you into those things, then he must have done something right."

She put her head on his shoulder. "Okay so maybe we're not basket cases. But we're not totally normal, either. Me with the husband checklist, and her with the inability to get close to people."

"Does this mean that you're giving up the list?"

She sat forward and laughed. "No."

He laughed, too. "Then why are you beating yourself up about it?"

"I guess I shouldn't be. Because someday the man from my list is going to appear, and I'll be living my dream life."

"As opposed to living with me in the dream cabin?

You keep talking like that and you're going to make me jealous of this guy you're going to marry."

She searched his gaze. "Are you being serious?"

Was he? J.D. wasn't sure. But he said, "No. I was just goofing around."

"I should have known better than to think you would be jealous."

"I'm all for you marrying someone else."

"Stop rubbing it in."

"I'm not rubbing it in, I'm being supportive."

"If you say so."

Before it turned into an argument, he said, "Why don't we settle this with a kiss?"

"I'd rather settle it with some butterscotch pudding. Do you still have some of those?"

"Yes." But it stung that she'd avoided kissing him. "I'll get you one." He went into the kitchen and returned with the pudding and a spoon.

"Thanks." She peeled the top off the container and proceeded to eat her favorite treat.

J.D. watched her. "Can I kiss you after you're done?"

Her lips curved into a smile. "Only if you admit that you're a little jealous of the prince who is going to marry me."

"The prince? Is that one of his requirements?"

"No. I was just being smart." She finished the pudding and set it aside. "You can kiss me if you want."

He put a hand on his heart, like a knight in a melodrama. "But I haven't sworn my jealousy yet."

"Now who's being smart?"

"Me. But I think maybe I am a little jealous. It's not that I want to be married." He sucked in his breath. "The idea of marriage still makes me panicky. But envisioning you with another man is a tough pill to swallow. Especially when I hear the way you talk about him."

"You've known from the beginning how important a husband is to me. But I'm glad you're jealous. It's better than you not caring."

"I do care. You're my lover and my friend. And I'm going to kiss you right proper. Naked and in bed."

He scooped her up and made her squeal. After carrying her to the bedroom, he plunked her down on the feather mattress, and she sank into it.

She grinned up at him. "Wow. This is comfy."

"I told you." He fell into bed with her. "I wonder if you're going to dream while you're here."

"My only dream is to be married someday, and I already know that's going to happen."

"Your list is your magic."

"I never thought of it that way before." She gazed into his eyes. "Thank you for saying that."

"What are friends for?" Immersed in her nearness, he peeled off her blouse and unhooked her bra. She in turn popped open the snaps on his shirt.

They removed the rest of their clothes and enjoyed the luxury of bared bodies. He inhaled the fragrance of her skin, and she roamed her hands over his.

The foreplay continued until he couldn't take another minute of not having her. He opened the nightstand drawer. It was time for him to glove up, as the saying went. "I put all of the protection in here."

She peered inside. "Good thinking."

"I wanted to be prepared for you."

"You always are."

Yes, but someday he wouldn't be. Someday she would belong to someone else. Forcing his thoughts in a different direction, he said, "Tell me your most romantic fantasy."

"Besides flower petals in my honeymoon bed?"

"Yes, something besides that." He didn't want to think about her wedding night.

"Sometimes I imagine messing around in a barn."

He entered her, surrounding himself with her warmth. "You mean making love in an empty stall? We could sneak out one night and do that."

She arched her hips. "What if we got caught?"

"We'd be careful that no one else is around." He twined a finger around one of her wavy tendrils. "I'd like to see you with hay in your hair."

"I won't get hay in my hair if we bring a blanket with us."

"You will if we roll off the blanket." To show her how it might feel, he rolled over the bed, making the covers tangle. "So, what do you say, should we slip out to the barn one night?"

"And embark on my fantasy?"

"It's *our* fantasy now."

"Living with you is going to be fun."

"That's the idea." *Fun,* he thought. *Free.* But in spite of that, he kept a dangerously possessive hold on her.

After their lovemaking ended, they broke apart, but it wasn't long before they were locked in each other's arms once again.

For now, J.D. just couldn't seem to let go.

Chapter 10

On Wednesday afternoon, Jenna, Donna and Tammy gathered on the porch of the main house with Tammy's brothers.

The women were seated in scattered chairs, and the men stood against the railing. Aidan, the older of the two, frowned and turned away from the sun, adjusting the brim of his hat. Jenna didn't know him very well, but if she had to describe him, she'd say he was the strong, silent type. Nathan was just the opposite. Already he'd been cracking silly jokes, even in the midst of turmoil.

Jenna glanced at Tammy. She looked so tiny next to her brothers. But she was also the most genuinely relaxed of anyone here. Jenna could barely breathe. Donna wasn't in any better shape. She had her hands clasped tightly on her lap.

On a side table was a pitcher of iced tea and plastic

tumblers that no one had touched. The lovely new porch swing was vacant, too, creaking softly from the wind and haunting the moment.

"Does anyone want to discuss this before we get started?" Tammy asked.

"Haven't we talked enough about it already?" Donna replied. "It's been consuming our lives."

That was true, Jenna thought. They were mired in it. She'd even skipped breakfast this morning, too anxious to eat. Soon it would be time for lunch, and her stomach would be growling like a junkyard dog.

Tammy replied, "We haven't discussed it at length with Aidan and Nathan."

Her brothers exchanged a glance. Was that good or bad? Jenna wondered.

"We talked amongst ourselves," Aidan said.

"You can share your thoughts with us," Tammy said.

"What for? This isn't a jury trial. We don't have to deliberate."

"I was just giving you a chance to speak your piece."

"We'll pass," Nathan said. "But thanks all the same, Tam-boy."

Tammy didn't flinch at the childhood nickname, but he'd said it affectionately. Besides, it was obvious that she wasn't a tomboy anymore. Then again, maybe she was. Maybe it would always be part of who she was—the old Tammy blending with the new.

Jenna glanced in the direction of the stables, where J.D. was working today. He'd wished her luck before she'd left the cabin, supporting her like the true friend he was. He was a prime example of an old/new person, except that he was still in the process of remembering his old self.

"Let's do this," Aidan said, cutting through the quiet.

Tammy volunteered to go first. "My vote is yes. I think we should hire the P.I."

No one reacted, but everyone already knew what her preference was.

"Who wants to be next?" she asked.

"I'll go." Jenna figured another yes was in order. "I'm in favor, too."

The men exchanged one of those private glances again. Had they been expecting Jenna to go the other way? Or had they guessed her right? It was obvious they'd tried to peg the women's votes ahead of time.

"How about you?" Nathan asked Donna.

"I'll wait until you boys have your say."

"All right. Then it's a no for me," Nathan said.

His brother concurred. "Also a no."

Jenna's heart sank. Donna was the tiebreaker, and that meant it was a lost cause. Clearly, she was going to side with the men.

"Come on, Donna," Nathan said. "Do us proud."

But instead of complying, she got up and poured herself a glass of tea. "I need to wet my whistle first."

Nathan chuffed. "And here I thought New Yorkers did everything fast."

Donna didn't falter. "A lady has the right to weigh her options."

Jenna's pulse pounded. Was her sister actually mulling it over at the last minute or just getting everyone's goat?

As she sipped her tea like a Southern belle, Nathan muttered, "Fiddle dee dee."

Tammy cracked a smile. Jenna thought it was funny, too, but she was too nervous to smile.

The wait continued.

Then Donna turned to Jenna. "I'm doing this for you, so remember that when Savannah hates us for invading her privacy or we end up butting heads with her disgruntled kid. If there is a kid," she concluded.

Jenna grinned. No matter what the future held, she adored her sister for thinking of her. "Okay."

The tiebreaker addressed the entire group. "Just to be clear, my vote is yes."

Aidan scowled. "You certainly had us fooled. We were sure that you were going to say no."

"I was. But women are notorious for changing their minds."

"Three to two," Tammy said. "The ayes have it."

Jenna's grin widened. "Who should we hire?"

Tammy had a ready answer. "How about Roland Walker? He's the P.I. Tex used to keep an eye on all of us, so he's already familiar with our family. I think it would be easier than bringing in someone new."

"Sure. Why not?" This from Donna. "Let's keep our scandals under one roof." She laughed a little. "And use the guy who knows how screwed up the Byrds are."

Everyone else laughed, too, even Aidan, which was saying a lot.

Soon the men went into the house, and Tammy followed them, giving the sisters a moment to themselves.

"Thank you," Jenna said. "What you did means everything to me."

"I knew how important it was to you. But I hope it doesn't come back to bite us in the butt."

"I don't think it will. But even if it does, I'll never forget that you sacrificed your vote for mine."

They got out of their chairs, and Jenna reached out to

hug her selfless sibling. She couldn't remember the last time she hugged Donna.

But it felt incredible.

J.D. glanced up and saw Jenna rushing toward him with exuberance. He struggled to collect his wits, preparing to greet her.

His day had started off fine, but as it wore on, dark and disturbing feelings had begun coming over him. And now here he was, trapped in the ache of a family he couldn't remember. But it wasn't just a case of not remembering them; he'd been dealing with that all along. It was the foreboding sense that whatever had gone wrong in his family couldn't be fixed.

As Jenna approached him, he slapped a smile on his face. He wasn't about to drag her down with his discomfort.

"It went well, I take it?" he asked.

"You wouldn't believe how well."

While she chattered about the outcome, giving him the details, he stood beside the barn, wearing damp jeans and a pair of rubber boots. Aside from having troublesome thoughts for the last few hours, he'd been bathing horses.

"Can you believe it?" she said. "Donna voted yes for me."

He'd never seen her so energized. If he wasn't so dirty and sweaty, and if his emotions weren't teetering on a thread, he would've lifted her off the ground and given her a little twirl. "I'm glad it worked out for you."

"It more than worked out. This mess with Savannah brought Donna and me closer. And you should have seen how funny she made it all seem. She had everyone laughing by the time it was over, and Aidan doesn't laugh that easily."

It was obvious how proud she was of her sister, and how much love there really was between them.

Jenna kept chattering. "We agreed to use the P.I. Tex had used. He must be good or Tex wouldn't have hired him. I'll bet he locates Savannah in no time."

"You have hope."

"Yes, I do. Donna warned me that it could turn out badly, but I don't think it will. I told her that it didn't matter, though, because what's most important is what she did for me."

"Happiness looks good on you."

"Thank you." She took a moment to catch her breath. "So how's your day going?"

The question hit him like the recoil from a high-powered rifle, nearly knocking the truth out of him. But he said, "Fine," determined not to spoil her mood.

Her stomach growled, and she laughed. "I knew that was going to happen. I still haven't eaten today."

"Then go get something."

"I will. And then you know what I'm going to do? I'm going to ask Tammy if she'll give me a cooking lesson."

"So you can feed your future husband?"

"Yes, but so I can make dinner sometime for you, too. You've been offering to be my guinea pig. You're still willing, aren't you?"

He nodded. "You can cook for me anytime you want."

"What should I focus on? What type of meal?"

"It doesn't matter."

"Of course it does. I want to learn to make your favorite food." She cocked her head. "Do you have a favorite that you're aware of? Or something you recently acquired a taste for?"

He roamed his gaze over her, pushing his bad feelings aside. "The only recent taste I acquired is for you."

She blushed. "I'm being serious, J.D."

So was he.

"There must be something you favor."

"I'm partial to Japanese food." The information zoomed right out, without him expecting it. He even jerked in surprise.

So did Jenna. "Oh, wow. Did you just remember that?"

"Yes." But he didn't have a clue why it was his food of choice. All he knew was that it was.

"That's so cool." She smiled at his horse-washing attire. "A sushi cowboy. Who would have guessed?"

Certainly not him.

She said, "As much as I'd like to accommodate your selection, I think Japanese might be a bit too ambitious for me to try. I doubt Tammy cooks in that style, either. Anything else?"

He gave her the option of choosing. "What's your favorite food? Or better yet, what do you want to learn to make? What do you see yourself cooking?"

She concentrated on the question. "Mom used to make spaghetti and meatballs, and sometimes I used to sing that silly parody of 'Old Smoky.'"

"The one where the meatball rolls on to the ground when somebody sneezed?"

She grinned. "Yep."

He grinned, too. She was improving his day, minute by confusing minute. "Now that I'd like to see."

"Me singing the song or the meatball rolling on to the ground?"

He chuckled. "Both."

"Here's an idea. I can turn my lesson into a family dinner. Tammy and I can fix the food, and maybe Donna, too, and you, Doc, Aidan and Nathan can hang out with us. Then, when it's ready, everyone can eat."

"Sounds great."

"I'm going to give the household staff the night off. I want to keep this low-key, without anyone else around, except the Savannah voters and our significant others."

He didn't deny that he was her significant other. Temporary as their agreement was, he still fit the bill. "I'll be there." And hopefully without a dark cloud hovering over his head.

Hours later, J.D. assessed the flock in the kitchen. By definition, "flock" meant a number of birds feeding, resting or traveling together, and these Byrds intended to eat together this evening.

And eat hearty.

The upcoming menu consisted of the aforementioned spaghetti and meatballs, along with deep-fried zucchini, garlic bread and a big green salad. For dessert—ice cream and fresh berries.

Jenna's lesson was a time-consuming project. To keep the masses from going hungry, Tammy had prepared a relish tray, and her Texas-size brothers were stuffing cold meats and cheeses in their mouths.

Nathan, the more talkative of the two, asked J.D., "So, who are you, exactly? Besides the guy who lost his memory? What's your role around here?"

"I work on the Flying B. I'm dating Jenna, too. She's staying with me in the dream cabin."

"You mean Savannah's old cabin? Maybe it should be called the nightmare cabin, considering everything that went on."

"Hey," Doc interjected. "That cabin helped me win my girl."

Tammy sent her fiancé a loving look.

Nathan rolled his eyes and spoke to Jenna. "You're the slowest cook I've ever seen. Isn't that a device of some kind? A slow cooker? Maybe that should be your ranch nickname." He cocked a gunslinger stance. "Slow Cooker, the pokiest chef in the West."

"Shut up, you big brute." She threw a dish towel at her jokester cousin, but missed him by a mile.

The Slow Cooker handle isn't half bad, J.D. thought. Jenna had only made two or three meatballs compared to the dozens Tammy had made. But J.D. thought Jenna looked damned cute doing it.

"I hope you don't plan on marrying her," Nathan said. "You'll starve."

Oh, cripes. J.D. didn't know how to react or how to respond. He certainly couldn't tell the other man how many marriage discussions he and Jenna had engaged in, but with a different groom in mind. Clearly Jenna wasn't going to say it, either.

Tammy came to the rescue. "Nobody is getting married, except Mike and me."

Nathan went with the flow. "Yep, my baby sister nabbed a doctor, and a damned fine one."

"Thanks," Doc said.

"Remember I said that when you're choosing your best man." Nathan grinned, then gauged the activity, his gaze landing on Donna and Aidan, who'd been staying quiet. "You know what this party needs? Some vino from Tex's cellar."

Aidan finally spoke up. "We're having Chianti with dinner."

"I know, but it'll be forever before we eat. I think we need to get buzzed now. Allow me to do the honors."

After he left to pilfer the spirits, Aidan said to J.D., "Sometimes my brother is full of himself. I hope he isn't offending you."

"None taken. But thank you."

Nathan returned with two bottles. He read from the first label. "This lovely vintage is a Montepulciana." He did the same thing with the second one. "And this robust selection is a Barbera." He dropped the act and grinned. "Mix your reds, I always say."

"That's because you don't know anything about wine," his brother commented.

"I know enough to enjoy them." He popped open the corks and poured everyone a drink, whether they wanted one or not. "How about a little music?" He turned on the radio and scanned the dial until he found a song that amused him.

He extended a hand to Donna, trying to persuade her to dance to Billy Ray Cyrus's anthem with him.

She rebuffed his attempt to make a Buckshot Hills filly out of her, shooing him away to "Achy Breaky" with someone else.

Nathan waggled his eyebrows at his brother.

"Me?" Aidan shook his head. "Get real."

The carefree Byrd danced by himself, creating an imaginary partner and swinging her around. Doc grinned and swept Tammy into his arms. When Jenna looked expectantly at J.D., he went for it, too. He led her into a two-step, and they laughed while they rocked to the rowdy beat.

The partnering didn't last long. Nathan started a line dance, and the rest of them followed. Even Aidan jumped in, kicking up his heels.

But not Donna. She darted over to the stove, as if she was saving the food from Billy Ray's old mullet.

"That one needs some country spirit," Nathan said. "Too bad there isn't a guy around to upset her Big City Apple cart."

Jenna and Tammy exchanged a behind-the-scenes glance, and J.D. assumed that they were thinking about Caleb Granger and his supposed attraction to Donna. But neither woman said anything to Nathan. Obviously they didn't trust him not to create a scene over it. Besides, Caleb was still out of town, and from what J.D. had heard about him from Manny, Caleb was a player with tons of women at his disposal. Donna didn't need her cart upset quite that far.

Soon the line dancers disbursed. Jenna and Tammy joined Donna at the stove, and the brothers went outside to grab some air.

Doc came over to J.D. and put his hand on his shoulder. "Tammy told me how your memory is starting to return. I'm glad you recalled some good things about yourself."

Good things. Doc was obviously referring to the Sam Houston/Cherokee information. J.D. wanted to tell him about the dark feelings he'd been dealing with today, but now wasn't the time. So he simply said, "Thanks."

"We'll miss you around here when you're gone."

"I'll miss this crazy clan, too." But mostly he would

miss Jenna. As she bustled around the kitchen, barely getting anything done, he thought about the man she was going to marry. Whoever he was, he would be a lucky guy.

Overall, the dinner was a success. The meal was delicious, and Jenna seemed proud of her Slow Cooker accomplishments. The newly formed group ate in the formal dining room, with a linen tablecloth, polished silverware and a floral centerpiece. *The Byrds,* J.D. thought as he glanced around at their faces.

A wonderfully mixed-up flock learning to be a family.

Chapter 11

The following morning at the cabin, J.D. and Jenna had breakfast—toaster waffles, doused in maple syrup.

She said, "I wonder if my next lesson should be waffles. Or do you like pancakes better?"

"I like either one." But mostly he liked her. She still had the same sunny disposition from yesterday. And he'd yet to tell her what was going on with him.

"Do you think it's the same batter?"

"What?"

"Pancakes and waffles?"

"I don't know."

"I'll have to talk to Tammy about it. She makes this really good chicken and waffles dish."

Barely hearing her, J.D. gazed at the clouds in his coffee.

"What's wrong? You seem preoccupied."

He glanced up. "I've been having bad feelings about my past."

She put down her fork. "What do you mean?"

He stopped eating, too. "I'm certain that whatever went wrong in my family can't be repaired."

"How can you be certain of something like that?"

"It's just what I feel, what I sense." Deep inside, where it counted.

"Do you have any memories to go along with those feelings?"

"No."

"Then I don't understand your certainty. You could be confused." She continued to evaluate the unknown situation. "What sort of thing could have happened that can't be repaired? Look at what's going on in my family and how we're coping with it."

"You haven't forgiven your dad."

"That's different."

"What makes your family different from mine?"

She clammed up.

"See," he said. "No difference."

"If I reached out to my dad, would you change your perspective about your family? Would you start to believe that whatever went wrong could be repaired?"

"I can't make a judgment call like that until I remember my past."

"We could hire Roland Walker to try to find out who you are. He would have a lot more time to devote to your case than the police."

He shook his head. "I appreciate the suggestion, but I'd rather let the sheriff's department handle it. Or better yet, to remember on my own."

"But you haven't remembered yet, and a P.I. would

delve deeper than the police. All they're doing is trying to find out your name and if you were carjacked."

"And that's exactly why I don't want Roland involved. I'm not comfortable with someone digging up bones."

"Does Doc know that you're having bad feelings?"

"I wanted to tell him last night, but it wasn't the right time."

"Would you mind if we talked to him together?"

"Not at all. In fact, I would prefer it." At this stage, he wanted to be as truthful as possible and for Jenna to know him as well as he knew himself, which wasn't saying much, he supposed. But it was the best he could do. "I'm not trying to hide anything from you. I think it's important to be honest. Otherwise our affair wouldn't seem right."

"Honesty is the very first quality on my list."

The vast blueness of her eyes nearly pulled him under, but her comment had packed an even bigger punch.

So much so, it became overly apparent.

"I'm sorry," she stammered. "I didn't mean to imply that you..."

He almost wished that she was, but it was wrong for him to feel that way, especially amid the murky waters in his mind. "I didn't think you were. We both know I'm not the guy from your list."

She went silent, and he studied her, intrigued by the way daylight zigzagged through the blinds and cast a glow on her hair. But there were always little things about her that fascinated him.

Interrupting the quiet, she picked up her fork. He resumed eating, as well.

She said, "I wonder if you're going to have any more

dreams while you're here. Or if your memories will return while you're awake."

"If my memories are bad, I hope they don't come in dreams. Because if they did, then Nathan would be right. This would be the nightmare cabin."

"That would be awful."

He nodded, then asked, "Are you ever going to reach out to your dad?"

"I would if it would help you come to terms with your family and whatever is causing the darkness."

"You can't fix me, Jenna. You can only fix what's broken within yourself."

"I know. But I want to make you feel better."

"You are. Believe me. Just knowing that you care matters."

"Same goes for me."

Before it got too emotional, he said, "We better finish up and get to work."

"When should we talk to Doc?"

"Tonight, if he's around."

They cleared the table and left the cabin. They walked to the stables together, then went their separate ways. He rode fence with Hugh, and she went into the barn to tend to her horses. And although J.D. was swamped with work, he thought about Jenna throughout the day and suspected that she was thinking of him, too.

Doc stopped by the cabin that evening, and Jenna listened while he and J.D. talked.

"Do you think my mind is playing tricks on me?" J.D. asked.

"Do you think that's what is happening?" the other man asked in return.

"No, but Jenna mentioned it."

Doc didn't ask her to expound on her opinion, but there was no need. It was obvious that she was troubled by J.D having a past that couldn't be repaired. Or a past that he didn't *think* could be repaired. There was a difference. She knew that better than anyone, and it was starting to make her guilty for hanging on to her Daddy resentments.

J.D. spoke to Doc again. "Jenna suggested hiring Roland Walker to hunt down my identity, but I don't want to do that. It's too personal to bring a P.I. into it."

"I understand," came the professional reply. "Another option would be to talk to a psychologist. I can recommend someone, if you'd like."

"Why do I need to talk to someone else? I'm already talking to you."

"This isn't my field of expertise, J.D."

"But I'm comfortable with you."

"Then you can continue to confide in me. I want to help in any way I can."

"Give me your opinion. I want to know what you think, regardless of your field of expertise."

"All right." Doc's voice was strong and steady, like the man he was. "I think that you need to relax and not worry so much about it. It seems obvious, to me anyway, that you need more time to address your feelings. And I think your memories will become clear when your mind is able to process the past and accept it, whatever it entails."

It was good advice, Jenna thought, and made complete sense to her.

"That's pretty much what you told me in the beginning," J.D. said. "To relax and let things happen naturally."

"And it still applies."

"I've had uneasy feelings about myself from the start, but it's getting harder to handle now that they're progressing."

"But what about the positive things you've recalled? It's not all bad."

J.D. furrowed his brows. "Meaning what? That every cloud has a silver lining, even the stormy ones?"

"I'd certainly like to think so."

"Ditto," Jenna said.

J.D. shook his head. "There you go ganging up on me. You two did that at the hospital, convincing me to stay here."

"That didn't turn out so badly, did it?" Doc asked.

J.D.'s expression softened, and when he glanced at Jenna, her heart went sweet and gooey.

"It turned out really nice," he said, still looking at her.

Her heart went even gooier. She was working so incredibly hard *not* to fall in love with him, and at this point, all she could do was keep praying that she didn't melt at his feet.

J.D. continued to look at her. She wanted him to break eye contact, but at the same time, she wanted to freeze this moment and keep it forever.

Forever. A dangerous word. A dangerous wish.

On and on it went. The look. The emotional push-pull. The fear of falling in love with him.

Then, thankfully, Doc cleared his throat, snaring J.D.'s attention and making Jenna breathe easier.

J.D. said to Doc, "I'll keep your advice in mind."

"Just let me know any time you need to talk."

"Thanks. I appreciate it."

Both men stood up and shook hands. Jenna got to her feet, too. Doc smiled at her, and she suspected it was his way of trying to help her relax. No doubt he could tell that she was fighting her feelings for J.D.

After Tammy's fiancé left, Jenna went into the kitchen to heat a pan of milk, her way of dealing with her feelings.

"Are you making hot chocolate?" J.D. asked.

"No. Just the milk. I can make hot chocolate for you, though."

"That's okay. I don't want anything." He leaned against the counter. "Remember when I made tea for you at the motel?"

She nodded.

"I think it was because I used to know someone who drank tea. Someone I was close to."

She started. "A former lover?"

"I don't know. It was a random feeling." He motioned to the pan she'd put on the stove. "I prefer cold milk."

"I like it cold, too. But Mom used to warm it for me when I was a kid. It's a comfort thing."

"That's nice." He came forward and slipped his arms around her. "You know what gives me comfort? Being around you."

She returned his hug, breathing in his masculine beauty and keeping him close. "What am I going to do after you're gone?"

"Find the man of your dreams," he whispered.

The man of my dreams, she thought. The man she loved. That was a lost cause. Because deep down, she knew that she'd already found him.

* * *

The week passed without incident. Roland Walker hadn't located Savannah yet or uncovered anything about her that indicated whether she'd had a child, J.D. hadn't remembered anything new about himself and Jenna was still struggling with the revelation that she loved him.

And now as she prepared to meet J.D. on their break, her pulse wouldn't stop pounding.

She removed their sack lunches from the fridge in the barn and headed to the spot they'd agreed upon, just east of the stables and beneath a shady tree.

Plunking down beneath the towering oak, she waited for him.

He arrived shortly, and as he walked toward her, he looked sinfully sexy, moving with a long, lean gait. He also had Tex's borrowed Stetson perched low on his head. Jenna was wearing a hat, too, with a red bandana tied around the outside of the crown.

"Afternoon," he said, and sat in the grass next to her.

She handed him his lunch, as nervous as a calf in the midst of being roped. Only it was her heart that was being lassoed.

"Are you okay?" he asked, obviously noticing that she seemed off. "Did something happen with Savannah?"

"No." Being honest about what was bothering her wasn't something she was capable of doing, not without admitting that she loved him. So she tried to wrangle in her emotions or at least not let them show. "There's no news. And I'm fine. Just hungry." She opened her sack and removed her sandwich, forcing a bite.

He didn't eat right away. Instead, he took a drink of his water. She watched him swallow, fascinated by the line of his neck and the way his Adam's apple bobbed with the effort.

"You were staring at me," he said afterward.

"Was I?"

"Uh-huh."

"Turnabout is fair play. You stare at me all the time, too."

"Guilty as charged. But neither of us should be doing it."

"Because it isn't polite to stare?"

"Yep." He leaned over and kissed her.

Heavens, he was the best kisser in the world. She wanted to crawl on to his lap and rub herself all over him, like a cat in heat. Or a woman in the throes of love.

"You taste like roast beef and avocado." He grinned. "Tastes good."

"I packed you the same lunch." She gestured to his sack. "Go for it."

"Don't mind if I do." He unwrapped his sandwich. "You're getting better at the kitchen stuff."

Wife practice, she thought, with a man who would never be her husband. "I'm trying."

He gazed at the bandana tied around her hat. Then blinked in an interested way.

"What?" she asked.

"The color just made me think of something. On the Native American medicine wheel, red symbolizes success and triumph."

"You just had another Cherokee memory."

"Apparently so." He sounded pleased. "And your hatband was the trigger."

She wasn't feeling triumphant or successful. But she summoned a smile, for his sake. "That's nice, J.D."

"It's a lot better than those dark feelings."

"Are you still having those?"

"Yes." They sat quietly and ate, then he said, "I hope this isn't going to sound like a loaded question, but how do you feel about the Savannah situation now that you're interested in meeting her? Do you want there to be another Byrd? Or would you prefer that there is no child?"

It *was* a loaded question, and she considered it carefully. "If there is no child, it will be a relief not to have to worry about who that person is and how he or she will fit into our lives. But on the other hand, if there isn't, I might actually be disappointed. Like I lost someone in my family that I never even got to know."

"I would feel that way, too." He glanced away and frowned.

Really, really frowned, she noticed.

"Did you just remember something bad?" she asked, analyzing how quickly his mood had changed.

"The children." He stared straight ahead. "I remember them. Or sort of remember..."

She leaned toward him. "What children?"

He discarded his lunch, crinkling the bag in his distress. "There were kids in my family who got left behind. I don't know who they were or how many of them there were, but I can feel their existence."

"What do you mean? Left behind?"

"In foster care. Kids who were supposed to get adopted but never were. That's why I know about the foster-care system. That's why it's been so important to me."

Her heart dropped to her stomach. Was it possible that they were his kids? That he was their biological father? Or that he'd actually been married? Was that why the thought of having a wife and kids made him panic?

No, she thought. He was too kind, too decent to have given up on his children or let them be taken away from him. And with the recurring talk of marriage, with it being a constant topic, wouldn't he have remembered having a wife, especially now with the foster-children memory?

"Was it you?" she asked, just to see what he would say.

He blinked. "What?"

"Did you father them?"

"No. God, no. I wasn't their dad."

"Are you sure?"

"Yes. I'm absolutely certain that I've never been a parent."

She gladly accepted his response, grateful that his feelings were so strong in that regard. "I didn't think you were, but I thought I should mention it, in case it was possible."

He was still frowning, still visibly troubled. "I don't know whose kids they were, but losing them is part of the darkness. Of what went wrong in my family and why it can't be fixed." He paused. "Doc said that I would remember things when I can handle it. But I don't want to remember anything else. Not today."

"Then don't think about it anymore."

"I'm not going to. It makes my head hurt."

It made his heart hurt, too, she thought, feeling sad for him. She wanted him to have a bright and happy future. She wanted that for herself, too.

And their families.

After work, Jenna thought long and hard about what she needed to do, and when she came to a decision, she told J.D. that she was going to go for a walk with her sister. But she didn't tell him why she'd summoned Donna. She didn't tell Donna, either.

So, as the women strolled along the ranch, a soft hush drifted between them.

"What's going on?" her sister finally asked.

"I have something important to talk to you about."

Donna stopped walking. Jenna did, too, and with the sun setting in the sky, she said, "I'm going to go see Dad on Saturday, and I'm going to ask him to tell me why he betrayed Uncle William and slept with Savannah. And no matter his excuse, I'm going to do my damnedest to forgive him."

Her sister took a step back, and a twig snapped beneath her shiny black boot. "Just like that? You're going to let him off the hook?"

"I'm in love with J.D."

Donna flinched in surprise or maybe it was confusion or both. "What does one have to do with the other?"

"J.D. has been saying that there are things in his family that can't be fixed, and now he's starting to remember some of those issues."

"So you're going to try to fix the way you feel about Dad? How is that going to help J.D.?"

"It isn't. But it's going to help me comes to terms with what Dad did. And hopefully it will help Dad in some way, too."

"Please don't ask me to go with you. I'm not ready to see him."

"I know you're not. I also know that this is more difficult for you than it is for me. I was always disappointed in him, but you used to idolize him."

The city girl set her jaw. "I did not."

"Say what you will, but I used to see the way you

looked at him. You aspired to be like him. He was strong and tough, and he was your role model. I never expected much of him, but you did. And he let you down."

Donna took another step back, and Jenna thought her big sis looked like she was ready to bolt, to run straight back to New York as swiftly as her long, gorgeous legs would take her.

Then Donna said, "I don't want to have this conversation with you."

"Yes, I can see that." Hence, Jenna wasn't going to push it. "I just wanted you to know that I was driving to Houston on Saturday."

"Don't give Dad my regards."

"I won't."

Donna turned and walked away, but she didn't go far. She came back with a concerned expression. "Does J.D. know that you love him?"

"No."

"Are you going to tell him?"

Her heart clenched. "No."

"Why not?"

"Because it won't change anything. And because I wasn't supposed to get attached. He and I talked about it ahead of time, and I kept insisting that I wouldn't."

"I'm sorry if you're hurting."

"Thank you." She longed to hug Donna the way she'd done on the day of the vote, but she feared that she might cry in her sister's arms. And that wouldn't do either of them any good.

They parted company, and Jenna continued to walk by herself, immersed in her surroundings. The Flying B was her home, the place that gave her hope, but would it be enough to sustain her after J.D. was gone?

She thought about Tammy and Doc and how lucky Tammy was. Her cousin had the ranch, but she had the man she loved, too. What if Jenna never found anyone to replace J.D.? What if she compared every man she met to him—to his qualities—instead of what was on her list?

Maybe she should throw that stupid list away.

She frowned at the path in front of her. She couldn't do it. She'd compiled it for a reason, and she was keeping it, especially since J.D had told her it was her magic.

Her magic. Her pain. Her confusion.

Before her emotions drove her straight into a ditch, she headed for the cabin, where she knew J.D. would be awaiting her return.

She went inside and came face-to-face with her lover, who was fresh from his evening shower and attired in a plain white T-shirt and crisply laundered jeans.

"How was your walk?" he asked.

She blew out the air in her lungs. "I told Donna what I needed to tell her." And now it was time to tell him, except for the part about loving him, of course. "I'm going to my dad's on Saturday."

"You are?" He widened his eyes. "To try to square things with him?"

She nodded. "What you recalled about your family has made me think deeper about mine. I can't keep letting my wound fester. I have to find a way to heal it."

"I'm so proud of you and the progress you've made." He took her in his arms. "Knowing that you're going to be okay will make my leaving easier when the time comes."

She buried her cheek against his neck, her emotions going haywire again. "What if I'm not okay? What if I turn into a lonely old spinster, waiting for a man who never appears?"

"Are you kidding? Your future husband is out there and he's going to be everything you imagined."

She buried her face deeper into the warmth of his skin. "Are you still jealous of him?"

"Hell, yes. But I'm glad he exists, too. That he'll be there when you need him."

What she needed was for him to be J.D., not a nameless, faceless stranger.

He said, "Someday you're going to get married with your entire family in attendance, and it will be the best day of your life."

How could it be the best day of her life unless she was marrying him? "I don't want to think about my wedding right now." Unable to let go, she clung to him, like a love-fraught reed in the wind. "I just need to deal with going to Houston on Saturday."

And the reconciliation with her father.

Chapter 12

As Jenna parked her truck and took in her surroundings, the familiar blue-and-white house stirred pangs of loneliness. But what did she expect, for this pristine suburban structure and its perfectly manicured lawn to give her a happy sense of home?

She would never forget the day she and Donna had moved in with their dad. They'd been two young girls raw from their mother's passing, and the ache was as vivid today as it had been then.

She exited her vehicle, her mind alive with deathly memories. The friends and neighbors who'd brought casseroles by had meant well, but their condolences hadn't helped. Dad, Donna and Jenna had made an awkward trio. The divorced father with his motherless children. The busy executive who'd been estranged from his own family. They'd been doomed from the start.

Jenna moved forward, taking the shrub-lined walkway toward the front door. She'd called ahead and let Dad know that she was coming, only now that she was here, she wanted to turn tail and run. But she quickened her pace and approached the awning-covered stoop. She no longer had a key. She'd gotten her own apartment ages ago, and now, of course, she was living at the Flying B.

She rang the bell, and Dad opened the door, appearing like a cautious mirage. They gazed uncomfortably at each other. He was an attractive man for his age, with striking blue eyes and graying brown hair. He stayed in shape by hitting the gym. His only lazy indulgence was the TV game show that he plunked himself in front of each night.

She went inside. He kept the place tidy, especially for a bachelor, but it lacked warmth. It had been that way ever since she was a child. Something had always been missing.

"Do you want a cola?" he asked.

She shook her head. He kept pop around for guests, but he rarely entertained. She couldn't actually remember him dating anyone, either. If he had lovers, he never brought them home for her and Donna to see.

He spoke again. "Where do you want to sit?"

"The living room is fine."

He offered her the sofa. "I'm not much of a talker, Jenna."

"I know, Dad. But this is a discussion we need to have." She hadn't told him that she wanted to make amends. She'd just said that she wanted to discuss their family.

He sat in his easy chair, the one from which he normally watched TV, only the television was off.

She said, "I have a lot of questions about the past. But first I wanted to check to see if anyone informed you about the outcome of the vote."

"William called me and said it went through. His kids gave him the details. Tammy was in favor of hiring the P.I. and Aidan and Nathan weren't, but their votes were canceled out by yours and Donna's. So now Roland Walker is searching for Savannah."

That pretty much summed it up. "I didn't know that you and Uncle William were on speaking terms, other than snapping at each other."

"We're not. He called out of anger, to remind me of what a mess I made out of everyone's lives. How many times do I have to hear that?"

"As many times as it takes."

He heaved a heavy sigh. "So you're here to berate me, too?"

"No. Actually, I came here to forgive you, Dad."

"You could have fooled me."

She bristled. This was going to be harder than she'd thought. "Maybe I should just leave and forget it."

"No, please. Stay. I miss you and Donna." He shifted in his chair, looking big and tough and troubled. "How is your sister?"

"She's fine."

"Why didn't she come with you?"

"She isn't ready to make amends with you."

He didn't reply, but he seemed wounded. Did he know that Donna used to idolize him? Or had he been too consumed with himself all these years to notice?

Jenna hoped and prayed that forgiving him was truly the right thing to do. Clearly he was hurting, but if it was self-indulgent pain, then it didn't count, not the way it should.

She asked, "How do you feel about us looking for Savannah and her possible child?"

He skirted the issue. "William is upset about it."

"I know. But how do *you* feel?"

He hesitated, obviously not keen about answering the question.

"Dad."

"I was in love with her, Jenna."

That was the last thing she'd expected to hear. And because it took her by complete surprise, she merely sat there, probably with a stupid look on her face.

He continued, "Out-of-my-head, out-of-my-young-heart in love. I even married your mother on the rebound because I'd lost Savannah. Your mom reminded me a bit of her, but they weren't the same woman, and I never got over Savannah. She was always there, like a ghost who wouldn't stop torturing me."

Conflicted by his admission, Jenna tensed, feeling sorry for him and hating him at the same time. "Did Mom know about Savannah?"

"No. I didn't tell her that I was estranged from my family because of a girl. I didn't make up a story, either. I just said that it was too painful to talk about, and she accepted it. I think in the beginning, my rebel-boy pain made me more appealing to your mom."

Jenna's voice went sharp. "She wouldn't have found it appealing if she'd known you were pining over another woman."

"I tried to make the marriage work. Honestly, I did. But I didn't love your mom the way I should have, and she began to lose feelings for me, too."

"I remember Mom being distraught over the divorce."

"You were six years old when we split up. How clear can your memories be?"

Clear enough, she thought. "I remember how often she cried. And how much time she started spending at her job. She didn't seem like the same Mommy anymore." But Jenna had stayed by her side, sticking like kindergarten paste, right up until the day she'd died.

He stared at the empty TV screen. "I never meant to hurt her."

"You hurt a lot of people."

"I didn't set out to do that."

She took an enormous breath, struggling to give him the benefit of the doubt. "Tell me more about Savannah and how your relationship with her unfolded."

"William and I were both home from school that summer. Me from Rice University and him from Texas A&M. It was our first year of college. William was majoring in animal husbandry so he could work beside Tex on the ranch, and I was majoring in business with a minor in economics, so I could get the hell off the Flying B someday."

She knew some of these details already, but she'd arranged this meeting to hear his version of the story, so she listened to the way he was telling it, concentrating on the emotional inflection in his voice.

He continued, "Right before summer break, William had gotten into a car accident and ended up with a fractured leg, a sprained wrist and some cuts and bruises on his face. So that's the condition he was in when he came home. He'd been dating Savannah for a while by then. She was a student at A&M, too. Since he was all banged up, she offered to drive him to the ranch and help nurse him back to health." He paused, then added, "I arrived a few days later, and from the moment I met Savannah, I was awestruck. But I kept telling myself that I was only attracted to her because she was William's girl. I'd always felt a raging sense of competition with my brother."

She interrupted. "Why, Dad?"

"Because Tex favored him. Tex never said so, but it was obvious to me from the time we were kids. William's love of the Flying B was a bond they shared, and it alienated me from them. I fought back by competing with William. But he was just as macho as I was, and he pushed back, competing with me, too. In retrospect, I probably created that holy-hell trait in him."

"Or maybe you both inherited it from Tex. Grandpa was an ornery old guy."

"That's for damn sure. Ornery when he was old. Ornery when he was young. Our father had always been a powerful force to be reckoned with." He glanced away.

She urged him on. "Finish telling me about Savannah."

He complied. "Since William was laid up, I spent a lot of time with her, entertaining her on the ranch. The Flying B was a heck of a lot more fun with her around. We took walks, we rode trail, we picnicked by the stream."

Jenna merely nodded. She'd been doing those same activities with J.D.

"She was charming and beautiful, and I started falling in love with her. Genuinely in love. I battled with my conscience every day, trying to make my feelings stop, but I couldn't. I wanted her so damned much. Finally, I reached the point of not caring that she was William's girl."

"How did she feel about you?"

"She went mad for me, too. In fact, she'd been awestruck over me from the moment we met, just the way I was over her. It wasn't the same between her and William. They had a nice easy relationship that she'd assumed was love. Only after she met me, she knew the difference. Of course she was terribly guilty over William, too. She kept saying that she needed to break the news to him. We even discussed coming clean and telling him together. One way or another, William had to be told."

"But neither of you followed through?"

He shook his head, frowned. "Actually, we did just the opposite. We kept sleeping together. But we'd never done it at the cabin until the night we got caught. Prior to that, we'd been having secret trysts, mostly in the hills, away from the Flying B."

Jenna went quiet. At this point she didn't know what to say. But her silence wasn't a problem, because her dad kept talking, as if he needed to get the whole sordid story off his chest.

He said, "Funny thing, too, when Savannah and William first arrived, Tex had insisted that she stay in the dream cabin because it was the farthest from the house. I think it was to stop her and William from getting frisky under his roof. He hadn't counted on me being tossed into the mix."

Once again, Jenna said nothing.

He spoke further. "After Savannah and I were together that night, I snuck out of there as fast I could, and ran smack dab into Tex, who'd gone for a walk to smoke one of his fancy-ass cigars. I was in the midst of tucking in my shirt and adjusting my belt. He knew instantly what I'd been doing with Savannah in the cabin. He lit into me, calling me every rotten name in the book. According to Tex, I was the biggest SOB that ever lived and Savannah was a trollop who'd cuckolded one twin for the other. He refused to listen to anything I had to say, so I didn't even bother trying to explain myself or tell him how much Savannah and I loved each other."

She went into question mode again. "So what did you do?"

"I blasted over to the main house to pack my things. But I was planning on going back to the cabin after Tex went to bed. To ask Savannah to run away with me." He gave a long drawn-out pause. "But later, when I returned to the cabin, she was gone. I figured that Tex had given her a piece of his mind and kicked her off the ranch. I left, too, and headed for A&M, where I thought she'd gone. But she didn't return to school. She just up and disappeared, and I never saw her again."

"And you had no idea that she'd taken a pregnancy test or that she suspected that she might be pregnant?"

"No. None."

"If there is a child, do you think it's yours? Or was she sleeping with William at the same time she was with you?"

"She wasn't with us at the same time. William will confirm that he hadn't slept with her after his accident. But he'd been with her before, so if there is a child, it could still be his. She could have been pregnant when she'd come to the ranch and not even known it."

"Tell me how you feel about the possibility of Savannah having a child, Dad."

"I'm hoping that there isn't one. I can't bear the thought of her and William having a son or daughter, for his sake as much as mine. But, by the same token,

I can't handle being a father again. I'm already a lousy parent to you and Donna."

She extended her heart to him. After everything he'd told her, she empathized with him now. "You did the best you could."

"Do you still think I'm a monster for having an affair with my brother's girlfriend?"

"No, but I think she should have broken it off with William first. You and Savannah should have showed more restraint."

"Being in love messes people up."

"I know," she replied, suddenly trapped in her own life, her own feelings.

His gaze zoomed in on hers, his blue eyes filled with fatherly concern. "Is there a young man I should know about?"

Unable to hold back, she nodded. Then she proceeded to tell him about J.D.

Afterward, he said, "You need to tell him that you love him."

"But I promised him that I wouldn't get attached, and he's determined to leave the ranch after his memory returns."

He got up and sat beside her. "My affair with Savannah turned into a disaster, but at least we spoke about our feelings. In that regard, I don't have any regrets."

"You're right." So very right. "If J.D. leaves the ranch without me telling him that I love him, I'll regret that for the rest of my life."

"It's possible that he loves you, too. But he's too mixed up with his amnesia to realize it. Once his memory comes back, it might work in your favor."

"Do you really think so?"

"Truthfully, I can't imagine him *not* loving you. You're a special girl, Jenna."

She put her head on his shoulder. "Thanks, Daddy."

"You haven't called me that since you were little."

They turned to look at each other, and she smiled. "I'm glad I came here. J.D. kept telling me that I should."

"I think I'd like that boy."

"I think so, too. There's a lot to like about him."

"There was a lot to like about Savannah, too. She was a foster child, and all she ever wanted was a family. I had a tough time understanding that since I was such an outsider in mine."

"J.D. has a connection to foster kids, too. Only he isn't quite sure who they are to him." She thought about his childhood dream, about his scattered memories. "Did Savannah dream while she was at the cabin?"

"I don't know. If she did, she never mentioned it."

"I haven't dreamed while I've been there."

"Not everyone does."

They sat quietly, then she asked, "Does Uncle William know that you loved Savannah? Have you ever told him?"

"No."

"You should tell him. You should apologize to him, too."

"After all of this time? Hell, we're practically old men now." He made a face, aging himself even more—the lines around his eyes crinkling, his lips thinning.

"Yes, after all of this time." She reprimanded him. "Your apology is long overdue."

"Do you know how difficult that's going to be for me?"

"No more difficult than me telling J.D. that I love him."

He cursed beneath his breath.

She stared him down.

"Okay." He held out his hands in surrender. "I'll go out on a limb if you will." He lowered his hands and gentled his voice. "It would be nice if you tried to talk me up to your sister, too."

"I'll try." But first she was going to talk to J.D. If she waited, she feared her nerves would explode. She gathered her purse. "I'm going to go home now."

"Call me later and tell me how it went."

"You, too."

He walked her to her truck, and she climbed behind the wheel, anxious to get back to the Flying B.

But in the evening when she arrived, Jenna entered the cabin and found J.D. staring into space.

Worried, she asked, "What happened?" He looked as if someone had just died.

"I know who I am." He turned in her direction, like a zombie with its heart falling out of its chest. "I remember everything, including the murder of my wife."

Chapter 13

"Your *wife?* Her *murder?*"

J.D. nodded, Jenna's choppy questions echoing in his ears. His memories had come crashing back, shaking him to the core. He'd spent the last few hours holed up in the cabin remembering the most painful things imaginable.

She dropped onto the sofa as if her knees had just buckled.

"Kimie was gunned down at a convenience store," he said, wishing he'd caught Jenna before she'd fallen onto the furniture. She looked as white as death. But it was Kimie who was dead. "There was a robbery in progress when she walked into the store. The gunman panicked and shot her, killing her instantly. Then he turned and fired at the clerk, a young guy who was scared out of his wits and had only worked there for a few weeks." J.D.

backed himself against the window, moving away from Jenna instead of toward her, with Kimie's lifeless body floating in his mind. "The clerk survived the injury and served as a witness in court."

"The gunman was apprehended?" Her voice vibrated.

He glanced out the window. The blinds were open, the darkness thick and vast. "He fled the scene, but he didn't get far. He was taken into custody the same night."

"I'm so sorry about your wife." She sounded tearful. "There was a moment, a couple of days ago, that I wondered if you'd been married. But it didn't seem possible. And I never would have thought..."

Was she misty-eyed? He didn't want to look at her to see. "There's nothing you can do. There isn't anything anyone can do."

"I wish there was."

He finally glanced at her. Her eyes *were* damp, and he suspected that she wanted to wrap him in her arms and to try to console him. But he couldn't bring himself to allow it, and she was obviously aware of how unapproachable he was. He stayed plastered against the window.

"When did you lose her?" she asked.

"Two years ago." But it seemed like yesterday, especially with the way his memories had come crashing back.

He glanced at Jenna again. By now she was sitting a little more forward on the sofa, and she looked as discomposed as he felt.

She spoke quietly. "What's your name?"

"Joel. Joel Daniel Newman."

"Do you want me to call you Joel?"

"No. I'm J.D. now. It still works as my initials." He didn't want to be Joel anymore. He'd been that to his wife. "Her full name was Kimie Ann Winters-Newman. We were married for six years. We were happy." His stomach went horribly tight. "I loved her, and she loved me. We were right together. So damned right. The only thing missing in our lives were children. We'd been trying to conceive, but couldn't. Kimie wasn't able to. So we decided to adopt. A whole passel of kids. That was our plan."

Jenna didn't reply, but she was riveted to his every word, gazing at him with her pretty blue eyes.

He went on. "We discovered how difficult it was to adopt an infant and learned how many foster kids were out there, needing homes."

"So the kids who'd been crowding your memories, who'd been left behind, are the ones you were hoping to adopt someday?"

He nodded. "The family that can never be repaired. Kimie and me and our nonexistent children." He paused to temper the quaver in his tone. He couldn't bear to break down in front of Jenna. "We were also looking into foreign adoption. With me being part Cherokee and her being part Japanese, we knew what it would take to raise kids from other cultures. We knew how important it would be to keep them connected to their roots and to teach them about ours." He considered the nickname Jenna had called him. "The sushi cowboy. Kimie would have liked that."

"Is she the tea drinker you were struggling to remember?"

"Yes. She had a cup of herb tea almost every night before we went to bed. Sometimes I fixed it for her. We had this easy rhythm, knowing each other's habits, catering to them."

She got teary again. "It makes sense now, the reason marriage and babies made you uncomfortable. It wasn't because you couldn't relate to that lifestyle. It's because you mourned it."

He didn't reply, and she went disturbingly quiet, too.

He shattered the silence. "Do you know why your hair fascinated me? Kimie said that some of our kids would be blond. Us with our dark hair, walking around with golden-haired children." Suddenly he wanted to touch Jenna's fair locks, to indulge in each wavy strand. But he stayed where he was. He was confused by his feelings. He shouldn't be thinking about Kimie while he was longing to touch Jenna. It only worsened the pain. "I should have never gotten you involved in my mixed-up life. I should have stayed at the homeless shelter."

"Don't talk like that."

"How else am I supposed to talk?" He could tell that she was confused, too, and that he'd dragged her into something neither of them could handle.

Jenna ached for J.D., but she also hurt for herself. His memories were like a boomerang flying between them.

Back and forth.

What a horrible twist of fate. At one time J.D. had been the ultimate family man, with the qualities from Jenna's list. Only he wasn't emotionally available anymore. His wife was gone, taken from him in a devastating way, and Jenna was sitting on the sidelines, wishing she could heal him, but knowing she couldn't. Telling him that she loved him was futile now.

"Where did you meet Kimie?" she asked, trying to envision him in happier times, trying to help him feel better.

"We went to the same high school. We saw each other around and flirted a little, but we didn't start dating until later."

"How old are you?" There was so much more she wanted to know about him—this man she loved, this man who would never belong to her.

"Thirty-three. I was twenty when Kimie and I first went out, twenty-five when we got married, and thirty-one when she died."

"I'm sorry," she said, not knowing what else to say yet realizing how meaningless those words were to him.

But even so, he moved forward, slowly, and joined her on the sofa. He still seemed dazed and distant, but he was coming out of his shell, at least a little.

"Have you talked to Doc?" she asked.

"Not yet." He exhaled an audible breath. "You're the first person I've told."

She wondered if he would flinch if she touched him. She didn't take the chance. They sat side by side, with no physical contact.

"How did your visit with your dad go?" he asked, as if suddenly becoming aware of where she had been when his memories surfaced.

"It went well. But we don't need to talk about that right now." There was still so much more she didn't know about him. "Why don't you tell me about your parents instead, and your brothers and sisters, if you have any?"

"I don't. But I had a happy childhood."

"Go on," she coaxed.

"My parents ran a horse farm in a small town in the Texas Panhandle, and that's where I grew up. I get my Cherokee blood from my mom. She taught me about our ancestors. She and Dad are good people, kind and loving." He paused. "When they retired, I purchased the farm from them, and they moved to Arizona. I loved that farm. So did Kimie." His voice cracked. "It's where we made our home together. After she died, my parents tried to talk me into going to Arizona and staying at their place, but I couldn't deal with being around anyone, not even them."

"So what did you do?"

"I sold the farm and started drifting. Sometimes I camped out in remote areas, for months at a time, where there wasn't another soul around. And sometimes I stayed at motels, staring at the walls and rarely leaving the room. I drifted all over Texas, going from town to town. Small towns, like the one I'd left behind."

Like Buckshot Hills, she thought. "Do you recall how you were injured?" The injury that had given him amnesia and had brought him to the Flying B. "Was it a carjacking?"

He nodded. "I stopped to help a man and a woman who appeared to be broken down by the side of the road. I was worried about the woman. That someone else might stop and something bad might happen to her. It never occurred to me that they were setting me up for a robbery."

Jenna understood why he'd been so quick to come to the couple's aid. He'd obviously been thinking about Kimie. "Your heart was in the right place."

He didn't comment on his heart. His broken heart, she thought.

He said, "They must have rigged their car so it wouldn't start. I think the woman struck me on the back of the head when I was leaning over the hood. I don't remember the blow itself, but I remember that the man was standing beside me, so he couldn't have been the one who hit me."

"Do you recall waking up?"

He nodded. "But I was too disoriented to think clearly, to contemplate where I was or why my head hurt so damned much."

"How long do you think you were like that before I found you?"

"The robbery took place about three miles from the Flying B Road. But how long I was wandering around is beyond me. They obviously stole my truck. They also got my cell phone, my ID and some cash and credit cards from my wallet, but my social-security card is in a safe-deposit box and the bulk of my money is in an investment account. There wasn't any evidence of the account in my belongings, so it's unlikely they know about it. And even if they discovered it existed, they wouldn't have been able to access it without drawing attention to themselves."

"Thank goodness for that. When are you going to call Deputy Tobbs and give him this information and tell him who you are?"

"Tomorrow. I'm too worn out to do it now. I've got too much going on inside me." He scrubbed a hand across his jaw. "How could I have forgotten her, Jenna?"

"Because it was too painful to remember." She stated the obvious, wishing, once again, that she could ease his sorrow, but knowing she couldn't. She'd never felt so helpless or so useless.

"It still seems wrong to have blocked her from my mind. Instead of remembering Kimie, I was falling for you."

Falling…

She'd been falling, too, only with the word *love* attached. J.D. wasn't making that claim. "You didn't do anything wrong. You have a right to keep living."

"I don't want that right. I want to disappear. I want to keep running."

"You can't drift forever."

"Yes, I can. I have enough money in my investment account to keep me going for a long time. And when it runs out, then I'll get ranch jobs, like this one. Temporary work so I don't have to put down roots. I don't ever want to put down roots again. It isn't worth it."

She looked into his eyes, trying to see the man he'd once been. But all she saw was emptiness. Still she said, "Maybe someday you'll feel differently."

He stood up and moved away from the sofa. "I'm going to pay you back for your hospitality, like I wanted to from the beginning."

"You know that doesn't matter to me."

"It matters to me, and now that I know I have money in the bank, I can give you what I owe you."

"If it makes you feel better, go ahead."

"I wonder if I should go to a motel tonight. I have enough cash from my wages for a few nights stay, and I—"

"What? Why?"

"I can't sleep in the same bed with you, Jenna. I wish I could, but after remembering Kimie…"

"Don't leave the ranch. Not this soon. Wait until you talk to Deputy Tobbs and get everything sorted out. I'll go back to the main house, and you can stay here by yourself."

"Are you sure? I don't want to put you out."

"You aren't putting me out. I wouldn't be staying in the cabin if you weren't here, anyway. Besides, maybe you'll have a comforting dream tonight."

"About Kimie?" His voice jumped. "Do you think that's possible?"

"I don't know. But it's worth a shot."

"Then I'll stay here. Thank you."

Jenna got up, and they gazed awkwardly at each other.

"You've been such a good friend all along," he said. "And you still are."

"I want what's best for you." And sharing his bed wasn't in his best interest, not when he wanted to be alone. "I should pack my things now."

She went into the bedroom, trying to hold herself together, to keep from crying in earnest. Finally she was ready, everything shoved into her suitcases.

He loaded them into her truck. "You look like you're going on a major trip."

But she was only going to another house on the same property. *So close, yet so incredibly far,* she thought. She was going to miss snuggling in J.D.'s arms tonight. She was going to miss him for the rest of her life.

"I'll talk to you tomorrow," he said. "And if you see Doc, will you tell him what's going on and that I'll talk to him tomorrow, too?"

"Of course."

"Night, Jenna."

"Sleep well, J.D."

"I will if I dream. God, I hope I dream."

"I hope so, too." He needed Kimie more than he needed her. Jenna couldn't compete with that. Nor was she going to try.

* * *

After hauling her luggage into the house, Jenna confided in Doc and Tammy, who were in the kitchen, where Tammy was baking a boysenberry pie.

Both were genuinely concerned and felt badly that J.D.'s memories had triggered such tragic news. Doc said that he would visit J.D. in the morning, and Tammy gave Jenna a sweet hug.

Later, Jenna talked to Donna. They sat on Jenna's bed in their pajamas, with plates of the leftover pie between them.

"This must be the worst night of your life," Donna said.

"It was a good day until I got home and found out about J.D. I think it's nice that Dad loved Savannah."

"And married Mom on the rebound? What's nice about that?"

"That part upset me, too. But I could tell that Dad had never meant to hurt Mom. And now that I feel about J.D. the way I do, I understand how conflicted Dad was."

"Love isn't an excuse to behave badly."

"No it isn't, but when you're caught up in it, you do things you wouldn't normally do. Who knows? Maybe I'll end up marrying someone on the rebound, too. I mean, honestly, Donna, how am I ever going to love someone the way I love J.D.? It seems impossible to love another man with the same intensity that I feel for him."

"Why do you have to get married at all? What's wrong with staying single?"

Laden with loneliness, Jenna sighed. She'd never told Donna about her list, and now wasn't the time, especially since she couldn't imagine anyone except J.D. fitting the bill. "How am I going to have children if I don't get married?"

"You don't have to be married to have kids. Single women can adopt these days or use a surrogate or go to a sperm bank."

"I know, but I can't picture myself in the role of being a single mom. And none of those methods sounds appealing to me. I want a family the traditional way."

"Then I hope you get what you want someday. I hate seeing you hurt."

"At least I squared things with Dad. He wants you to forgive him, too."

Donna shook her head. "I can't deal with Dad's issues right now."

"He's going to make amends with Uncle William. He's going to call him and apologize."

"Really?" Donna arched a delicate brow. "And whose idea what that? Yours or his?"

"I suggested it, but he agreed fairly easily. We made a pact—I would tell J.D. that I loved him, and he would apologize to William."

"You're not keeping your end of the bargain."

"How can I, knowing what I know about his past?"

"You can't, I guess. But it seems sad for you to keep it a secret. It doesn't seem right for him to stop living, either."

"That's what I told him. Maybe if he has a dream about Kimie, he'll realize that."

"An angel dream?"

"I hadn't thought about it that way. But yes, I suppose so. Kimie would be his angel if she appears to him in a dream."

Donna reached for her hand. "I hope it happens the way you want it to."

The sisterly solace was much needed. Both of them went silent for a while, even after their fingers drifted apart and Jenna managed to stave off her tears, as she'd been doing for most of the night. Donna truly cared, and it truly mattered.

Jenna caught her breath and said, "What I want is for him to love me and want to be with me. Dad said that he couldn't imagine J.D. not being in love with me."

"Dad isn't the authority on love, but I agree, I can't imagine J.D not loving you."

"Thank you. But I actually think Dad is an authority. The way he talked about Savannah. About the way both of them felt about each other."

But it wasn't a comforting thought, considering how their father's life had turned out, and Jenna could only pray that she wasn't destined to follow in his shaky footsteps.

Chapter 14

In the morning, all Jenna could do was think about J.D. and how he was faring. But she wasn't going to go down to the cabin until Doc returned, and Doc was there now.

She looked across the breakfast table at Tammy. Her cousin had fixed the meal—pancakes—and they were waiting together.

Jenna took small bites, trying not to heighten the tightness in her stomach. Earlier she'd questioned Tammy about the preparation of the food. Not because this was the time to continue her cooking lessons, but because she was trying to keep her mind engaged. The batters for pancakes and waffles, she'd learned, were similar but not the same. Traditionally waffle batter was made with egg yolks and the whites were whipped separately and folded in just before cooking. It sounded complicated to her, but at the moment, everything was complicated.

"How are you holding up?" Tammy asked.

"Not well. I—"

The sound of footsteps interrupted their conversation. Doc entered the kitchen, and Jenna nearly knocked over her juice, catching the glass before it fell.

"Did J.D. dream last night?" she blurted, asking him the first thing that popped into her head.

"No, he didn't," Doc replied. "I suggested grief counseling, but he refuses. As you're aware, he was already struggling with this, drifting around aimlessly. But the amnesia has only made things worse."

Jenna understood. Now that J.D. was remembering the details of his wife's death, he was reliving the horror all over again. "I wish he would listen to you and see a grief counselor."

"Maybe you can talk him into it."

"I'll try." She left the table and her pancakes half eaten, but she knew that Tammy didn't mind.

When she arrived at the cabin, J.D. was sitting on one of the mismatched porch chairs, with shadows beneath his eyes. Obviously he'd had a restless night. She'd tossed and turned, too.

"Doc was just here," he said.

"I know. I spoke to him. Why don't you want to get grief counseling?"

"It won't do any good."

"How do you know it won't?"

"Counseling won't bring Kimie back." He frowned into the sun. "Why didn't I dream about her last night? Why didn't she appear to me? I wanted her to, so damned badly."

She wasn't able to answer his questions. "When I

told Donna what you were hoping for, she called it an angel dream."

"That's nice. I like that."

"I think so, too." She sat beside him. "And there's still time to dream about her. You can stay at the cabin for as long as you need to."

"What if it doesn't happen?"

"Don't lose hope."

"My hope ended on the day she died. Besides, who am I trying to kid? How is a dream going to help? Even if she came to see me, she would only disappear again."

She didn't know what to say to comfort him. She wasn't able to comfort herself, either.

He left his chair, and the timeworn planks that made up the porch creaked beneath his feet. He stood beside the chipped wood rail, with the Flying B as his backdrop.

Jenna stayed seated and studied him. He was dressed in his original clothes, the jeans and shirt he'd been wearing on the afternoon she'd found him stumbling along the road. His hair was tousled, too, most likely from running his hands through it, also mirroring how he'd looked that day. She'd been attracted to him from the start, but she'd never imagined falling in love with him. Nor could she have predicted what his memories would unveil.

He said, "I called Deputy Tobbs earlier, before Doc came to see me. Now that the police know who I am, they're going to run a search on my stolen credit cards, my cell phone, my vehicle and everything else that might lead them to the carjackers. In the meantime, I need to apply for a temporary license and replacement credit cards. After I get my new ID, I can go to the bank and withdraw the money I owe you. I'm going to get a new cell, too, and buy a used truck."

"Did you contact your bank?"

He nodded. "My investment account is secure, like I assumed it would be."

She couldn't help but ask, "Did you tell Deputy Tobbs about your past? Did you tell him about Kimie?"

"Yes, and he said that he was sorry. That's what people always say."

"Because they are sorry."

"I know. But to me, they've become empty words. I've heard them more times than I could ever count." He changed the subject. "I'm still interested in hearing about your meeting with your dad. Will you tell me about it now?"

"Yes, of course." She relayed the details to him.

"Your Dad and Savannah were in love? None of us saw that coming."

"No, we didn't, and neither did they. Neither of them expected to feel that way about each other." She crossed her arms over her chest, hugging herself in a protective manner. Then she asked, "When did you know that you loved Kimie?"

"I don't recall the exact moment. But it happened easily." He frowned. "Everything came easily to me then. I lived a charmed life. Supportive parents, a thriving horse farm, a great girlfriend that I was looking forward to marrying."

Jenna kept questioning him, her curiosity too intense to ignore. "How did you propose?"

"The usual way, I guess. I bought a ring, took her out to dinner and popped the question." He smiled a little. "I wasn't nervous because I knew she would say yes."

"Where was the wedding?"

"On the farm." He gazed out at the Flying B. "This would be a nice place for a wedding, too."

Her throat went dry. She could imagine marrying him here. "Donna is working on making it into a wedding location. She's designing a garden with a gazebo for those types of events."

He kept gazing at the ranch. "That sounds pretty."

"It will be."

He turned to look at her. "When I'm gone, I'm going to envision you in the gazebo with your groom by your side, taking the vows you've always wanted to take."

Tears banked her eyes. "And how should I envision you, J.D., drifting from town to town, lonely and filled with despair? You should stay here. You should live on the Flying B and make this your home."

"I can't."

"You could if you wanted to. Hugh would be glad to create a permanent position for you. You're an asset to the ranch."

"It would never work. Besides, it would be weird later when your husband is around."

Her husband? A stranger who no longer mattered? Her resolve snapped. "You're the man I want. *You.* Damn it, I love you, J.D.!" The crimson-hot admission flew out of her mouth so quickly, so violently, it could have been blood.

The image made her think of Kimie, and she flinched from the visual. His wife, dead on the convenience-store floor, soaked in red.

J.D. reacted just as badly. He gripped the railing behind him so tightly he was probably getting splinters from the wood. She waited for him to speak.

When he did, his expression was as taut as his hands. "Don't love me. Please, don't."

"I didn't mean for it to happen."

"Oh, Jenna." He returned to his seat. "You promised you wouldn't get attached." His tone was sad, not accusatory, but that only exaggerated her pain.

"I tried not to."

He leaned forward and put his forehead against hers. Her pulse jumped like a rocket. His skin was incredibly warm, and he was close enough to kiss. She envied Kimie for how desperately he'd loved her. That made Jenna's pain more pronounced, too. Envying a dead woman.

"You and I aren't meant to be," he told her, his breaths whispering across her face.

"I wish we were."

"So do I. But I can't be the man you need."

He pulled back, leaving her bereft. She merely sat there, aware of how broken she must look—glassy-eyed, unblinking.

"I'm sorry," he said, then scoffed at his own words. "Sorry. As if that helps, right?"

"Actually, it does. A little." Unlike him, she longed to be consoled. Regardless, she got to her feet. She couldn't remain on his porch, torturing herself with his presence. "We should probably keep our distance now."

"I'll try to get everything in order as soon as I can. Then I can leave, and you can try to forget that you were ever with me."

She shook her head. "I'll never forget, J.D."

"Nor will I," he replied as she walked away. "Never again."

* * *

J.D. followed through. He got his license, his new truck, a cell phone and everything else as quickly as possible. And now, on the day he was leaving, he made a point of saying goodbye to everyone on the ranch. He'd spent the morning with the ranch hands, portions of the afternoon with Doc and Tammy, and now, as dusk neared, he prepared to see Jenna.

He knew she was in the barn, avoiding him and working her tail off. That was mostly what she'd been doing since she'd told him that she loved him.

He never should've started the affair with her. He had no right to mess with her feelings when his had been so damned jumbled. A man with amnesia wasn't what Jenna needed. Of course a man with horrific memories wasn't what she needed, either. He was no good for her, either way.

J.D. entered the barn and headed for the section of the stables that housed the school horses. When he saw her, he released a rough breath. She was cleaning the hooves of one of the new geldings. She looked intent on her task, too intent, too focused. She was well aware that this was the day he was leaving, with no plan to ever come back.

He waited until she finished with the hooves, then he said her name, softer than he should have. "Jenna."

She glanced up, and their gazes met.

"J.D." She spoke his name just as softly.

He moved closer, and she exited the gelding's stall and met him in the breezeway.

"My truck is all packed," he said.

"So this is it?"

"Yes." The end. Their final farewell. "I don't know

where I'm going. I'm just going to drive and see where the road takes me."

"It's supposed to rain later. A quick summer storm."

Somehow that seemed fitting. "I can handle the rain."

"Just be careful."

As their conversation faded, he looked around at the barn. They'd never crept out here on a moonlit night to make love. Heaven help him, he still had fantasies of Jenna with hay in her hair. He longed to kiss her goodbye, to feel her lips against his, but he refrained from suggesting it, knowing it would only make his departure more difficult.

Instead he said, "I never did have that dream. But it's probably my own fault for not believing that it would matter, anyway. Or maybe Kimie is just too far away to connect with me." He was beyond trying to figure anything out.

"Did you have any pictures of her in your truck? Did those get stolen, too?"

"I had a photograph in my wallet of the two of us together." So far the police had yet to solve his case, and he doubted that even if his vehicle was recovered, his belongings would still be in it. "But I have more pictures of her. The rest of them are in my safe-deposit box, back in the town where we lived."

She glanced at his hand. "Did you ever wear a wedding ring?"

"I did when she was alive."

"What did you do with it after she died?"

"I buried it with her."

"You buried everything with her—your heart, your soul, your life."

"I know, but I can't cope any other way."

"I think she would want a happier existence for you."

"I spent eleven years with Kimie, five as her boyfriend and six as her husband. Being happy without her isn't in my realm of thinking."

Yet, suddenly, he was worried about missing Jenna as badly as he'd been missing Kimie, and Jenna was still alive, standing right before him and willing to be his partner. But he wouldn't be good for her, he reiterated. She deserved someone new and fresh, not someone damaged from the past.

She said, "You should get going before the rain starts."

Yes, he should. But it wasn't the rain that concerned him. He needed to get away from Jenna before the thought of losing her worsened. He didn't have amnesia anymore, but he was as mixed-up as ever.

"Bye, Jenna."

"Goodbye, J.D. Joel Daniel," she added, using his birth name. "Strange, how I got your initials right."

"You got everything right. It's me that screwed things up."

"That isn't true. I'm the one who fell in love when I wasn't supposed to."

"People can't help falling in love." He took a chance and drew her into his arms, wrapping her in a hug that made him want to stay.

Jenna clutched his shoulders, holding him like a lifeline. Only he wasn't her salvation. Someday, the right man would come along and fill her with joy.

He ended the embrace, and they gazed at each other in a blaze of pain.

He walked away. She didn't follow him, and he didn't glance back to see what she was doing. But he suspected that her eyes were rimmed with tears.

He strode swiftly to his truck, got behind the wheel and steered it in the direction of nowhere, realizing that he was in love with Jenna, too.

Yes, by God, he *loved* her. Still, he didn't turn his vehicle around. He kept going.

Hours later, he drove straight into the rain. He drove and drove, the windshield wipers clapping, washing the water aside, only to have it return again.

As the night got darker and wetter, he squinted at the misty highway. Then, finally, he stopped at an average little motel, ready to rest his weary bones.

And when he crawled into bed, it was with Jenna Byrd on his mind.

Jenna went to bed that night in the dream cabin. She wanted to sleep where J.D. had been sleeping, to inhale his scent on the sheets, to hug a pillow to her body and imagine that he was holding her the way he used to.

As she closed her eyes, she wondered where he was. She missed him beyond reason. But she knew that she would.

She slept fitfully, dozing in and out of repose. But eventually she fell into uninterrupted slumber.

And dreamed.

She saw herself on the Flying B, walking barefoot through the grass, only there were clouds billowing near her feet, hovering just above the ground. She couldn't feel them, but they went on forever, stretching beyond the boundaries of her vision.

She kept walking toward something or someone, uncertain of her final destination.

Then the scene changed, and she was on another ranch. No, not a ranch. A horse-breeding farm. Outdoor pens shimmered with mares and foals, frolicking among the grass-level clouds, which looked more like spun sugar here.

Then she remembered J.D.'s youthful dream and the boy he'd once been, with sugar cubes in his pocket. This was his horse farm, she realized. His old place.

Jenna glanced across the farm and saw a dark-haired woman coming toward her. Kimie. J.D.'s murdered wife. There was no gunshot wound, no blood, nothing to indicate that she was dead, except the sweet heavenly groundcover.

Small and lean with exotic features, Kimie wore a simple ensemble—a denim shirt and blue jeans. Like Jenna, her feet were bare. Only she wasn't alone. She carried a child on her hip. A little girl, no more than two, with wavy blond hair, similar to Jenna's. Clearly, she represented one of the many foster kids Kimie and J.D. had hoped to adopt, and Kimie had chosen her because she was a delicate reminder of why J.D. had become fascinated with Jenna's sunny-colored hair.

Kimie stopped and put the child down, smoothed her pink dress and patted her on the bottom. The toddler smiled and started running toward Jenna, going as fast as her sturdy little legs would go. She tripped and disappeared in the cotton candy clouds. A millisecond later, she popped back up and continued to run.

Instinctively, Jenna got down on her knees and opened her arms, welcoming the child into her embrace. Scooping her up, she hugged her close.

Kimie didn't come any closer. She watched from afar. Then she lifted her hand in a wave and vanished, an angel returning to her ethereal world and taking the clouds with her.

The little girl said, "Bye-bye," in a tiny voice, making tears come to Jenna's eyes.

The scene changed again, and she and the child were back on the Flying B. Jenna kissed the little girl's cheek, and more children appeared.

Hundreds of them.

They were everywhere, chattering and playing. All ages, all sizes, all nationalities. Every adoptable foster child in Texas was here, she thought, along with potential adoptees from other countries. Kimie had sent them, offering them to Jenna.

But what about J.D.? He was nowhere to be seen.

Still clutching the original girl, Jenna looked for him. The other children helped search, too, running all over the ranch, shouting his name. But no one found him.

Soon Jenna awakened, shrouded in darkness. She reached out to gather the children, but they were gone, even the little one she'd been carrying.

She turned on the light and burst into tears. She wanted to call J.D., but she couldn't. He hadn't given her his number. He was unreachable.

Just like in the dream.

Chapter 15

J.D. woke up with a start. He'd just had the most vivid dream, only he wasn't in it. But Jenna and Kimie were, along with scores of kids. They'd been calling his name at the end of the dream, but he wasn't able to answer because he wasn't there. He was here, alone in a pitch-black motel room.

He switched on the lamp and squinted at the invasion of the light. When he'd hoped for a dream, he'd never fathomed anything like this—Kimie and Jenna together, with depictions of the children he and Kimie had lost.

Jenna had looked so natural, holding the toddler in her arms. And his wife—clever, beautiful Kimie—making certain that the first child who appeared was blonde, like Jenna.

It didn't take a psychologist to figure out what it meant. Kimie was telling J.D. that she approved of Jenna, as a woman and a future mother, but Kimie wasn't telling J.D. what to do. The choice was his. He could keep drifting or return to Jenna and create a family with her.

Really, it was a no-brainer and something he should have done without Kimie's intervention. But he'd been locked so deeply in his pain, he'd run off, even after he'd acknowledged to himself that he loved Jenna.

He glanced at the clock. It was four in the morning, or nearly four. 3:56 a.m.

He got out of bed. He wanted to call Jenna, but at this ungodly hour? It didn't seem right to rip her from sleep. Still, he wanted to hear her voice, to tell her that he'd made a mistake and that he loved her.

Would she appreciate his dream? Or would she feel slighted that he hadn't come to his senses until after Kimie had appeared?

There was only one way to know. He needed to call her. But he fixed a cup of coffee first, waiting for daylight.

And it was the longest wait of his life. He felt as if he might go mad with it. The numbers on the clock moved so slowly, he considering yelling at them to hurry.

To keep himself occupied, he opened the window and peered outside. The ground was damp with rain, but drops were no longer falling.

The wait continued.

Finally, *finally,* dawn broke through the gray-scattered sky, and he lifted his cell phone from the nightstand and dialed Jenna's cell. It rang and rang, until her voice mail came on. He didn't leave a message; he wanted to talk to her in person.

But he couldn't just sit around until she became available. He was already going stir-crazy. He took a shower and got dressed. Grabbing his bag, he made a beeline for his truck. He was hours away from the Flying B, but by damn, he was going there, as quickly as he could.

Then a terrible thought struck him. What if something deterred him? What if he was in an accident? He knew how quickly the unexpected could happen. Look at Kimie. After a hectic night of birthing foals, she'd dashed down to the corner store to buy a few things. Never in a million years could J.D. have imagined her not coming back.

Or coming back in a box.

His mind drifted to her funeral—the scrolled-wood coffin, the flickering candles, the wreaths of flowers, her family clutching each other and crying. J.D. hadn't cried, not in front of everyone. He'd kept his tears private. But he'd been inconsolable, nonetheless.

There were no guarantees that he was going to live happily-ever-after with Jenna. Something could happen to Jenna as easily as it could happen to him.

The thought of losing her someday nearly sent him into a panic. But he forced himself to breathe. He was sitting in the parking lot, obsessing about the darkness associated with death, even after he'd seen an angelic version of Kimie in a dream.

Doc had been right. J.D. needed grief counseling.

And he needed to leave Jenna a message, too, to tell her that he loved her, just in case he never made it back to the ranch. He dialed the number again, preparing for her voice mail. But Jenna answered.

"Hello?" she said in the customary way, and her voice was the most beautiful sound he'd ever heard.

"It's me," he replied. "J.D."

"Oh, my God." She gasped. "I'm so glad it's you. I

slept in the dream cabin last night, and I had a dream where I was searching for you. Kimie was there in the beginning, and she…"

Jenna went on to describe the dream J.D. had experienced. Every detail was exact. Wonderfully astounded, he listened while she relayed every moment.

Afterward, he said, "Me, too."

"You, too, what?"

"I had the same dream."

The shock in her voice was evident. "You did?"

"Identical. I woke up with you and the kids calling my name." He told her his interpretation of it. Then he said, "I love you, Jenna, and I shouldn't have walked away. I knew that I loved you when I left. But I was scared. I'm still scared."

"Of what?"

"Losing each other."

"We aren't going to lose each other, J.D. We belong together."

"I belonged with Kimie, too, and look what happened to her." He paused to quell his shiver. "I'm going to get the grief counseling Doc recommended. I know I need it."

"Maybe that's the most important message Kimie was trying to convey."

That until he found himself, no one could find him, either? "I'm going to learn to tackle my fears, and I want to be with you while I'm working on it. I want to be with you for as long as God allows."

"Then come to me. Come home now."

"I will. I am." He started his engine, destined for the Flying B.

* * *

Jenna waited for J.D. at the dream cabin. In fact, she sat on the porch, wanting to see his truck as it rolled up.

Hours later, he was there, climbing out of his vehicle and coming toward her. She held out her arms, and he enfolded her in his. They held each other so tightly, air whooshed from her lungs, but she didn't care. All that mattered was that they were together.

He kissed her, and she melted from the feeling. It was the most powerful kiss they'd exchanged, the connection warm and soulful. When it ended, they caressed each other's faces, fingers gliding over familiar features.

"Will you marry me?" he asked. "Not right away. After I get the counseling I need."

Her heart soared. "You know I will."

He flashed his crooked grin. "And adopt hundreds of children with me?"

Shc laughed. She knew he was referring to the kids in the dream. "I don't think Kimie meant for us to take all of them. But we'll adopt as many as we can."

He lowered a hand to her stomach. "I'm going to plant some babes in your womb, too." He grinned again. "You're going to be one busy little mama."

"And you'll be a busy papa."

"Maybe we really will end up with hundreds of them."

"Goodness, can you imagine?"

"Not really, no." But he was still grinning. "We can use my money to build a house. A big, kid-friendly house."

"On the Flying B," she added. "There's plenty of room for us to put down roots here."

"We should have the ceremony on the ranch, too. In

the garden and gazebo Donna is designing. Ours will be the first Flying B wedding."

"Unless Doc and Tammy beat us to it."

He shrugged. "It's okay if they do. They already have a jump start on the engagement. But it's going to be fun to plan our wedding. 'Let's Make Love' is going to be our song."

"It already is." It was from the moment they'd danced to it at Lucy's. "I'll wear a long silky dress and those old-fashioned western boots. The kind that lace up the front."

"That works for me. I can already see you in my mind. The elegant country bride."

She thought about his other wife. The lovely young woman in the dream. The lady who'd blessed them with the gift of hope. "What did Kimie wear when you married her?"

"Her dress had a Japanese flair. Her mother made it for her. My mom got involved, too, and beaded a Native design on my jacket. I can show you the pictures from our wedding album when I go to my safe-deposit box and bring everything here."

"I'd love to see them." She was thrilled that he was able to talk about Kimie in a positive way. It was a good start and was only going to get better. "Do you think your parents are going to like me?"

"Are you kidding? They're going to adore you, and they're going to be grateful that I'm not drifting all over Texas any more. I know they've been praying for me to make a new life."

"And now you are."

"Because of you." He looped her into his arms again. "I'm going to make sure that our bed is filled with rose petals on our wedding night. I want to make that fantasy happen for you."

"You still owe me a naughty night in the barn, too."

"I know. I thought about that when I left the ranch. How we hadn't done it. How I'd been missing out on seeing you with hay in your hair." He nuzzled her cheek. "We could do it tonight."

Sweet chills shimmied up and down her spine. She couldn't imagine a more romantic homecoming. She wanted to do luscious things with J.D.

Tonight, and every night thereafter.

They slipped into an empty stall at midnight, and J.D. spread a blanket on the ground. He'd brought a battery-operated lantern, too. He kept it on low, so it shone gently.

Jenna stood quietly, watching him with a loving expression, her hair tumbling over her shoulders and her dress flowing around booted ankles. She'd deliberately worn something that would be easy to remove, and he knew that she was naked underneath.

This was their moment. Their fantasy.

He extended his hand, and she came forward, joining him on the blanket. They kissed soft and slow, immersed in a bond only lovers could share.

He lifted her dress above her head. She'd become everything to him, everything good and pure. His future wife. The mother of his future children. The woman who loved him enough to help him heal.

J.D. didn't get undressed all the way. He merely opened his shirt and undid his pants.

"That's cheating," she said.

"Not if someone happens by. I can right myself real quick."

She lay there, all sweet and seductive, bare, except for her boots. Looking up at him, she asked, "What about me?"

"You, I'll wrap in the blanket."

"And ruin my good-girl reputation? That's not fair." But she was smiling as she said it.

"Your reputation won't be ruined." He smiled, too. "I'm going to marry you, remember? Right here on the ranch." He realized that he'd omitted a significant part of the wedding plans. "Do you want to shop for a ring tomorrow?" He held her hand up to the light. "A diamond we can pick out together."

"Of course I want to shop with you."

"We'll go bright and early. I want you to have a ring as soon as possible." To reflect their commitment and symbolize their unity. "God gave me a second chance to be with someone I love."

"And He gave me the man from my list." She pressed her lips to his ear. "I can't show it to you, not at the moment. But I can tell you what's on it."

Talk about sexy, whispering to him about her infamous list. "Yes, ma'am, you can. But I'm already familiar with some of it." Things she'd mentioned over the course of their affair. He recited what he knew. "You want an honest, marriage-minded, family oriented man who shares your love of horses and embraces the Flying B as his home."

"So far so good." She tugged him closer. "Chivalry is high on my priorities. Kindness, too. He must be giving and caring."

"That's understandable. Is there more?"

"Strong work ethic. Integrity. I also appreciate a man who has a sense of humor."

"Do you?" He circled her nipples, coaxing them into pearly pink nubs. "Because I seem to recall my sense of humor grating on you."

She made a breathy sound. "Yours is exceptionally wicked. It took some getting used to."

"Glad we cleared that up." He caressed her curves, up, down and all around. "What else?"

She leaned into him. "His physical attributes—tall, dark and handsome."

"That's a cliché."

"Not to me. I'm partial to dark hair and dark eyes."

He slipped his fingers between her legs and elicited a moan. "Anything else?"

"A man who knows how to make me…"

"Make you what?"

"Orgasm."

"You're a bad girl for including that." He sent her a dastardly smile. He'd always wondered if she'd put her sexual preferences on it. He'd even teased her in that regard, just as he couldn't help teasing her now, rubbing her most sensitive spot. "A very bad girl."

She arched under his ministrations. "If I'm going to spend the rest of my life with someone, he needs to know what's what."

He heightened the foreplay. "Like this?"

"Yes, just like that."

He continued to pleasure her, with his hands, his mouth. In response, she tunneled her fingers through his hair and lifted her hips, rife with sensual energy.

When he gave her the Big O, she muffled her excitement, biting down on her bottom lip to keep from crying out.

J.D. couldn't be more aroused. He snagged the condom from his pocket, shoved his jeans down, sheathed himself and entered her, full and deep. He made damned sure that they rolled off the blanket, too, and she got bits of hay in her hair.

They made love in a fever, each touch wild and thrilling. Heat pounded in his loins. Need shivered through his veins. She kissed him so hard, he dragged her on to his lap, encouraging her to ride him to completion.

Afterward, they collapsed in a heap of tangled limbs. Once they were able to move, she put her dress back on, and he fastened his clothes.

Quietly, they returned to the dream cabin. Not to dream, but to sleep. The new couple. In each other's arms.

Where they belonged.

A week later, Jenna, Tammy and Donna went into town, where they met with Roland Walker for an update. He told him exactly what he'd been doing to search Savannah, and even though he still didn't have any news of her, he was convinced that he would locate her. Roland was a confident man.

He was also a tad gruff, but Jenna liked him. She understood why Tex had hired him at one time, too. The P.I. was a good old boy, much like Tex had been.

Jenna considered Tex and his sons. By now, Dad had apologized to Uncle William, and they were working on making amends. They'd even planned a fishing trip.

She glanced over at Tammy. Her cousin was glad, of

course, that their dads were trying to be brothers. Jenna was, too. But Donna hadn't said much about it.

After their meeting with Roland, they stopped by the local ice-cream parlor, shared a cafe table and ate dessert. Tammy got two scoops of vanilla, smothered in fruit toppings and colorful sprinkles, Jenna went for a banana split and Donna got frozen yogurt.

Donna, always the odd girl out.

Jenna and Tammy were both engaged and living at the Flying B, the future B and B, with their men. But Donna was busting her butt to get the heck out of Texas and return to New York, where she would continue to work day and night, trying to resume her city-girl career.

It made Jenna feel guilty for being so happy, so settled. The marquee-cut diamond on her finger was dazzling, and she was elated to have it. Tammy had a gorgeous engagement ring, too.

Again, Donna with nothing.

"I have something I want to show you," Jenna said to her sister. She reached into her purse and handed over her list.

Donna began reading. "What in the world is this?"

Jenna explained when she'd first written it, how she'd revised it to include the Flying B, how important it was to her, how J.D. had called it her magic and finally, how J.D. turned out to have every single quality she'd imagined in a man.

"That's wonderful," her sister said, "but I don't see how this has anything to do with me."

"I wanted you to see it because I wanted you to be part of it somehow. But I was also hoping that it would inspire you. Not to find a husband, necessarily, but to find whatever it is you need to be joyful."

"Really? Oh." Donna hugged the list close to her heart. "No one has ever said anything like that to me before."

"I should have said it a long time ago. You're my sister, and I love you."

Was Donna holding back tears? She blinked her glamorous lashes, a bit too rapidly. "I love you, too."

Tammy smiled around her next bite. Then she said, "Can I get in on some of that love?"

Jenna grinned and leaned toward her cousin. "Of course you can. Tex knew exactly what he was doing when he brought us together. We're the best trio ever."

"We absolutely are." Tammy ate more ice cream to celebrate.

Jenna glanced at Donna. "You know, sis. It's okay if you secretly want a husband."

Donna shook her head. She laughed a little laugh. "Seriously, Jenna. Where do you come up with this stuff?"

"Most women want to get married someday."

"I'm not most women."

That was true, but still…

"Well, whatever it is you want, I hope you attain it."

"Thank you. That means a lot to me. But all I want is to get my career back on track."

Following Tammy's lead, Jenna attacked the ice cream in her dish. Then she said to Donna, "Since J.D. and I aren't staying at the dream cabin anymore, you can sleep there now if you want."

"Whatever for?"

"To have a life-altering dream."

"I think I'll let nature take its course." Donna returned the list. "Why did you move out of the cabin?"

"It doesn't make sense for us to horde it." They were

living in the main house while he was working on the plans for their custom home. In fact, he was going to hire Aidan and Nathan to build it. "We have everything we need."

"I'm happy for you," Donna told her. She turned to Tammy. "And you, too."

Jenna tucked the paper back into her purse. Donna might not want a husband, but that was what Jenna wanted for her.

Eventually.

For now, a hot fling with a sinful playboy would do. She smiled to herself. Maybe after Caleb returned from his leave of absence, he would take Donna for a sexy spin. Then later, she could marry the right man, a polished New Yorker or whatever.

"We better get back to the ranch soon," Donna said. "I've got a slew of work to do."

Yep, Jenna thought, *if anyone needed a little fun, it was my sister.*

A short while later Donna got her wish and they were back at the ranch, each going her own way.

Jenna met up with J.D., where he'd just turned some horses out into the arena, and he rewarded her with a tender kiss. Although he was making great strides on his own, he was scheduled to begin his grief counseling soon. Determined, Jenna thought, to keep his fears at bay and live life to the fullest. She couldn't be prouder.

Luckily, the robbery was behind him, too. The police had arrested the offenders, discovering that they were part of a carjacking ring that had been committing similar crimes all over the country. J.D. had already pressed charges, and Jenna was glad it was over.

In the quiet, they both turned toward the arena and watched the equine activity.

Then J.D. said, "How would you feel if I went back to breeding horses? Not a full-time operation, but just enough to bring some of my expertise to the Flying B. After the B and B is underway and after our house is built."

"I think that's a great idea." She remembered the precious foals she'd seen in the dream at his previous farm. "Mares and their babies."

"To go with Mama Jenna and our babies." He reached out and cradled her in his arms.

She put her head against his shoulder, and they stood in the sun, a wondrous future unfolding before them.

* * * * *

USA TODAY bestselling author **Judy Duarte** has written over forty books for Harlequin Special Edition, earned two RITA® Award nominations, won two Maggie Awards and received a National Readers' Choice Award. When she's not cooped up in her writing cave, she enjoys traveling with her husband and spending quality time with her grandchildren. You can learn more about Judy and her books at her website, judyduarte.com, or at Facebook.com/judyduartenovelist.

Books by Judy Duarte

Harlequin Special Edition

Rocking Chair Rodeo

Roping in the Cowgirl
The Bronc Rider's Baby

The Fortunes of Texas: The Secret Fortunes

From Fortune to Family Man

The Fortunes of Texas: All Fortune's Children

Wed by Fortune

Brighton Valley Cowboys

The Cowboy's Double Trouble
Having the Cowboy's Baby
The Boss, the Bride & the Baby

Return to Brighton Valley

The Soldier's Holiday Homecoming
The Bachelor's Brighton Valley Bride
The Daddy Secret

The Fortunes of Texas: Cowboy Country

A Royal Fortune

The Fortunes of Texas: Welcome to Horseback Hollow

A House Full of Fortunes!

Visit the Author Profile page at Harlequin.com for more titles.

THE RANCHER'S HIRED FIANCÉE

JUDY DUARTE

To Mark Winch, who reads every book I write.

I hope you enjoy this one, too, Mark.

Chapter 1

Catherine Loza napped in a child's bedroom at the Walker family's ranch in Texas, dreaming of sold-out nights on Broadway, the heady sound of applause and the pounding of her heart after a well-executed performance.

She took a bow, then straightened and glanced out into the audience, only to see an empty stall and a bale of straw in an illuminated old barn, where a group of children clapped their hands in delight.

Their faces were a blur until two of them glided toward the stage, greeting her with red rosebuds, their long stems free of thorns.

Recognizing Sofia and Stephen, Dan and Eva Walker's youngest twins, Catherine knelt and received the flowers. Then the darling two-year-olds wrapped their pudgy arms around her and placed soft, moist kisses on her cheeks, on her forehead, on her chin.

How strange, she thought, but so sweet.

She'd no more than thanked them and sent them on their way when she heard a light tapping noise in the distance.

Thoughts and visions tumbled together in her sleepy mind—until another knock sounded, this time on the bedroom door.

"Yes?" she said, realizing she'd dozed off after reading a storybook to the children. Now, as she scanned the empty room, she saw that they'd both slipped off, leaving her to nap alone.

Eva opened the door and peered into the darkened bedroom. "I'm sorry to bother you, but we're having company for dinner tonight, and I thought you might want to know."

Catherine glanced out the window, which was shuttered tight, only a faint light creeping through the slats. She tried to guess the time of day but didn't have a clue—other than it was obviously nearing the dinner hour.

"A lot of help I am," Catherine said. "I wasn't the one who was supposed to fall asleep."

Eva chuckled softly. "Sofia and Stephen woke up a few minutes ago. Now they're in the kitchen, coloring and playing with their sticker books."

Catherine never had been one to nap during the day. Apparently the fresh air, sunshine and the rural Texas setting had a calming effect on her.

"If you'd like to rest a little longer," Eva said, "it's not a problem. You've been burning the candle at both ends for so long. Your body probably needs the sleep."

"Who's coming for dinner tonight?" Catherine asked.

"Ray Mendez. He's a local rancher and a neighbor. In fact, he'll be here any minute."

"Thanks for the heads-up." As Eva closed the bedroom door, Catherine raked her fingers through her hair, her nails catching on a couple of snags in her long curls. She probably looked a fright, with eyes puffy from sleep, but she wouldn't stress about it. This was supposed to be a vacation of sorts.

Ever since her arrival on the ranch, she'd decided to go au natural—no makeup, no fancy hairstyles. She was also kicking back for a change—no schedules, no grueling workouts, no rehearsals. And quite frankly, she was looking forward to having a break from the hectic life she'd once known in Manhattan.

Catherine rolled to the side of the bed and got to her feet. Then she straightened the pillows, as well as the coverlet, before opening the door and stepping into the hall.

She'd taken only two steps when the doorbell rang. The rancher had just arrived. Wanting to make herself useful, she detoured to answer the door. What had Eva said his name was? Ray something.

Catherine had never met any of the Walkers' neighbors, but she assumed Ray must be one of Hank's friends. Hank, Dan's elderly uncle, who'd once owned the ranch and now lived in a guesthouse Dan had built for him, always ate dinner with them in the main dining room.

Not seeing anyone else in the room, Catherine opened the front door.

She expected to see a weathered rancher who resembled Dan's uncle, a sweet but crotchety old cowboy who reminded her of Robert Duvall when he'd played in *Lonesome Dove* or *Open Range*. But nothing had prepared her for the tall, dark-haired visitor who stood on the porch.

The man, whose expression revealed that he was just as surprised to see her as she was to see him, didn't look anything like the grizzled Texan she'd envisioned just moments before. At first glance, he bore enough resemblance to Antonio Banderas to be his younger brother—all decked out in Western wear, of course.

A sense of awkwardness rose up inside, and she tried to tamp it down the best she could. She might be dressed like a barefoot street urchin in a pair of gray sweatpants, an old NYU T-shirt and no makeup to speak of, but she was actually an accomplished woman who'd performed on Broadway several times in the past—and would do so again.

"I'm Catherine Loza," she said. "You must be Ray…?"

"Mendez." His voice held the slightest bit of a Spanish accent, which made him all the more intriguing.

She reached up to flick a wild strand of her sleep-tousled curls from her eyes, only to feel something papery stuck to her face. She peeled it off, and when she looked at her fingers to see what it was, she spotted a child's butterfly sticker.

Oh, for Pete's sake. How had that gotten there?

It must have been on the bedspread or pillow, and she'd probably rolled over on it.

Determined to shake the flush from her face and to pretend that her ankles weren't bound together with duct tape, that her brain hadn't been abducted by aliens, Catherine forced herself to step forward and reach out to shake the neighboring rancher's hand. "It's nice to meet you, Ray. Eva said you'd be coming to dinner tonight. Please come in."

The handsome rancher's smile deepened, lighting his eyes, which were a vibrant shade of green.

As he released his grip on her hand, leaving her skin warm and tingling, he lifted a lazy index finger and peeled another sticker from her face.

Her lips parted as he showed her a little pink heart.

"You missed a couple of them," he said.

Huh? A couple of…what?

He removed a gold star from over her brow and a unicorn from her chin.

Catherine blinked back her surprise, as well as her embarrassment. Then she swiped her hand first over one cheek and then the other, discovering that either Sofia or Stephen had decorated her face while she'd slept.

Goodness. What else had the twins done to her while she'd been asleep? Surely they hadn't used their Magic Markers on her, too?

She hadn't felt the least bit self-conscious in years, but it all came rushing back at her now. She must look like a clown. What must the man be thinking?

Calling on her acting skills and her ability to ad-lib on stage, she gave a little shrug, as if this sort of thing happened all the time. "Well, what do you know? The sticker fairies stopped by while I napped."

Ray tossed her a crooked grin, humor sparking in his eyes. "You've got to watch out for those fairies, especially on the Walker Ranch. There's no telling what they'll do next."

"I'm afraid he's right about that," Dan said as he entered the living room. "Our younger twins can be little rascals at times."

Before Catherine could respond, Dan greeted his

friend with a handshake, then invited him to take a seat, suggesting that she do the same.

But there was no way Catherine wanted to remain in the living room looking like a ragamuffin, so she said, "I'd better help Eva in the kitchen."

"I was just in there," Dan said. "And she has everything under control."

Catherine didn't care where she went—to the kitchen, her bedroom or the barn. All she wanted to do was to disappear from the handsome rancher's sight until she could find a mirror before dinner.

"Well, since Eva doesn't need my help, I'll just go freshen up." She lobbed Ray Mendez her best, unaffected smile. "It was nice meeting you."

"The pleasure was mine."

The sound of the word *pleasure* on the lips of a man who not only resembled a Latin lover but sounded like one, too, was enough to knock her little Texas world off its axis.

And until she flew back to Manhattan, she'd do whatever it took to keep her feet on solid ground in Brighton Valley.

One screwed-up world was more than she cared to handle.

Ray Mendez had no idea who Catherine Loza was, why she'd been napping this late in the afternoon or why she'd been included to have dinner at the Walkers' ranch. He watched her leave the room, turn down the hall and walk toward the bedrooms.

The minute she was out of hearing range, he turned to his neighbor and friend. "You're not starting in on me, too, are you?"

"*Starting in* on you? What do you mean?"

Ray crossed his arms and tensed. "Is this dinner supposed to be a setup?"

Dan looked a little confused by the question—or rather the accusation. "A *setup?* You mean, with you and *Catherine?* No, I wouldn't do that." Then he glanced toward the kitchen, as if realizing his pretty wife might have had a plan of her own.

But why wouldn't she? Every time Ray turned around, one of the women in town was trying to play matchmaker.

"Eva called and asked you to dinner because we hadn't seen you in a while," Dan said. "Why would you think we had anything else in mind?"

"Because ever since word got out that my divorce was final, the local matchmakers have come out of the woodwork, determined to find the perfect second wife for me. And the last thing I'm looking for right now is romance. I've got my hands full trying to run my ranch from a distance and finish out the term of the previous mayor."

"Has it been that bad?" Dan asked.

"You have no idea."

"For the record," Dan said, "Catherine is a great woman. She's beautiful, talented and has a heart of gold. But she's just visiting us. Her life is in New York, and yours is here. So it would be a waste of time to try my hand at matchmaking."

That was a relief. Thank God Ray's friends hadn't joined every marriage-minded woman in town—or her well-intentioned best friend, mother or neighbor.

He unfolded his arms and let down his guard.

As he did so, he glanced down the hall just as Catherine returned with her hair combed, those wild platinum curls controlled by a clip of some kind.

She'd changed into a pair of black jeans and a crisp, white blouse—nothing fancy. She'd also applied a light coat of pink lipstick and slipped on a pair of ballet flats.

For a moment, Ray wondered if she had romance on her mind. But the cynical thought passed as quickly as it had struck.

If Catherine had expected to meet someone special tonight, she wouldn't have opened the door with her hair a mess, stickers all over her face and no makeup whatsoever.

Although he had to admit, she'd looked pretty darn cute standing at the door, blue eyes wide, lips parted….

As Catherine crossed through the living room on her way to the kitchen, she gave him a passing smile.

And when she was again out of hearing range, Ray turned back to Dan. "Where'd you meet her?"

"She used to be Jenny's roommate."

Dan's sister, Jenny Walker, had left Brighton Valley after graduating from high school. She'd gone to college in the Midwest, majored in music or dance and moved to New York, where she'd done some singing and acting off-Broadway.

About eight or nine years ago, Jenny gave birth to twins, although she died when Kevin and Kaylee were in kindergarten. Dan and Eva adopted the kids and were now raising them, as well as their own younger set of twins.

"Catherine has come out a time or two to visit," Dan added, "but she never stayed long. She's an actress and a dancer, so she usually has a Broadway show of some kind going on."

"Is that what she's doing here now? Visiting the kids?"

"Actually, this time I'm not sure how long she'll be with us. She broke up with some hot-shot producer back in New York and wanted to get away for a while. I don't know all of the details, but it really doesn't matter. She stepped up to the plate and helped me and the kids out when we really needed her, so I'm happy to return the favor now."

Ray raked his hand through his hair. "I'm sorry for jumping to conclusions. I should have known you wouldn't have invited me to come over with more than dinner on your mind."

Dan studied him for a moment. "Is the matchmaking really that bad?"

He chuffed. "I can't make it through a single day without someone trying to set me up with a single daughter, niece or neighbor. And that's not counting the unmarried ladies who approach me on their own behalf." Ray grumbled under his breath, wishing he'd stayed out of politics and had remained on his ranch full-time.

"Well, I guess that's to be expected." A grin tugged at one side of Dan's lips, and his eyes lit up with mirth. "You're not a bad-looking fellow. And you've got a little cash put away. I guess that makes you an eligible bachelor in anyone's book."

"Very funny." Ray had never been full of himself, but most women considered him to be the tall, dark and handsome type. He also had a head for business, which had allowed him to parlay a couple of inheritances into millions. As a result, he had more money and property than he could shake a stick at, something that made every unattached female between the ages of 18 and 40 seem to think he was a prime catch.

He could always give them the cold shoulder, but his mother had taught him to be polite and courteous—a habit he found hard to shake. Besides, he didn't know how to keep the women at arm's distance without alienating half the voters in town.

"To top it off," Dan added, "you being the mayor gives you a little more status than just being a run-of-the-mill Texas rancher, which the ladies undoubtedly find even more appealing."

Ray sighed. "That's the problem. I'm not looking for romance. And if the time ever comes that I'm interested again, I'm perfectly capable of finding a woman without help."

Dan, who'd been biting back a full-on smile, let it go and chuckled. "There's got to be a lot of guys who'd be happy to trade places with you."

"Maybe, but only for a couple of days. Then they'd get fed up, too. This has been going on since…well, since word got out that my divorce was final. And now I can hardly get any work done—in town or on the ranch."

"Why *not* date someone, just so word will spread that you're already taken?"

Ray shook his head. "No, I'm not going to do that. After the marriage I had, I'm steering clear of women in general. But even if I wanted to ask someone out, I don't have the time to add anything else to my calendar. As it is, I've been spending the bulk of my day driving back and forth to the ranch, making sure Mark and Darren have everything under control, then zipping back to town for one meeting or another."

"I don't blame you for not wanting to jump back into another relationship, especially after the hell Heather put you through over the past two years."

Dan had that right. Ray's ex-wife had not only cheated on him, she'd turned out to be a heartless gold digger. And after the long legal battle she'd waged, Ray wasn't about to make a mistake like that again.

"You know," Dan said, "it might not be a bad idea to spread the rumor that you're already taken. Maybe that way, the matchmaking mamas and their starry-eyed daughters will give you a break and let you get some work done."

"That's an idea, but as simple and easy as it sounds, I'm afraid it won't work."

"Why not?"

"Because I'd keep showing up alone at all the various community events I'm required to attend, and people will begin to realize the woman is only a myth. And then I'll be right back where I started. I'm afraid I'd need the real thing, and that would defeat the purpose of creating a fictitious woman."

"Too bad you can't rent an escort," Dan said.

"Yeah, right."

At that moment, Catherine reentered the living room and called Dan's name. "Eva said to tell you that dinner's ready. She's already called Hank, and he's heading over here now."

"Thanks," Dan said. "We'll be right there."

As Catherine returned to the kitchen, Ray watched the sway of her denim-clad hips. It was hard to imagine her as a woman who was at home on the stage, especially since she had a wholesome, girl-next-door appeal. But then again, she *was* an actress....

Suddenly, an idea began to form.

"How long does Catherine plan to be in town?" he asked.

"I'm not sure. Why?"

"Do you think she'd want a job?"

"Probably. Just this morning she mentioned that she'd like to find something part-time and temporary. Why?"

"Because I want to hire her, if she's interested."

"What did you have in mind? Something clerical?"

"No, it would be an acting job."

Dan looked confused. "I'm not following you."

A slow smile stretched across Ray's face. "I'd like to hire Catherine to be my fiancée."

After dinner and dessert had been served, Dan's uncle thanked Eva for another wonderful meal, then headed back to his place so he could watch his favorite TV show.

Eva sent the older twins to get ready for bed, then she and Dan gathered up the preschoolers and told them it was bath time, leaving Catherine and Ray in the dining room.

"Can I get you another cup of coffee?" Catherine asked.

"That sounds good. Thanks."

Minutes later she returned with the carafe and filled his cup, then her own.

"Dan told me that you might be interested in some part-time work," Ray said.

Catherine had no idea how long she'd be in Brighton Valley, but it would probably be at least a month. So she'd thought about trying to earn a little cash while she was here.

Of course, if truth be told, she didn't have many skills that would come in handy in a place like Brighton Valley.

"I'm interested," she said, lifting her coffee cup and

taking a sip. "As long as it was only temporary. Do you know of a position that's open?"

"Yes, I do. And it's probably right up your alley."

Catherine couldn't imagine what it might be. She was just about to ask for more details when she realized that Ray had zeroed in on her again, as if mesmerized or intrigued by her.

If she were in Manhattan, dressed to the nines, she might have taken his interest as a compliment. As it was, she didn't know what to think.

"What kind of job is it?" she asked.

"It's a little unorthodox," he admitted, "but it's only part-time, and the money's good."

"Who would I be working for? And what would I be doing?"

"You'd be working for me. I need an actress, and you'd be perfect for the part."

"I don't understand." Catherine lifted her cup and took another sip.

"I need a fiancée," Ray said.

Catherine choked on her coffee. "*Excuse* me?"

"I want people in town to think that I'm in a committed relationship. And Dan thinks you have the acting skills to pull it off."

"Why in the world would a man like you need to hire a girlfriend?" Once the words were off her tongue, she wanted to take them back. "I'm sorry," she said. "I'm not sure I'm following you."

"Okay, let me explain. I need a temporary escort to attend various community functions with me, and it would be best if people had the idea that we were serious about each other."

Did he think that was an explanation? He'd merely reworded the job description.

"There are a lot of single women in town who've been making my life difficult," he added. "And for some reason, they seem to think I'm actively looking for another wife."

"But you're *not?*"

"No. At least, not for the foreseeable future. My divorce became final a month ago, although my ex-wife moved out nearly two years ago. So I'm not in any hurry to jump into another relationship. I've tried to explain that to people, but apparently they don't believe me."

"Maybe you should be more direct."

"I thought I was. And I'd rather not alienate or anger any of my constituents."

Constituents? Oh, yes. Eva had mentioned he was also the mayor of Brighton Valley. So that meant he was dealing with small-town politics.

Either way Catherine thought the whole idea was a little weird—if not a bit laughable. But then again, she could use the work—and she *was* an actress.

"How long do you need my help?" she asked.

"Until my interim position as mayor is over—or for as long as you're in town. Whichever comes first."

He seemed to have it all planned out.

"I'll pay you a thousand dollars a week," he added.

Catherine was still trying to wrap her mind around his job offer, which was crazy. But the money he would pay spoke louder than the craziness, and against her better judgment, she found herself leaning toward an agreement.

"What would your fiancée have to do?" she asked.

Ray sketched an appreciative gaze over her that sent

her senses reeling and had her wondering just how far he'd want her to go in playing the part.

"I have to attend a lot of events and fundraisers, so it would be nice to have you go with me whenever possible. I even have a ring for you to wear on your left hand, which you can return when the job is over."

He was including the props?

This was wild. Pretending to be engaged to Ray Mendez was probably the craziest job offer she'd ever had, but she supposed it really didn't matter. If he was willing to pay for her acting skills, then why not go along with it?

"All right," she finally said. "You've got yourself a deal. When do I start?"

"Why don't you meet me for lunch at Caroline's tomorrow? A lot of the locals will be there, so it'll be a good way to send out the message that I'm already taken."

"And then…?"

"I don't know." He stroked his square-cut jaw. "Maybe I could greet you with a kiss, then we'll play it by ear. Hopefully, the rumor mill will kick into gear right away."

"What if it doesn't?"

He gave a half shrug. "I guess we'll have to take things day by day."

"So you just want me to have lunch with you tomorrow?"

"Actually, later that evening, I also have a charity event to attend at the Brighton Valley Medical Center. It's a benefit for the new neonatal intensive care unit, and it would probably be a good idea if we walked in together, holding hands. Maybe, if you looked at me a little starry-eyed, people would get the message."

"You want me to look at you *starry-eyed?*"

"Hell, I don't know how to explain it. You're a woman—and an actress. Just do whatever you'd do if we were actually engaged or at least committed to each other. I want people to think we're a real couple."

"Okay. I can do that. But what's the dress code tomorrow night?"

"I'll be wearing a sport jacket."

She bit down on her bottom lip, then glanced down at the simple blouse and black jeans she was wearing now. If truth be told, it was the fanciest outfit she'd brought with her.

"What's the matter?" he asked.

"If we were in New York, it wouldn't be a problem for me to find the right thing to wear. But I'm afraid I didn't plan to do anything other than kick back on the ranch and play with the kids while I'm here, so I only packed casual outfits."

"That's not a problem." He scooted back his chair and reached into the pocket of his jeans. He pulled out a money clip with a wad of bills, peeled off three hundred dollars and handed it to her. "After lunch tomorrow you can walk down the street to The Boutique. It's a shop located a few doors down from the diner."

Catherine couldn't imagine what type of clothing she'd find in Brighton Valley, but then again, she'd chosen to come to Texas because it was light-years from Manhattan and her memories there. She supposed she would have to adjust her tastes to the styles small-town women found appealing—or at least affordable.

She stole another glance at the handsome rancher seated across the table from her to find that he was studying her, too. Sexual awareness fluttered through her like a swarm of lovesick butterflies.

But that shouldn't surprise her. Ray Mendez was a handsome man. No wonder every woman in town was after him.

Of course, he was paying her to keep the other women at bay.

It would be an easy job, she decided—and one she might actually enjoy. Her biggest Broadway role had been the mistress of a 1920s Chicago mobster. The actor who'd played her lover had been twenty years older than she and about forty pounds overweight. His ruddy appearance had suited the character he'd played, although it had taken some real skills on her part to pretend she was sexually attracted to him.

Ray Mendez was going to make a much better costar, though—especially if her role was going to require a few starry-eyed gazes, some hand-holding and maybe a kiss or two.

For the first time since leaving Manhattan, she was actually looking forward to getting on stage again.

Chapter 2

At a few minutes before noon, Ray stood in front of Caroline's Diner, waiting for his hired fiancée to arrive. The plan had been for Catherine to borrow Eva's minivan, then to meet him in town.

To his surprise, he was actually looking forward to seeing her again—and not just because she was the solution to one of his many problems.

Even when she'd been wearing sweatpants and an oversize T-shirt, the tall, leggy blonde with bed-head curls had been a lovely sight. Her blue-green eyes—almost a turquoise shade, really—and an expressive smile only added to the overall effect.

Of course, those little heart and flower stickers that the younger Walker twins had stuck on her face while she'd slept had been an interesting touch.

When Ray had pointed them out, she'd made a joke

of it without missing a beat. And that meant she would probably be able to handle anything the townspeople might throw at her. If anyone quizzed her about their past or their plans for the future, she'd be quick on her feet.

They hadn't talked much after dinner last night, since Dan and Eva had returned to the table once they'd gotten the kids in bed. But they'd managed to concoct a believable past for their imaginary romance.

Fortunately, she wasn't a well-known Broadway actress, so they'd agreed to tell people they'd met in Houston six months ago and that they'd been dating ever since.

The day Ray's divorce had been final—after two long years in legal limbo—he'd proposed over a glass of champagne during a candlelit dinner in the city. She'd accepted, although they'd decided not to make an official announcement of their engagement until she could take some vacation time and come to Brighton Valley.

So now here he was, standing outside Caroline's Diner, ready to reveal their phony engagement to the locals who'd already begun to file into the small restaurant and fill the tables.

Ray glanced at his wristwatch again, knowing that he'd arrived a few minutes early and realizing that Catherine really wasn't late. Rather, he was a little nervous. Could they pull it off?

"Hello, Mayor," a woman called out in a chipper voice.

Ray glanced up to see Melanie Robertson approaching the diner wearing a smile.

Aw, man. This was just the kind of thing he'd been trying to avoid. Where was his "fiancée" when he needed her?

"Are you waiting for someone?" Melanie asked. "Or would you like to join Carla Guerrero and me for lunch?"

"Thanks for the offer, but I am meeting someone."

"Is it business or pleasure?" she asked, her lashes fluttering in a flirtatious manner.

"It's definitely pleasure." Out of the corner of his eye he spotted Catherine walking down the street. At least, that tall, blonde stranger striding toward him appeared to be the woman he'd met last night.

She'd told him that she hadn't brought anything fancy to Texas, but…hot damn. She hadn't needed a shopping trip for their lunch today. A pair of tight jeans, a little makeup and a dab of lipstick had made a stunning transformation from attractive girl next door to dazzling.

"Hi, honey." Catherine burst into a smile as she reached him. "I'm sorry I'm late."

Then she leaned forward and brushed her lips across his, giving him a brief hint of peppermint breath mints.

Her fragrance—something light and exotic—snaked around him, squeezing the air out of his lungs and making it nearly impossible to speak.

Then she turned to Melanie, offered a confident, bright-eyed smile and reached out her hand in greeting. "Hi, I'm Catherine Loza."

The same pesky cat that seemed to have gotten Ray's tongue appeared to have captured Melanie's, as well. He could understand her surprised reaction to Catherine's arrival and greeting, but not his own. Not when he'd been the one to set up the whole fake fiancée thing in the first place.

So why had Catherine's performance set *him* off balance?

Because she was so damn good at what she was doing, he supposed.

Shaking off the real effects of the pretend kiss, he introduced the women, adding, "Melanie's family owns the ice cream shop down the street."

"It's nice to meet you," Catherine said.

Melanie, whose eyes kept bouncing from Ray to his "date" and back again, said, "Same here. I…uh…" She nodded toward the entrance of Caroline's Diner. "I came to have lunch with a coworker, so I guess I'll see you two inside." Then she reached for the door and let herself in.

Well, what do you know? Catherine had been on the job only a minute or two, and the ploy was already working like a charm.

When they were alone, she asked, "So how did I do?"

"You were great." In fact, she was better than great. She both looked and acted the part of a loving fiancée, and even Ray found himself believing the romantic story they'd concocted was true.

"Now what?" she asked. "Did you want to go inside?"

"Yes, but I've got something to give you first. Come with me." Ray led her to the street corner, then turned to the left. When they reached the alley, he made a second left.

Once they were out of plain sight, he reached into the lapel pocket of his leather jacket and removed a small, velvet-covered box. Then he lifted the lid and revealed an engagement ring.

"Will this work?" he asked.

Catherine's breath caught as she peered at what appeared to be an antique, which had been cleaned and polished. The diamond, while fairly small, glistened in the sunlight.

"It was my grandmother's," he said.

"It's beautiful." She doubted the ring was costly, but

she imagined that the sentimental value was priceless. "I've never had an heirloom, so I'll take good care of it."

Then she removed the ring from the box and slipped it on the ring finger of her left hand, surprised that it actually fit.

For a moment, she wondered about the woman who'd worn it before her, about the relationship she'd had with her husband—and with her grandson. She suspected they'd been close.

When she looked at Ray, when their eyes met and their gazes locked, she asked, "What was her name?"

The question seemed to sideswipe him. *"Who?"*

"Your grandmother."

He paused, as if the reminder had surprised him as much as the question had, then said, "Her name was Elena."

Catherine lifted her hand and studied the setting a bit longer. It was an old-fashioned piece of jewelry, yet it had been polished to a pretty shine.

When she looked up again, he was watching her intently.

"What's the matter?" she asked.

He didn't respond right away, and when she thought that he might not, he said, "I know that ring isn't anything most people would consider impressive, but it meant a lot to my grandmother."

Catherine's mother had worn a single gold band, although she wasn't sure it had meant much to her. And when she'd passed away, the family had buried her with it still on her finger. As far as Catherine knew, not one of her siblings had mentioned wanting to inherit it.

But Ray's ring was different—special.

"It's actually an honor to wear this." She studied the

setting a moment longer, then turned to Ray, whose gaze nearly set her heart on end.

So she repeated what she'd told him before, "I'll take good care of it while it's in my possession."

"Thanks. I'm glad you can appreciate the sentiment attached to it. Not all women can."

He'd mentioned being recently divorced, so she couldn't help wondering if he was talking about his ex-wife.

Had she worn it? Had she given it back to him when they'd split?

Not that it mattered, she supposed.

"So," he said, "are you ready to have lunch now?"

When she nodded, he took her hand and led her back to the diner, where they would begin their performance. They were a team, she supposed. Costars in a sense.

They also had something else in common—hearts on the mend.

Ray opened the glass door, allowing Catherine to enter first. While waiting for him to choose a table, she scanned the quaint interior of the small-town eatery, with its white café-style curtains on the front windows, as well as the yellow walls that were adorned by a trellis of daisies on the wallpaper border.

To the right of an old-fashioned cash register stood a refrigerated display case filled with pies and cakes—each one clearly homemade.

She glanced at a blackboard that advertised a full meal for only $7.99.

In bright yellow chalk, someone had written, *What the Sheriff Ate,* followed by, *Chicken-Fried Steak, Buttered Green Beans, Mashed Potatoes, Country Gravy and Apple Pie.*

The advertised special sounded delicious, but she'd have to watch what she ate today. When she'd gotten dressed back at the ranch, she'd struggled to zip her jeans and found them so snug in the waist that she'd been tempted to leave the top button undone or to wear something else.

If she didn't start cutting out all the fat and the carbs she'd been consuming since arriving in Brighton Valley, she was going to return to New York twenty pounds heavier. And where would that leave her when it came time to audition for her next part?

Of course, after that stunt Erik Carmichael had pulled, she'd be lucky if other producers didn't blackball her by association alone.

How could she have been so gullible, so blind? The one person she'd trusted completely had pulled the cashmere over her eyes. And while she feared that she'd been hard-pressed to trust another man again, it was her own gullibility that frightened her the most.

As Ray placed his hand on her lower back, claiming her in an intimate way, she shook off the bad memories and focused on the here and now.

"There's a place for us to sit." With his hand still warming her back, he ushered her to a table for two in the center of the restaurant, then pulled out her chair.

It was the perfect spot, she supposed. Everyone in the diner would see them together, which was what Ray had planned—and what he was paying for. So as soon as he'd taken the seat across from hers, she leaned forward, placed her hand over the top of his and put on her happiest smile. "I've missed you, Ray. It's so good to be together again."

His lips quirked into a crooked grin, and his green eyes sparked. "It's been rough, hasn't it?"

When she nodded, he tilted his hand to the side, wrapped his fingers around hers and gave them a gentle, affectionate squeeze. "I'm glad to have you with me for a change."

Before Catherine could manage a response, a salt-and-pepper-haired waitress stopped by their table and smiled. "Hello, Mayor. Can I get you and your friend something to drink?"

"You sure can, Margie. I'd like a glass of iced tea." Ray gave Catherine's hand another little squeeze. "What would you like, honey?"

"Water will be fine."

At the term of endearment, Margie's head tilted to the side. Then her gaze zeroed in on their clasped hands. Instead of heading for the kitchen, she paused, her eyes widening and her lips parting.

"We'll need a few minutes to look over the menu," Ray told the stunned waitress.

Margie lingered a moment, as if she'd lost track of what she was doing. Then she addressed Catherine. "I haven't seen you in town before. Are you new or just passing through?"

Catherine offered her a friendly smile. "I'm visiting for the next couple of weeks, but I'm not really passing through. I plan to move here before the end of summer."

"Well, now. Isn't that nice." Margie shifted her weight to one hip, clearly intrigued by Catherine. "Where are you staying?"

"With *me*," Ray said. "You're the first one outside the Walker family to meet my fiancée, Margie."

"Well, now. Imagine that." The waitress beamed, her

cheeks growing rosy. "What a nice surprise. Of course, there's going to be a lot of heartbroken young women in town when they learn that our handsome young mayor is…already taken."

"I doubt that anyone will shed a tear over that," Ray said, turning to Catherine and giving her a wink. "But I'm definitely taken. And I was from the very first moment I laid eyes on her in Houston."

Catherine reached for the menu with her left hand, taking care to flash the diamond on her finger. Then she stole a peek at Margie to see if the older woman had noticed—and she had.

When the waitress finally left the table, Ray said, "Margie is a great gal, but she's a real talker. By nightfall, the news of our engagement will be all over town."

As Catherine scanned the diner, which had filled with the lunch crowd, she realized that Margie might not have to say much at all, since everyone else seemed to be focusing their attention on her and coming to their own conclusions.

"So what are you going to have?" she asked as she opened the menu and tried to get back into character.

"If I hadn't already eaten a good breakfast at the Rotary Club meeting this morning, I'd have the daily special. But Caroline's helpings are usually more than filling, so I'll probably get a sandwich instead."

Moments later, Margie returned with her pad and pencil, ready to take their orders. "So what'll you have?"

"I'd like the cottage cheese and fruit," Catherine said.

Ray asked for a BLT with fries.

After jotting down their requests, Margie remained at the table, her eyes on Catherine. "So what do you think of Brighton Valley so far?"

"It's a lovely town. I'm going to like living here."

"I'm sure you will." Margie smiled wistfully. "My husband and I came here to visit his sister one summer, and we were so impressed with the people and the small-town atmosphere that we went back to Austin, sold our house and moved out here for good. In fact, it was the single best thing we ever did for our family. Brighton Valley has got to be the greatest place in the world to raise kids."

"That's what I've been telling her," Ray said. "So I'm glad you're backing me up."

"Well, let me be the first to congratulate you on your engagement," Margie said, "and to welcome you to the best little town in all of Texas."

"Thank you."

Margie nodded toward the kitchen. "Well, it was nice meeting you, but I'd better turn in your orders before you die of hunger."

When the waitress left them alone again, Ray reached into his pocket, pulled out a single key, as well as a business card, and handed it to Catherine. "This will get you into the apartment I keep in town, which is just down the street. I'll point it out to you later."

She placed the key into the pocket on the inside of her purse, then fingered the card with his contact information at both the Broken M Ranch and City Hall.

"After you go shopping at The Boutique," he added, "you can hang out and wait for me at my place. I should be home by five or five-thirty."

"All right. I'll be dressed and ready to go by the time you get there."

"Good. I've got some snacks in the pantry and drinks

in the fridge. But if there's anything else you need, give me a call and I'll pick it up for you."

Anything she needed?

For the hospital benefit? Or was he talking about the duration of her acting gig?

She recalled the day Erik Carmichael had given her the key to his place, pretty much telling her the same thing, so she wasn't sure.

"Did you bring an overnight bag?" he asked.

No, only her makeup pouch. He hadn't said anything about spending the night.

Where are you staying? Margie had asked Ray just moments ago. And without batting an eye, he'd said, *With me.*

Was he expecting Catherine to actually move into his apartment while they pretended to be lovers? He hadn't mentioned anything about that when they'd discussed the job and his expectations last night.

"We'll probably be out late this evening," he added, then he bent forward and lowered his voice to a whisper. "It'll be easier that way."

She supposed it would be. And if they wanted everyone in town to assume they were lovers, staying together would make the whole idea a lot more believable.

They could, she supposed, talk about the sleeping arrangements later, but she assumed that she'd be using the sofa.

Of course, she wasn't sure what he had in mind, but she'd have to deal with that when the time came. Right now, she had a job to do.

She had to convince everyone in town that she was Ray Mendez's fiancée.

* * *

After Ray had paid the bill and left Margie a generous tip, he opened the door for Catherine and waited for her to exit. Once he'd followed her outside, they would be the talk of the diner, and that was just what he'd wanted.

Catherine had done all he'd asked of her. She'd looked at him a little starry-eyed, and she'd also used her hands when she'd talked, which had shown off the diamond his grandfather had placed upon his grandmother's finger more than seventy-five years ago.

She'd seemed to be genuinely impressed by the ring, although he supposed that could have been part of the act. But something told him that wasn't the case, which was more than a little surprising.

Before offering the ring to Heather, he'd had it cleaned and polished. But she'd turned up her nose at wearing something that wasn't brand-new and expensive. So, like a fool, he'd gone into Houston and purchased her a two-carat diamond, which she'd taken with her when she'd told him she wanted a divorce and moved out of the ranch house.

He supposed he'd have to be thankful for Heather's greed in that respect. Otherwise, he would have lost his grandmother's ring completely—or paid through the nose to get it back, since Heather had known how much it had meant to him. And if she'd had one more thing to hold over him, they might still be in the midst of divorce negotiations.

On the other hand, Catherine seemed to have a lot more respect for the family heirloom. When she'd studied the diamond in the sunlight, she'd even asked his grandmother's name, although Ray had been so caught up in the memory of Heather scrunching up her face at the ring that Catherine's question had completely side-swiped him.

Now, as they stood outside the diner, in the mottled shade of one of the many elm trees that lined Main Street, Ray pointed to his right. "The Boutique is located right next to the ice cream shop. And several doors down, you'll see the drugstore. There's a little red door to the left of it, which is the stairway that leads to my apartment."

"Thanks. After I buy the dress, I'll probably do some window shopping while I'm here. If anyone asks me who I am, I'll tell them I'm your fiancée. And that I'm staying with you."

"That's a good idea." He probably ought to start the walk back to City Hall, but for some reason, he couldn't quite tear himself away.

Outside, even in the dappled sunlight, the platinum strands of her hair glistened like white gold. And when she looked at him like that, smiling as though they were both involved in some kind of romantic secret, he noticed the green flecks in her irises that made her eyes appear to be a turquoise shade. It was an amazing color.

And she was an amazing...*actress.*

In fact, she was so good at what she did that he'd have to be careful not to confuse what was real and what wasn't.

"Thanks for helping me out," he said.

"You're welcome." She didn't budge either, which meant she was waiting for him to make the first move. But there were people seated near the windows of Caroline's Diner, people who were watching the two phony lovers through the glass.

"Well, I'd better go," he said. "I've got to get back to

City Hall before it gets much later. Do you have enough money to cover the dress and any incidentals you might need?"

She patted the side of her purse. "I sure do. And it's plenty. I'll probably have change to give you this evening when you get home."

Change? Now, that was a surprise. Even when they'd only been dating, Heather would have spent the entire wad and then some. And once he'd slipped a ring on her finger…well, things had just gone from bad to worse.

He was just about to say goodbye and send Catherine on her way when she eased forward, rose on tiptoe and lifted her lips to kiss him goodbye.

Of course.

Great idea.

There was an audience present, and they were two people in love. A goodbye kiss was definitely in order.

Ray stepped in and lowered his mouth to hers, but as their lips met, he found himself wrapping his arms around her and pulling her close, savoring the feel of her in his arms, the scent of her shampoo, the taste of her…

Oh, wow.

As he slipped into fiancé mode, the kiss seemed to take on a life of its own, deepening—although not in a sexual or inappropriate public display. In fact, to anyone who might be peering at them from inside the diner, their parting kiss would appear to be sweet and affectionate.

Yet on the inside of Ray, where no one else was privy, it caused his gut to clench and his blood to stir.

She placed her hand—the one that bore his grandmother's ring—on his face and smiled adoringly. As she slowly dropped her left hand, her fingers trailed down his cheek, sending ripples of heat radiating to his jaw and taunting him with sexual awareness.

Damn she was good. She even had *him* thinking there was something going on between them. No wonder Hollywood actors and actresses were constantly switching partners.

He'd best keep that fact in mind. The last thing in the world he needed to do was to get caught up in the act and to confuse fantasy with reality.

Chapter 3

When Ray entered his apartment at a quarter to five, he found Catherine seated on the sofa, watching television.

"You're home early," she said, reaching for the remote. After turning off the power, she stood to greet him.

But just the sight of the tall, shapely blonde wearing a classic black dress and heels made him freeze in his tracks.

"What do you think?" She turned around, showing him the new outfit she'd chosen.

"It's amazing," he said. And he wasn't just talking about the dress. Her transformation from actress to cover model had nearly thrown him for a loop.

Each time he saw Catherine, she morphed into a woman who was even more beautiful than the last.

Is that what dating an actress would be like? Having a different woman each time they went out?

If so, the part of him that enjoyed an occasional male fantasy sat up and took notice.

"I even found a pair of heels and an evening bag," she said, striding for the lamp table to show him a small beaded purse.

"You found all of that at The Boutique?" He'd expected her to complain about the out-of-date inventory at Brighton Valley's only ladies dress shop. Heather, who wasn't even from a place as style conscious as New York, certainly had.

"No," Catherine said, "I had to go to Zapatos, the shoe store across the street, for the heels and bag. What do you think? Will this do?"

Would it *do?*

"Absolutely." She looked like a million bucks, which had him thinking he'd better reach for his wallet. "I couldn't have given you enough money to pay for all of that."

"Oh, yes, you did." She smiled, lighting those blue-green eyes and revealing two of the prettiest dimples he'd ever seen. "I even have a few dollars change for you."

Again, the compulsion to compare her to his ex-wife struck him hard, but he shook it off. Heather was long gone—thank goodness. And now, thanks to Catherine, Ray wouldn't need to weed out the gold diggers from the dating pool until he was ready to.

"I'll take a quick shower," he said. "Just give me a couple of minutes."

After snatching his clothes from the bedroom, he headed for the bathroom. Then, once inside, he turned on the spigot and waited for the water to heat.

Surprisingly, he was actually looking forward to attending the hospital benefit tonight, especially since he would walk in with Catherine on his arm. A man could get used to looking at a woman like her—and talking to her, too.

Of course, he was paying her to be pleasant and agreeable. If they'd met on different terms, it might be another story altogether.

He had to admit that he'd gone out on a limb by hiring a fake fiancée, but after all he'd been through with Heather, after all their divorce had cost him, he wasn't ready to date again. And even when he was ready to give it another go, he didn't think he'd ever want to get married again.

What a nightmare his marriage had turned out to be.

Of course, if he wanted to have a child, he'd have to reconsider. After all, as the only son of an only son, Ray had no one to leave his ranch and holdings to unless he had an heir. But he was still young—thirty-six on his next birthday—so he had plenty of time to think about having children.

He reached into the shower stall and felt the water growing warm, so he peeled off his clothes and stepped under the steady stream of water. As he reached for the bar of soap, he found Catherine's lavender-colored razor resting next to it, along with her yellow bath gel.

It was weird to see feminine toiletries in his bathroom again. He'd been living without a woman under his roof for nearly two years, so he'd gotten used to having the place to himself.

Still, he reached for the plastic bottle, popped open the lid and took a whiff of Catherine's soap. The exotic floral fragrance reminded him of her.

Again he realized that he could get used to coming home to a beautiful blonde like Catherine, to having her ask how his day went, to stepping into her embrace and breathing in her scent. But the Catherine who'd spent the lunch hour with him earlier today wasn't real.

He'd employed her to be the perfect fiancée, and she was merely doing her job.

Even if he got caught up in the act, if he let down his guard, believing Catherine was different and allowing himself to see her in a romantic light, he'd be making another big mistake.

After all, he'd made up his mind to steer clear of big-city women from here on out—and cities didn't get much bigger than Manhattan.

Besides, he now realized that he needed someone with both of her feet firmly planted on Brighton Valley soil.

And Catherine was only passing through.

Ray snatched one of the brown fluffy towels from the rack on the wall and dried off. After shaving and splashing on a bit of cologne, he put on his clothes—black slacks and a white dress shirt, which he left open at the collar.

After he'd combed his hair, he removed his black, Western-cut jacket from the hanger and slipped it on. Then he returned to the living room where Catherine waited for him.

She wasn't watching television this time. She was standing near the window, looking out onto Main Street. She turned when she heard his footsteps, gave him a once-over and smiled. "You look great."

He didn't know about that, but he figured people were going to think that they'd planned coordinating outfits.

"Thanks," he said. "So do you. You're going to knock the socks off every man at the benefit—married or not."

"Well, you're no slouch, Mayor. Especially when you

get all dressed up. So maybe I ought to worry about running into a few jealous women tonight." A slow smile stretched across her face. "I might have to charge hazard pay."

He chuckled. "There might be a few who'll be sorry to learn I'm taken, but they'll be polite about it." He nodded toward the bedroom door. "I need to get my boots. I'll be right back."

Minutes later, he returned to the living room, ready to go.

"So tell me," Catherine said, as she reached for her small, beaded evening bag. "What made you decide to run for mayor of Brighton Valley?"

"I didn't actually run for mayor. Six months ago, after a couple of beers down at the Stagecoach Inn, I had a weak moment and agreed to run for a vacant city council seat. I'd never really wanted to get involved in politics, so I almost backed out the next day. But then I realized I might be able to make a difference in the community, so I went through with it."

"Apparently the citizens of Brighton Valley agreed with you."

"I guess you're right, because I won hands down. Then, a few weeks ago, Jim Cornwall, the elected mayor, was trimming a tree in his backyard and fell off the ladder. He suffered a skull fracture, as well as several other serious injuries. He'll be laid up for some time, so I was asked to fill the position until he returns."

"That's quite the compliment," she said.

"You're right, which is why I reluctantly agreed. Trouble was, I had enough on my plate already, with a land deal I'm in the midst of negotiating and a new horse-breeding operation that's just getting under way."

Then, on top of that, his life had been further complicated by all the single women coming out of the woodwork, now that he was single again. And if there was anything he didn't need in his life right now, it was more complications—especially of the female variety.

"Something tells me you'll be able to handle it."

She was right, of course. Ray Mendez was no quitter. He was also an idea man who could think himself out of most any dilemma.

So here he was, preparing to go to a charity event at the Brighton Valley Medical Center with a hired fiancée, albeit a lovely woman who was sure to make a splash when they walked into the hospital side by side.

Ray had never been one to want center stage, yet he didn't really mind it tonight, since he knew he'd be in good hands with an accomplished actress. So, with their employment agreement binding them, they were about to make their evening debut.

Now, as he opened the door of his apartment, the curtain was going up and the show was on. He probably ought to have a little stage fright, but he wasn't the least bit apprehensive.

Catherine, as he'd found out at their matinee performance earlier today, just outside Caroline's Diner, was one heck of an actress. All he had to do was to follow her lead.

In fact, he was looking forward to being with her tonight, to watching their act unfold.

When it was over, they'd head back to his place. He wasn't sure what would happen after that. They'd have a debriefing, he supposed. And maybe they'd kick back and watch a little TV.

He really hadn't given the rest of the evening any

thought. Yet something told him he should have. He was finding his hired fiancée a little too attractive to just let the chips fall where they might.

As Catherine and Ray entered the hospital pavilion, which had been decorated with blinking white lights, black tablecloths and vases of red roses, she instinctively reached for his hand.

She wished she could say it had been part of the act, but the truth was, she was having a bit of stage fright—as unusual as that was.

He wrapped his fingers around hers and gave them a conspiratorial squeeze. "Good idea."

She wished she could have taken full credit for the hand-holding, but she'd done it without any forethought.

During the ten-minute drive from his downtown apartment to the medical center, she'd been so engrossed by the tall, dark and handsome man across the seat from her, so mesmerized by his sexy Texas drawl, that she couldn't help thinking of this evening as a date, rather than a job. So when they'd entered the pavilion and she'd spotted a sea of strangers, she'd reached for a friend.

At least, that's the way it had felt at the time.

But he was right; slipping her hand into his had been the perfect move—under the circumstances.

So what if his warm grip was actually comforting and she found herself feeling energized by the connection, strengthened by it.

Ray led her toward a petite Latina who was greeting an older man dressed in a gray suit and bold tie.

"I want to introduce you to Dr. Ramirez," he said upon their approach. "She's one of the major players trying to fund a neonatal intensive care unit at Brighton Valley Medical Center."

The attractive doctor who, even in high heels, didn't appear to be much taller than five foot two, was stylishly dressed in turquoise and black.

"Selena," Ray said, "I'd like you to meet my fiancée, Catherine Loza."

The doctor brightened, and as she reached out in greeting, Catherine released her hold on Ray long enough to give the woman a polite shake.

"I didn't realize Ray was engaged," Selena Ramirez said, "but it's no surprise. He's a great guy."

"I couldn't agree more." Catherine wondered if Selena had been one of the single women in town who'd been after Ray, although she certainly wasn't giving off those kinds of vibes now.

Even Melanie Robertson, the woman she'd met in front of the diner, had seemed a little disappointed—and maybe even envious—when she'd gotten the message that the handsome, single mayor was now taken.

"Selena is an obstetrician," Ray added. "She's been actively working with the city council to support the efforts to build the NICU."

"As it is," Selena explained, "our smallest preemies have to be airlifted to Houston. And I'd like to provide our mothers with the assurance that their babies are getting the best care available here at the medical center."

Ray nodded in agreement. "That reality really hit home for all of us when one of the councilmen's granddaughter was born. She had some serious problems at birth and had to be transported to the nearest neonatal unit. That's when we agreed to open our wallets and do whatever we could to help."

"That must have been a scary time for the councilman's family," Catherine said.

"It was." Selena's face grew solemn. "And sadly, their baby didn't make it."

Just hearing of a new mother's loss tore at Catherine's heart. She loved children and had hoped to have one or two of her own someday, but she'd had so many female problems in the past, including cysts on one of her ovaries and surgery to remove it, that the doctors had told her years ago that she wasn't likely to conceive. So her chances of having a baby of her own were slim to none.

She'd been more than a little disappointed upon learning the news, but she'd come to grips with it.

"I'd be happy to lend my support," Catherine said. "When Jennifer Walker's twins were born, they were several weeks early. But thanks to their time spent in a top-notch neonatal unit, they came home healthy and were soon thriving. So I know how valuable it is to have a NICU at the medical center."

"Jennifer Walker's twins? Are you talking about Kaylee and Kevin?"

Catherine nodded. "I used to be Jenn's roommate in New York."

"So that's how you met Ray," Selena surmised, "through Dan and Eva."

Uh-oh. That hadn't been part of the story she and Ray had created last night, but it was the truth, so she nodded in agreement. "That's how we first met, of course. But nothing came of it. Then we ran into each other again in Houston six months ago. He attended one of my performances and came to visit me backstage—just to say hello. He asked me to have a drink with him, and one thing led to another."

"You're a performer?" Selena asked.

"I sing a little and dance." Catherine thought it might be a good idea to downplay the acting.

"That's wonderful. Our next benefit is a talent show, so it would be nice if you took part in it."

Catherine was at a loss, and she glanced at Ray, hoping he'd toss her a lifeline of some kind.

"That's on the second Saturday of this month," Ray said. "Right?"

Selena nodded. "Can we count on you to perform?"

Good grief, Ray was leaving it up to her. But then again, she supposed that was only fair. He couldn't very well schedule her every waking moment.

"I'll see what kind of act I can come up with," Catherine said.

"That's great," Selena said. "Clarissa Eubanks is in charge of the talent show. I'll tell her to call the mayor's office for contact information."

"I'll make it easy on both of you," Ray said. "Catherine's staying with me."

They made the usual small talk for a while, then Selena saw someone else she needed to greet.

"Congratulations on your engagement," she said as she prepared to walk away. "I hope you'll be very happy together."

"Thank you. I'm sure we will." Catherine turned to Ray and blessed him with a lover's smile, which he returned in full force.

For a moment, as their gazes zeroed in on each other again, something she couldn't quite define passed between them, something warm and filling.

He reached to take her hand again, and as his fingers wrapped around hers, the shattered edges of her heart, which had been damaged by Erik's deceit, melded into one another, as if beginning a much-needed healing process.

Coming to Brighton Valley had been a good idea, she decided.

With her hand tucked in Ray's, reinforcing whatever tentative bond they'd forged just moments ago, her past turned a brand-new corner, revealing a future rife with promise and possibilities.

And for one brief moment in time, she could almost imagine that future including Ray Mendez.

Ever since Ray had agreed to take the job as the interim mayor of Brighton Valley, he'd spent more time at various benefits, ribbon-cutting ceremonies and dinner meetings than he'd imagined possible.

In fact, just thirty-six hours ago, he'd dreaded attending this very event.

Not that he didn't fully support the building of a new neonatal intensive care unit. He did, but he'd been waking up each morning at four, just so he could tend to his personal business commitments, as well as the political obligations that now filled his calendar.

Yet tonight, with lovely Catherine on his arm, the hospital benefit had not only been tolerable, but surprisingly pleasant.

Of course, now as the evening was winding down, he and Catherine had become separated once again. Usually they'd split up due to someone wanting to speak to him privately about one matter or another. But a couple of times, someone else had whisked Catherine away to introduce her to somebody she "just had to meet."

However, they'd always managed to find each other in the midst of the milling crowd.

Even from across the room, their gazes would meet. And when they did, Catherine would look at Ray with a lover's yearning. At least, that's the way it felt to him.

The first time it had happened, he'd been so unbalanced by the expression on her face that his breath had caught. But after a while he'd actually come to look forward to their eye contact.

What was with that?

He knew that their so-called romance was all an act, but he'd gotten so caught up in their performance that he'd found himself seeking her out, just to catch her eye.

And there she was now, standing next to a potted palm, talking to one of the doctors' wives. And here it came—the glance his way, the look, the smile, the expression that announced she would much rather be curled up in bed with him.

She was good. *Really* good. And it was all he could do to remember that they'd only just met, that she was his employee, that they hadn't slept together—and that they would never even consider it.

Well, hell. Okay, so he probably would consider it—if it ever came to that. But it wouldn't.

The affectionate glances, the touches, were all just for show. Things would be much different when they returned to his apartment.

So why was all that phony longing driving him nuts now?

Because she was such a good actress that he was buying it all—hook, line and sinker. How was that for bad luck and a lousy roll of the dice?

Still, he planned to take one last opportunity to claim

his fiancée this evening. Then he'd take her home and end it all.

After checking his wristwatch and deciding now was the time, Ray made his way across the room to where Catherine was speaking to Margo Reinhold, the wife of one of the city councilmen.

"Your fiancée and I have been talking," Margo said to Ray. "I suggested that she join the Brighton Valley Women's Club. We're having a luncheon and fashion show next month, so it would be a fun meeting to attend. We're also looking for more models, so I hope she'll consider volunteering for that, as well."

There was no guarantee Catherine would still be in town this summer, so she couldn't very well commit to anything that far in advance without letting someone down.

Realizing her dilemma and seeing the indecision in her eyes, Ray stepped in to help. "I'm sure Catherine would love to join you ladies, but she has plans to…take a cruise with a couple of her girlfriends."

"Oh, yes," Catherine said, taking the baton he'd passed. "When is the fashion show?"

"It's on August the tenth."

Catherine's expression fell—just as if she were shattered that her previously made plans wouldn't allow her to take part in the event.

"Wouldn't you know it?" she said. "That's the day I set sail for the Caribbean."

"I'm so sorry to hear that," Margo said. "But there's always next year."

"Oh, of course." Catherine tossed Ray another one of those bright-eyed, I-love-you grins. Or maybe it was one of those saved-by-the-bell smiles.

"Since you won't be leaving until mid-August," Margo continued, "maybe you'd like to help with the high school dance recital. It's on the last Saturday in July. I'm sure the young people would love to have some advice from a pro."

Had Catherine told Mary that she was a dancer? And a professional? Or had Selena Ramirez spread the word?

Ray supposed it was okay that the news was out, but something told him they'd better go over their story again so they didn't get mixed up and tell on themselves.

"I'd love to work with the kids," Catherine said.

Now, wait a minute. Catherine was working for *him*. How was she going to schedule practices at the high school when he might have need of her? And what if…

Well, what if she decided to stick around in Brighton Valley indefinitely? What would happen when he decided to end…her employment?

Of course, that could become a problem whether she started volunteering in the community or not.

Catherine placed a hand on his arm. "You don't mind, do you, honey?"

Had she read something in his expression? If so, he hadn't wanted anyone to know he was a little uneasy about their future together in Brighton Valley.

"Of course I don't mind," he said.

The women chatted a moment longer, then Margo handed Catherine a business card with her contact information. "Give me a call sometime tomorrow, and I'll schedule a meeting between you and the dance teacher at the high school."

At that point, Ray decided it was time to cut out. Who knew what else Margo had up her sleeve or what she might try to rope his pretty fiancée into?

"Are you ready to go home?" he asked Catherine.

"Yes, I am." Then she slipped her arm through his and said goodbye to Margo.

Five minutes later they were in his Cadillac Escalade and headed back to his apartment.

"Something tells me you didn't want me to volunteer to work with the dance recital," she said.

"It just took me by surprise, that's all."

"Why?"

He glanced across the seat and saw her studying him, her brow furrowed.

"I don't know," he said. "I'd hate to see you get more involved with the locals than you have to."

"Actually, I'd love to work with the kids. It will be a way for me to pay it forward."

"I don't understand."

After a beat, she said, "I grew up in a family that was both large and dysfunctional. Music was my escape from the noise and hubbub. I would have loved to have taken dance or piano lessons when I was a child, but my dad was chronically unemployed, and my mom used to spend her extra cash on beer and cigarettes for the two of them. So there wasn't any money available for the extras."

"So how'd you become a dancer?"

"In high school, I chose every music, dance or drama class I could fit into my schedule. The teachers insisted I had a natural talent, and after a while I began to believe them. I also knew that an education was my way out of the small town where we lived, so I studied hard and landed a scholarship at a small liberal arts college in the Midwest."

"And from there you decided to go to New York?"

"In a way. I met Jenn Walker at college, and she insisted that we try our luck on Broadway. But it was Miss Hankin, my high school dance teacher, and Mr. Pretz, the choral director, who convinced me that I could actually have a career doing what I loved."

So that's what she meant by paying it forward. She wanted to encourage other talented students to reach for their dreams. He had to admire that, he supposed.

"Do you miss it?" he asked. "Being on Broadway?"

"Yes, although I was ready for a break."

Dan had mentioned that she was recovering from a bad relationship. And now that Ray knew her better, he was curious about the details. And about the guy who'd broken her heart.

"Why did you need to get away?" he asked.

She paused for the longest while, then said, "The man I was involved with turned out to be a jerk. So I wanted to distance myself for a while."

"From him?"

"And from everything that reminded me of him."

She didn't say any more, and he didn't want to pry. After all, he'd had his own ways of shutting Heather out of his life after their split. So who was he to criticize someone else's way of dealing with a bad and painful situation?

After he pulled into the parking lot in back of the drugstore, he found a space and turned off the ignition.

When Catherine reached for the handle to let herself out, he said, "Hold on. I'll get it for you." Then he slid out from behind the wheel, went around to the passenger side and opened the door for her.

"I could have gotten it," she said. "There's no one around who'd see me do it."

"We don't need an audience for me to be polite."

She graced him with a moonlit smile. "Then thank you."

A shade in one of the upstairs windows opened, letting a soft light pour out from the apartment over Caroline's Diner.

Apparently they weren't entirely alone and unnoticed.

As they started back across the dimly lit parking lot, Catherine's ankle wobbled, and she reached for Ray to steady herself.

As her fingers pressed into his forearm, setting off a surge of hormones in his bloodstream, he asked, "Are you okay?"

"Yes. I stepped in an uneven spot and lost my balance."

"Those high heels look great on you, but it's got to be tough walking in them, especially out here."

"Yes, it is." Still gripping his arm, she looked up at him. And as she did so, their gazes met—and held.

There it went again, that rush of attraction. And while he knew whatever they were feeling for each other was purely sexual, he couldn't help basking in it longer than was wise.

Then, as one heartbeat lapsed into a second and a third, he reached for her waist.

"We've got an audience," he whispered, making an excuse to hold her, to draw her close.

He doubted that was really the case, though. But he didn't care. All he wanted to do right this moment was to extend the act they'd been playing a little while longer. To push for just a bit more of that heated rush.

To maybe even push for another brief kiss…

As his blood began to race, he didn't think one that was brief would be quite enough.

Besides, he told himself, a kiss from Catherine, albeit a phony one, just might help him forget all the crap Heather had put him through.

Oh, what the heck. Who was he trying to kid? He wanted to kiss Catherine senseless—even if he'd pay for it later.

So he lowered his mouth to hers.

Chapter 4

The last thing Catherine expected this evening was for Ray to kiss her goodbye while they stood in the parking lot behind his apartment.

Not that she minded.

In fact, as she stepped right into his arms, her heart raced in anticipation as if she'd been waiting all evening to get her hands on him.

And maybe, somewhere deep inside, that's just what she'd been doing, because the moment their lips touched, the kiss, which she assumed was also a thank you for a job well done, intensified.

As tongues met, their breaths caught and desire sparked, turning something that began tender and sweet into something heated and sexual.

Before long, Catherine wasn't so sure who ought to be thanking or praising whom.

In fact, right this moment, all she wanted to do was to kiss Ray back and let nature run its course. And if truth be known, she wasn't doing this for the benefit of any neighbors who might be watching.

No, her motive was a bit more selfish than that.

Over the years, she'd kissed quite a few men—most of them her costars on stage. And not a single one of those kisses had come anywhere near to moving her as much as Ray's did.

She supposed this was a nice perk that went along with the job she'd been hired to do.

As the kiss ended, Ray placed a hand on her cheek. "You were great tonight."

He'd been *great,* too—especially right now.

Somehow, she managed an unaffected smile. She'd planned to thank him and tell him it had been easy, yet as his gaze settled on hers and his fingers trailed along her cheek, she found it difficult to speak.

On the other hand, his eyes were speaking volumes to her—if she could trust them. Maybe she was misreading something that was merely appreciation for affection.

The acting was over for tonight, wasn't it?

Sometimes, when she really got into a role, she became the character she portrayed. Is that what was happening now? Had she actually become Mendez's fiancée for the past couple of hours?

If so, she'd better shake that role on her drive back to the ranch.

"Well," she said, finding the words to segue back to reality. "I guess I'd better go. I don't want Dan and Eva worrying about me."

"I hate to have you drive back to the ranch this late at

night. The road isn't well lit, and some of those curves are tough to make in the daylight."

So what was he suggesting?

"You're more than welcome to stay in town with me," he added. "We can call the Walkers and tell them you'll be bringing the car back in the morning."

He wanted her to spend the night with him? She probably ought to be a little concerned by his expectations, yet she didn't find the idea of a sleepover all that out of line. And she wasn't sure why.

The kiss maybe? The temptation to see where another one might lead?

No, she needed to keep things a little more professional than that.

"Thanks for the offer," she said, "but I think I can make the drive without any problems. If I'd had more to drink than club soda, I might take you up on it."

Still, in spite of the decision she'd made, Catherine knew it wouldn't take much of an argument from Ray for her to call Eva and tell her there'd been a change of plans. Her knees were still wobbly from the kiss. And the chemistry the two of them shared—on or off the stage—promised to be explosive.

"Just for the record," he added. "I'll sleep on the sofa and you can have the bed."

"That's tempting," she admitted. And not only because she was tired and didn't want to make the drive back to the ranch.

"Then what's holding you back?"

The truth? Not trusting herself when her senses were still reeling from that last kiss.

Instead, she said, "I don't like to change plans after they've been made, but I'll keep your offer in mind next time—assuming there'll be another event we need to attend together."

"It's going to take more than a couple of sightings for people to realize I'm engaged."

He was probably right.

"So what's next on the agenda?" she asked.

"How about lunch tomorrow? We can meet at City Hall around noon, then walk a couple of blocks to an Italian restaurant that just opened up. The owner's grandfather is a member of the city council, and I'd like to be supportive of a new local business endeavor."

"All right. I'll see you then."

She started toward the parked minivan, and Ray followed. When she reached the driver's door, he placed his hand on her shoulder. She turned, and as their eyes met, she sensed another goodbye kiss coming her way.

"Just in case someone's watching from one of the apartment windows," he said, as he slipped his arms around her.

Yet as their lips met, she had a feeling he would have kissed her a second time tonight, even if no one was looking down at them.

And if that had been the case, she would have let him.

The chemistry between them was much stronger than she'd anticipated, which might prove to be a real problem for her in the very near future.

The handsome Brighton Valley mayor was paying her to keep the single women at bay—not to join their ranks.

Sofia, one of the younger Walker twins, had awakened with an earache. So Eva had needed her car to drive the child to the pediatrician, which meant Catherine's only mode of transportation was one of the ranch pickups.

So, after getting directions to the Brighton Valley City Hall, an ornate brick building that the town fathers had built nearly a hundred years ago, Catherine drove into town to meet Ray for lunch.

As the beat-up old pickup chugged down Main Street, past Caroline's Diner and the other quaint little shops, Catherine held tight to the steering wheel, looking for town square and the public parking lot Dan had told her about.

Sure enough, it was right where he'd told her it would be. Once she'd found the automatic dispenser and paid for the two-hour minimum, she took the ticket back to the pickup. Then she crossed the street, entered the hundred-year-old brick building and made her way to a reception desk, where a middle-age woman with graying hair sat.

"Can I help you?" the woman asked.

Catherine offered a friendly smile. "I'm here to see Ray Mendez."

The woman's pleasant expression faded. "Do you have an appointment?"

"Not exactly. I came to have lunch with him."

"You don't say." The woman arched a brow, as if she found that hard to believe. "I'm not sure if he's available. I'll have to give him a call."

Did she treat every visitor this way?

Catherine crossed her arms and shifted her weight to one hip. "Tell him that Catherine Loza is here."

The woman lifted the telephone from its receiver, then pushed an intercom button. When someone on the other end answered, she brightened. "Hello, Mayor. It's Millie. There's a young woman named Catherine here to see you."

Millie's smile faded, and her eyes widened.

"Your…fiancée?" She took another gander at Catherine, her expression softening. "Of course. I'll tell her you'll be right down."

Millie hung up the phone, then offered Catherine a sheepish grin. "I'm *so* sorry, Ms. Loza. It's just that I had no idea he… That you…"

"That's okay." Catherine lifted her left hand and flashed the diamond. "We haven't told many people yet."

"Still, I'm sorry. I didn't mean to be rude. It's just that I was asked to screen his calls and his visitors."

"I understand," Catherine said, realizing that Ray hadn't been exaggerating when he'd said the single women in town were making it difficult for him to get any work done.

Millie pointed to a row of chairs near her desk. "You can have a seat, if you'd like. But he said he'd be right down."

"Thank you."

Within moments Ray came sauntering down the hall, a dazzling smile stretched across his face. "Hi, honey. Did you have any trouble finding the place?"

"No, not at all."

They kissed briefly in greeting, then Ray turned to the receptionist and said, "Thanks, Millie. I see you met Catherine. What do you think?"

"I think the local girls are going to be brokenhearted, especially when they realize they can't compete with the future Mrs. Mendez." Millie chuckled. "And once word gets out, it'll make my job easier. Now I won't have to stretch the truth and come up with excuses for you anymore."

"I guess my engagement is a win-win for all of us."

Ray placed a hand on Catherine's back. "Are you ready to go, honey?"

"Whenever you are."

Ray took her by the hand, and after a two-block walk, they crossed the street to a small restaurant that offered curbside dining under the shade of a black awning.

"It's a nice day," Ray said. "Why don't we sit outside?"

"That sounds good to me."

After Ray told the hostess their preference, they were led to a linen-draped table and handed menus.

Ray held Catherine's chair as she took her seat. Then he sat across from her.

"I heard the manicotti was pretty good," he said.

Catherine scanned the menu, tempted to choose the pasta, but knowing she didn't need the carbs when she wasn't having regular workouts each day.

"What looks good to you?" Ray asked.

"I'd like the vegetarian antipasto salad—the oil and vinegar on the side. And a glass of water with lemon."

"That's it?"

"Yes, but I might try to steal a bite of whatever you're having—as long as it's high in carbs and covered in cheese."

He tossed her a boyish grin. "Be my guest."

Fifteen minutes later, after several of the townspeople stopped to say hello to the mayor and were pleasantly surprised to meet his "future bride," the waiter brought out their meals.

"Can I get you anything else?" the young man asked.

"No, this is fine for now." Ray glanced down at the lasagna he'd ordered. "I had no idea the servings would be this large. I'll give you half of it."

"Oh, no you don't. I just want a taste."

Ray cut off a good size chunk anyway, placed it on a bread plate, then passed it to her.

It was, she decided, just the kind of thing that lovers and friends did while eating. Yet she hadn't given their roles any thought when she'd asked to sample his meal.

Were they becoming friends?

Before she would even risk pondering the idea of them ever becoming lovers, she asked, "Do you have anything special on the calendar this week?"

"There's a community barbecue in the town square on Saturday afternoon. Besides having the best rib eye you've ever tasted, they'll have a pie-eating contest and a line-dance competition."

That sounded like fun. "What's the dress code?"

"I suppose you'd call it country casual, with denim being the only requirement."

"I can handle that." Catherine cut into the lasagna Ray had given her with a fork and took a bite. The minute it hit her mouth, she wished she'd agreed to split their meals.

"Do you have any Western boots?" Ray asked.

"No. Do I need a pair?"

"Not really. You'll be fine in jeans."

Maybe Eva would have a pair she could borrow. She'd ask her as soon as she got home.

They ate in silence for a while, and when Catherine reached for her glass of water, she caught Ray staring at her.

"What's wrong?" she asked.

"Nothing."

She didn't believe him.

Finally, he said, "You're a good sport."

She always tried to be. But something told her his comment held a deeper meaning. "What makes you say that?"

"Because you're a big-city girl. All this country-bumpkin stuff has to be pretty foreign to you. Are you that good of an actress?"

She laughed. "I'm a pretty good actress, but I wasn't always a big-city girl. I grew up in a small town in New Mexico, although it wasn't anything like Brighton Valley."

"You mentioned that to me before, but I still have trouble imagining you as anything other than a big-city girl."

"Why is that?"

He shrugged. "The way you carry yourself, I suppose. And because of your background on the Broadway stage."

"I've spent the past ten years surrounded by bright lights and skyscrapers, but that wasn't always the case."

"What was it like growing up in a small New Mexico community?" he asked.

"It was dry, hot and dusty for the most part. And I couldn't wait to leave it all behind."

He took a bite of garlic bread. "What about your family? Do they still live there?"

"A few of them do. My dad died when I was twelve, and my mother passed on about five years ago. Most of my siblings cut out the minute they turned eighteen, just like I did."

"*Most* of them? How many brothers and sisters do you have?"

"There were seven of us—three boys and four girls."

"I was an only child," he said. "I always wondered what it would have been like to have had siblings."

"Big families aren't always what they're cracked up to be. Mine was pretty loud and dysfunctional, and so I escaped through reading or listening to music."

"Is that when you decided to be an actress?"

She'd been gone so long and traveled so far, that whenever she looked back on those days, it was hard to believe she'd ever been that lonely girl with big dreams.

"I knew that an education was my only way out of that town—and school provided the lessons I wanted. So I studied hard and landed a scholarship."

"At the college where you met Dan's sister?"

"Yes. Jennifer was determined to perform on Broadway, and her dreams were contagious. I began to think that I might be able to make the cut, too."

"And you did." He smiled, his eyes beaming as though he was proud of her.

Her heart skipped a beat at his belief in her, at his pride in her accomplishment. She hadn't had a cheerleader since Jenn died. And while Dan and Eva had always liked hearing about her successes, she'd never been able to share her failures with them in hopes of getting a pep talk.

She offered Ray a wistful smile. "After we graduated from college Jenn and I moved to New York, rented a small apartment in the Bronx and then tried out for every off-Broadway play or musical available. In time, we began to make names for ourselves, first with bit parts, then with an occasional lead role."

"Sounds like the perfect world—at least, for you."

"Yes and no. When Jennifer got pregnant with the twins and feared she'd have to call it quits, I was afraid

I couldn't make it on my own. Not because I didn't have the talent, but Jenn was the one with the determination and the perseverance, the one who kept me going when things didn't work out as hoped or planned. So I offered to support her any way I could—*if* she'd stay in New York."

"Support? You mean financially or with the kids?"

"Both. I had no idea how difficult it would be to bring home two newborns."

"I'll bet that changed both of your lives."

It certainly had. And in a good way. A lot of roommates might have had qualms about having crying babies in the house, but Catherine and Jennifer had become a team—and a family.

But then again, Catherine had suffered a lot of female problems in the past. Since she'd been told that having a child of her own wasn't likely, it was only natural that she grew exceptionally close to Kaylee and Kevin.

"It must have been tough when Jennifer died."

Catherine nodded. Just the thought of losing the young woman who'd been both her best friend and a better sister than the three she'd had brought tears to her eyes.

It might have been four years ago, but the grief sometimes still struck hard and swift.

She could still recall that awful day as though it had been yesterday. She'd been home watching the kids and practicing the lines for a new part in an off-Broadway production when the doorbell rang. And when she'd answered, she'd found an NYPD officer on the stoop, who'd told her the news: Jennifer had been killed while crossing a busy Manhattan street—struck by a car.

At that time, Jennifer and her brother Dan, the twins' only surviving relative, had been estranged. He'd been devastated to learn of his sister's death and had flown to New York to do whatever he could. But the twins weren't quite five years old and hardly knew him. So Catherine had volunteered to keep the children for a few months to help them through the grieving process and to allow them time to get to know their uncle better.

When the kids finally moved to Brighton Valley, Catherine had missed them terribly, but she knew it was for the best. Still, she called regularly and visited them in Texas as often as her work would allow—although it wasn't nearly as often as she would have liked.

"I'm sorry," Ray said. "I didn't mean to bring up something painful and turn your afternoon into a downer."

Catherine lifted her napkin and dabbed it under her eyes. "That's okay. It happens sometimes. We were very close. And I still miss her." Then she managed a smile. "I really don't mind talking about her. And I don't usually cry."

As Ray watched Catherine wipe the tears from her eyes, he regretted the questions that had stirred up her grief. He'd only wanted to learn more about her, to get to know her better.

If they'd actually been dating, if he'd had the right to quiz her about her past, it might have been different.

She glanced at the napkin, noting black streaks on the white linen.

"My mascara is running," she said.

"Just a bit."

"I probably look like a raccoon." She smiled through her tears, relieving the tension, as well as his guilt. "Excuse me for a minute. I'm going to find the ladies' room and see if I can repair the damages."

Catherine had no more than entered the restaurant

when Ray spotted Beverly Garrison getting out of her parked car. Beverly was the president of her homeowners' association and made it a point to attend every city council meeting, whether the agenda had anything to do with her neighborhood or not.

When Beverly saw him, she brightened and waved. "You're just the one I wanted to see, Mayor. I have something to give you."

Then she reached into the passenger seat and pulled out a yellow plastic tub.

What the heck was in it? Margarine?

"I looked for you over at Caroline's Diner," she said, as she bumped her hip against the car door to shut it. "But you weren't there. Someone suggested I look for you here."

She headed for his table. "I brought you a treat."

"What is it?" Ray asked.

"Two dozen of the best homemade oatmeal-raisin cookies you've ever eaten in your life. My daughter baked a fresh batch this morning. Carol Ann is a little shy, so she asked me to give them to you."

As Ray glanced down at the yellow tub, Beverly reached for the lid, peeled it off and revealed a stack of cookies that certainly looked delicious.

"Thanks for thinking of *me,*" he said, a little surprised that she'd go so far as to chase him down.

"Oh, it wasn't me." Beverly's hand flew up to her chest, as she took a little step back. "It was my *daughter.* You remember Carol Ann, don't you? She's the pretty blonde who showed up at the last city council meeting with me."

Ray remembered, but poor Carol Ann, who'd spent most of the time with her nose stuck in a book, was neither pretty nor blond. At best, she was a rather nondescript woman with stringy, light brown hair. She was also in her forties, which meant she was five to ten years older than him.

Not that age was that big of an issue. But Ray wasn't looking for a date.

Of course, he didn't want to hurt the woman or her daughter's feelings, so he kept those thoughts to himself.

"You'll have to thank Carol Ann for me," he said.

"I can certainly do that, but why don't I give you her telephone number instead? That way, you can call her yourself. It'd be a nice thing for you to do."

Ray took a deep breath, then glanced to the doorway of the restaurant, where Catherine stood, watching the matchmaking mama do her thing.

Catherine's lips quirked into a crooked grin, clearly finding a little humor in the situation.

Beverly reached into her black vinyl handbag and pulled out a pen and notepad. Then she scratched out Carol Ann's contact information, tore out the sheet she'd written upon and handed it to Ray. "Carol Ann has plenty of time on her hands these days. She and Artie Draper broke up a few months back, and...well, what with your recent divorce and all, I'm sure you understand how tough it is to get back into the dating world again."

It actually wouldn't be tough at all for him to start dating—if he were inclined to do so. There were single women ready, willing and able at every turn.

"I'll be sure to call Carol Ann and thank her for the cookies," Ray said, getting to his feet and glancing to the doorway where Catherine stood by.

"That would be wonderful," Beverly said.

Taking her cue, Catherine approached the table.

"Beverly," Ray said, "I'd like to introduce you to my fiancée, Catherine Loza."

"How do you do," Catherine said. "Goodness, will you look at those yummy cookies."

Beverly's eyes widened and her lips parted as she ran an assessing gaze over Catherine. "I… I…um, didn't know you were engaged, Mayor…."

"It's only been official for a few days," Catherine said with a gracious smile. "And we haven't made any formal announcements."

Beverly took a step back, then fingered the top button of her blouse. "You know, I can probably thank Carol Ann for you, Mayor. There's probably no need for you to call her. She's pretty shy. And well, I'd hate to see her embarrassed. She…uh…"

"I understand," Ray said. "I wouldn't want to cause her any discomfort, especially after her recent breakup. But please give her my best. Tell her the right guy will come along. And before she knows it, she'll be happy again."

"Well," Beverly said, nodding toward her car. "I really need to get going. I have a lot of errands to run."

"Thank you for the cookies," Ray said. "Do you want me to return the container?"

"No, don't bother. You can just recycle it when you're through." Then she turned and strode to her car.

Ray pulled out Catherine's chair, and when she took a seat, he followed suit.

Once Beverly had closed her car door and backed out of her parking space, Ray glanced across the table, his gaze meeting Catherine's.

"See what I mean?" he asked. "That kind of thing happens to me all the time. And most of them don't know how to take a polite no for an answer."

"Well, hopefully, once word gets out that you're taken, you won't have to deal with those kinds of distractions anymore."

That was his plan. Having a hired fiancée seemed to be working like a charm, thank goodness. Although he had to admit, another actress might not have been able to pull it off with Catherine's grace and style.

Ray studied the beautiful blonde as she ate the last of her salad.

The sunlight glimmered in her hair, making the strands shine like white gold… The teal-colored blouse she wore made her blue-green eyes especially vivid today.

While in the restroom, she'd reapplied her mascara, as well as her pink lipstick.

Damn, she was attractive. And not just because of her appearance. In a matter of two days, she'd added something to his life—smiles, camaraderie…

Of all the women he'd met since his split from Heather, Catherine seemed to be the only one who might not complicate things.

Of course, she was an actress, so who knew if he was seeing the real Catherine. She also lived—and no doubt thrived—in Manhattan, which was worlds away from Brighton Valley.

Still, if things were different…

If he could trust that the woman who'd revealed herself to him was real…

If she were a normal, down-home type…

If she planned to escape the city lights and excitement and move to a small Texas town…

…then Ray would be sorely tempted to ask her out on a real date.

Chapter 5

On Saturday afternoon Catherine climbed into the same old ranch pickup she'd driven before and headed for Ray's apartment, but she wasn't sure if she would make it or not. Each time she stopped at an intersection, the engine sputtered and chugged as though it might stall at any moment.

Thankfully, she reached the alley behind the drugstore and parked in the lot next to a battered green Dumpster.

Before climbing out of the cab, she reached into her purse, pulled out her cell and called Dan.

"I'm sorry to bother you," she said, "but there's something wrong with the pickup."

"Are you stranded along the road?"

"No, I made it. But I'm not sure if I'll be able to get home or not."

He paused a moment, then said, "The ranch hands

have all left for the day. And I'm still waiting for the vet. But I'll try to get out there as soon as I can."

Dan had a broodmare that was sick. And earlier this morning, while climbing on the corral near the barn, Kevin had fallen down and sprained his ankle, which was why Dan, Eva and the kids wouldn't be coming to the town barbecue.

"Don't give it another thought," Catherine said. "I just wanted to let you know. I'll ask Ray to look under the hood. And I'll also have him bring me home this evening."

"Don't bother asking Ray to look at the truck," Dan said. "As long as it won't put you in a bind or strand you in town, you can leave it right where it is. I'll call a towing service and have it brought home on Monday."

After she ended the call, Catherine got out of the pickup and crossed the parking lot. She'd borrowed a pair of cowboy boots from Eva, as well as faded jeans and a blue-and-white gingham blouse. She was certainly going to fit right in with the other Brighton Valley residents today, which ought to please Ray.

A smile tugged at her lips as she climbed the stairs to the small apartment, then used the key Ray had given her. She was a few minutes early, so once she was inside, she made herself at home—just as he'd told her to do.

The sparsely furnished apartment, while clean, tidy and functional, lacked any artwork on the walls or accent colors. She was tempted to pick up a couple of throw pillows, something to brighten up the place and make it a bit homier. But she supposed it didn't matter. Ray stayed here only on the nights he didn't want to drive all the way back to the ranch.

Catherine turned on the television. Then after finding the Hallmark channel, she took a seat on the brown leather sofa and watched the last half of a romantic comedy about a woman who was snowbound in a cabin with her ex-husband.

It wasn't until the ending credits began to roll that she heard another key in the lock, alerting her to Ray's arrival.

"I'm sorry I'm late," he said as he closed the door and stepped into the small living area that opened up to a kitchen and makeshift dining room. "I meant to get here sooner, but I was at a funeral of an old friend of my parents, and his widow asked me to meet with her and her attorney."

"Please don't apologize." Using the remote, she shut off the power on the television, then got to her feet. "I'm so sorry to hear that."

"Thanks. It wasn't a surprise. He'd been sick for a long time, so it was probably for the best." He loosened his tie.

Not only was Ray a successful rancher, he was also a loyal friend, which Catherine found admirable. No wonder he'd been elected to the city council and appointed mayor.

"Look at you," he said, breaking into a smile. "You're going to be the prettiest cowgirl at the barbecue."

Catherine didn't know about that, but she thanked him just the same.

"I need to change into something more appropriate," he said. "I'll only be a minute or two."

She knew he'd planned to be home a lot sooner than this. "Is there anything I can do to help? I know you'd wanted to arrive early."

"I was going to welcome everyone before the music

started, but that's not going to happen now. I'll just have to do that at the halfway point." His steps slowed. "In fact, I'm even going to take time to get a drink of water."

"Is your life always like this?" Catherine asked as she returned to her seat on the sofa. "Do you run from one event or meeting to another?"

"Yep. That's pretty much the way each day goes."

She smiled. "I'll have to keep that in mind if I ever decide to run for public office."

"Actually," he said, removing his jacket, "I never planned on going into politics, but a few of my friends and neighbors—including Dan Walker—had been urging me to run for the city council. I'd put them off for a while, but..."

"Now here you are," she said, "the mayor of Brighton Valley."

"The *interim* mayor," he corrected. "I'm covering for Jim Cornwall, remember?"

"Are you sorry you took on the extra work?" she asked.

"I really don't mind the job itself. The biggest problem I have is balancing all of my other responsibilities."

"Such as...?"

"The day-to-day duties on my ranch, as well as the new horse-breeding operation I'm just starting up with Dan." He blew out a sigh, and his shoulders seemed to slump a bit. "I hate leaving others to do the work I should be doing myself. And it's not easy being pulled in a hundred different directions. But I can handle it. Besides, now that you've stepped in as my 'fiancée,' things are a lot easier. I don't have to fend off the single ladies in town."

"That surprises me."

"What does?" He hung his jacket on the back of one of the dinette chairs. "That the women are interested in me?"

"No, not that." Goodness, not *that.* The man was successful, well-respected, personable and drop-dead gorgeous. "I'm just a little surprised that you're not the least bit interested in dating."

"I don't have time for a relationship. And even if I did, I'm not ready to get involved in another one."

If that was the case, then his ex-wife must have done a real number on him—just as Erik had done to her.

"Not that it's really any of my business," she said, "but why aren't you ready to start dating?"

"My divorce got ugly." He strode to the kitchen area, pulled a glass from the cupboard, then filled it with water from the tap. "And when the one person in the world you depend on to have your back kicks you in the ass instead…well, even a cowboy isn't too eager to get back in the saddle again."

She knew exactly what he meant. That's why she was in Brighton Valley these days, rather than in Manhattan.

After Ray had quenched his thirst and put the empty glass in the sink, Catherine said, "You mentioned that your divorce got ugly. I assume your marriage started out all right. When did things go south?"

"Probably after the first few weeks. But our relationship was wrong from the get-go. And it's my fault for not realizing that."

Catherine should have seen Erik's flaws, too, but love—or whatever she'd felt for him—had blinded her to them. She'd not only been hurt, but she'd felt pretty stupid, too. So it was nice to know she wasn't the only one who'd been snowballed by someone she'd cared about, someone she'd trusted.

"What clues did you miss?" she asked.

"First of all, Heather was a city girl who didn't like living on a ranch. And I was crazy for thinking she'd eventually get used to it." He clucked his tongue and shook his head. "She was also selfish and greedy. I'd noticed it going in, I suppose. But I hadn't realized just how bad it really was." He pointed to Catherine's left hand. "When I asked Heather to marry me, she turned up her nose at the ring you're wearing. I know it isn't much, but she couldn't see the value in it—the vows made and kept over the years."

Catherine lifted her finger, studied the small stone. Again she thought about Ray's grandmother, the woman who'd worn it and cherished the love and the promises it had represented.

"I should have taken a step back and reconsidered my proposal at that point," Ray said as he left the kitchen area, "but I stuck the ring in the safe, then went out and purchased a two-carat diamond for her instead."

Catherine had always believed there were two sides to every story—until she'd met Erik and fallen for his lies. So she found herself disliking Ray's ex-wife, even though they'd never met.

"Were the two of you ever happy?" she asked.

"At first, but once we got home from our honeymoon, the complaints started. And it became clear that she hated everything about my life—and me, too. Before long, she was spending more time in the city than she was in Brighton Valley. The day we split, she finally admitted that she was having an affair with a plastic surgeon."

"I'm sorry."

"About the divorce? Don't be. It was for the best. Trouble was, she hired a high-priced attorney out of Houston, and even though I'd expected to pay a hefty settlement, I hadn't been prepared for a legal battle. Each time I thought we'd reached some kind of agreement, she'd ask for something else. The whole thing dragged on for nearly two years."

Catherine didn't know what to say. Another *I'm sorry* seemed not only redundant but inadequate.

"I'm just glad it's finally over," he said. "So you can see why I'd be hesitant to get involved with someone else again—especially a woman who's only interested in me because she thinks I'd make a good catch."

Ray Mendez would make a *wonderful catch* for any woman, so Catherine could certainly understand why every Tamara, Diane and Mary in town was trying her best to snag his attention or set him up with someone she knew.

Yet Ray had a lot more going for him than his financial portfolio and political standing in the community. And he deserved a woman who'd be true blue and a helpmate to him.

"Dan said you'd been through a breakup, too," Ray said.

Catherine hadn't meant to bring up the subject. Goodness, she was trying to forget Erik and all he'd put her through. But after Ray's heartfelt disclosure, it seemed only fair to admit that she'd been hurt and disappointed, too.

"Last year I met a producer who'd recently moved to Manhattan from London. He asked me out, and we started dating. Before long, he promised me a starring role in the play he was producing, and I was thrilled. In fact, he also gave me an opportunity to invest in the production, which meant I'd reap some of the profit.

"For the first time in my life, I began to believe that I might finally be able to have it all—a successful career and a happy marriage. But he turned out to be a scam artist who ran off, taking the funding for a production that never came to pass."

"I'm sorry to hear that."

Catherine had not only been crushed and embarrassed by his deception, but she'd also lost a large chunk of her savings to the lying jerk.

"So you decided to get away for a while?" Ray asked.

That was about the size of it. She'd sublet her brownstone for three months and flown to Texas to stay with Dan and Eva.

"I figured that Brighton Valley would be a great place to lick my wounds and to sort out my options," she admitted.

And while she was here, she'd use the downtime to allow her body to mend. Like many professional dancers, she'd suffered a couple of injuries that made it difficult for her to continue performing in musicals.

To be honest, she hoped to land more singing or acting roles from now on. But she'd deal with that once she got back to Manhattan.

In the meantime, she tossed Ray an appreciative smile. "And thanks to you, I'll not only be able to stay longer, I'll also be able practice my acting skills while I'm here."

"I'm glad to do my part. You've been a real godsend. If things continue to go well, I'll have to give you a bonus."

With finances being what they were, she could certainly use the extra cash, but she couldn't take any more money for doing a job that came so easily to her.

"That's not necessary," she said. "I get a lot of perks working for you."

"Such as…?"

"Meals and entertainment."

As their gazes met, as their time so far together came to mind, another perk crossed her mind: heart-spinning kisses that turned her every which way but loose.

Her cheeks warmed at the memory. Afraid to let him know what she was thinking, she turned away, walked several steps to the window and peered at the street below just so she could break eye contact.

"When do you plan to return to New York?" he asked.

"I don't know. In a couple of months, maybe. I don't have a return flight scheduled."

She liked knowing she could leave whenever she grew tired of being in Brighton Valley, although she found the rural Texas setting both quaint and restful. But she'd grown up in a small town and had found it to be stifling.

In Manhattan, she'd thrived and had finally become the woman she was meant to be.

"Well, I'd better get into my boots and jeans," he said, removing his wristwatch and leaving it on the dinette table, "or we'll end up arriving even later than we already are."

Minutes later, Ray sauntered into the living room in his Western wear, his Stetson in hand. His bright-eyed, sexy grin was so mesmerizing that Catherine couldn't help thinking that he made the perfect cowboy hero to play opposite her.

How did Brighton Valley's most handsome and eligible bachelor get better-looking each time she laid eyes on him?

"I'm sorry I kept you waiting," he said.

She offered him a breezy smile and said, "No problem," even though she could see a huge one looming on the horizon.

Ray had hired her to keep the local ladies from setting their romantic sights on him, and she had no reason to doubt that they'd respect the phony engagement.

Catherine would respect the role she was playing, too. And there was the problem.

As Ray opened the door for her, she grabbed her purse and proceeded downstairs. In a matter of minutes she'd be strolling along the street with the hottest cowboy in town.

She'd pretend to be in love with the handsome mayor, although it wouldn't take much acting on her part to feign her affection or her attraction to him.

No, the real difficulty would be in forgetting that it was all part of the act.

Ray and Catherine decided to walk to the community barbecue, since the town square was just down the street. In fact, it was so close that they'd barely stepped onto the sidewalk when they caught a hearty whiff of mesquite-grilled meat and heard the sound of bluegrass music.

"It sure smells good," Catherine said.

"Wait until you taste it. Brighton Valley goes all out for this event."

Ray, who'd been fighting the urge to hold her hand while they'd made the five-block walk, reached for it now.

It was all part of the act, he told himself. Yet there

was something very appealing about Catherine. Something that made him happy to be with her.

Maybe it was the fact that she wasn't batting her eyelashes at him, that she wasn't delivering homemade cookies and hinting that she'd like more than a friendship.

Yeah, he told himself. That had to be it.

But as she slipped her hand into his, as their fingers threaded together, a burst of pride shot through him.

Or was it more than that?

Unwilling to let the possibility of anything "more" take root, he said, "I think you'll have a good time. Besides having the best barbecue food you've ever eaten, several of the local bands will be playing and trying to outdo each other as a way of promoting themselves for future parties and performances."

"Is it all bluegrass and country-western music?" she asked.

"For the most part. You'll hear some banjo groups and a couple of fiddlers. But there'll probably be some classic rock, too."

"It sounds fun."

He'd always liked attending the event, but something told him he was going to enjoy it a whole lot more with Catherine as his date.

Well, not a date in the classic sense of the word.

As they turned the corner and caught the first glimpse of the town square, Ray gave her hand a gentle squeeze. "Here we are."

The parklike area had already begun to fill with local residents, who stood in small groups on the grass or sat in some of the white chairs and tables they'd gotten from the party-rental company.

Near the courthouse, the Barbecue Pit, a local restaurant known for its great sauce, had set up an old-style chuck wagon, as well as a portable barbecue grill, where several men with white aprons watched the meat cook over mesquite chips.

Over by the restrooms, Charlie Biller's bluegrass band played their last set, as the Dave Hawkins Trio stood by, waiting to take their place on stage.

Now would be a good time for Ray to walk up to the microphone and welcome everyone to the event that had become one of the highlights of the year.

They'd barely stepped off the sidewalk and onto the grass when they were met by Buddy Elkins, one of the older city council members. Buddy was dressed in his cowboy finest—complete with boots, a silver buckle and a Stetson.

As recognition dawned, the silver-haired councilman headed straight for Ray with a big grin on his face. "I'd heard you snatched up the prettiest little gal in these parts, but I gotta tell ya', Mayor, the rumor mill didn't do this young lady justice. You really hit the jackpot this time."

Ray winked at Catherine, then released her hand so he could shake Buddy's. "You've got that right. I'm a lucky man. Catherine has renewed my faith in women."

That same surge of pride returned as Ray watched Buddy tip his hat to Catherine. "I'm pleased to meet you, ma'am."

She thanked him, then blessed him with a pretty smile.

Buddy elbowed Ray. "There'll be a hundred young men who'll be chomping at the bit to take your place—

and a few my age who'd like to give you a run for your money. So you'd better treat her right."

"You can bet on it." Ray stole a glance at Catherine, and she gave him one of those starry-eyed smiles he'd suggested she throw his way every now and again. But this one shot right to his heart—or somewhere thereabouts. In fact, if he didn't know better, he'd think it was real.

Too bad it wasn't. He could get used to having a woman look at him like that—especially if the lady was her.

Shaking off the effects of their playacting, Ray said, "I'm going to head over to the stage and welcome people to the barbecue. But I'll be right back, Buddy. So don't try to steal my girl from me."

Buddy, who was nearing seventy, chuckled. "I'll keep my eye on her and chase off any riffraff who might not be as honorable as I am."

Ray brushed a kiss on Catherine's cheek, but as he did so, he caught a whiff of her floral scent, which taunted him to distraction. But he didn't dare stray from his task, so he excused himself and headed for the bandstand.

Along the way, several of the local townspeople stopped him to ask about one thing or another—but mostly to congratulate him on his engagement. For the first time in what seemed like ages, no one tried to hit on him or introduce him to the perfect woman.

Apparently the Brighton Valley residents had begun to realize that he'd already found her.

Of course, when it came to hired fiancées, he certainly had. Catherine was not only classy and sophisticated, but she also seemed to have a down-to-earth way about her.

Ray reminded himself that she was a talented actress who was able to immerse herself in a role. And even though a bucolic setting and small-town personalities held little appeal to a woman who'd moved on to the big city, Catherine appeared to be in her element and charmed everyone she met.

In fact, Ray felt a little bewitched by her, too.

When Charlie Biller, the leader of the bluegrass band, noticed Ray standing near the stage, he nodded to acknowledge him.

As soon as the song ended, the audience broke into applause. Charlie thanked them, then announced, "Let's all give a hand to Mayor Mendez."

Once Ray stood at the microphone, he welcomed everyone to the barbecue, then thanked the committee members who'd worked so hard to put on the event, as well as the local businesses and citizens who'd made donations of both money and goods.

"Before I turn the stage over to Dave and his trio," Ray said, "I'd like to take a minute to thank you for offering your best wishes on my engagement."

A brief hush fell on the crowd, followed by a gasp or two and some startled looks.

Ray scanned the grounds, looking for Catherine, finding her in the same place he'd left her. "Honey? Where are you?"

The townspeople, many of whom hadn't heard the news, began to crane their necks, seeking the woman in question.

Catherine, who wore a pretty smile, lifted her hand and fluttered her fingers. Then she blew Ray a little kiss.

Damn. She was good. And so *natural*....

So believable.

But Ray couldn't very well stand there and gawk at her like everyone else. So he said, "Let's get on with the show."

As the trio of banjo players took their place onstage, Ray stepped onto the lawn, only to be stopped by Clyde Wilkerson, one of the local ranchers.

"I had no idea you were engaged," Clyde said. "When in the world did that happen? My wife was planning to invite you to dinner so she could introduce you to our niece."

"I kept things quiet until I popped the question and she said yes."

Clyde took another gander at Catherine. "Lucky you. She's certainly a pretty one."

"Yes, she is." Ray found himself craning his neck, looking for her. And wanting to make his way back to her.

"Where'd you find her?" Clyde asked.

"In Houston. I saw her dance on stage at the Yellow Rose Theater, and I knew right then and there that I had to meet her. We've been seeing each other for several months now."

"I don't suppose she has a sister," Clyde said. "I'd sure like to see my son Grady find a lady like that."

Catherine, who'd managed to break free of Buddy, made her way to where Ray and Clyde were standing. She offered Ray an I-missed-you-baby smile, then slipped her arm through his.

Trouble was, Ray had kind of missed her, too.

He supposed he ought to be glad his ploy was working—and he was. The whole town square was abuzz with whispers about the mayor's new lady and nods of approval, indicating they were all clearly impressed by the match.

Thank goodness for that small miracle.

Some bachelors might find it nice to have nearly every single woman in town trying to catch their eye. And while Ray had spent more than his share of lonely nights during the months leading to his divorce and the two years after he and Heather had split, he'd put it all behind him now. And it grated on him to have anyone assume that he'd never be a whole man until he landed another wife, when that couldn't be any further from the truth.

Heck, even if he were the needy kind, he wasn't interested in complicating his life with romance until long after his job as interim mayor was finished. And to be honest, the jury was still out on whether he ever wanted another wife or not. His divorce had left him more than a little gun-shy when it came to trusting his heart to anyone again. So he wasn't going to give matrimony another try anytime soon.

Of course, it was a little weird and disconcerting to think that he'd not only had to pay through the nose to divorce the ex-wife who'd made his life a living hell, but that he was now paying a fake fiancée to keep his life simple and maintain his privacy.

On the other hand, he found himself enjoying Catherine's attentions far more than he could have imagined.

So he placed his hand on her lower back. "Come on, honey. Let's get something to eat."

They'd no more than taken a couple of steps when an old pickup started up, then backfired.

Catherine jumped. "What was that? A gunshot?"

Ray slipped his arm around her and smiled. "No, it was just an old truck that needs a tune-up."

“Oh, thank goodness.” As they walked toward the chuck wagon, she leaned into him, just as if it was the most natural thing in the world to do.

And maybe it was.

“Speaking of old trucks,” she said, “I completely forgot to mention this. Dan’s pickup, which I drove into town today, isn’t running very well. So I’m going to need a ride home this evening—unless you don’t mind me sleeping on your sofa.”

No kidding? Ray would love to have her stay the night with him in town. And she didn’t need to take the sofa. She could sleep anywhere she liked.

“If you spend the night,” he said, “I’ll take you to Caroline’s Diner for breakfast in the morning. The Brighton Valley Rotary is meeting in the back room, and that way, people will assume we’re not only engaged but sleeping together.”

It was kind of a lame excuse, especially since Ray hadn’t even planned to attend the meeting. But if it meant having Catherine to himself this evening, then so be it.

“Sounds good to me.”

It did? Was she feeling that comfortable with him, too? Or did spending the night just make her job easier?

The only way to find out for sure was to ask, and he wasn’t about to do that.

They continued on to the chuck wagon and the spread of food that had been set out on long tables, but it took nearly twenty minutes to get there, thanks to all the folks who stopped them to offer their congratulations.

Each time it happened, Catherine lit up like a happy bride at her wedding.

Needless to say, the phony engagement was working

beautifully, and Ray couldn't imagine anyone thinking that Catherine wasn't in love with "her man."

He supposed he ought to be pleased, but for some reason, he felt compelled to steal her away from the crowd, to find someplace quiet and romantic where they could spend the rest of the evening alone.

And he didn't dare contemplate why.

Chapter 6

As the sun set over Brighton Valley, black, wrought-iron gas lamps that had been spaced throughout the town square came on, bathing the parklike grounds in a soft glow.

An hour earlier, Ray had introduced Catherine to Shane and Jillian Hollister, then asked the couple to join them at their table when they ate dinner. Shane, who'd once been a detective with the Houston Police Department, had worked on Dan Walker's ranch prior to being appointed as the Brighton Valley sheriff.

Shane was off duty today, yet he continued to make the rounds, just as Ray did. But Catherine didn't mind fending for herself. She'd hit it off with Jillian. And she also enjoyed holding Mary Rose, the Hollisters' three-month-old daughter.

"It must be tough leaving the baby with a sitter while you do your student teaching," Catherine said.

"Yes, it is, but my grandmother recently moved to Brighton Valley and watches Mary Rose for me. In fact, Gram loves providing child care and even has her own little nursery set up. So I'm really fortunate in that respect."

Catherine studied the infant in her arms and smiled. "It seems like ages since I've held a little one."

"Did you have brothers and sisters?"

"Yes, but by the time I left for college, I was so eager to get a break from them that I didn't think I'd ever want to have kids of my own."

"Have you changed your mind?"

"I suppose," Catherine said wistfully, "but I've had a lot of female problems, including endometriosis. The doctor told me that I'd probably never conceive."

"I'm sorry to hear that," Jillian said.

"Me, too." Catherine glanced up and gave her an I've-accepted-it smile. "But the Walker twins have become the children I'll never have. After Kaylee and Kevin were born, I fell in love with them. And since their mother was my roommate, the kids lived with me for the first five years of their lives. So at least I've had the whole baby experience—times two."

Catherine glanced down at Mary Rose, realizing that holding someone else's child wasn't the same as holding her own.

The thought of adopting someday struck again, which was comforting. At least she had options available to her.

"You know," Jillian said, "my doctor, Selena Ramirez, is a great obstetrician/gynecologist. She was a resident at the Brighton Valley Medical Center, but started up her own practice last year. You might want to check with her and get a second opinion. She also treats infertility."

If Catherine were going to stay in town, she'd give it some thought. But she had no business even thinking about home and hearth and families at this point in her life.

Still, she scanned the town square, searching for Ray and finding him talking to Jillian's husband. As their gazes met, a warm feeling spread throughout her chest, setting off a yearning she couldn't quite explain.

What was that all about? It's not as though she and Ray actually had a future together.

Jillian glanced at the bangle watch she wore on her wrist, then sighed. "As much as I'd like to stay here, I need to take Mary Rose home. It's getting close to her bedtime."

Catherine took one last look at the precious infant in her arms, then handed her back to her mommy.

"I need to let Shane know I'm leaving," Jillian said. "That is, if I can find him."

"He's over there," Catherine said, pointing toward the chuck wagon, "talking to Ray."

"Oh, yes. I see them." Jillian reached for the diaper bag, then paused. "I hate to leave you sitting by yourself."

"Don't feel bad about that. I like sitting here, listening to the music." She'd also enjoyed talking to Jillian, as well as the various townspeople who occasionally stopped by to introduce themselves and to welcome her to Brighton Valley.

"Shane and I will be inviting you and Ray for dinner one day soon," Jillian said, as she prepared to leave.

"I'd like that." Catherine had found it easy to talk to Jillian. And the fact that she was also a friend of Eva's made it all the nicer.

"Hopefully, Ray will come back soon."

"I'm sure he will." Catherine offered her new friend a smile. "And even if he doesn't, I'm in no hurry to leave. I'm having a good time."

As Jillian crossed the lawn and approached her husband, Catherine watched her go. Once she'd reached Shane's side, Ray spoke to them both for a moment longer, then he softly stroked Mary Rose's dark hair before returning to Catherine's table.

"How are you holding up?" he asked as he took a seat beside her.

"I'm fine. How about you?"

"Winding down." He lifted his Stetson with one hand, then combed his fingers through his dark hair with the other. "It's been a long day, and I'd really like to say my goodbyes and get away from the crowd and all the noise."

It must have been especially tiring for him. Even though he wasn't being bombarded by matchmakers, a lot of people continued to drag him off to talk about a project or a problem they had.

"Will you be able to leave soon?" Catherine asked. "Or do you need to stay until it's over?"

"It's supposed to go on for another hour, but I don't need to stay that long."

As she studied him in the soft light created by one of the gas lamps, she noticed that his expression had turned serious, creating a furrowed brow.

Was something weighing on his mind? Or was he just tired, as he'd implied?

When his gaze caught hers, he seemed to shake the serious thoughts. "You've got to be worn to a frazzle."

"Not really." She'd been able to kick back and enjoy the day, but he hadn't been that lucky. He'd had to work.

In a sense, she supposed she'd been working, too.

But being Ray's fiancée hadn't required much effort on her part. It had been an easy role to fall into. In fact, at times it felt as though the two of them were a real couple.

But even if it was real, long-distance relationships had two strikes against them already. Not that Ray had indicated he'd like to become involved in something like that.

As the country-western band began to play a slow and sultry love song, Catherine stood and reached out her hand to him. "Okay, Mr. Mayor. I've been patient long enough. You've been so busy with your civic duties that you haven't even gotten around to dancing with the woman you love, and I think it's high time you did."

He tilted his head slightly, then when he caught her wink, he smiled, slipped his hand into hers and let her lead him to the dance floor.

On the stage, an attractive young brunette vocalist sang "Breathe," the hit song that had earned Faith Hill a Grammy.

The local singer certainly wasn't as talented as Faith, but she gave it her all, and the other couples who'd gathered on the dance floor seemed to appreciate her efforts.

"I should have thought of this earlier," Ray whispered, as they walked across the lawn. "People are probably wondering why I haven't been courting my fiancée properly."

"I'm not so sure about that," she said, lowering her voice to match his. "We put on a believable act for them."

In fact, there'd been times throughout the day that she'd nearly forgotten that she really wasn't his lover, that he'd only hired her to play the part.

When they reached the dance floor, Catherine turned to Ray, whose smile had lit his face and completely chased away that furrowed brow.

"I'm not a bad dancer," he said as they came together, "for an amateur. But I'm sure you're used to guys with a lot more talent than I've got. So take it easy on me, okay?"

As she peered into his eyes and saw them sparkle with mirth, she returned his grin. "I'm not looking for any fancy footwork, Ray. All you need to do is sway to the music, and I'll follow your lead."

As he opened his arms, she stepped into his embrace, savoring the warmth of his body and the musky scent of his cologne.

It's an act, she told herself. But as she felt the strength of his arms, as they melded into one on the dance floor, she couldn't help wishing there was something more going on between them.

If things were different…

If she were going to stay in Texas indefinitely…

If she didn't have a career waiting for her in New York, directors who'd like to cast her again…

But how crazy was that? If she stayed in Brighton Valley, she'd have to give up all she'd ever wanted, all she'd worked so hard to achieve.

No, they just had this time together—today, tonight, next week. Who knew how long she'd stay in town? Who knew when the urge to return to the stage would strike?

The song, it seemed, ended all too soon. And as Ray released her, she hadn't been ready to let him go.

That is, until their eyes met and she spotted the intensity burning in his gaze.

Well, what do you know? The dance had affected him, too.

"Come on," he said, taking her by the hand. "Let's go home."

Her heart skipped a beat, then slipped into overdrive.

Home, he'd said. But right now, she'd follow him anywhere—no matter what role she was playing, even if she were merely being herself.

Ray had taken Catherine's hand when they'd walked off the dance floor, and he continued to hold it as they left the town square and headed back to his apartment.

He wasn't sure what he'd expected when he'd taken her into his arms—just a run of the mill slow dance, he supposed. But when his hands had glided along the curve of her back and he'd drawn her close, there'd been more than a seductive tune and lyrics swirling around them.

No one ever told him that acting could be so much fun—or so arousing. He could almost imagine their phony romance taking a turn toward the real thing.

Would he ever find a woman like Catherine—or like the woman she was pretending to be?

Again, he wondered how much was acting and how much of it was genuine. After all, he was only human. And he'd been celibate for nearly two years.

Damn, had it really been that long?

He had no idea what to expect when they returned to his apartment—a good-night kiss or maybe one of appreciation? It was hard to say, but something told him that any kiss they shared was going to consume him with lust for the beautiful woman who had the ability to turn him inside out with just a smile.

Still, he was glad to know she'd be going home with him. Even if it meant one of them would be sleeping on the sofa.

As they walked down Main Street, which was quiet

now that the stores had closed, their boot soles crunched along the sidewalk.

"There's something appealing about Brighton Valley," she said.

"I think so."

"How'd you like growing up here?"

He wasn't sure why she'd asked, but he gave her an honest answer. "It was great. I can't imagine living anywhere else."

She seemed to think on that for a moment, then she nudged her arm against his. "You mentioned being an only child. That must have been nice—and peaceful. The house I grew up in was just one drama after another."

"My home life was nice and quiet, but it was lonely at times."

She smiled. "Sometimes people can be lonely in a crowd."

He supposed she might be right about that. "It wasn't so bad, though. My parents wanted me to socialize, so they let me invite plenty of friends to come to the ranch."

"Did you have any cousins?" she asked.

"Nope. It was just one set of grandparents, my folks and me. In fact, I was the only son of an only son."

"I'm sorry," she said.

"Don't be. It wasn't so bad." A smile tugged at Ray's lips, as he thought back to the loving home in which he'd grown up. "I was a late-in-life baby, whose birth was an answer to my mother's prayers. Needless to say, all the adults in my life doted on me."

Catherine's smile deepened, setting off her pretty dimples. "I'll bet they're proud of the man you've grown up to be."

"They were. They sat in the front row of every school

play I was in, every Little League game I played. And they cheered, even if I messed up, telling me that it didn't matter."

"Do they live with you?" she asked. "I mean, it being a family ranch and all."

"No. My grandpa passed away when I was a junior in high school, and my dad died three years later. I lost my grandmother next, and my mom right before my thirtieth birthday."

"That's too bad. I'm sorry."

He was, too. "I guess that's the downside of having older parents. You usually lose them a lot sooner than most of your friends."

He sensed her grieving for him, and he appreciated the sentiment—whether sincere or not. Heather hadn't fully understood or sympathized with his loss—and she hadn't even tried to fake it. Instead, she'd thought he was lucky to have been the sole heir of the family ranch, the biggest spread in Brighton Valley and all the investments his family had accrued over two generations.

But he would have given it all up just to have his family still with him.

As they neared the drugstore, he realized they'd be at his apartment in no time at all and he found himself looking forward to having some time alone with the woman who was unlike any other he'd ever known.

"So what about school?" she asked. "Did you attend college?"

He wasn't sure what had triggered her curiosity, yet he didn't mind her interest in his past. So he said, "I went to Texas A and M."

There didn't seem to be any reason to mention that he'd graduated at the top of his class and received several job offers before his last semester—a couple in the Dallas area and one near Houston. He'd turned them down, though. Instead, he'd come home and taken over the family ranch, which he'd made even more successful than his grandfather and father had made it.

As they continued to hold hands and to make their way down the quiet, deserted downtown street, Ray relished the intimacy they shared.

"What about you?" he asked.

There wasn't much to tell—at least, when it came to her childhood—but Catherine supposed it was only fair that he quizzed her, too.

"I don't have too many good memories of growing up. By the time I graduated from high school, all I wanted to do was get on the first bus heading to Ohio."

"Ohio?" he asked.

"I had a scholarship to Crandall School of Fine Arts. It wasn't my first choice of colleges, but it had offered the best scholarship and was the farthest from home. So I jumped at it."

"And that's where you met Jenny Walker?"

She nodded. "Then we both moved to Manhattan."

Once she'd left New Mexico, she'd really begun to thrive in the college setting—and even more so in the metropolis, where she'd finally become the woman she was meant to be.

"I've never gone to New York," he said. "Brighton Valley must be a huge culture shock for someone used to a city that's open twenty-four hours a day."

"That's for sure."

Their boots continued to crunch on a light film of grit on the sidewalk that lined the empty street, reminding her just how huge the difference was. Still, there was something appealing about the community, as well as the people she'd met so far.

When they reached the drugstore and the stairwell that led to Ray's apartment, his steps slowed. Then he withdrew his hand from hers and motioned for her to go first.

As she started up the lit steps, she wondered what the evening would bring. More disclosures, she supposed.

Would he kiss her again? Probably not. Once they were completely out of sight from any passersby, it wouldn't be necessary.

Still, she couldn't help but hope that he would, and by the time they reached his front door, her heart rate kicked up a notch.

Ray pulled out his keys, slipped them into the lock, then let her in. Once inside the small apartment, he hung his hat on the hook by the door.

She scanned the sparsely decorated living area, again tempted to do something to help him add a little color. In one of several small apartments inside of an old brownstone in Greenwich Village she called home, she'd done her best to brighten up the drab rooms by using vivid shades of red, yellow and blue, then adding a splash of purple here and there.

Even her furniture back home—a selection of black, glass and chrome—was modern in style.

Still, she supposed there was no need for him to go all out on the decor of the place when he spent only occasional nights.

She wondered what his ranch was like—and whether he'd ever invite her to go out there with him. She'd really like to see it.

"I can put on a pot of coffee or decaf," he said. "I also have a bottle of merlot."

Coffee probably was the safest bet, but she liked the idea of kicking back with him and having a glass of wine.

"The merlot sounds good," she said.

"I think so, too. Why don't you have a seat while I open the bottle."

Catherine made her way to the leather sofa and settled herself near one of the armrests, leaving room for Ray to join her. Then she watched him move about in the kitchen area as he removed a wine bottle from the pantry, two goblets from the cupboard near the sink and a corkscrew from the drawer.

He wasn't at all like the men she'd known in Manhattan, although he was pure eye candy, no matter how he was dressed. His dark hair, which was mussed from the Stetson he'd worn earlier, was a bit long and curled at his collar. She supposed some women might think it needed a trim, but she wasn't one of them. In fact, she didn't think she'd change a thing about the man.

Broad shoulders tapered down into a narrow waist, and—

Before she could continue her perusal, he turned and smiled at her.

Did he realize she'd been making an intense assessment of his lean, cowboy body, appreciating both his form and his style?

She hoped not, yet her cheeks flushed warm.

He carried the wineglasses to the sofa, then handed her one. "Here you go."

When she thanked him, he took a seat beside her.

The lamplight cast a romantic glow in the room, but it

was the handsome cowboy who'd set her heart spinning, her hormones pumping and her imagination soaring.

She remembered something one of her friends had told her in Manhattan. *Once you meet another man—even if it's just a one-night stand—you'll forget all about Erik Carmichael.*

At the time, Catherine hadn't been interested in anyone else—not even to go out for a cup of coffee.

But what about Ray? Would he make the perfect transitional relationship?

She took a sip of wine, hoping to shake the thoughts that began to plague her. She couldn't very well suggest that they have an affair while she was in town, could she?

No, that would have to be Ray's idea.

"You know," he said, "I'd like to make a toast to the best hired fiancée I've ever had."

Catherine smiled, then clinked her wineglass against his. "And to the best male lead an actress ever had."

Did she dare tell him how easy her role had been? How tempted she was to stop playacting and see what developed between the two of them?

Not that she'd want to actually be engaged or marry him one day, but would making love with him be out of line? After all, if the man's kisses turned her inside out, what would a full-on sexual encounter be like?

Just the thought of it shot a warm, intoxicating buzz right through her, and she hadn't taken more than a couple of sips of wine.

"I'll sleep on the sofa tonight," he said. "You can have my room."

"That isn't fair."

"What isn't?" A boyish grin tugged at his lips, and

a spark of mischief lit his eyes. "Did you want to fight me for the sofa?"

"Maybe," she said, teasing him right back.

Truth was, she'd seen his room—and the size of his bed. It was plenty big enough for both of them.

She told herself that she was just being thoughtful when she said, "There's no reason for you to sleep out here and be uncomfortable. I don't mind sharing the bed, if you don't."

The mischievous glimmer in his gaze disappeared, and something else took its place—something intense. Something masculine.

"It's not like we'd do anything other than sleep," she added by way of explanation. Yet the moment the words left her mouth, she realized she wouldn't be doing much sleeping if he were lying beside her, just an arm's reach away.

Goodness. What had she done?

She wished she could blame it on the wine, but her thoughts had taken a sexual turn the moment she'd entered his house.

When they finished their first glass, Ray poured them a second.

"Just half for me," she said. "Thank you."

After filling his glass, he walked over to the stereo and turned on the radio to a country-western station. She didn't recognize the artist or the song, but she liked the music.

"This is really nice," she said, lifting her glass and studying the deep burgundy color in the lamplight.

Yet she was talking about more than the music or the wine. She meant this moment, this man.

She was tempted to suggest something they might

both regret. And with a man who was her employer. Wasn't there something unethical or inappropriate about that?

"You know," she said, "I'm going to need something to sleep in tonight. Do you have an old shirt and a pair of shorts I can use?"

"Sure." He placed his goblet on the coffee table, then strode to the bedroom.

She heard the closet door open and shut, followed by a bureau drawer.

When he returned, he held a large maroon T-shirt that sported a white Texas A and M logo on the front, as well as a pair of black boxer shorts. "How's this?"

"Perfect."

"I've also got a new toothbrush you can use," he added. "It's in the right-hand drawer in the bathroom."

"Then I'm all set." She got to her feet and took the makeshift nightwear he'd given her. "Thanks."

"You may as well take the bathroom first. You'll find clean towels hanging on the rack, in case you'd like a shower."

She offered him an appreciative smile, then headed for the bathroom, wondering what he'd say if she offered him a lot more than a smile upon her return.

Chapter 7

While Catherine was in the bathroom, Ray walked to the window and looked out into the darkened street below. He'd been both surprised and pleased when she'd agreed to stay with him tonight. But that had nothing to do with the long drive back to the ranch and everything to do with the fact that he wanted to spend more time with her, to have her to himself for a while.

He actually looked forward to being around her, and not just because she was a pleasure to look at. He enjoyed talking to her, too. There was something very appealing about her, something alluring that went beyond sexual fascination.

Maybe it was due in part to the fact that he was safe with her. She understood that he didn't want to get romantically involved with anyone right now, so she hadn't pressed him for anything other than friendship.

Of course, if things were different, if she planned to stay in Brighton Valley—and more important, if he could be sure that the persona she'd revealed to him wasn't just part of an act—he might even ask her out on a real date, complete with soft music, candlelight, roses and wine.

But even if she was just as sincere, considerate and sweet as she appeared to be, she was going back to New York one of these days. So he'd just have to enjoy their friendship and whatever time they had left.

Now here they were, tiptoeing around all the sweet dreams and bedtime stuff.

The water shut off in the bathroom, which meant she was probably climbing from the shower and reaching for a towel, naked and wet.

That particular vision was a lot more arousing than it ought to be, but then again, the tall, leggy blonde was a beautiful woman who also seemed to have a good heart.

To top that off, he'd been serving a nearly two-year term of self-imposed celibacy, which was really starting to eat at him now—big time.

He tried to shake it off—the sexual thoughts, the arousal, but he wasn't having much luck.

Had she dried off yet? Had she slipped on his shorts and his shirt?

She'd mentioned that they could sleep together tonight, although he supposed she was only being practical. But the moment she'd suggested sharing the bed, his thoughts had taken a sexual detour.

And that's exactly where his thoughts were right now.

He could almost see her in the bathroom, wrapped in a towel and facing the fogged-up mirror. In his mind, he stood behind her, damp from the shower, too. His hands reaching for the edge of the towel, tugging it gently, removing it. Revealing that lithe dancer's body in the flesh.

He was going to drive himself crazy before she even left the bathroom.

As a soft, country love song began to play on the radio, setting off a romantic aura in the room, his libido began to battle with his good sense. In spite of his better judgment, the idea of making love with Catherine grew stronger by the heartbeat.

He probably ought to change the station and find something with a livelier beat, but he didn't make a move toward the stereo.

Instead, when the bathroom door opened, he turned to face the woman he'd envisioned naked just moments before.

Her platinum-blond hair had been swept up into a sexy twist, revealing a ballerina's neck, just begging for hot, breathy kisses.

She smiled when she spotted him, her eyes lighting up. He probably should have responded with a platonic grin of his own. Instead, he allowed his gaze to sweep over her, amazed by those long, shapely legs that could wrap around a man and make him cry uncle. Or aunt. Or whatever else she had in mind.

"It's a little steamy in there," she said.

Hell, it was even steamier out *here.* And while he had no business making any kind of sexual innuendo, he couldn't help speaking his mind. "Seeing you like that..." His gaze sketched over her again, making it difficult to continue without acting upon his arousal.

"I can change into something else," she said, glancing down at the shirt she wore, "if you'd be more comfortable. Or..."

Or *what?* Was she going to suggest that they let nature take its course this evening?

Sure, why not? he wanted to say.

She didn't continue the open-ended option, but the way she was looking at him—which had to be the same way he was looking at her—didn't leave a whole lot of doubt that her thoughts had taken a sexual turn, too. But hey, why shouldn't they?

He could throw out the idea, he supposed, laying it on the table—or wherever else they might end up. But what would he do if she told him it wasn't in her job description?

Then again, he might kick himself later for letting a once-in-a-lifetime opportunity slip through his hands.

"How long has it been for you?" he asked, stepping out on a limb that swayed under the weight of the question.

"Since I've had sex?" She gave a little shrug. "Quite a while. How about you?"

Had he actually been celibate for two long years?

After he and his ex had split, it had seemed like a good way to avoid getting caught in another bad relationship before he had time to get over the last one. But now?

He couldn't imagine going without sex for a minute longer.

They stood like that for a moment—too far away from each other to touch, yet connected in a way he hadn't expected.

"I know that a short-term affair wasn't part of our bargain," she said, "but I wouldn't be opposed to it."

At that, his pulse rate shot through the roof, and his mouth went dry, then wet. Before meeting Catherine, he hadn't really missed sex all that much. Not that he'd planned to give it up for good.

But now? When the opportunity of a lifetime was knocking?

He took a step forward, then another. "I wouldn't be opposed to it, either."

"It might actually help us both move along in the healing process," she said.

There was no doubt about that. Just the thought of taking Catherine in his arms had his heart spinning—and all in one piece—strong, vibrant, whole.

"We've definitely got chemistry," he said as they met in the middle of the room.

"That's true. If the kisses we shared were any indication of how good it would be between us..."

He finished the thought for her. "Then making love is going to be off the charts."

She nodded.

Still, he didn't make a move.

And neither did she.

When she bit down on her bottom lip, he wondered if it was a shy reaction to what was going on between them or if it was... No, it wasn't part of her act. Neither of them were playing a role right now. This—whatever *this* was—had to be real.

For a while, he'd wondered where fantasy ended and reality began when it came to his feelings for her. But when push came to shove, he had to admit that he'd quit playacting about the time of their very first kiss.

In fact, he'd even become intrigued by the idea of dating her and... What? Pursuing her?

Maybe so—at least, that was his game plan tonight.

When Ray opened his arms and Catherine stepped

into his embrace, he relished her clean, fresh-from-the-shower scent, as well as the feel of her soft breasts pressed against his chest.

He realized she must be entertaining a similar game plan because she wrapped her arms around his neck and drew his lips to hers. As their tongues met, their kiss exploded with passion, with heat.

She tasted of peppermint, of sunshine and dreams, and he couldn't get enough of her. His hands sought, stroked and explored every uncovered inch of her, but still he wanted more, needed more. He reached for the hemline of her T-shirt, lifting the fabric, revealing her bare waist, her taut belly, her perfect curves....

When his hand reached her breasts, he cupped the soft mounds, caressed them. As his thumb skimmed across her nipple, her breath caught.

Damn. He couldn't believe his good fortune. They were actually going through with this, and he couldn't be happier—no matter what tomorrow brought. And by the way Catherine was responding to his touch, to his kiss, he had a feeling she felt the very same way.

Caught up in an amazing swirl of heat and desire, Catherine leaned into the rugged cowboy and gripped his shoulders as if she might collapse if she hadn't. And who knew? Maybe she would have.

Never had she wanted a man so badly, so desperately. If she didn't know better, she'd swear that they'd been made for each other—their bodies, their hearts, their souls.

She kissed him back for all she was worth, wanting him, wanting this.

There might be a hundred reasons they shouldn't

allow themselves to get carried away tonight, but tell that to her raging hormones. Right now, all she wanted to do was let him work his cowboy magic on her and take her someplace she'd never been.

As the kiss ended, they clung to each other, their breaths ragged, their hearts pounding.

"Let's take this to the bedroom," Ray whispered against her cheek.

She didn't trust herself to speak, so she slipped her hand in his and allowed him to take her anywhere he wanted to go.

They padded across the hardwood floor, and moments later, when they reached the bed, he took her in his arms again and kissed her until her thoughts spun out of control, until nothing else mattered other than this man and this night.

His hands slid along the curves of her back, then he pulled her hips forward, against his erection. She arched forward, showing him her need, as well as her willingness to make love to him.

When she thought she'd melt into a puddle if they didn't climb into bed and finish what they'd started, she ended the kiss, then she removed the T-shirt he'd loaned her. As she let the garment drop to the floor, she stood before him in nothing but the boxers he'd loaned her.

His gaze caressed her as intimately as his hands had done just seconds earlier. "You're beautiful, Catherine."

Her only response was to reach for his belt buckle and to begin removing his clothing, too. She needed to feel his bare skin against hers, and she couldn't wait another minute.

Together, they removed his shirt, and she marveled at his broad chest, his six-pack abs.

Catherine wasn't a novice at lovemaking. She'd had lovers before—two, in fact. But neither of those men had been built as strong and sturdy as Ray, whose muscles were a result of both genetics and hard work.

"You're beautiful, too," she said.

After they'd drawn back the spread and slipped into bed, Ray showed her how a cowboy loved a lady, creating a memory she'd never forget.

They moved together in rhythm that built until they reached a breath-stealing peak. As she cried out with her release, he let go, too, climaxing in a burst of fireworks and spinning stars.

Never had she felt such passion or experienced such an earth-shattering orgasm.

As she lay in Ray's arms, relishing the stunning afterglow, a sated smile stretched across her face. She'd expected their lovemaking to be good, but she'd never imagined it would be like this.

She tried to tell herself that it was merely a physical act, that there wasn't anything emotional going on. Making love with Ray had been a great way to completely shake any lingering disillusionment she'd had after her breakup with Erik. Yet she found herself wading through a rush of emotions she hadn't expected.

As she pondered those budding feelings, Ray stiffened, then rolled to the side.

Was something wrong?

"I, uh...hate to put a damper on things," he said, propping himself up on an elbow and casting a shadow over the sweet afterglow she'd thought they'd both been enjoying.

Her stomach knotted, and disappointment flared. Just

moments ago, everything had seemed right—perfect, if not promising. Was he regretting what they'd done?

The possibility sent her tender emotions into a tailspin, making her question the value she'd placed on their lovemaking. As her mind scampered to make sense of it all—not only the budding emotion their joining had stirred within her, but also her agreement to enter into a fake engagement in the first place. What had she been thinking?

Determined to protect herself, she decided to downplay their joining and her unexpected emotional reaction to it.

"It was just a physical act," she said, "something we both needed."

"Yes, I know." He brushed a strand of hair from her brow in a sweet and gentle manner, yet the look on his face remained serious, sending her a mixed message.

"This doesn't mean we have to change our employment agreement," she said, taking a guess as to what might be bothering him. "And don't worry. I'm not going to ask for any kind of commitment or chase after you like some of the local women have done."

"I know that." While his expression seemed to soften, his demeanor remained tense, maybe even defensive.

"Then what's bothering you?" she asked.

"You don't know?"

No, she didn't. That's why she'd assumed that he was regretting what they'd done. And why she'd tried to assuage whatever worry he might have.

As he slowly shook his head and clicked his tongue, she braced herself for the worst.

"We didn't use any protection," he said.

Oh, no. He was right. They hadn't.

"And it's not like me to be irresponsible."

It wasn't like her to neglect something important like that, either. But apparently, they'd gotten so carried away with the passion that they'd lost their heads.

"You might have gotten pregnant," he added. "And that's a complication neither of us needs right now."

She appreciated his concern, but at least she could put his worries about that to rest. "It's not the right time of the month for me to conceive. And even if it were, it isn't likely. I've been told my chances of having a baby are slim."

"I'm sorry to hear that."

She was sorry, too, but she'd come to accept it. "It was depressing to hear that news when the doctor told me, but I'm okay with it now. Dan and Eva's twins have adopted me as their auntie, so I'm glad to be a part of their lives."

The conversation was getting entirely too heavy and too sad to deal with after such an amazing bout of love-making. And while Ray might have said that he hadn't wanted to put a damper on things, he'd done just that.

She rolled slightly, moving away from him. Then she slipped out of his arms, climbed from bed and headed for the bathroom.

"Are you okay?" he asked.

She turned, glanced over her shoulder and offered him her brightest smile. "Of course."

But she *wasn't* okay. She was struggling with rejection, disappointment and the sudden reminder that she'd never have a baby of her own. Not that she'd expected to have one with Ray, but at least for a moment or two while making love, she'd entertained the brief fantasy of having it all someday: a husband and children, a home in the suburbs. Yet for some reason, and without any warning, that dream fell apart before it could even begin.

She had to find some solid ground on which to stand and some time to ponder what they'd just done, what she'd briefly imagined it to be and what she would do about it now.

When she'd kissed him, when she'd agreed to make love, she'd only thought of it as a sexual act. Yet thanks to the chemistry between them, it had been even better than she'd anticipated. Amazing, actually. And it had seemed to be a whole lot more than physical.

Surely, she'd only imagined the emotional side of it—at least, on her part. So until she could sort through it all and figure out a way out of it, she needed to be alone for a while.

If that darn pickup wasn't having engine trouble, she'd tell Ray that she was driving back to the ranch tonight. But as it was, she was stuck here until morning.

After their lovemaking last night, Catherine had stayed in the bathroom for what had seemed like hours, although it was probably only a matter of minutes. She hadn't seemed the least bit concerned about pregnancy, which should have made Ray feel better. But for some reason, it hadn't helped at all. He'd still been uneasy about the whole thing.

Not that he regretted making love with her. The time spent in her arms had been incredible, a real fantasy come true. But now that the new day had dawned, so had reality.

A relationship between the two of them, which had seemed so feasible in the heat of the moment, was no longer viable. The possibility had dissipated the moment

Catherine had returned to the bedroom, only to curl up on her side of the mattress, rather than cuddle with him.

Now, as he lay stretched out on the bed, trying to set aside the uneasiness that had niggled at him all through the night, he tried to focus on the memory of their love-making. Of course, any sexual encounter would have been great after a two-year dry spell.

Or would it?

When he tried to imagine being in bed with another woman, each time he gazed into the fantasy woman's eyes, he saw Catherine smiling back at him, urging him on.

He told himself that was because the memory of their lovemaking was so fresh in his mind, so *real.* In that one, amazing moment, when the two of them had become one, climaxing at the same time, he'd wanted to hold on to her and never let her go. He'd also been tempted to spill his heart and soul to her—if he'd actually thought that what he'd been feeling for her had been real. But as his heart rate and his breathing slowed to a normal pace, he'd realized that he'd neglected to use a condom, that he hadn't even had the foresight to purchase any ahead of time. And the irresponsibility left him completely unbalanced.

He appreciated the fact that pregnancy wasn't an issue, but he had other concerns, too. Like becoming emotionally attached to a woman who wouldn't be in Brighton Valley forever.

Besides, just because sex between a couple was absolutely incredible, especially the very first time, didn't mean that they'd be compatible.

When the bathroom door clicked open, and Catherine walked out wearing the clothes she'd worn to the community barbecue last night, she cast a friendly smile his way. Yet they really weren't friends at this point. In fact, he wasn't sure what they were to each other. He supposed they were lovers, but would that be true if this was just a one-night thing?

He had no idea. Still, he sat up in bed, determined to face the uncertainty of the day.

"Would you like to eat breakfast here or at Caroline's Diner?" he asked.

"If you don't mind, I'd really like to get back to the ranch. I promised Eva I'd help her with the kids this morning."

He wished he could say he was relieved, yet for some reason, he hated to see her go, which made no sense.

Nevertheless, he threw off the covers and climbed out of bed. "No problem. I'll take a quick shower, then I'll drive you back to the ranch."

"Thanks."

Again she smiled.

And again, he sensed there was something missing in her expression.

He'd never seen her like this—wrapped up in some kind of invisible armor, her thoughts a million miles away.

She'd withdrawn last night, right after their climax. Had she been truthful when she'd told him not to worry about pregnancy?

Or was she angry that he hadn't been more responsible?

No, she couldn't be mad about that. She should have thought about the consequences of unprotected sex, too.

Was she kicking herself for letting it happen? He supposed he wouldn't know unless he addressed the issue.

"Is everything okay?" he asked.

"Yes, it's fine." She crossed the room and placed a kiss on his cheek as if trying to convince him, yet failing miserably.

Something still wasn't right.

"Are you sorry about what we did last night?" he asked.

"No, not at all." She offered him another smile he couldn't trust. "How about you?"

"I'm not the least bit sorry." Okay, so that wasn't entirely true. He wasn't sorry about having sex—and he doubted that he ever would be. His only real regret stemmed from her mood change and the distance between them.

As Ray went into the bathroom and shut the door, he tried to rehash everything that had gone on the night before so he could figure out what went wrong—and *when.*

The lovemaking itself seemed perfect.

When he'd rolled to the side and gazed at her, she'd been wearing a serene smile—a *real* one. And that proved that they'd shared the same pleasure.

It was only after she'd returned from the bathroom that things had grown a little…chilly.

Shouldn't he be happy that she wasn't putting any pressure on him, especially when she'd be moving back to New York soon?

Or had he begun to fall in love with an actress? A woman who pretended to be someone else?

By the time he got out of the shower, he wasn't any closer to having an answer than he'd been last night.

Even after he'd dried off and gotten dressed, he still wasn't sure what was going on between them—or how he ought to feel about it. But there was one thing he did know. He was in danger of falling in love with a woman who might not exist.

When he entered the living area, Catherine was seated on the sofa, waiting for him.

"You know," he said, as he grabbed his keys from the dinette table, "I was thinking. We've done a good job convincing everyone in town that I'm engaged. And after that announcement at the barbecue last night, people will know I'm off-limits. We probably don't need to be seen together constantly."

"You're probably right." She got to her feet. "Just give me a call at the ranch if you need me again."

For what? Another date to a community event he had to attend. Or for another night of lovemaking?

Damn. It almost sounded as if she was ending it all—their employment, their friendship, their… What? Their star-crossed affair?

An ache burrowed deep in his chest, and he wished that he could roll back the clock twelve hours and start over. But it was too late to backpedal now.

"There's not much going on for another week," he said, "but I'm sure I'll need you again."

"No problem. Just let me know when."

He locked up his apartment, then followed her down the stairwell.

"How much longer do you plan to be in town?" he asked.

"I'm not entirely sure. But probably as long as you might need me."

For a moment, he was tempted to say that he'd like for her to extend her visit, that he had a feeling he would need her for a long, long time. But he couldn't say that. Instead, he thanked her for all she'd done to help him.

"And I'd also like to thank you for…last night. It was amazing. Maybe we can do it again sometime. But if not, that's okay, too."

"I feel the same way."

Did she?

He certainly hoped they weren't on the same page, because he hated not having a game plan. And he had no idea where to go from here.

Chapter 8

The drive back to the Walker ranch was fairly quiet, other than the sound of the music playing softly on the car radio.

Catherine hoped that she'd put Ray's worries to rest, although she wished she could say the same for herself. What had happened last night?

If she didn't know better, she'd think that she might actually fall for Ray—if she wasn't careful.

And if that was the case, then it really was for the best that they slow down their time spent together. Ray had made it more than clear that he didn't have any interest in striking up a romance—with *anyone.*

Besides, she had a life in New York. Getting involved with the Brighton Valley mayor wasn't a good idea. And if she let her feelings get in the way, their relationship—or whatever it was—could end in disappointment or heartbreak. And heaven knew she didn't need to risk having something like that happen.

When they arrived at the ranch, Ray kept the engine running.

"I have a meeting in Wexler with a couple of investors at noon," he said. "And while I'm in the area, I thought it would be a good idea if I talked to my foreman first. So, if you don't mind, I'm just going to drop you off. Can you tell Dan and Eva I said hello?"

"Of course."

His gaze zeroed in on hers, reaching out in a way that gripped her heart and nearly squeezed the beat right out of it.

"One more thing," he said.

She stiffened, and her breathing slowed to a near stop as she readied herself for whatever he had to say.

"Thanks again for last night. It was *amazing. You* were amazing. And it was both a gift and a memory I'll cherish."

Emotion balled up in her throat, making it difficult to speak. Yet, somehow, she found her voice and mustered a smile. "I thought it was special, too. And, for the record, I'm not sorry about it." At least, she didn't regret making love with him. It was the unexpected emotional fallout that had her scampering to make sense of it all.

"I'll give you a call in a day or two," he said.

"Sounds good." She lifted her hand in a wave, then watched him back up his SUV, as if he was backing out of her life forever.

She'd told him that she wasn't sorry, and in a sense, that was true. But now that she'd opened up to him, now that they'd shared a physical intimacy as well, she had to admit that she grieved for what might have developed between them. Because, if truth be told, she would have been tempted to remain in Brighton Valley indefinitely if he'd given her any reason to think that he'd wanted her to.

And how crazy was that? Her life and her career were in Manhattan. Giving up everything she'd ever wanted, everything she'd achieved, for a man was unthinkable. Yet the thought had crossed her mind just the same.

Catherine turned and headed for the ranch house. After climbing the steps and crossing the porch, she opened the front door and entered the living room, where Kaylee and a little red-haired girl sat beside a pink-and-chrome child's karaoke machine, five or six dolls surrounding them.

Upon seeing Catherine, Kaylee brightened. "You're home!"

She smiled, glad that she'd been missed. But at this point in time, she wasn't really sure where "home" was. Her apartment in Greenwich Village had been sublet for six more weeks, so she couldn't even fly back to New York if she wanted to. Still, she said to the child she thought of as a daughter, "Yes, sweetie. I'm home."

She watched the two girls set the dolls in a semicircle. "What are you doing, Kaylee-bug?"

"Me and my new friend, Shauna, are making a Broadway show for our dolls, just like you do. And after we practice, we're going to invite you and our moms to watch it. Well, not her mom. But her..." Kaylee turned to the red-haired girl. "Who is she again?"

"She's my foster mom, I guess." Shauna, a tall, gangly child who appeared to be a year or so older than Kaylee, gave a little shrug. "Her name is Jane Morrison. And she's a lot nicer than the last one I had before."

Catherine's heart went out to the girl, with big green eyes haunted by sadness.

In an effort to let Shauna know that her situation wasn't all that unusual, Catherine said, "I'm kind of like Kaylee's foster mom, too."

"Yeah," Kaylee said. "When my mommy died, me and my brother lived with Catherine. Then we moved to the ranch with my Uncle Dan and Aunt Eva. But now that we're adopted, they're our dad and mom."

"Sometimes life gets complicated," Catherine said to the child, yet the reality of the words echoed in her mind, reminding her of Ray and of the awkward situation she'd created for herself.

"Shauna goes to my church," Kaylee added. "And on Monday, she gets to go to my school. I'm going to ask Mrs. Parker, the principal, to let her be in my class."

"It's nice to meet you," Catherine said. "And I'm glad you'll have at least one friend when Monday comes around."

"That's why Mrs. Morrison brought her to our house today," Kaylee said. "She's already gone to about a hundred different schools."

"Only four," Shauna corrected. "But that's okay. I'm used to being a new kid."

Catherine doubted anyone ever got used to being moved around that much or placed in new households, but she let the subject drop and asked, "Where's your mom, Kaylee?"

"She's in the kitchen."

Catherine set her purse on the bottom step of the stairway, planning to carry it up later. Then she made her way through the house, eager to find Eva and seek some advice—that is, if she had the courage to tell her what she'd done.

When she entered the kitchen, she spotted her friend standing at the sink, chopping vegetables to add to the Crock-Pot on the counter.

"Need any help?" Catherine asked.

Eva turned and smiled. "Thanks, but I've got it under control. How was the barbecue?"

"It was fun. The food was great, the music, too. And I really enjoyed the people I met."

"I'm sorry we missed it, but I couldn't take Kevin after he twisted his ankle."

"Where is he?"

"Dan took him to the Urgent Care in town to have an X-ray. We really don't think he fractured it, but it was still swollen and sore this morning. So we wanted to get a doctor's opinion—and to make sure he didn't have any serious tissue damage."

"I'm sorry I wasn't here earlier," Catherine said. "I could have watched the kids for you. Then you both could have taken him to the doctor."

"No, Dan can handle it. Besides, Kaylee has a friend over today, and it was important that I stayed home for that."

Catherine took a seat at the table. As she did so, she realized that the house was unusually quiet. "Where are the little ones?"

"Uncle Pete took them on a nature walk. Then he's going to put on a cartoon movie at his house and feed them lunch. I wanted Kaylee and Shauna to have some time alone so they could get to know each other better."

"Kaylee introduced me to her. She seems like a nice little girl, but I feel sorry for her."

"You don't know the half of it," Eva said, her voice lowered. "Her mother died when she was just a toddler. And somehow, she ended up with the stepfather. When he went to prison, she was placed in foster care. From what I understand, her maternal grandmother finally got custody, only to be diagnosed with terminal cancer a few months later. The poor kid has really been through a lot."

"I'm glad Kaylee is reaching out to her. How did you meet her?"

"Jane Morrison, one of the women in our church, is her new foster parent. And she asked if we could help with the transition." Eva turned back to her work long enough to put the veggies into the Crock-Pot, then she washed her hands at the sink. "How about a cup of herbal tea? I just put on a pot of water to heat."

"Sounds good."

Eva carried the sugar bowl, spoons and a variety of tea bags she kept in a small wicker basket to the table. Then she filled two cups with hot water, setting one in front of Catherine. She'd no sooner taken a seat when she asked, "What's the matter?"

"Nothing." Catherine opened a packet of Earl Grey, then dropped the tea bag into her cup of water. "Why?"

"I don't know. You look a little tired, I guess."

It was, Catherine decided, a perfect opening to tell Eva why she felt so uneasy, what she and Ray had done. But she wasn't sure if she was ready to admit to all of that—or if she'd ever be ready. So she said, "I guess I'm just a little tired. I didn't get much sleep last night."

"Sometimes that happens when you sleep in an unfamiliar bed."

"Yes, I'm sure that's it." Catherine glanced down at the steeping tea bag, wishing the leaves were loose instead of contained, wishing she could empty the cup and read her future.

"Uh-oh," Eva said.

Catherine glanced up at her friend, and as their gazes met, Eva cocked her head to the side as if she'd read Catherine's mind.

"I sense that something's either *very* right," Eva said, "or *very* wrong."

At first, Catherine assumed she was talking about the children, but when she caught the knowing look in Eva's eyes, she realized the conversation had taken a personal turn.

"What do you mean?" she asked.

"You and Ray might be faking an engagement, but you look good together. And you're both as nice as can be. If you lived in town, or had plans to stay, I'd probably encourage you to consider him as a romantic possibility."

"But I *don't* plan to stay in town," Catherine said, more determined to leave now than ever.

"I know." Eva took a sip of tea, and a smile tugged across her lips. "The two of you would make a great couple. And since you're both nursing broken hearts, it seems natural that one or the other or both of you would find the other attractive. And that in itself might be the cause for a restless night."

Yes, and so would the emotional aftereffects of great sex, especially when a romantic future didn't look the least bit promising.

Before Catherine was forced to either lie or to admit more than she was willing to share, Kaylee came bounding into the kitchen. "It's time for the show. Will you please come and watch us?"

"I wouldn't miss it for the world." Eva picked up her

cup and looked at Catherine. "Do you mind bringing your tea into the living room? They've been practicing all morning."

"No, not at all." Catherine picked up her cup and saucer, then followed Eva and Kaylee back to the living room.

"There's going to be a talent show in our school cafeteria," Kaylee told Catherine. "And me and Shauna are going to be in it. We're going to sing and dance, just like you and my mommy."

Shauna kind of scrunched up her face. "It's Kaylee's idea. She wants me to be the singer, and she's going to dance."

"There's a talent show at the kids' school?" Catherine asked Eva. Could it be the same one she'd heard about while attending the hospital benefit with Ray? The one Dr. Ramirez had suggested she take part in?

"The Brighton Valley Junior Women's Club is sponsoring it," Eva explained. "There's been a lot of talk about building a center for the arts on the new side of town, and they'd wanted a fundraiser. They're even encouraging the school children who sing, dance or play an instrument to participate."

"That's really nice." Catherine would have loved getting involved in a community event like that when she'd been a girl.

"And Catherine," Kaylee said, "you can be in it, too. You could sing that song about the raindrops on roses, the one you used to sing to me and Kevin."

Catherine smiled, remembering the days when she lived with the twins. "You're talking about 'My Favorite Things' from *The Sound of Music*."

"Yes, that's the one," Kaylee said. "Will you sing it at

our school? And can you wear a beautiful costume like the ones you have in New York?"

Kaylee had been only five when her mother died, but she still remembered the times Jennifer and Catherine would take her backstage to see the costumes and props. One set in particular had been a pirate ship, and Kevin had loved the tour one of the stagehands had given him. But Kaylee had especially enjoyed seeing some of the gowns up close.

"It would be really nice if you participated," Eva added, "especially since you're 'engaged' to the mayor. I'm sure he'd be pleased if you did."

Catherine wasn't sure what would please Ray these days, although she suspected he'd like the idea. And she missed performing for an audience—no matter what the size. But she didn't want to upstage any of the local talent—not when she was a professional.

"I don't mind getting involved with the talent show," Catherine said, "but I don't think it's a good idea if I compete with any of the local townspeople."

"I understand," Eva said. "It might not be fair to everyone involved. But maybe you could perform at the end of the evening. Or what if the grand prize was a voice or dance lesson from you?"

"It would have to be up to the committee heading up the event," Catherine said, "but I'm willing to do anything I can to help out."

"What about *us?*" Kaylee said. "You can give lessons to me and Shauna so we can be the winners."

"You'll always be a winner in my heart," Catherine said. "And I'd love to give you two a few pointers."

The girls clapped their hands with glee, then turned

on the karaoke machine. Within minutes, they put on a darling show.

Shauna, who belted out a Hannah Montana/Miley Cyrus hit, had a natural talent that nearly knocked Catherine off her chair. On the other hand, Kaylee, bless her heart, hadn't inherited her mother's dancing ability.

Then again, maybe she just needed a few pointers. Either way, the kid had heart. And their performance brought maternal tears to Catherine's eyes.

When the "show" ended, the women broke into applause, praising both girls.

"I'll tell you what," Catherine said as she swiped at her watery eyes with her fingers. "I'd be happy to coach you girls for the community talent show."

Kaylee squealed in delight, while Shauna smiled.

"And I'll make the costumes," Eva added as she placed her hand on the red-haired girl's shoulder. "I'm also going to ask Shauna's foster mom to help me. This is going to be so much fun."

She was right. Catherine was going to enjoy helping the girls. She was also looking forward to having something to do over the next few weeks that would help to keep her mind not only off Ray, but off the mess she might have made out of their budding friendship.

After dropping Catherine off at the Walkers' place, Ray had driven twenty minutes to his own ranch to talk to Mark Halstead, his foreman. He could have used his cell phone rather than make the trip in person, but he'd needed to get some perspective, and there was no better way to do that than to step onto the old family homestead, to breathe in the country air, to see the cattle grazing in the pastures.

The bluebonnets his mother had loved dotted the hillsides these days, and while seeing them wasn't the same as entering her kitchen and finding her baking homemade cinnamon rolls as a treat, it was the best he could do.

He'd hoped that once Catherine had gotten out of his Escalade, he'd be able to sort through what had happened, and then decide what he wanted to do about it—if anything.

All morning long, he'd been beating himself up, although he wasn't sure why. He wasn't sorry they'd had sex, although it had definitely changed things between them. And he had no idea if that change had been good or not.

For one thing, he'd come pretty damn close to falling for Catherine Loza, another city girl who'd never want to be a rancher's wife. And to make matters worse, she would be leaving soon—and taking a part of his heart with him, if he was fool enough to offer it to her.

You'd think that after all the hell his ex-wife had put him through, he'd be fighting to remain single and unattached for the rest of his life. Not that he would ever broach the idea of a commitment with Catherine.

Besides, she'd said it herself. *It was just a physical act, something we both needed.*

And she'd certainly been right about that. He'd needed the release more than he'd realized. Maybe he'd needed the intimacy, too. He'd come from a very small but close family who'd been both loving and supportive. But as each family member had died, one after the other, he'd slowly lost parts of his connection to someone who'd loved him unconditionally.

He'd actually hoped that Heather would have stepped

up to the plate in that respect, but whatever connection they'd had began to fray the day she'd moved in with him. And that was fine with him. He'd learned to get by without those family ties.

Besides, he had good friends who'd been supportive, like Dan Walker and Shane Hollister.

Yet in just a few days, he'd begun to feel that bond and the sense of kinship again—*with Catherine,* as strange as that might seem. Their whole relationship, whether they were friends or lovers, had been based upon a lie. So how could he place any value on whatever feelings he might be having for her, especially when he had no idea how much—if any—of the real Catherine she'd actually revealed to him. She could be putting on one hell of a show, and he wouldn't know the difference.

Still, he couldn't quite bring himself to let her go. It might be foolishness on his part—or a bad case of lust—but he didn't like the idea of ending her employment just yet. If he did, he'd have to explain their breakup to everyone in town.

Okay, so that's the excuse he was making to continue their charade—and he hadn't even reached the family homestead yet or breathed the country air that seemed to clear his mind.

As he neared the feed lot, which was only five miles from the long, graveled driveway that led to his ranch, he began to realize that he had another reason for maintaining the phony fiancée plan, and it wasn't nearly as practical.

Or maybe it was. He'd been yearning for something elusive, something he seemed to have temporarily found with Catherine.

Call him a fool, but after allowing them both some

time to think, some time to put things into perspective, he was going to ask her to attend another function with him.

So what was next on his calendar?

The only thing he could think of was that birthday dinner at the American Legion Hall to honor Ernie Tucker.

Ernie, who'd been the first sheriff in Brighton Valley, was going to be one hundred years old on the fourteenth of the month. So the town had planned to have festivities all weekend long, beginning with the fancy dinner. There was going to be a parade down Main Street on Saturday, and finally, on Sunday morning, the Brighton Valley Community Church would have an ice cream social in his honor.

If you asked Ray, it seemed a bit much. Poor old Ernie was going to be plumb worn out from celebrating come Monday. But not many folks could claim to reach a milestone birthday like that, especially when they were still spry and sharp as a tack.

So now he had a good reason to call Catherine and set up another date—so to speak.

Why was it that he couldn't wait to distance himself from her just moments ago, yet now he was thinking about seeing her again?

He wasn't going to ponder the answer to that, but attending a birthday celebration with her seemed safe enough.

When he spotted the three oak trees that grew near the county road, marking the property line at the southernmost part of his ranch, he imagined being with her on the night of Ernie's dinner party, walking down the quiet city street, feeling the heat of her touch as his hand reached for hers.

And as he let the fantasy take wing, he imagined taking her back to his apartment, this time with a game plan that included a night's supply of condoms, a room full of candles and anything else he could think of to create the perfect romantic setting.

It was a risky thing to do, he supposed, especially since any kind of a relationship between them would last as long as an icicle in hell.

But then, tell that to his libido.

Every day that following week, after Kaylee and Shauna got out of school, Catherine worked with them on their dance steps, as well as on the song they planned to perform for the talent show. Eva had insisted that the other children stay out of the way so the girls could practice without interruption. And while there were a few complaints from the younger twins, they forgot their disappointment as soon as Eva suggested a new outdoor activity to keep them occupied.

As a result, Kaylee and Shauna worked hard. It didn't take Catherine long to realize they stood a chance to win, especially if the competition was divided into age groups.

"Shauna," she said, "I think it's time you tried to sing without using the karaoke screen."

"I don't know about that." The shy, gangly girl bit down on her bottom lip. "I'm not sure I can do it without the words."

Catherine smiled. "Actually, you haven't been relying on the screen that much anyway. Why don't you give it a try and see how it goes?"

"O-kay."

Before Catherine could start the music, her cell phone rang. She would have ignored the call completely, but it might be Ray. And she…

Well, they hadn't seen each other since last Saturday, although things seemed to be okay both times they'd talked on the phone. So she was eager to…

What? Hear his voice?

She clicked her tongue as she glanced at the lighted display, and when she recognized his number, her heart stopped momentarily, then spun in a perfect pirouette.

You'd think she'd been waiting for days to hear from him. And, well…okay, she *had.*

"Excuse me, girls. I need to take this call." As she prepared to answer, she walked out of the living room and onto the porch, telling herself he probably had something work-related to say and nothing that would require her to seek privacy. But she still didn't want an audience, just in case.

Once she was out of earshot, she said, "Hello."

"Hey, it's me." They were just three little words—not even three that held any real importance, yet the deep timbre of his voice shot a thrill clean through her.

"Hey, yourself," she responded.

"Am I bothering you?"

"No, not at all."

"Good. I called to ask if you were available to attend a few functions with me next weekend."

Not until then? She shook off a tinge of disappointment. "Sure, what's up?"

"There's a birthday party at the American Legion Hall on Friday night for Ernie Tucker, one of Brighton Valley's oldest residents. There's also a parade in his honor on Saturday and an ice-cream social at the community church after services on Sunday. Can you attend all of them with me?"

She didn't see any reason why not.

"You're welcome to stay with me in town," he added, "if you'd like to."

Her heart thumped and bumped around in her chest like the worn-out rods and pistons in the ranch pickup she'd driven into town last week. The one that hadn't been safe for her to drive home.

You're welcome to stay with me in town...if you'd like to.

Oh, she'd like to all right. Her thoughts drifted to the night she and Ray had slept together, and she was sorely tempted to agree. At least her body was eager. But her heart and mind were telling her to slow down and give it some careful thought.

Was he actually suggesting that she spend three days and two nights with him in his apartment in town?

"We can always figure something else out," he added. "I can take you home between the events—or you can drive yourself. It's really up to you."

"Let's take one day at a time."

At least that would give her time to think things through.

"By the way," she said, "what's the dress code on Friday night?"

"Whatever you're comfortable wearing. Some people will be casual, while others might get dressed up. I'll probably wear a sport jacket."

"And for the parade?" she asked.

"Slacks, I guess. Or maybe jeans, if you'd prefer. Nothing fancy."

"How about the ice-cream social?"

"Well, that's casual, too. But I suspect some people will have on their church clothes." He paused for a moment, as though wanting to say something else.

When it became apparent that he had nothing more to add, she said, "I'll be glad to go with you. Why don't I meet you in town on Friday evening?"

"You mean at my apartment, right?"

She wasn't sure what she meant. "Okay, I'll meet you there. We can talk about the sleeping arrangements later."

He paused a beat. "Fair enough."

There was so much left unsaid that the silence filled the line until it grew too heavy to ignore. But instead of mentioning the chasm their lovemaking had created between them, she told him goodbye and promised that they'd talk again—soon.

Yet thoughts about the future followed her back to the living room, where the girls had continued to practice without her.

She'd no more than taken a seat when her cell phone rang again. She glanced at the display, thinking Ray might have forgotten to tell her something, but she recognized Zoe Grimwood's number.

"I'm so sorry," she told the girls. "But I need to take this call, too."

As Catherine returned to the patio, eager to hear what was going on in Manhattan, she greeted her friend.

"Guess what?" Zoe said. "Word is out that Paul De Santos has managed to pull things together financially. And he's going to start casting parts for *Dancing the Night Away*."

That was the show Erik had been producing when he'd left town, taking several large investments with him.

"I saw the script," Zoe added. "And the lead would be perfect for you."

Erik had said the same thing—before he'd talked Catherine into investing fifty thousand dollars of her own money into the project. The man she'd trusted had burned her in many ways when he'd left. The most difficult, of course, had been facing the irate investors and telling them she had no answers for any of their questions.

"I'm not sure how Paul would feel about me auditioning for any of the parts," Catherine said. "He probably blames me. Erik left him holding the bag. He had to deal with the investors who'd lost their money and try to make things right."

"Paul can't hold you responsible," Zoe said. "You invested in the project, too."

Still, Catherine had been dating Erik, so she should have been able to see through him. If Paul considered her guilty by association, she'd never land the part. So, no matter how badly she wanted it, why should she even audition?

"I'll have to think about it," she said.

"Why? That part was made for you. And Paul has to know it."

She was certainly tempted. If she went back to New York and landed a role in the very musical Erik had been trying to produce, it might vindicate her in the eyes of everyone she'd ever known or worked with on Broadway.

Catherine crossed the porch and peered through the window, into the living room, where the girls continued to practice their dance steps.

"I've got a commitment here for the next couple of weeks," Catherine said. "I can't come immediately."

She also had a commitment to Ray, the job he'd asked her to do. And then there was their budding romance or whatever they'd been tiptoeing around.

Tiptoeing around? That sounded as if they were both considering some kind of relationship, when she didn't know *what* either of them were actually thinking, let alone feeling.

She slowly shook her head. She'd better get the stars out of her eyes, or she could end up brokenhearted again. Ray had made it clear that he didn't want to date anyone. Otherwise, he wouldn't have hired her to keep the women at bay.

So what made her think he'd be interested in her—other than the fact that she was safe and would be leaving soon?

And worse, what if she was wrong? What if he actually considered striking up a romance with her? And what if she were foolish enough to go along with it?

She might end up married to the guy—and stuck in a small town forever.

"How's your knee?" Zoe asked.

When Catherine had been in New York, she'd been having a little trouble with it. She'd considered seeing a specialist, but the down time had really helped. "It's a lot better than it was—in fact, I think it's completely healed, although it's still a little stiff."

And that reminded her. If she was going to return to Broadway, she'd have to start working out again. She'd also have to lose a couple of pounds.

"Okay," she told Zoe. "I'll do it. Once I have my flight scheduled, I'll give you a call."

At that moment, Kaylee ran out to the patio and

tugged at Catherine's sleeve. Then she pointed toward the living room, where Shauna was belting out the song.

"She's not looking at the screen," Kaylee whispered, her eyes bright. "She's doing it, just like Hannah Montana!"

Catherine smiled at the child she thought of as a daughter and gave her a wink, then returned to her telephone conversation with Zoe. "I can return in a little over two weeks, but I won't have access to my apartment for another three. Will you let me stay with you for a while?"

"Absolutely."

"Okay, then. It's all set."

As she ended the call, she told herself it was time to go home. It was the right thing to do.

The *only* thing.

Chapter 9

On Friday night, twenty minutes before the birthday party was scheduled to start, Catherine arrived at Ray's apartment.

And he was ready for her.

He'd stocked a box of condoms in the drawer of his nightstand—just in case. He also had two selections of wine—a nice merlot lying on its side in the pantry, as well as a pinot grigio chilling in the fridge.

Not that he was going to try and seduce her. But this time, he was prepared for a romantic evening, especially since he hadn't been ready the last time.

As he swung open the door, he found her waiting for him, her striking blond hair glossy and curled at the shoulders. She'd chosen a festive red dress for the party, one that was both modest and heart-stopping at the same time.

What other woman could pull off something like that?

The moment their eyes met, all was lost—every thought, every plan, every dream he'd ever had.

What was it about Catherine that had him wishing things were real? That their feelings for each other were mutual? That their engagement wasn't just an act?

"I'm sorry I'm late," she said. "I'd meant to get here sooner."

"No problem." He slipped aside and let her in. "The American Legion Hall is just a short walk from here. We ought to arrive in plenty of time—that is, if you're ready to go."

In the soft living room light, he scanned the length of her one more time, deciding she was as dazzling as ever in that simple red dress and heels.

Yet when he spotted the little black clutch she carried and realized it was too small to hold much of anything, even a toothbrush, a pang of disappointment shot through him.

She'd said that they could talk about the sleeping arrangements later, although he suspected she'd already made up her mind. That is, unless she left an overnight bag in her car—just in case.

A guy could hope, he supposed.

"Do you want to come in for a drink or something?" he asked. "Or do you want to head for the party?"

"I'm ready whenever you are."

"All right, then." He lifted his arm in an after-you manner, then stepped out the door, locked up the apartment and followed her down the stairs.

She looked hot tonight—like a model striding down a runway, all legs and sway. And for the next couple of hours, she was all his.

Another pang of disappointment shot through him. What he wouldn't give to know that she was here because she wanted to be. Would she have come if he'd actually asked her to be his date?

He supposed he'd never know, because he sure wasn't going to ask her.

As they continued out onto the sidewalk and started down Main Street, she slowed in front of the florist shop, where a variety of potted orchids were displayed in the window.

"I love exotic flowers," she said.

He'd have to remember that.

When they reached the beauty shop, which had a Closed sign in the window, Ray came to a stop. "I'm sure you'd never consider getting your hair done in a small town like this, but you ought to check it out sometime. Darla Ortiz, the owner, used to be a Hollywood actress back in the sixties. And she's decorated the place with all kinds of memorabilia."

"No kidding?" Catherine stopped, too, then peered through the window and into the darkened shop that had closed an hour earlier.

Ray caught a whiff of Catherine's floral-scented body lotion, something exotic, something to be handled with care—or cherished from a distance like those orchids at the floral shop.

He did his best to shake it off, as he stood next to her and looked into the darkened hair salon.

"It's pretty cool inside," he said. "Darla has a wall full of framed headshots of various movie stars who were popular forty and fifty years ago. Some are even black-and-whites from the post–World War II era. And each one is autographed to her."

"I'll make a point of stopping by to see them," Catherine said.

Feeling a little too much like one of the older women in town who worked for the local welcoming committee or a fast-talking real estate agent bent on selling the community to a new buyer, Ray said, "Come on. We'd better get moving."

As they started down the street again, he couldn't help adding, "Brighton Valley is a small town with a big heart."

"I've sensed that."

He wanted to say that the same was true of most of the residents, including the mayor, but he decided he'd better reel in his wild and stray thoughts before he went and said something stupid. Something he might not be able to take back.

Instead, he decided to enjoy the evening with Catherine—whatever that might bring.

The Ernie Tucker birthday committee had gone all out in decorating the American Legion Hall for the celebration, complete with red, white and blue balloons and matching crepe-paper streamers. Several picture collages on poster board had been placed at the entrance, as well as in various spots around the room.

Each board had a slew of photographs—old brown and whites, a few Polaroids and some in color. They each provided a view of Ernie's life from the time he was a baby until present day.

"There's a lot of history here," Ray said.

"I can see that."

One particular photograph caught Ray's eye. Ernie

was a kid, standing barefoot next to the original Brighton Valley Community Church.

"For example," he said, pointing to the picture. "That church burned down nearly sixty years ago. And the congregation rebuilt it in its present location on Third Street."

"How did it happen?"

Ray chuckled. "Fred Quade and Randall Boswell who, according to my grandmother, never did amount to much, snuck out of Sunday services one summer day. They hid out in the choir room, where they decided to drink a beer and light up a smoke. Before long, they were both sicker than dogs and ran outside, leaving two smoldering cigars next to the robes hanging in the closet. And before long, the church was on fire.

"It seems that old Reverend McCoy was giving one of those fire and brimstone sermons. My grandmother said there were a few people who thought that brimstone was raining down on Brighton Valley."

Catherine smiled, then pointed at a picture of Ernie receiving a Hero of the Year award from the city council back in the 70s. A young boy, Danny Marquez, stood next to him. "Is that Ernie and his son?"

"No, it's the kid whose life he saved. There'd been a car accident, and the vehicle slammed up against a brick building. When it caught fire, the boy was trapped inside. His mother was thrown from the car, but she was seriously injured and couldn't get to her son.

"Ernie came along and, using a tire iron, broke out the front window and pulled him to safety. Ernie suffered some burns in the process, but he became a local hero that night."

"The community must love him." Catherine scanned

the crowded room. "Looks like quite of few of them have come out to celebrate his birthday."

"Yep. Ernie has always been one of the white hats, as far as people in Brighton Valley are concerned. Not only was he the town sheriff for nearly forty years, he was also a veteran of World War II and received a Bronze Star. There are a lot of people in town who will tell you that they don't make 'em like Ernie Tucker anymore."

Ray's granddad had been a local hero, too, and if he'd lived to be one hundred, the town would have also come out in droves. But Ray didn't see any need to comment. This was Ernie's big day—and one that was well deserved.

"Come on." Ray nudged Catherine's arm. "Let's go wish ol' Ernie a happy birthday."

They did just that, and for the next two hours, Ray and Catherine made the rounds at the party, talking to one person or another.

Finally, after cake and ice cream had been served, Ray and Catherine wished Ernie the best, then made their way to the door and out onto Main Street.

Just as they were leaving, Kitty Mahoney, one of the local matrons who'd been trying to set him up with her daughter, stopped them and congratulated them on their engagement.

"You're a lucky gal," Kitty told Catherine.

Ray wrapped an arm around Catherine's shoulder. "I'm the fortunate one. I thank my lucky stars every day that this lady agreed to be my wife."

For a moment, he actually believed it—that they truly were a couple, that they had a future together.

Kitty smiled, then went about her way.

Ray loosened his hold on Catherine, letting his hand

trail down her back before releasing her altogether. They might have been more affectionate before—the hand-holding, the starry-eyed gazes. But it wasn't so easy pretending anymore, and he wasn't sure why.

He supposed it was because he was having a hard time deciding what was real and what wasn't.

Once they'd stepped outside, where a full moon lit their path, Ray said, "That was probably a boring evening for you, so thank you for being a good sport."

"It wasn't so bad. I've never had the chance to meet a man who was a hundred years old before. That's actually amazing, don't you think? And he seems so sharp."

"He sure is."

They continued their walk down Main Street, which was fairly quiet, now that the stores had all closed. Yet they weren't doing much talking, either.

Ray wondered if she was pondering the sleeping arrangements—or if she'd already made up her mind.

When their shoulders brushed against each other, he had the strongest urge to reach for her hand—and he might have done it, if she hadn't been holding her small handbag between them.

Was that on purpose? A way to keep her distance?

When they neared the drugstore and the entrance to his apartment, he slowed and nodded toward the front window. "Have you ever been inside?"

"Of the drugstore? No, why?"

"Uriah Ellsworth runs the place, and he just refurbished the old-style soda fountain in back. It's kind of a treat to go in, sit at one of the red-vinyl-covered stools and sip on a chocolate milkshake or a root beer float. I'll have to bring you here one day."

"That sounds like fun."

Did it? Was she enjoying herself in Brighton Valley? Did she have any longing whatsoever to stick around town?

And more important, did she suspect that Ray would like it if she did?

When they reached the stairwell that led to his apartment, Ray slowed to a stop. “Why don’t you come up and have some coffee? Or maybe even a nightcap?”

“I’d really like to, but I need to get home. I promised to help Eva work on the girls’ costumes for the talent show.”

“What girls?”

“Kaylee and her friend Shauna. They created an act, which is pretty good. I choreographed the dance steps for them and have been coaching them.”

“No kidding?”

Catherine cocked her head slightly. “What do you find hard to believe? That the girls are actually pretty good? Or that I’m helping them?”

“A little of both, I guess. But I mean that in a good way.”

She smiled. And in the golden glow of the streetlight, he could see the pride shining in her eyes. Could he see something else in there, too?

Either way, it didn’t seem like something he should put too much stock in. Her feelings—whatever they might be—would only complicate the issue. So he said, “I’m glad you’re helping out. It’s…a nice thing for the mayor’s fiancée to be personally involved in one of the community events. So you can bet I’ll be at the talent show, cheering them on.”

“Thanks. The girls have really worked hard. I think you’ll be pleasantly surprised.”

"I already am." And not just about the girls.

He paused for a moment, giving her a chance to change her mind about coming upstairs with him. When she didn't, he said, "Come on, I'll walk you to the parking lot."

They continued to the intersection of Main and First, then they turned left and headed for the alley where she'd left her car.

"You'll never guess what else I'm going to do," she said.

She was full of surprises this evening, it seemed.

"I have no idea," he said. "We haven't had a chance to talk much this past week."

Okay, so maybe that was partly his fault. He'd made a point of not calling her each time he'd thought of her, each time he remembered the night they'd made love.

Her steps slowed as she reached Eva's minivan, and she turned to face him with a bright-eyed smile. "I'm going to help out in the Fine Arts Department at Wexler High School starting next Monday."

She'd been right—he wouldn't have guessed that in a week of Mondays. Maybe he'd been wrong about her hightailing it back to New York and leaving him in the dust. Maybe she was finding her niche in Brighton Valley.

"How did that come about?" he asked, wondering if it meant she had plans to stay in town indefinitely.

"A couple of days ago, Jillian Hollister stopped by the Walker Ranch. I was in the living room, coaching Kaylee and Shauna on their routine. She watched for a while, and then she suddenly lit up and told me that the Wexler High dance teacher is out on maternity leave. Apparently, some of the kids in class had wanted to perform in the talent show, but the substitute teacher they'd brought in has no dancing experience—if you can imagine that."

Actually, he was still trying to wrap his mind around the idea of her taking on a job like that. "So you volunteered to help?" Ray asked.

"Well, when Jillian asked if I'd work with them, I told her I'd be happy to—at least until the night of the talent show."

That was great news. And promising. He liked thinking that she was getting more involved in the community. Maybe she wouldn't be so eager to leave town.

"Sounds like you're settling in," he said.

Settling in?

Oh, *no.* Catherine didn't want him to get *that* idea. Her life, her career, her very identity was in New York. And with *Dancing the Night Away* now a go, she had no reason to stay in Brighton Valley much longer.

Well, no reason other than Ray and the twins she'd come to love. And standing outside with him in the silver glow of a lover's moon, she was almost tempted to reconsider.

Almost.

As she struggled to shake off the sentiment that tempted her to change her course and ruin her chances to ever perform on the Broadway stage again, Ray placed his hand on her back, sending a spiral of heat to her core.

"Are you sure you don't want to spend the night with me?" he asked.

No, she wasn't sure. In fact, she wasn't sure about anything at all right now, especially with that blasted full moon shining overhead and the musky scent of Ray's cologne taunting her with the promise of another wonderful evening spent in his bed.

But if she weakened, then where would she be?

As if he might somehow hold the clue, she looked into his eyes, where the intensity of his gaze dared her to change her mind about staying with him, not only tonight, but in Brighton Valley indefinitely.

Yet how could she give it all up—the dream career, the bright lights, not to mention the culture-rich opportunities in a metropolis she'd grown to love?

As they continued to study each other in silence, his hand remained on her back. He stroked his thumb in a gentle caress, setting her heart on end.

How could such a simple movement be so arousing, so alluring?

She pressed her lips together, forcing herself to remain strong. After a beat, she said, "Staying with you tonight isn't a good idea. My life is in Manhattan. And I'll be going back one day soon. When that happens, it'll be easier if we haven't grown too attached to each other."

His thumb stopped moving, then his hand slowly lowered until he pulled it away altogether. The loss of his touch stirred up a chill in the night air, leaving her to crave his warmth.

And to crave him.

"You're probably right," he said.

Under normal circumstances, she would have been happy to have him agree with her. Yet there was something bittersweet about being right, especially on a night like this.

As they faced each other in the moonlight, Ray reached out again, this time placing his hand along her jaw. His thumb brushed her cheek, warming her once again and deepening her craving for more of him.

"Would it also be a bad idea if I kissed you good-night?" he asked.

She opened her mouth to tell him yes. But would it be so bad to end their evening together with a kiss?

Oh, for Pete's sake. Her better judgment, which had been battling desire as if her life depended upon it, lost the will to fight any longer and surrendered to temptation.

She slipped her arms around his neck, and with her lips parting, raised her mouth to his. The moment their tongues touched, the memory of their lovemaking came rushing back, making her relive each stroke, each caress, each ragged breath until she was lost in a swirl of heat.

This was *so* not a good-night kiss. Instead, it whispered, *Take me to bed and stay with me forever.*

When they finally came up for air, Catherine's head was spinning.

Really spinning.

She blinked, trying to right her world, yet a burst of vertigo slammed into her. As she grabbed on to Ray to steady herself, her fingers dug into his shoulder. Still, she swayed on her feet.

If he hadn't caught her, she might have collapsed on the ground.

What in the world was happening to her?

"Are you okay?" he asked, humor lacing his voice as if he thought the kiss had a bigger effect on her than it had.

Again, she blinked. Moments earlier, when she'd been kissing him, she'd been so overcome with passion and desire, that she might have described it as head-spinning and knee-buckling. But the buzz she was feeling right now was much more than that.

She was actually dizzy.

Was there any chance she might faint?

"Are you sure you're okay?" he asked again, this time taking her reaction a little more seriously.

As her head began to clear, she managed a smile and tried to downplay whatever had happened. "I guess I lost my head for a moment."

"Me, too. And you can't tell me that's a bad thing."

Sure it was. Losing her head might lead to losing her heart, and that would be a *very* bad thing.

But she wasn't sure where the dizziness had come from. It seemed to be easing now. But was it safe for her to drive home? The winding road that led to the ranch was pretty dark in spots.

"You know," she said, "I'm feeling a little lightheaded. I must have eaten something that didn't sit right with me. Maybe I should stay the night."

He brightened. "If that's the case, you shouldn't be driving."

"But I'll sleep on the sofa," she added.

He stiffened, as if her sudden change of course took him completely aback. But then, why wouldn't it? She'd been struggling with her feelings for him ever since the night they'd slept together. And she was still vacillating when it came to knowing what to do about it.

"No," he said, slowly shaking his head. "You take the bed. I'll sleep on the sofa."

"But I'm the one making unreasonable demands," she said.

He placed his hand on her back, disregarding her comment. "Come on. Let's go inside."

She didn't know what he would expect of her once they entered his apartment, but she'd meant what she'd said. She would stay the night, but they wouldn't be sleeping together.

Too bad her hormones were insisting otherwise.

Chapter 10

Once inside the apartment, Ray told Catherine to sit on the sofa. Then he went into the kitchen, filled a glass with water and took it to her.

He watched her take several sips, all the while checking out her coloring, which was a little pale.

"Are you feeling any better now?" he asked.

She nodded. "That dizzy spell seems to be over. If I wait a little while, I can probably drive home—"

"You're not going anywhere. There's no need to risk driving home in the dark when you can stay here."

She nodded, then glanced down at the glass of water she held. When she looked up, her gaze snagged his. "Thank you, Ray."

"For what?"

"I don't know. Understanding, I guess."

To be honest, he didn't understand any of it—her dizziness, of course. But her reluctance to make love again, when it had been so good between them, confused him. So did her change in attitude toward him, the distance between them, the stilted conversations that had once flowed so smoothly.

What had happened to the old Catherine, the woman he'd hired to be his fiancée, the one who'd at least pretended to hang on his every word and to gaze in his eyes with love?

He'd come to appreciate that woman. Not that he didn't appreciate the new Catherine. He just didn't understand her, that's all.

Was she playing some kind of game with him?

He hoped that wasn't the case.

"Listen," he said. "There's something we need to talk about."

His comment hung in the air for a couple of beats, then she slowly nodded. "You're probably right."

Then why was it so hard to broach the subject, to throw it out there? To encourage her to share her thoughts?

Finally, he said, "I miss the camaraderie we once had."

"So do I. But making love…changed things."

It certainly had. He supposed it always did—no matter who the couple was or what their stories.

"Why do you think that happened?" He had his own ideas, of course. But how did *she* feel about it?

"Because a relationship between us won't work. I mean, your life is clearly in Brighton Valley, and mine is in Manhattan. So even though the sex was incredible—and we seem to…care and respect each other—

getting any further involved will only make it difficult for us when I leave."

She had a point, because he would damn sure miss her when she left town. And while it made sense that they protect themselves from getting in too deep, he couldn't help wishing that things could be different. That she would decide to make a life for herself in Texas.

But that was as unlikely as him selling his ranch and moving to New York City.

It would never happen.

"Are you sorry we made love?" he asked.

She smiled, her eyes filling with a sentiment he couldn't quite peg. "No, I don't regret that at all. But I do regret knowing nothing will ever become of it."

The truth in her words poked a tender spot inside him, just like a spur jabbing him in the flanks. And he had to concede that she was right.

"At this point," she added, "we can walk away with a nice memory. But if we get any more involved—or if that involvement is emotional—it might be tough to say goodbye."

It might be tough to do that anyway. But he shook off that thought as well as the implication that she could actually develop feelings for him.

"You've got a point," he admitted. "We don't live in the same worlds."

"If we did, things would be different."

Again the truth she spoke, the reality of the situation in which they'd found themselves, gave Ray another spurlike jab.

If he could come up with any kind of argument, he would have laid it on the table. But there wasn't one to be had.

"I'm glad we got that out of the way," he said. "Now all we have to do is decide on the sleeping arrangements. And like I told you before, I'm taking the sofa."

It had been an easy decision to make—the only one.

Yet three hours later, Ray lay stretched out on the sofa in the living room, trying his best to sleep and not having any luck at all.

She'd told him that she didn't want to risk an emotional involvement with him. And he could see the wisdom in that.

But each time he closed his eyes and tried to drift off, he wondered if he'd already gotten in too deep.

If so, she'd been right.

It was going to hurt like hell when she left town.

Over the next two weeks, Catherine got so caught up at Wexler High School with the talent show rehearsals, as well as with Kaylee and Shauna, that she hadn't been able to spend much time with Ray or go to many of those social engagements he'd been paying her to attend.

Okay, so that was the excuse she'd been giving him.

He didn't seem to mind, though. And that made things easier. After the heart-to-heart chat they'd had the night of Ernie Tucker's birthday dinner, their conversations had been better, but they were still…a bit awkward.

They'd attended the parade in Ernie's honor the next morning, but that afternoon she'd felt a little nauseous and had decided to drive back to the Walker ranch instead of staying over to attend the ice cream social on Sunday.

"I must have picked up a bug of some kind," she'd told Ray, as she got ready to leave the parade. "First the dizziness last night, and now an upset stomach."

"Take care of yourself," he'd said.

And she had. She'd gone straight home, slipped into her nightgown and taken a nap.

The dizziness and nausea had plagued her off and on for a while, although never enough to make her consider calling a doctor. And the busier she kept herself, the better she seemed to feel.

Still, if she didn't kick that bug soon, she'd have to make an appointment with a doctor, and she hated to see someone she didn't know in Brighton Valley. But she'd deal with that if and when the time came.

Now, as she prepared to walk up the stairwell to Ray's apartment, she reached into her purse for the key. She'd told him she'd meet him at his place so they could attend an auction tonight, and she was a little early. But she'd just finished working with the high school dance troupe and couldn't see any reason to drive all the way back to the ranch, then to town again.

She carried a garment bag that held a dress she'd borrowed from Eva, as well as a pair of heels. So she had to transfer everything to one hand so she could fit the key into the lock.

Once inside, she carried her change of clothes to the bathroom, where she would get dressed.

Thirty minutes later, she'd taken a shower and slipped into the light blue dress. Then she'd freshened up her makeup and swept her hair into an elegant twist. By the time Ray arrived, she was ready to go.

"I'm sorry I'm late," he said as he entered the apartment. When he spotted her in the kitchen, pouring herself a glass of club soda, he froze in his tracks. As his gaze swept over her, an appreciative smile stretched across his face. "Nice dress. Is it new?"

"Merely borrowed."

Something borrowed, something blue…

Shaking off the thoughts of the wedding day ditty, she asked, "Did you have a good day?"

"I sure did. And better yet, I heard that Jim Cornwall is doing much better and would like his job back in the not-so-distant future."

She took another sip of her drink, wishing it was ginger ale instead. Her stomach was feeling a little woozy again. "Have I met Jim?"

"No, not yet. He's the elected mayor, the one I've been filling in for."

Oh, that's right. He'd fallen off a ladder while trimming a tree in his yard and had been seriously injured—a skull fracture if she remembered correctly.

Catherine offered Ray a smile. "So that's good news, isn't it?"

"You bet it is. I had no idea how demanding the job would be, especially when it comes to all the social events I have to attend—like this one tonight." Ray nodded toward the bedroom. "Give me a minute, and I'll change clothes. Then we can go."

Catherine didn't have to wait long. True to his word, Ray returned within minutes, wearing a sport jacket and tie. And they were soon in his car and on the way to the Wexler Valley Country Club.

Tonight's event was a dinner and an auction, which would benefit a local Boys and Girls Club that serviced both Brighton Valley and Wexler, the neighboring town.

"You know," she said, as they turned into the country club, "you make a great mayor. And the townspeople really seem to like you."

"Thanks. It's been a good experience. But I'm eager to go back home and be a rancher again."

She could understand that.

Ray parked his SUV in the lower lot, and the two made the uphill walk to the main dining room, where the dinner and silent auction would take place. As he opened the door for Catherine, they were met by the sound of a harpist playing just beyond the entry.

"The music is a nice touch," Catherine said.

"Isn't it?" He smiled, then placed his hand on her back as if nothing had changed between them. "That's got to be Margo Reinhold, the wife of one of our councilmen. She's the only one I know who plays the harp."

They'd no more than entered the main dining room, when Margo's husband approached Ray, taking time to greet Catherine first.

Ray turned to Catherine. "You remember Dale Reinhold, don't you, honey?"

"Yes, I do." She reached out a hand to greet him. "It's good to see you again."

After a little small talk, Dale said, "You heard the news about Jim Cornwall, didn't you?"

"I sure did." Ray lobbed him a bright-eyed grin. "And I'll be counting the days until he comes back."

"Maybe so. But you've been a darn good mayor. You really ought to think about running in the next election."

"Thanks. I'll have to give it some thought."

Catherine had expected Ray to bring up all the work he needed to do on his ranch, but he didn't. Was that because he'd actually enjoyed his stint as mayor?

Either way, she had to agree with Dale. Ray had been doing a great job as mayor. And he was clearly respected by everyone in the community.

As the men continued to talk, a waiter walked by with a tray of hors d'oeuvres—something deep fried and wrapped in bacon. The aroma snaked around Catherine, setting off a wave of nausea.

Oh, dear. Not again. And not here.

"Would you…" She cleared her throat, then issued an "Excuse me" before dashing off to find the ladies' restroom.

Thankfully, just putting some distance between her and the waiter's tray was enough to settle her stomach.

Good grief. What was that all about? Why hadn't she kicked that flu bug?

When she spotted a matronly woman wearing a tennis outfit, she asked where she could find the nearest restroom and was directed to her left.

Once inside, she found a sitting area and took a seat in an overstuffed chair. Her game plan had been to call a doctor once she got back to New York if she hadn't gotten any better. But maybe she ought to see someone while she was in Brighton Valley. What if the nausea and dizziness were symptoms of something other than a bug, something serious?

If she hadn't already been told that her chances of getting pregnant were slim, she might even wonder about that. But she'd learned a long time ago not to pin her hopes on having a child of her own.

Minutes later, the nausea passed. As she got to her feet, a silver-haired woman entered the room wearing a cream-colored dress and heels. Catherine had met her a time or two, but to be honest, she'd completely forgotten her name or her connection to Ray.

"Well, hello," the woman said. "What a lovely dress. That color really brings out the blue of your eyes."

"Thank you."

"I haven't seen you around lately," the woman added, offering a friendly smile. "It's good to see you and our mayor together."

"I've been busy," Catherine said.

"I heard that." The woman brightened. "You've been helping out with the high school dance group. That's a wonderful thing for you to do. But then again, you are the mayor's fiancée, so it makes sense that you'd jump right in and get involved in the community."

Catherine returned her smile, although she was still at a complete loss when it came to remembering the woman's name. Was she the wife of one of the councilmen?

Maybe she was a councilwoman herself.

"Have you and Ray set a date for your wedding?" the woman asked.

"No, not yet."

"I couldn't wait to set a date when Roger and I became engaged."

Catherine wasn't sure what to say to that.

"June weddings are always nice," the woman added. "Roger and I figured that early summer would be a nice time to take a vacation, if we ever wanted to celebrate our anniversary out of town."

"Now there's a thought."

"Well, all I can say is that you're going to make a beautiful bride."

"Thank you." Catherine fought the urge to check her watch. Ray had to be wondering where she was.

"I hope you plan to have a big wedding."

"Why?" Catherine asked.

"Because everyone in this county loves Ray. And

they're going to want to attend so they can wish the two of you their best."

"You're probably right." Catherine offered the woman her sweetest smile, then excused herself and left the bathroom.

She and Ray were going to have to talk about dates all right. Dates for their breakup.

And they'd also need to come up with a good reason for a perfect couple to split and go their own ways.

Catherine had been fairly quiet all evening, which really shouldn't surprise Ray. She'd been introspective ever since they'd made love. Even the heart-to-heart talk they'd had the other day hadn't made things any clearer.

She'd been right about not getting emotionally involved, but that didn't mean he was happy about the decision to take a step back—no matter what the future might bring.

Ray reached for his steak knife, cut into the filet mignon and took a bite. He'd eaten his share of fancy meals, but he had to admit the chef at the Wexler Valley Country Club had gone above and beyond tonight.

"Are you sure you don't want to have some of my steak?" he asked Catherine.

She'd passed on dinner, choosing only the salad with lemon instead of a dressing. She'd mentioned watching her weight, which he thought was silly. If ever a woman had a perfect shape, it was Catherine. But he decided it wasn't his place to tell her what to eat.

When the people at their table had finished their meals, the wait staff brought out cheesecake for dessert.

"Would you like a bite?" Ray asked Catherine.

"No, thank you."

She certainly had a lot of willpower. Heather, his ex, would have taken her spoon and at least had a taste.

After the waiter picked up the empty dessert plates, Ray placed his hand on Catherine's. "Are you ready to go, honey?"

"I am, if you are."

He nodded, then stood and pulled out her chair.

One nice thing about these public dinners was being able to pretend that everything was still good between them—even if there really wasn't a "them."

Still, he had to admit that it would have been nice if they really were a couple, if their fake relationship was real. There was something very appealing about being with Catherine, sharing an intimacy he'd never known with anyone else—even if it was all an act.

Would he ever share that kind of relationship with anyone? He hoped so.

Somewhere, deep inside, he was sorry that it might be with a woman he hadn't met, a woman who wasn't Catherine.

After saying their goodbyes to the others at their table, they made their way to the entrance.

"How much money do you think the auction brought in?" she asked.

"Quite a bit. Last year they made ten thousand dollars, and I suspect they did better this time. There had to be at least twenty more people. And they had a lot of nice donations for the silent auction." Ray opened the door, and when he asked Catherine to step outside, she swayed on her feet.

He reached out and grabbed her arm, steadying her. "Are you okay?"

His first thought was that she'd lost a heel or something.

"Yes," she said. "But can we stand here a minute?"

"Sure. Why?"

"I'm a little dizzy again."

His gut clenched. "*Again?* How often have you been having these spells?"

"A few times. Maybe three or four."

He'd been with her on two of those occasions—both of them in the evening. "Where were you when you had the other dizzy spells?"

"Once I was in the bathroom at the Walker ranch. And then it happened again when I was at the high school. But if I sit down for a while, it passes."

He hated the thought of her being sick. "That's a little worrisome, don't you think?"

"I suppose so. But in this case, I didn't eat much for dinner, so maybe that caused me to be a little lightheaded. I probably need to have some protein."

She might be right, but that didn't make him feel much better. What if there was something wrong? Something serious?

"I'll fix you a ham sandwich when we get back to my place," he said.

"That might be too heavy. If you have any cottage cheese, I might have a spoonful."

He never ate cottage cheese, let alone put it on his shopping list. And even if he did, he would insist that she eat more than that.

"I'll tell you what," he said. "Once I get you to the car, I'll go back inside and ask them to put one of those steak dinners in a take-home box."

"Please don't bother the chef with a request like that. I'll find something to eat when we get home."

Home. Just the sound of the word coming from Catherine's lips made Ray wonder what it would be like if the two of them actually lived together, but given their different ways of life, that would never happen.

"Do you think you can walk to the car now?" he asked.

She nodded. "Yes, let's go."

He slipped an arm around her—just in case she wasn't as steady on her feet as she implied she was—and walked her to the lower parking lot, where he'd left his SUV.

"You're staying with me tonight," he added.

She didn't object, which was good.

The next step was to insist that she make a doctor's appointment first thing Monday morning—whether she wanted to or not.

Once they'd gotten back to Ray's apartment, Catherine gave Eva a call and told her she'd bring the minivan back in the morning.

Ray had insisted that she make an appointment with one of the doctors at the Brighton Valley Medical Center on Monday morning, and she promised to do so—if she had another dizzy spell.

"I'm sure it's nothing to worry about," she added, although she wasn't entirely convinced of that. "I was probably just a little lightheaded from not eating much today."

"Then come into the kitchen with me," he said. "I'll fix you a sandwich."

"All right. But if you don't mind, I'd like you to leave

it open-faced. No mayonnaise, please. And can I please see the nutrition label on that ham?"

He reached for her hand and gave it a warm, gentle squeeze that nearly stole her breath away.

"Okay," he said, letting go. "But you need to understand something. I'm worried about you skipping meals—or relying on rabbit food to keep you going. And while we're on the subject, I'm not sure why in the hell you think you have to diet. You look great."

"I… Well, thank you." She rubbed the hand he'd been holding just moments before. "But just so you know, I've put on ten pounds since arriving. And I don't want it to get out of hand."

She also needed to lose at least that much if she wanted to land the lead role in *Dancing the Night Away,* but she wasn't ready to tell him that.

"You can lose that extra weight without starving yourself." He nodded toward the open kitchen. "Come on. Let's get you some nourishment."

After pulling the ham from the fridge, he handed it over to her to look at the packaging. Then he took a loaf of bread from the pantry.

Catherine read the nutrition label. The deli meat was a low-fat version, so she decided not to stress about it.

Within minutes, Ray had made the sandwich, just the way she'd asked—with one slice of bread and no mayo. He also added some lettuce and tomato, leaving them on the side. Then he carried her plate to the dining area.

"Thanks," she said, taking a seat at the table. "It actually looks pretty good."

"I'm glad." Ray removed his sport jacket, then he carried it into the bedroom, leaving her to eat.

When she'd popped the last bite of the sandwich into

her mouth, she took the empty plate back to the kitchen and put it in the sink.

Ray, who'd come out of the bedroom, slipped up behind her. She'd heard him coming, then caught a whiff of his musky aftershave as he placed his hands on her shoulders and slowly turned her around.

"Now that you've eaten," he said, "I have another request."

"What's that?"

His gaze, as intense and arousing as she'd ever seen it, locked onto hers, causing her heart to rumble and her pulse to kick up a notch. But it was the husky tone of his voice and the suggestive words he uttered that nearly dropped her to her knees.

"I want to sleep with you tonight, Catherine."

If she were going to be honest—with him, as well as herself—she would admit that there wasn't anything she'd like better. But making love with him, as star-spinning and mind-boggling as it had been, had left them both on edge around each other. And if she weren't careful, she could ruin whatever friendship they had.

And Ray knew how she felt. He'd even agreed with her.

Of course, that didn't mean she wasn't sorely tempted to make love with him again. And obviously, he was dealing with the same temptation.

The hormones and pheromones that swarmed around them became so strong, so heady, that she could almost see them. But she forced herself to hold steady. "I told you that, under the circumstances, having a sexual relationship wasn't a good idea."

"I said *sleep*. Not make love."

She paused for a beat, thinking about it—and actually liking the idea.

"Even if we don't ever become lovers again," he added, "I'd like for us to be friends. I care about you, Catherine. And I want to share my bed with you."

She cared about him, too. Way more than she dared to admit—to him or to herself. But she would be leaving soon. She'd even purchased her flight back to JFK for the day after the talent show, although she hadn't told Ray yet.

And why hadn't she?

Maybe because she was afraid he had some warped idea that they might actually have a future together. That he'd ask her to stay in Brighton Valley, to be his real fiancée.

If he did, what would she say?

Could she give up her life and her dreams for a man?

Maybe.

And maybe not.

Yet a better question might be: Could she give it all up for Ray? And if so, would she grow to resent him in the long run?

Her heart clamored in her chest, begging to get out and to have a say about it, urging her to agree to more than just sleeping with him, to make love one more time.

And maybe even to cancel her flight back to New York.

But she had to go. And leaving Brighton Valley—leaving *Ray*—was going to be tough enough without running the risk of an emotional attachment, which she feared she already had.

Yet against her better judgment, she said, "Okay. I'll sleep with you."

She told herself she'd made that decision because she hated to have him sleep on the sofa, and she knew he'd insist that she take the bed.

But in truth?

If she was leaving on Sunday, she wanted to sleep next to him tonight.

And even more than that, she wanted to wake up wrapped in his arms.

Chapter 11

Ray woke the next morning with Catherine's back nestled against his chest, his arms wrapped around her.

He'd thought that once they'd drifted off to sleep last night, they'd end up on their own sides of the bed, but he'd been wrong. They'd cuddled together until dawn.

As Catherine began to stir, he took one last moment to breathe in the faint floral scent of her shampoo, to relish the feel of her breasts splayed against his forearm.

She turned, adjusting her body so that she faced him, and smiled. "Good morning."

He returned her smile. "'Morning."

"How'd you sleep?"

"Great." Much better than if he'd slept on the sofa, holding on to his pillow. "How 'bout you?"

"Not bad."

"Are you feeling any better?" he asked.

"Yes. I guess I just needed a bite to eat and a good night's sleep."

He hoped so. He'd been worried about her last night.

"Do you want to use the shower first?" he asked.

"All right."

After she climbed from bed, he headed into the kitchen, where he brewed a fresh pot of coffee and searched the fridge for something to make for their breakfast.

He settled on bacon and eggs, although he figured it might be best to ask what she'd like to eat. Maybe she'd rather go to Caroline's Diner.

Minutes later, Catherine entered the kitchen, fresh from the shower.

"Coffee's ready," he said. "Would you like me to make some scrambled eggs? Or would you rather go down to Caroline's? She makes the best cinnamon rolls."

"I'll pass on a big breakfast," she said. "Coffee will be fine for now."

There she went with the dieting again. Hadn't she learned her lesson?

He crossed his arms and leaned his weight onto one leg. "Remember what happened last night? You need more than that to get by on. I don't want you getting dizzy again."

"Okay," she said. "I'll have an egg."

Just one? What was he going to do with her?

Love her came to mind. But he shook off that thought as quickly as it had popped up. All he needed to do was to fall for a woman who was supposed to be leaving town in the near future.

"There's something I need to tell you," she said, taking a seat at the dining room table.

"What's that?" He pulled two mugs from the kitchen cupboard, his back to her as he filled them with coffee.

"I've made plans to return to Manhattan."

His pulse, as well as his breathing, stopped for several beats, and when it started up again, he turned to face her. "When?"

"A week from next Sunday."

Eight short days from now.

"I hope that's okay with you," she added.

Wouldn't it have to be? He'd known it was coming, although it still took him by surprise and left him unbalanced.

"I know we had an agreement," she said, "but the length of it had been indefinite. And, well, I have an opportunity to audition for the lead in a musical, one I'd really like to have."

His heart sank to the pit of his stomach. Not only was she leaving Texas, but she was going back to the life she'd created for herself, the life she loved.

He couldn't fault her for it, but it still…well, it hurt to know she was leaving—and before he was ready to let her go.

Her news had jerked the rug right out from under his feet, toppling the phony world they'd created for themselves in Brighton Valley.

"We'll have to come up with a reason for our breakup," she added.

It would have to be a damn good one. Everyone in Brighton Valley seemed to like her—and to think of them as a couple. A perfect one at that.

The phony engagement may have worked like a charm, but now he would have to deal with the repercussions of ending it.

Too bad one of those repercussions had just hit him personally like a wild bronc coming out of the chute.

"Are you okay?" she asked.

Hell no. He wasn't okay. But he didn't want her to know that. Or to think that her leaving was going to be any more than a little inconvenience to him. So he glanced at his bare feet, then back up to her face. "I'm sorry, Catherine. I didn't mean to ignore you. I had a couple of things scheduled for later in the month, and I was trying to figure out how I'd manage without you. But you're right. We'll have to concoct a story for everyone—something believable that won't make either one of us look like the bad guy. Can I have some time to think about it?"

"Of course. I'll try to come up with an excuse for our breakup, too."

He handed her a cup of coffee, then grabbed his and took a drink of the rich, morning brew. He hoped the familiar taste, as well as the caffeine, would right his world again.

Three sips later, it hadn't helped a bit.

He'd known this day would come. Why hadn't he planned for it? Why hadn't he realized they'd need an explanation?

Or *did* they?

Compelled to drag his feet, he asked, "Would it be so bad to let things ride a while?"

"What do you mean?"

"Well… Maybe we can tell people you had to go to take care of business in New York. We can let them think you'll be returning. That would keep the marriage-minded women in town at bay for a bit longer. And by then, maybe Jim will be back on the job as mayor, and I'll be at my ranch more often than not."

She seemed to chew on that for a moment, then began to nod. "That sounds like it might work."

It also bought him some valuable time. Time for Catherine to change her mind about leaving. Or, if she got to Manhattan and missed the small-town life and wanted to return to Brighton Valley, it provided them with an opportunity to pick up right where they'd left off.

At least that's the excuse he seemed to be hanging on to.

What the hell was happening to him? Why the uneasiness about her plans to leave, especially when that had always been part of the plan?

Why was he missing the idea of having her around, when she'd never even hinted that she was looking for a husband or a home, let alone relocating to a town that must seem like Podunk, Texas, after living in a metropolis?

Damn. If he didn't know better, he'd think that he'd fallen in love with another woman who didn't share the same affection for him. And if anyone ought to know better than to imagine a woman having loving feelings where none existed, it was Ray. Heather hadn't placed any value on love, marriage or promises. And when she left the ranch, she'd never looked back.

Of course, Catherine wasn't at all like his ex-wife. She didn't have a selfish or greedy side. At least, not that he'd noticed.

Catherine lifted her cup and took a sip. Then she grimaced and set it down.

"What's the matter?"

"I don't know. It doesn't…taste very good."

"Really? Mine tastes fine." And just the way he liked it, just the way he made it every day.

"I guess it just isn't hitting the spot." She picked up the mug, carried it to the sink, then poured it out. "I'm sorry. I can't drink it."

"Would you rather have some orange juice?"

"I'm not sure. Maybe."

"It would be a lot more nutritious." He strode to the fridge and pulled out the container. "Wouldn't that be better?"

"I think so."

As he poured her a glass, he wondered if she was having any reservations about leaving. Maybe second thoughts, instead of the coffee, had left a bitter taste in her mouth.

Or maybe that was just wishful thinking on his part.

Either way, he was going to have to get used to the idea—no matter how much it weighed him down.

As he handed her the glass of OJ, he thought of something his grandma used to say: *You don't miss your water until the well runs dry.*

It hadn't been the case for him when Heather had moved out. By then, he'd actually been glad to see her go. But that certainly seemed to be the case now. He felt empty, just at the thought of Catherine going away.

"You know," she said, "if we put our heads together, I'm sure we can think of a good reason for us to break up."

He'd rather come up with a reason for her to *stay.* But she was right. They lived in two different worlds. Forcing her to clip her wings and remain on a ranch or in a small town like Brighton Valley would destroy a part of her—maybe even the part that appealed to him most.

But how was he going to get by without water, now that his well had gone dry?

* * *

The night of the talent show finally arrived, and no one was more excited than Catherine. Working with Kaylee and Shauna had been an amazing experience, and so had coaching the Wexler High School students.

Ray had been tied up at a meeting all afternoon, so he told her he'd meet her there and asked her to save him a seat. He'd also mentioned that he had something to talk to her about and suggested she bring an overnight bag so she could stay in town with him.

If her flight had been another week out, she might have refused, fearing that her resolve to leave might weaken. As it was, she'd be flying out of Houston on Sunday afternoon—just a little under twenty-four hours from now.

In all honesty, she was going to miss Ray when she went to New York—more than she'd realized. And certainly more than he would ever know.

So what harm would there be in having one last evening together?

After dressing for the talent show and telling Kaylee she'd see her there, she borrowed one of the ranch pickups and drove to town. Instead of going straight to the theater, she first stopped at the florist shop on Main Street.

Three days ago, she'd ordered two bouquets of red roses to give to her favorite stars after tonight's performances. Wouldn't Shauna and Kaylee be surprised?

Next she drove to the Lone Star Theater, which had been built sixty years ago. When the owner died, his widow hadn't been able to find an investor or a buyer. Upon her death, she donated it to the city.

From what Catherine understood, it wasn't used very

often. But it certainly made a perfect place for a talent show, with its old-fashioned curtain, stage and lighting.

Catherine sought a seat in the front section that was reserved for the families of those performing.

Eva and Jane, along with the parents of the younger contestants, had been allowed backstage to wait with the girls. That left Jerald Morrison, Dan and Hank Walker, as well as Kaylee's siblings to sit in the same row as Catherine.

Knowing she would need to get up and present the flowers to the girls, Catherine took an aisle seat, then placed her purse on the one next to it, saving it for Ray. Rather than hold the flowers and be unable to clap or to read the program, she slipped the bouquets under her chair, where they'd be safe.

Ray, who'd just arrived, greeted the others in the row before slipping into place, next to Catherine. Then he reached for her hand and gave it a squeeze. "Would it be appropriate for me to say 'Break a leg' to the dance coach?"

"Absolutely." She returned his smile.

Moments later, the show began, and Catherine sat back, waiting for the act she hoped would win in the ten-and-under division.

When the time came, and the girls finally stepped onto the stage, looking darling in the costumes Eva had made, Catherine sat upright and leaned forward. Her heart soared at the sight of them, at the smiles on their faces.

Eva and Jane had come around to the front part of the theater and knelt in the aisle, taking pictures. Somehow, even Jerald Morrison had managed to get out of his seat and film the girls using the video camera on his cell phone.

It was nice to see Shauna's new foster family being so supportive of her. The poor kid certainly deserved to finally have a stable, loving home. It was also high time someone recognized how sweet she was, how pretty and talented. And Catherine was thrilled to have the opportunity to encourage her.

As the girls performed on stage, it was clear to everyone that all their practice in the Walkers' living room had paid off. Shauna, who also had a solo part, brought down the house when she belted out the song's refrain.

And no one's heart swelled as much as Catherine's. In a way, she was paying it forward, encouraging young talent to reach their dreams.

When the song ended, Ray rose from his seat, clapping and cheering with all the rest. Yet when his eyes met hers, they seemed to tell her how very proud he was…of *her*.

In all her many performances, going back to those in the high school auditorium, on to college and even those on and off Broadway, no one had cheered like that for her. Sure, she'd been proud of her own success. And so had Jennifer Walker. But it wasn't quite the same as…

Shaking off the sentiment and the memories, Catherine reached for two of the small bouquets she'd set under her chair, but couldn't quite get a grip on them. So she stood and bent over to retrieve them.

The dizziness that had plagued her earlier in the week struck again as she stood upright. But she couldn't miss the chance to offer roses to Brighton Valley's newest and youngest stars. As she headed for the stage, she blinked her eyes, trying to clear her vision.

When she reached the bottom of the stage, she handed one bouquet to Kaylee and the next to Shauna.

"I'm so proud of you two," she said, realizing she would have given anything to have had someone say the same thing to her—and to truly mean it.

The lights up front glared, causing the dizziness to increase. Wanting to find an empty chair in which she could sit until her head cleared, she made her way to the far side of the stage.

In the meantime, Jane Morrison, who was standing in the wings, snapped a photo of the girls holding their roses. The camera's flash set the theater walls spinning.

Oh, God. No, Catherine thought as everything faded to black.

It had taken Ray a moment before he realized that Catherine had disappeared from his vision, and only half that time to see that she'd collapsed on the floor.

He rushed forward, nearly knocking over a couple of parents with cameras. He mumbled an apology, but all he could think of was getting to Catherine. The thought that she was hurt, that she was sick, nearly tore him apart.

When he reached her side, she was just starting to come to.

"What happened?" he asked, his gaze raking over her, trying to assure himself that she was okay.

"I..." She blinked. "When I...bent to pick up those roses... I got a little dizzy. I probably should have asked you to...pass them out for me. But I...wanted to be the one..."

Ray turned to a guy who'd been holding a cell phone, taking a video of the two girls on stage. "Hey, buddy. Will you call an ambulance?"

"Oh, Ray," Catherine said. "Please don't let anyone

interrupt the show. If you want me to see a doctor, I will. Can't you take me?"

"Yes, of course." He scooped her into his arms, holding her close to his chest. The thought of losing her, of…

Hell, if she went back to New York, he was going to lose her anyway, and the truth nearly tore him apart. Because either way, he didn't want to let her go. He…

He loved her came to mind, but he couldn't even consider telling her, not when he knew she was leaving.

The man using his cell phone to film the girls, who Ray now realized was Jerald Morrison, said, "I've got my truck parked right outside the door, Mayor. I'll give you the keys, if you want to take it. I can ride home with my wife."

"Thanks." Ray knew his vehicle was several blocks away, thanks to his late arrival. And he was eager to get her to the E.R. as soon as he could.

"I don't think the girls saw anything," Catherine told Jerald. "But if they did, tell them that I'm fine."

"Don't you worry," he said. "I'll reassure them." Then he reached into his pocket and handed Ray a set of keys. "It's a black Dodge Ram."

Ten minutes later Ray had placed Catherine in the borrowed truck and driven her to the E.R. at the Brighton Valley Medical Center. He parked as close to the entrance as he could.

"I can walk, Ray. The night air has cleared my head. I'm not feeling dizzy anymore."

He agreed to let her give it a try, but he wrapped his arm around her for support and held her close.

Upon entering the two double doors, they headed for a triage area, where they spoke to a nurse. Catherine told her about the fainting spell, the dizziness and the occasional bouts of nausea.

After making note of it, the nurse sent Catherine to the registration desk. There she provided them with the pertinent information, as well as her insurance card.

Fortunately, the waiting room was fairly empty, which was unusual for a Saturday night. But that, Ray realized, could change in a heartbeat.

They chose seats near a television monitor that was set on the Discovery Channel. Catherine seemed to tune in to whatever show was on, but Ray couldn't help thinking about the various diagnoses that they might hear—things like brain tumors, aneurisms…

He supposed it could also be something less scary, like an inner-ear problem. He certainly hoped it was something that minor with an easy fix.

When his cell phone bleeped, indicating a text, Ray read the display and saw that the message was from Dan and read it.

How is Catherine? Dan asked.

So far, so good, Ray texted back. Waiting to see the doctor.

Let us know what he says.

Will do.

Kaylee and Shauna won the ten-and-under competition, Dan added. Both families are thrilled. Please tell Catherine.

After typing in OK, Ray turned to Catherine and gave her Dan's message.

"They won?" A broad smile stretched across her

pretty face, lighting her eyes and making her look well and whole again. "I had a feeling they would. They worked so hard."

Ray reached out and caressed her leg. "They did a great job. You did wonders with them."

"Thanks, but it was my pleasure to help out. I really enjoyed watching Shauna come out of her shell. I'm so glad she found a loving home. Jane, her foster mom, has been *so* supportive. And did you see Jerald? He's taking an active paternal role, too. Hopefully, she can remain in the Morrisons' home until she's able to move out and live on her own."

"I hope so, too. The Morrisons raised three kids of their own. When the youngest went to college, they signed up to become foster parents."

While Ray was happy to know about Shauna's good fortune, he couldn't help worrying about Catherine. In fact, he'd been concerned about her ever since she'd had that first dizzy spell on Friday night. And while he hadn't seen her again until this evening, he'd called her every day to ask how she was feeling.

According to Catherine, she hadn't been dizzy since Ernie's birthday dinner. At least, that's what she'd told Ray. And he had no reason to doubt her. But then it had happened again.

Ray glanced at his wristwatch. What was taking so long? He really wanted Catherine to see a doctor.

Twenty minutes later, a tall red-haired nurse called Catherine's name, and Ray got right to his feet.

The nurse let them inside, then took them down one hall and then another. "Here we go," she said as she pulled back a screen and pointed out the hospital exam room assigned to Catherine. "Why don't you take a seat on the bed while I get your vitals."

After taking Catherine's temperature and blood pressure, the nurse checked her pulse, then made note of it on a temporary chart.

"The doctor will be here in a minute or two," she said, before whipping back the curtain and walking off.

That minute stretched out to ten or more. Finally, a lean young man wearing glasses and a lab coat pulled back the curtain and introduced himself as Dr. Mills. He talked to Catherine about her symptoms, then looked at the nurse's notes.

After listening to Catherine's heart and examining her ears, nose and throat, he took a step back. "Everything appears to be normal, but I'm going to ask a lab tech to come in and draw some blood. As soon as I get the results, I'll be back to talk to you."

"Thank you," Ray said.

When the doctor left and they were alone, Ray was finally able to relax long enough to take a seat near Catherine's bed.

"I'm sure it's nothing to worry about," he said, although he wasn't nearly as confident as his words and his voice might imply.

He prayed silently, *God, please don't let it be anything serious.*

Moments later, a balding, middle-age man came in and drew Catherine's blood, then he took the vials to the lab.

To pass the time, Ray tried to make small talk, to keep both their minds off the possibility that there might actually be something seriously wrong.

Earlier today, when he'd told her to bring her overnight bag and stay with him after the talent show, he'd planned a romantic evening alone. He'd hoped to talk her into making love one more time before she left for New York.

Now, with her health in doubt, he wouldn't think of suggesting sex, which was out of the question. Instead, he'd be content to sleep with her and hold her all night long.

Damn. What was taking so long?

In what seemed like forever, but was less than an hour, the doctor returned.

Catherine, who was sitting on the bed fully dressed, her feet hanging over the edge, bit down on her bottom lip, preparing for whatever news he had to give her.

Ray got to his feet and made his way to her side, taking her by the hand.

"Well," Dr. Mills said, sitting in the swivel chair and wheeling a little closer to Catherine. "I think I have an answer for what's been causing the dizziness and the nausea."

Ray hoped for the best, but braced himself for the worst. Yet nothing prepared him for what the doctor announced.

"You're pregnant."

Chapter 12

Pregnant?

Catherine wasn't sure she'd heard him correctly. There had to be some mistake. The other doctor, her gynecologist in New York, had said that it was unlikely she'd conceive, that…

"Are you sure about those results?" Catherine asked Dr. Mills.

"I'm afraid so. You're definitely pregnant, Ms. Loza. And that's probably what's causing you to feel dizzy and nauseous."

Yes, of course. That made sense. But still…

She was pregnant?

Her mind was awhirl. A *baby.* She would have a child of her own, a family…

But what about the upcoming audition? No way could she consider taking the role, even if they offered it to her.

So what would she do? How would she support herself in New York?

"She's been dieting," Ray told the doctor. "That can't be good for her."

Oh, goodness. *Ray.* Did he realize the baby was his? And if so, how had he taken the news?

She shot a glance his way, saw the seriousness of his expression. But then, why wouldn't he be uneasy? He'd been so stressed about the fact that they'd had unprotected sex, so worried about an unexpected pregnancy.

And now this…

On the bright side, he was still holding her hand. And he hadn't scrunched her fingers in a death grip.

"I don't think the dieting is a problem," Dr. Mills said. "At least, not as long as she starts eating nutritiously from now on. You can ask one of the resident obstetricians about that, but I suspect it's fairly early in the pregnancy. When was your last menstrual cycle?"

"I…" Catherine tried to think. "I guess it's been a while. I've been so busy that I haven't even thought about it."

"She's only about four weeks along," Ray said.

He was right, of course. Catherine, whose mind was still reeling in awe at the news—she was going to have a *baby?*—nodded her agreement. They both knew the exact night it had happened.

"We have several good obstetricians at the Brighton Valley Medical Center," Dr. Mills said. "So if you'd like me to refer you to someone, I can."

But Catherine wouldn't be staying in Brighton Valley.

Of course, if she couldn't dance or act on stage, she had no idea how she'd support herself and a child in New York. Things were horribly expensive there.

Jennifer Walker had faced the same dilemma when she'd gotten pregnant with twins, but Catherine had stepped in to help her out.

When Catherine didn't answer the doctor right away, Ray said, "We'd like you to give us those names."

Surely Ray didn't expect her to stay in Brighton Valley, did he? Supporting herself and a baby here wouldn't be easy, either. What would she do?

Or was he still playing the role of her future husband—just in case word of this got out into the community in spite of all the privacy laws.

Uh-oh. Speaking of their role-playing, what were they going to tell everyone now? "Breaking up" was one thing. But when there was a baby involved? People might not be so understanding of those involved.

Boy, had things gotten complicated.

She and Ray certainly had a lot to talk about, a lot to decide. But he'd paid her to pretend to be his fiancée while she was still in town, so she'd continue to do that, at least until they came up with a breakup plan.

"We won't need those names," she told the doctor.

Ray stiffened, as if she'd somehow challenged him, threatened him. But she hadn't meant to.

"I already know which doctor I'd like to see," she explained. "It'll be Dr. Ramirez, Eva's obstetrician."

Ray relaxed his stance, as well as his grip.

Still, the enormity of the problem facing them was staggering.

"I have to admit," Catherine finally said, "this is quite a surprise for both of us. We're going to have a lot to talk about when we get home."

But where was home? New York? Brighton Valley? Someplace altogether different?

Life as she knew it was over. Maybe not in a bad way, since she was actually thrilled to learn about the baby. But she had no idea how the father-to-be felt about the news.

She shot a glance at Ray, the man who ought to have a say in all of this, the man who was probably going through his own emotional turmoil right now, but she didn't have a clue.

On the other hand, Ray was still trying to wrap his mind around the fact that Catherine was pregnant.

He supposed he'd better thank the good Lord that she was healthy and whole, since that had been his prayer earlier. But she was also expecting his baby.

His baby.

Talk about major dilemmas…

"I'm sure you're right," the doctor said, getting to his feet. "You do have a lot to talk about. I'll finish up the paperwork. Once you check out, you're free to leave."

"Thank you," Catherine said.

Neither of them spoke until after they'd left the hospital and climbed into his car.

"I'm sorry about this," she said.

About what? Getting pregnant?

"Do you plan to keep the baby?" he asked.

"Absolutely. I didn't think I would ever conceive, but that doesn't mean I didn't want a child—or a family."

That was good, wasn't it? He wouldn't have wanted her to consider adoption or anything else. Because even if he didn't have a wife or have any plans to get married again, that didn't mean he never wanted to have any kids.

So that was one hurdle solved.

"I'd like to be a part of the baby's life," he added.

"That might be a little difficult," she said.

Not if she stayed in Brighton Valley.

"Are you still going to leave tomorrow?" he asked.

"I don't know. I'd planned to audition for a part, but if I'm pregnant, there's no way I'll get it."

He wished he could apologize, but he wanted her to stay here. How the heck could he be a part of their child's life if he had to fly back and forth to New York every other month?

"There's a lot to think about," she added.

She had that right. He sucked in a breath, then blew it out again. "Here's something else you ought to consider."

"What's that?"

"We can always get married."

She turned to him, lips parted, as if the suggestion had taken her completely by surprise. Hell, by the look on her face, she'd either been swept off her feet or shocked by the preposterous notion.

But then again, he hadn't expected to propose to her this evening, either. Not when he feared the answer would be no.

"What's the matter?" he asked. "Was the idea too wild for you to even ponder?"

"No, it just took me aback, that's all."

Yeah, well he was a little off-kilter, too. But he didn't like the idea of losing her, especially when he'd be losing his child, too. How was he going to parent a kid who lived in New York?

"You're offering to marry me so the baby has your name?"

For starters, he supposed. He'd kind of like her to have his name, too.

"Marriages should be built on love," she said, "especially if they're meant to last."

"That's true." Sarcasm laced his tone as he thought about the woman who'd promised to love him until death, the woman who'd felt no such thing.

Trouble was, he knew darn well that Catherine wasn't anything like Heather. And he suspected that if she made a commitment to love someone, she would keep it.

But she hadn't said anything about love. And while he'd begun to realize that's what he was feeling for her, he didn't want to lay his heart on the line, then have her throw it right back at him.

Then again, he now had a son or daughter to consider. And he had a chance to have a family again.

"Marriage is still an option," he said. "I care for you. And I think you have feelings for me, too. To top that off, if we did get married, neither you nor the baby would lack anything. In fact, it might even solve some of our problems."

At least when it came to the phony engagement they'd created, it would help.

"You'd go so far as to marry me?" she asked, the sadness in her voice leaving him a bit unbalanced.

Did she think marrying him was a step down from what she deserved? Heather certainly had.

"Do you want to be a single mother?" he asked.

"At this point, I really don't mind. I'm actually glad to know that I was able to conceive. Being unwed and pregnant doesn't have the stigma it once did."

Maybe not. But what were all the townspeople going to think when they learned that Ray had fathered a baby and didn't marry the child's mother, especially when the woman was one who'd charmed her way into their hearts within a matter of weeks?

And it wasn't just the townspeople he worried about. His parents and grandparents would rise from their graves and haunt him like crazy if he didn't do the right thing by the woman he...*loved.* What was he going to do without her? Just thinking about losing her hurt like hell.

But what options did he have? He couldn't hire Catherine to be a *pretend* wife.

"It's really not a big deal," she added.

Oh, no? It seemed like a very big deal to him. After all, the woman he loved was taking his child and leaving him. And that hurt far more than anything Heather had ever said or done to him.

"I guess we can talk about it more when we get home," he said.

Silence stretched between them for a mile or two, and as he neared Main Street, she said, "You know what? I'm really exhausted. I'd like to go back to the ranch tonight. Would you mind dropping me off at the theater? I left Dan's truck there."

"I thought we had a lot to talk about."

"It might be better to sleep on it and talk tomorrow."

He glanced across the console at her, only to see her looking out the passenger window, her thoughts as far from him as the mountain in the distance.

What had happened? What was bothering her?

Ray was tempted to ask, but hell. He'd already had one city woman turn on him. What made him think Catherine wasn't doing the same damn thing?

He'd been down that painful road before. And he knew how badly things could end when two mismatched people said "I do."

But were they really mismatched and destined for heartbreak?

He wished he could say for sure. And while he was tempted to ask her to reconsider, he wouldn't.

The only thing worse than losing the love of his life would be chasing after her and begging her to stay when she was dead set on leaving.

So after dropping Catherine off at Dan and Eva's, he walked her to the door. Instead of the goodbye kiss he'd been tempted to give her, if she'd seemed to be willing, he gave her something to think about instead.

"No matter what happens, I want you to know that I'm happy about the baby. The pregnancy might have blindsided me, but I'm getting used to the idea of being a father. And no matter what you decide, I want to be a part of the baby's life."

"That might not be easy."

"Yeah, well, sometimes the best things in life are worth fighting for."

She seemed to think about that for a moment, then said, "Thanks, Ray. That helps."

He hoped so, because it certainly hadn't seemed to help him.

"Good night," he said. "I'll talk to you in the morning."

Then he climbed into Jerald Morrison's truck, which he was going to have to return tomorrow, and drove back to his ranch.

Still, as he entered the empty, sprawling house, he was glad to be home, the memory-filled place where he'd grown up.

It was odd, he thought. When he and Heather had split, and she'd left him alone in this house, he hadn't been swamped in memories of childhood, of fishing with his grandpa or riding fence with his dad.

Instead he'd been angry and driven to shake every last thing that reminded him of her, every dream he'd ever had, every memory he'd ever cherished.

If it came right down to it, he might have run for city councilman as a way to get off the ranch, to shake the reminder of a marriage gone bad.

But Catherine had changed all that. And now, walking through the living room, where his mother used to sit with her knitting needles, crocheting baby blankets for the various expectant mothers she knew from church, Ray remembered it all.

And he missed it more than he'd ever thought possible.

Why was that?

What had Catherine done to him?

Somehow, in the midst of all the playacting, the pretending, he'd found the love of his life. Thanks to Catherine, he'd shaken all the anger, all the bad memories. And he was ready to reclaim all that had once been good and right.

As he climbed the stairs and headed for his bedroom, he wondered if he'd ever have a loving marriage with a woman who would stick by him through thick and thin.

As much as the dilemma perplexed him, he couldn't help wanting to make things right with Catherine—and by that, he meant making them real.

After Ray had dropped Catherine off at the ranch, Eva and Dan met her at the front door, worry sketched across their faces.

"Are you okay?" Eva asked. "What did the doctor have to say?"

Catherine might have kept the news to herself, but she'd been alone and on her own for so very long that she needed to confide in someone. And Dan and Eva were more like family to her than her many siblings.

"I'm not sure how Ray will feel about me telling you this," Catherine began, "especially so soon, but..." She took a deep, fortifying breath, then slowly blew it out. "I'm pregnant."

Dan blinked and cocked his head, as if he'd been as surprised by the news as she'd been.

But Eva, who'd known that Catherine hadn't expected to have a baby of her own, even though she'd secretly longed for one, wrapped her in a warm embrace. "I'm so happy for you."

"Thanks."

As Eva slowly lowered her arms, she gazed into Catherine's eyes. "You *are* happy about the baby, aren't you?"

"Yes, of course I am. But it certainly complicates things."

"Does it change your plans to leave?" Dan asked.

"It changes *everything*—and in ways I can't quite comprehend right now." Catherine blew out another heavy sigh.

"How does Ray feel about it?" Eva asked.

"He's taking it pretty well—at least for a man who went so far as to hire a fiancée so the single women in town would realize he wasn't interested in love or romance."

"Sounds like he wasn't too down on the *romance* part," Dan said with a grin.

Eva gave her husband a little elbow jab, as if his humor might not be appreciated. But it's not as though there'd been any seduction going on. They'd both been willing.

"It just…well, it just happened," Catherine said. "Neither of us planned on…"

What? Falling in love?

She certainly hadn't expected a feeling like that to develop. And what made it worse was that Ray had never given her reason to believe that he was feeling the same way about her.

Sure, he'd suggested marriage. But she'd be darned if she'd marry someone just because it was the honorable thing to do.

If he'd told her that he loved her, if he'd been sincere, she might have considered accepting his proposal. But she couldn't get involved with another man who didn't love her. And she couldn't "pretend" that a wedding ring was the solution to their problem.

Speaking of rings, she glanced down at her left hand, at the heirloom Ray had loaned her to wear. She'd have to give it back to him before she left town. That is, if she left.

What was she going to do?

"Maybe I should put on a pot of chamomile tea," Eva said. "It sounds as if you might need it after all you've been through this evening."

As much as Catherine would like to have a confidant tonight, a woman who would understand why she couldn't accept Ray's proposal—if you could call it that since it had merely been a suggestion—she wanted to retreat to her bedroom, where she might be able to come up with a game plan she could live with.

"Thanks, Eva. But I'm really tired. It's been a taxing day and evening. And what I really need is a good night's sleep."

But even after Catherine had shed her clothes, put on a nightgown and climbed into bed, sleep had been a long time coming.

And morning arrived too soon.

Ray waited until nearly seven o'clock before driving to the Walkers' ranch. It was probably way too early for a Sunday morning visit, but he didn't want to wait much longer. Catherine was still holding a ticket for a flight leaving this afternoon, and he didn't want her to go before he had a chance to tell her what he had to say.

Last night, while he'd tossed and turned, thinking about what all he stood to lose, he realized that he hadn't told Catherine how he'd come to feel about her. She might throw it right back at him, but it was a risk he had to take.

What if she left and he'd never told her how he felt? Would he regret it for the rest of his life? After all, what were the odds that he'd meet another woman who would touch his heart the way Catherine had?

Probably slim to none.

So he parked Jerald's pickup near the Walkers' barn, then made his way to the front door and knocked.

Kevin, who was still in his pajamas, answered. "My dad already went out to the barn. You can find him there."

Ray figured as much. Ranchers didn't lollygag over coffee, even on Sundays. "Actually, Kevin, I came to talk to Catherine. Is she here?"

"I think she's still asleep. Want me to wake her up?"

"Sure. Go ahead."

Ray took a seat on the sofa, but he didn't have to wait long. Catherine came into the living room just moments later, wearing a light blue robe over a white cotton gown. Her hair was tousled from sleep, and her feet were bare.

Ray stood, then nodded toward the door. "I need to talk to you. Do you mind going out on the porch with me?"

She fiddled with the lapel of her robe for a moment, then said, "All right."

As Catherine followed Ray outside, she couldn't imagine what he had to say. Would he bring up marriage again? Or maybe ask her to stay in town and give up her career?

She might have to do that anyway, although now, with a baby on the way, performing on Broadway had lost some of its appeal. Besides, she'd like to be near family when the baby came. And Dan and Eva, who'd become so much more than friends to her, held that place in her heart.

Maybe she could find her niche in a small town. She'd enjoyed working with the kids… And there was a theater that wasn't used nearly as much as it ought to be.

But that was wishful thinking. Ray didn't love her. And he didn't really want a wife. So how could she consider staying, especially when people learned she was carrying the mayor's illegitimate baby?

Once the door to the house was closed, and they were standing on the porch, Catherine asked, "What did you come to say?"

"Something I should have told you last night."

"What's that?"

He waited a beat, then said, "I may have hired you to be my fiancée, but along the way, I fell in love with you, Catherine. And I should have told you that when I suggested we get married. I liked the roles we played. And I'd want them to be real."

She liked being with Ray, too. And she'd even begun to like the woman she'd pretended to be, thinking that might be the person who lived deep within. But did she dare hope… Did she dare believe…

"You *love* me?" she asked, trying to wrap her heart and mind around his confession, needing to hear him say it again, wanting to believe him.

"Yes, I love you. And even if that doesn't make any difference to you, I wanted you to know."

"Why didn't you say anything last night?"

"Because I couldn't believe a woman like you would love a guy like me. And with you leaving…"

"You *love* me?" she repeated. That was even more amazing than finding out they were having a baby.

He smiled, and a glimmer lit his eyes. "I think I fell for you the first day I saw you and spotted all those stickers on your face."

"You're kidding. I think that's when I started falling for you, too."

He cocked his head slightly, his smile fading into seriousness. "Are you saying that you feel the same way about me?"

"Yes, Ray. I love you, too."

He let out a whoop that might surprise any of his conservative constituents. "Then it looks like we've pretty much worked through all the complications that matter."

That was true. And she was beginning to believe that she could finally have it all—marriage to the man she loved, a wonderful father for her baby, the family she'd always wanted.

“So does that mean you’ll marry me?” he asked.

“If you’re asking me again, then I’m saying yes this time around. There's nothing more in the world I want than to be your real wife and the mother of our baby.”

Then she wrapped her arms around him and kissed him with all the love in her heart.

The love they professed, the love they felt, was the real deal—and it promised to be the kind to last a lifetime.

* * * * *

SPECIAL EXCERPT FROM

HARLEQUIN®

SPECIAL EDITION

Single parents Liam Mercer and Shelby Ingalls just found out their little boys were switched in the hospital six months ago! Will they find a way to stay in the lives of both boys they've come to love?

Read on for a sneak preview of
THE BABY SWITCH!
the first book in the brand-new series
THE WYOMING MULTIPLES
by Melissa Senate, also known as Meg Maxwell!

"Are you going to switch the babies back?"

Shelby froze.

Liam felt momentarily sick.

It was the first time anyone had actually asked that question.

"No, ma'am," Liam said. "I have a better idea."

Shelby glanced at him, questions in her eyes.

"Where is my soup!" Kate's mother called again.

"You go ahead, Kate," Shelby said, stepping out onto the porch. "Thanks for talking to us."

Kate nodded and shut the door behind them.

Liam leaned his head back and he started down the porch steps. "I need about ten cups of coffee or a bottle of scotch."

"I thought I might fall over when she asked about switching the babies back," Shelby said, her face pale, her green eyes troubled. She stared at him. "You said you had a better idea. What is it? I sure need to hear it. Because switching the babies is not an option. Right?"

"Damned straight it's not. Never will be. Shane is your son. Alexander is my son. No matter what. Alexander will also become your son and Shane will also become my son as the days pass and all this sinks in."

"I think so, too," she said. "Right now it's like we can't even process that babies we didn't know until Friday are ours biologically. But as we begin to accept it, I'll start to feel a connection to Alexander. Same with you and Shane."

He nodded. "Exactly. Which is why on the way here, I started thinking about a way to ease us into that, to give us both what we need and want."

She tilted her head, waiting.

He thought he had the perfect solution. The only solution.

"I called the lab running the DNA tests and threw a bucket of money at them to expedite the results. On Monday," he continued, "we will officially know for absolute certain that our babies were switched. Of course we're not going to switch them back. I'd sooner cut off my arm."

"Me, too," Shelby said, staring at him. "So what's your plan?"

"The plan is for us to get married."

Shelby's mouth dropped open. "What? We've been living together for a day. Now we're getting married. Legally wed? Till death do us part?"